Printed in the United States of America
First Printing, 2020

The characters and events portrayed in this book are fictitious. Any similarity to real
persons, living or dead, is coincidental and not intended by the author.

ISBN 0578674491 (Paperback) / 9780578674490 (Paperback) / 2940162719083
(eBook) / B0882NDJ68 (eBook)

10 9 8 7 6 5 4 3 2 1

Forever

Burn

TRINITY LEMM

Chapter One
The Stranger

Strobe lights flashed throughout the room. The entire basement of the fraternity house was packed. People bumped into me left and right and although it was extremely annoying, I just focused on having fun. The music blared so loud that it was nearly impossible to hear anyone talking to you unless they were screaming in your face.

I had been in a good mood all night, not just part of it, and when nights like that came along, it was important for me to take advantage of it, because nights like these were few and far between.

Claire, Gianna, and I danced our way around the basement. We drank a bit before we got there, so we were already a little tipsy. The boys of Alpha Tau Alpha scouted all the girls at the party, trying their best to find one girl dumb enough to want to go upstairs with them. I had a few guy friends in this frat and although most of the guys in the frat were kind gentlemen, they were only that way towards the girls that they were strictly friends with. The rest of the girls were fair game.

I came to Western Michigan University for a new start. I had gone the past few years dying to get out of Wilmot and now that I finally had, I was happy– for the most part at least. My past had always come around to bite me in the ass.

I had known Claire and Gianna for two or so years now. We used to go to the same dance studio back home, so when we all decided to go to the same college, I was ecstatic. Knowing that I would have friends with me lessened my stress on move in day.

We didn't pay attention to the dozens of guys around us or the couples that were dancing against each other. I didn't care enough to look at any of them or to find my own guy to dance with. All I wanted to do was be invisible to guys until I could figure my shit out.

Claire stopped moving for a second, her eyes hovering past me. She looked alarmed.

"What's wrong?" I asked.

"That guy over there. He's been staring at you for the past fifteen minutes."

I furrowed my brows, confused as to why any guy would be staring at me when there were dozens of other girls here to be looking at. I whipped around, making eye contact with the mysterious boy and immediately regretting it. He stood tall. His wide frame took up a good amount of the wall that he was leaning against. His brown curls were the perfect amount of clean, yet messy and even from across the room, I could see his defined jawline. He grinned while watching me curiously.

I turned back towards Claire. She could tell I was uncomfortable. "Who is that?" I screamed over the music. My red lipstick formed a straight line as I pressed my lips together. Claire shrugged her shoulders, clearly just as confused as I was. Gianna stepped into the conversation.

"Axel Burne!" she yelled, barely loud enough to hear over the deafening music. After hearing the name come out of Gianna's mouth, Claire knew exactly who he was. A look of worry came over her and she grabbed my wrist, pulling me in close enough to hear her every word.

"I've heard about him. He's bad news, Tatum. Everyone says he's a piece of shit. Don't even look at him twice," Claire said. I nodded. Of course, he was a piece of shit. Most guys were. And by simply looking at him once, I could tell. He looked like the typical college douchebag.

I kept my back to where I last saw Axel standing. I'll admit that he was hot as hell, but I knew that the last thing I needed was to become involved with him in any way possible. The three of us continued to dance and after another ten or so minutes, curiosity got the best of me. I quickly looked to see if Axel was still there. An empty spot was all that was left of where he once stood and I was both disappointed and relieved at the sight.

4

When I turned back around, a tall, wide frame stood in front of me. I could see Axel's muscles bulging out the sleeves of his white t-shirt. Tattoos were scattered across both of his arms. Damn.

He leaned in so that his mouth was directly next to my ear.

"Dance with me."

I was slightly taken aback. I could smell the alcohol on his breath, and I didn't know how to react. I glanced behind me to see Claire and Gianna dancing with two random guys. My mouth fell slightly open and my eyebrows shot up for a quick second, before dropping back down.

Fuck it.

I turned my backside towards Axel, backing up until I was against him and began to sway side to side. He placed his hands on my hips and pulled me closer to him. His fingers laid on the skin between my black crop top and my jeans, sending electricity through my body. After a few songs, I could feel the bulge in his pants pressed up against me. It made me feel accomplished.

I had no intentions of getting to know Axel or of dancing with him again after tonight. Even though he was gorgeous and was making my heart pound with the way he held me to him, it was evident that he was no good for me. Hookups had never been my thing and relationships weren't really my thing either— at least not anymore. I kept my distance from guys at all costs.

I was surprised with the amount of calmness I contained while dancing with Axel. It was my only motivation to keep going. Every now and then, I would look over towards Claire and Gianna to make sure they were still in sight. The last thing I needed was to lose them in the crowd.

Axel picked up a hand off of my hip and moved my long brown hair, that I had curled a few hours before, over to one side. Once he had my neck in sight, he buried his head into the crook. I could feel his chestnut brown curls against the side of my face, but I didn't mind. The alcohol in my system ignited my adrenaline as he slowly and carefully brought his lips to my neck. I was a little confused with how gentle his lips were against my skin. I figured he was the aggressive type. The type that went in for the kill as soon as he got the chance. His kisses moved up my neck until he was by my ear. I could feel his hot breath on me, and I'm not going to lie, the feeling made me smirk.

"Tate, let's go!" Claire shouted towards me. I fell out of the trance that I was in and slight disappointment came about when I realized that our dance session was over. My hips stopped moving and I stood up straight, taking a deep breath as Gianna grabbed my hand and yanked me over to her. I turned around as she pulled me away, shooting one last shy smile in Axel's direction. He had a mixture of disappointment and confusion on his face as he kept his eyes on me. I watched as he disappeared in the flood of people.

Stepping outside felt so refreshing after being stuck in the middle of people for nearly three hours. On top of it already being so hot in the party, dancing for so long with Axel made me break a small sweat, so the quiet breeze felt good. We started walking towards our dorm. Stanley Hall wasn't too far from Fraternity Village, a little less than a mile or so. But it was so nice out that we didn't mind walking. We knew that the warm, mid-September air would turn to cold Michigan weather sooner or later, so we wanted to take advantage of it while we could.

"So, are you gonna spill or what?" Claire started. It was obvious that she was referring to Axel, but I didn't feel like explaining, mainly because I barely even knew what the hell happened back there. Her bright blonde hair cascaded down her back as her hazel irises glared into me harshly.

"Spill what?" I looked ahead instead of at her, hoping that playing dumb would force her to just drop it. Claire had always been more curious and straightforward than Gianna. I loved her, but goddamn she was always nosy. I could see the disapproval in her face as I glanced over at her.

"Um, Axel? I thought I told you he was *no bueno*. His body count is like twenty."

"I heard it was thirty," Gianna chimed in.

Even though the conversation annoyed me, I felt truly blessed to have friends that cared that much. "Claire, we were just dancing. I wouldn't have even danced with him in the first place if I hadn't seen you and Gi dancing with those two dipwads. And plus, you know I can't date people or even talk to guys for that matter, so it's really nothing to worry about."

I had no intent on allowing the conversation to continue, so I made sure it ended there. There was no point in trying to argue what I already knew. Axel was just some guy I danced with for twenty simple

6

minutes. It meant nothing and it never would mean anything. Him holding me tight and kissing my neck was just a normal, horny, college boy thing. It wasn't any new behavior and it was nothing to read into. My control over my thoughts and emotions had come too far to allow anyone, especially some guy that I didn't even know, to mess it up. I saw my strength as the ability to resist. I saw it as control over myself and each situation I was in. The memory of the lack of control I had over the past four years flickered into my head, but I quickly pushed it away. There was no need to go down that road right now.

I laid down in bed once we got back and fell asleep within minutes. The thought of Axel was already out of my mind, and I planned on keeping it that way.

The next couple of days were nothing special. I spent all my time at class, studying, or with the girls, waiting patiently for the weekend to come so that we could go out and have fun. I was so proud of myself for having a good time the weekend before, uninterrupted by intrusive thoughts or fears or remembering things that I didn't want to.

Before I knew it, Friday had rolled around. We all got ready in Claire and Gianna's room. I had bought a new white shirt a few weeks prior and I was too excited to be wearing it. It crossed over and tied in the front, tight enough to make my decently sized breasts look slightly bigger. My curled brown hair rested gently against my back as I slipped my black heels on. I stood directly in front of the mirror on the wall, slowly tracing my red lipstick over my mouth. The goal was to have another good night. No anxiety. And certainly, no triggers.

We made our way to Fraternity Village with the slightest bit of alcohol resting in our systems, as always.

"Where do we wanna start tonight?" Gianna asked, chin up. Her short, light brown hair rested directly above the powdered blue strapless shirt she wore that fit her as if it was made for her. It was impossible to ignore the fact that she illuminated kindness and confidence, both traits that I wish I had more of.

Claire usually chose which frats we went to. She was always good at sniffing out which ones had the best parties of the night. She stopped walking for a second and looked in all directions of Fratville, taking in which ways sounded the loudest and rowdiest. Her pointer finger rose to our left, so that's the way we began to walk towards. ATA was that way, and although we never tended to go there at the beginning of the night, we usually ended up there by the end of it.

"Sig Omega?"

Gianna and I both nodded, not having a single care as to where Claire lead us, as long as it would be fun and trigger free. There was a group behind us, all girls, except for two guys. Claire noticed them too, shaking her head with the knowledge that they didn't have a chance of getting into any party on the block. We walked past the guys at the front without a single issue, hearing the annoyed groans and sighs of the group behind us. They were denied. It was well known that guys wouldn't be allowed into any frat party, unless they knew specific people in the frat or were in Greek life.

I could feel eyes on me as I made my way inside. I glanced around myself. One of the guys of the group stared me down, bright blue eyes penetrating into my soul. He was kind of cute, but there was no way I was going to cross paths with him again tonight and even if I had, I wouldn't be able to talk to him. My courage was too low, and my guard was up too high.

Like every other frat in the neighborhood, the lights flashed sporadically on the dance floor. The smell of alcohol and marijuana flooded the house, enough to make my nose wrinkle in disgust. We began to dance like the freakshows we were and after thirty minutes, we were already bored. The music wasn't that good anymore and it was clear that Claire and Gianna felt the same way.

We made our way to Pi Rho. A small sigh escaped my mouth as we got closer, knowing that Claire only wanted to come here to see Jason, the guy she's had a crush on since orientation. But truly, I didn't mind Jason. I only minded Lucas, his best friend and fraternity brother. Lucas was sweet and fairly attractive, but he had been trying to get with me since orientation. His continuous efforts were just annoying and cringey by now. If I wasn't so paranoid, maybe I would've gone for him too. The past wasn't around the corner type recent, but it still felt fresh, and it would feel that way for a very long time. Hence the constant paranoia.

8

The entrance to Pi Rho was around the side of the house and Jason was already waiting there with a smile on his face for Claire, who ran into his arms at the sight of him. He lifted her feet off the ground for a second as Gianna and I took our time to catch up with them. People walked past on both sides of us, minding their own business. I tried to look around at them rather than to make eye contact with Lucas, whom I knew was standing near Jason, waiting for me to meet his gaze.

Pi Rho usually threw their parties half inside and half outside. Their backyard was massive enough to fit hundreds of people. I was internally praying that we would stay outside so that Lucas wouldn't try to back up behind me on the dance floor.

"Hey, beautiful!" His ecstatic tone made me shudder. I gave a shy smile, one that I didn't actually mean. His arms wrapped around me, making me feel the responsibility to hug back, so that I wouldn't look like such a bitch. "How have you been?"

"I'm good, how are you?"

"I'm great now that you're here," he winked. Oof. Didn't he understand by now that I wasn't interested? If Claire hadn't wanted to see Jason so bad, then there was no way in hell that I would even be at Pi Rho. She was the only reason why I sucked it up to deal with Lucas.

I didn't even respond to his cheesy remark. I had no reason to. So, instead, I just gave another meaningless grin. His hand made his way to mine and I quickly moved mine away at the touch.

Hell no.

That hug was enough action for him from me. That was all he was getting tonight, and he should've felt lucky that he even got that.

Lucas clearly noticed my hesitation but disregarded it. "I've been meaning to ask you... do you maybe want to..." he paused for a quick second. I could tell he was nervous. I knew he was about to ask me on a date, and I was dreading to hear him finish the question. "Um, go get dinner with me either tomorrow night or next weekend?" He had been asking since the second school started, and I had turned him down every time. I didn't understand why he thought asking again would make me give him a different answer.

"I, um, don't really know if I can tomorrow or if that's really a good idea for me right now." I was certainly harsh in my head, but I didn't have the guts to be harsh in person too. The goal was to let him down as easily as possible, but it got difficult when you kept denying and denying and denying the same person over and over and over again. Lucas deserved an explanation as to why I was constantly turning him down, but I didn't have the courage to give him one. My past and my current issues were things that I didn't like to talk about. I was embarrassed and shameful, both symptoms of the disorder that branded me. If Claire and Gianna hadn't been around when everything was happening, then even they probably wouldn't know anything at all. That's how much I hated discussing the topic and how much I hated thinking about it.

Disappointment dawned on Lucas's face. "Oh, uh, that's alright. No worries." I felt bad, but at the same time, was he really expecting a different answer than the one I had given him five hundred times before?

We made our way around the side of the house to where the actual party was. The backyard was full of frat boys and girls so drunk that they were falling over. Jason grabbed Claire's hand and led her inside through the back door to where the dance floor was. I glanced over at Gianna, giving her a look that screamed *let's get the fuck outta here.*

Her bright blue eyes widened, and she nodded in agreement, but both of us knew that we couldn't leave Claire here. We had made a pact that none of us would ever be left behind and even though she was with Jason, it was still sketchy. Lucas stayed by my side, the awkward tension sticking in the air from my denial of him a few minutes prior. Why wasn't he inside already, finding another girl to dance with?

Gianna could sense my frustration. "Lucas, you don't have to stay out here with Tatum and I." She motioned toward the house. "You can go inside if you want."

"No that's okay." His attention was on me. "I don't mind." His mouth turned upwards.

Well I minded. I didn't want him here.

After fifteen minutes of small talk and awkwardness, Claire and Jason came outside, sweat formed on the sides of their temples. The brightest smile was on Claire's face. My only reason for ever coming here.

"Ready to go?" Gianna's voice echoed annoyance, fully aware that Claire's only incentive for coming to Pi Rho had everything to do with her own wants, not ours. Claire nodded, happily accepting a kiss on the cheek from Jason. I waved to the boys and we set off towards our next destination. It was already midnight, meaning we only had another hour or two before we would head back to Stanley.

Gianna broke the silence. "ATA?"

Thank God she said it. ATA always threw the best parties and after going to two that were mild, I was ready for a rager. Again, we walked in without a problem. It was the only time I was blessed to be a girl.

The party was very much alive when we walked in. Empty beer bottles were lined along the floor and a majority of everyone we passed by had a drink in their hand. Western Michigan University was always known as Western, because everyone was constantly wasted. Our school most definitely lived up to its nickname.

We found a spot on the floor near the DJ. The other girls dancing near us wore even skimpier clothes than us, with caked makeup on their faces. A couple of them eyed me viciously and it wasn't until I looked to my right that I understood why.

Axel stood in the spot he was in before, resting against the wall. Did he always stand there watching all the girls at the party and picking out which one or ones he wanted for the night? Gross. I was disgusted knowing that I was one of many of the girls he must have danced with last weekend.

He wore a dark blue short sleeved flannel with the sleeves rolled up. His black jeans hugged his legs the perfect amount and his curls rested effortlessly on top of his head. Once again, his eyes were on me and even when I looked back, making it evident that I knew he was staring, he didn't look away. Axel was truly a beautiful sight, but that didn't even matter because he was still a douche.

I turned back around, pretending not to notice. I didn't understand why these girls were giving me that look. Were they jealous that he was looking at me and not them? It almost made me feel good about myself. A guy staring at me on one side and a group of girls jealous of me on the other? Legendary.

I had slightly sobered up after the first two stops we had and even though a little bit of alcohol was still in my system, it most definitely wasn't enough to get me to dance with Axel again if he asked. Part of me wanted to move out of his sight so that he couldn't see me, but the other part of me didn't want him to know that I cared.

The song changed. *This* song. I paused as the music made its way through my ears. Frozen in place, I looked straight ahead of me, with no idea what I was looking at. The memories flooded. I saw *his* devious smile for only a second before it went away, overtaken by *him* throwing the blame in my face. It quickly faded and was replaced with the carelessness in *his* eyes before seeing the sight of a ring on a finger, a finger that wasn't mine. A hundred other glimpses of memories flashed through my mind, a million miles per hour. My body started to shake. I could feel my heart rapidly pound as my lungs struggled with each breath. I needed to get the fuck out of there.

Without thinking, I pushed through all the people around me and got out of the crowd as quickly as I could. Once the outdoors was in sight, I ran. I ran until I was far enough away from the house to feel safe. I rubbed my arms until it had successfully occurred to me that I was in the present time, not the past. Out of breath and still in my fight or flight mode, I started to feel myself calm down. There was no way I could go back in there. Gianna and Claire might be pissed that I left without them, and as guilty as I felt about breaking the pact, I was sure they'd understand.

As bad of an idea as it was to walk back to Stanley by myself at night, I didn't care at the moment. Anything was better than going back into that party. I shot my friends a quick text that I urgently had to leave and then started to walk, on high alert for any sign of danger. Footsteps crept up behind me and before I could even react, Axel was by my side.

"What the fuck are you doing going around Fratville by yourself at night?"

This was really the only time he had ever talked to me other than when he asked me to dance, and that's what he decided to say to me? Just more evidence of why he was a douche.

"Walking," I snapped back at him.

"Well aren't your friends still at the party?" Damn, he was nosy. I kept my focus in front of me, knowing he was looking at me, but refusing to meet his gaze. I didn't want to explain myself to him and I didn't have to. I owed him no answers.

"Who are you again?" I asked with the bitchiest tone I could manage.

He gave a short chuckle. "C'mon, you know who I am." His cockiness annoyed me. Reminded me of a person that I didn't want to be reminded of. The thought made my hands start to shake again, but I managed to stop them immediately this time.

I absolutely knew who he was, but it occurred to me that we never officially introduced ourselves to each other, only danced against each other last weekend. I didn't want him to know that I was aware of his existence or of his notorious name.

"If I knew who you were, then I wouldn't have asked." I didn't allow my legs to stop walking and he made sure to keep up to my pace, moving just as quickly as I was. As bothered as I was that he was walking next to me, I was a little relieved knowing that I was walking with at least someone and not alone at night.

"Axel Burne," he paused, waiting for me to say my name as well. "And you?"

"Tatum," I shortly stated.

"Last name?"

Why was he so nosy? I already barely wanted him walking with me, let alone talking to me. "Does it matter?" I shot back. He raised an eyebrow and I sighed, "Everley."

His mischievous grin appeared, and as it did, so did his dimples. "Alright, Tatum Everley, so my next question is— are you actually a bitch or are you just pretending to be?"

I could hear the playfulness in his tone, but the question still caught me off guard. Not only did I not know *how* to answer, but I didn't even *know* the answer.

I scrunched my face together, unhappy with the question. "Oof, yeah I am the biggest bitch around actually. And are you *actually* a douche or are *you* just pretending to be?" I was doing my best to scare him off, but my response caused his mouth to slowly turn upwards.

"How 'bout you come to my apartment with me?" he said, putting his hands in his jean pockets.

I stifled a laugh. "Absolutely not."

His face fell, disappointed with my answer. It seemed as if he wasn't very used to girls telling him no. I thought about how perfect he probably looked under that flannel, but there was no way in hell that I would allow myself to go down that road.

We rounded the corner and Stanley came into sight. I was relieved knowing that I would only have to deal with Axel for another five minutes, if that. Realization hit him that his time was running out and I could tell he was trying to come up with a quick way to convince me to go back with him.

"We could just hang out. We wouldn't even have to do anything." His proposal was weak. Why would I want to hang out with someone who not only annoyed me, but would most definitely try to make a move even if he said he wouldn't?

I took out my school ID to swipe me access into the building. "Let me think about it... umm, no." I responded, never taking my eyes off what I was doing. He let out a sigh. I finally looked at him. "Bye, Axel." My flirtatious tone echoed into the night, and I pulled my red lips over to a small, sexy grin.

Axel stood under the lights in front of the building, highlighting the green of his eyes. He watched me walk inside with a bitter, yet motivated look on his face.

Either I had successfully scared him off, or he was about to come at me harder. Either way, I had awoken a beast.

Chapter Two
The Beast

I was sitting at my desk doing homework when Penelope walked in. Her golden, wavy hair bobbed as she strode in, tugging her backpack behind her. Claire and Gianna roomed together, so I had to find a roommate on my own. At first, it was upsetting, but at the end of the day, what set of cousins wouldn't room together? Claire and Gianna were in the room right next to us, so I was at least thankful that we were neighbors. I met Penelope at orientation and our personalities clicked right away. We had become fairly close already and our friendship was only growing.

"Uh, dude?" She sounded concerned and out of breath as she spoke, setting her two-thousand-pound backpack down on the ground.

I turned around in my desk. "What's up?"

She brought her lips together into a hard line. "So, I just got back from class," she paused, "and Axel Burne was standing outside the building asking for you."

What the hell? I stood up angrily without saying anything else to Penelope, and immediately headed downstairs. I pulled the front door of the hall open and Axel turned towards me as I did.

I sighed as loud as I could. "What are you doing here?"

His green eyes were much easier to notice in the broad daylight. They shimmered as he spoke. "I just wanted to say I'm sorry for being a dick the other night." He scratched his head. "And I wanted to make it up to you by taking you out to dinner."

Dinner? As in a date? No way. Dates weren't my thing. And as far as I knew, dates weren't his thing either. What shit was he trying to pull now? If I turned down Lucas, then I most definitely should turn down Axel too.

"I don't really think that's a good idea..."

"C'mon, just dinner, not even an actual date. And I promise I won't try to get in your pants after," he playfully rolled his eyes as he finished his sentence.

I didn't know what the best option was. Okay, that was a complete lie. I knew that the best option was to stay as far away from Axel as possible, but a small part of me didn't really want to. I was intrigued by the way that he was so intrigued by me. Both Lucas and Axel were desperate to take me out, but the difference was that Lucas wanted a relationship with me, whereas Axel clearly did not. That wasn't the way he rolled, and it wasn't the way I rolled either. But hey, a free meal was always a good idea— as long as it wasn't with Lucas, of course.

"Okay, fine. But this is a one-time thing."

His dimples appeared as his smile lit up. "Tomorrow night?"

"Yeah, that works." I was confused as to what his true intentions were, but as long as no feelings were caught, it didn't really matter. And at the end of the day, my guard was up too high to even allow that possibility.

Claire and I sat on the futon a few hours later, snuggled up in blankets as we watched tv.

"So," I started.

"Yeah?"

"What do you really know about Axel Burne?"

Claire shrugged. "Not too much other than the fact that he's never had a girlfriend in his life and he's a walking one-night stand." I opened my mouth to respond, but Claire beat me to it. "Oh, and he always gets into fights."

"So, basically, he's a total douche?"

"Yeah, pretty much. He's constantly going from girl to girl. Normal frat boy things, but probably ten times worse than a normal frat boy." She brought her brows together. "Why are you asking? You're not thinking of talking to him, right?"

16

I faked a laugh, trying to hide the fact that I had plans with him tomorrow. "No. God, no. Of course not. I was just curious because we saw him at ATA. You know I like to know all the tea."

"Oh, okay. Understandable. I mean, I'd be lying if I said he wasn't hot as hell, but... he sucks."

"You can say that again," I agreed, taking a deep breath as I prepared myself for the tornado that tomorrow would be.

I was almost done getting ready when I heard a knock on my door. "Come in!" I shouted, adjusting the necklace that lay carefully on my chest.

Gianna strolled in with a smile on her face. "You ready for wine night?" Her excitement traveled throughout the room and it suddenly hit me that I hadn't told her I was going to dinner with Axel.

Shit.

"Um," I started. I didn't even know if telling her was a good idea or not, but lying didn't seem like a great way to go either. "I can't go to wine night tonight."

A pouty lip plastered on her face and my nerves slightly amplified at how she would react to the truth. "Why not?"

"Well," I gave a nervous laugh, "don't be mad at me... but I'm going to get dinner with Axel."

Her eyes grew wide. "The fuck! You heard Claire, Tate. He's a total man whore and has a bad temper. Why the hell would you think that's a good idea!"

I thought about her question for a second, wondering the answer myself. "Because it's the only way to get him to leave me alone. It's just a one-time thing. You and I both know the last thing I would do is get into a relationship right now, especially with someone like him."

She narrowed her eyes at me. "I'm telling Claire on you."

"No, no, no," I shook my head, grabbing her wrist as she tried leaving to go into her and Claire's room. "Please, Gi. Don't tell her. I'll never hear the end of it."

She sighed and looked at me sympathetically. "Alright, fine. I'll cover for you tonight when she asks where you are. But this better be a one-time thing, Tatum!" I nodded, agreeing to her every word. "And Tate?"

"Yeah?"

"Don't sleep with him. He's probably got some fucked up STD's," she said with a laugh, before opening the door and making her way out.

I shook my head, giggling at her comment as I stood in front of the mirror in my room, making sure I looked decent. My blue velvet romper was snug in all the right places and instead of applying my red lipstick, I decided to do clear gloss instead. After checking the time again, I made my way downstairs.

A douchey black Mustang sat in front of Stanley. Axel got out of the driver's seat and jogged around the front of the car as I approached, opening the passenger side door for me. He flashed that beautiful smirk of his, gesturing for me to get in. I was surprised at how gentleman-like he was, but I knew better than to be impressed.

When we walked into the restaurant, I gasped quietly to myself. I had no idea he was taking me somewhere so fancy. Beautiful chandeliers hung from the ceiling and the lights throughout the place were dimmed, giving off a romantic vibe. I slid into the booth that the hostess led us to, sitting across from Axel.

When I looked up, Axel was already looking at me. His eyes watched me deeply, taking in every inch of me. It made me shift around in my seat.

"You look really beautiful by the way," he said, finally breaking his stare. I couldn't help but blush at his comment. I wasn't used to being taken to a fancy restaurant or being complimented so directly. I was used to never being taken out to dinner and being compared to another girl, rather than having full focus on me, or being admired. It was refreshing, but dangerous.

"Thank you," I responded kindly. The last thing I ever wanted to do in the first place was be a bitch, but it was my only defense mechanism. For some reason, I felt sort of comfortable being with him, but that's the exact feeling I wanted to ignore. I would have to turn my bitch mode back on.

I skimmed the menu, amazed at how expensive everything was. Axel spoke as if he had read my mind. "Get whatever you want. Price doesn't matter."

18

I gave a shy smile, but still ordered the least expensive thing I saw as our waitress made her rounds. I had no idea why he was so okay with spending so much money on someone that he had just met, especially when I was so mean to him all the time.

He folded his hands on the table. "So, what's your backstory?"

I had a feeling he would ask me questions about my past, so I responded the same way I usually would when people asked. I steered clear of anything regarding my disorder or of *him* and stuck to the other parts of my life. "Um, I've got a big family and I eat ice cream religiously. That basically sums me up." I tried to look anywhere and everywhere other than at him when I spoke.

He seemed dissatisfied with my answer, tilting his head. "C'mon Tatum, gimme some of the under the surface stuff."

I disliked the way he was so insistent on digging into my life. It made it much easier for me to turn bitch mode back on. "Well what about you?" My defensive tone could be heard from across the room. He didn't seem the least bit affected by my question, or even by the tone of it.

"I'm from Battle Creek. I've got a small family, just my brother, sister, and I. My bro and I share an apartment. He's like my best friend. I used to play football but quit after high school. My favorite movie of all time is *The Godfather*. I'm a chemical engineering major, and turtles freak me out." I wrinkled my nose. "What?" he asked.

"Chemical engineering? Gross. I hate chemistry," I explained. It was impressive that he was studying such a difficult and elevated major. I guess when I met him, I assumed he was just another frat-boy who was all party and no school.

He laughed, "Out of all of that, that's the only part you caught?" Each time he smiled, it became harder and harder to hold mine back. Damn it. I wasn't being a big enough bitch. I needed to make him hate me, not want a second date.

"Yeah, pretty much," I said blankly. "I zoned out a bit, not gonna lie." But the truth was that I heard every word. I was listening closely to everything he had said, but there was no way I was going to let him know that.

Axel shook his head, maintaining a grin as he grabbed his drink and took a sip. "You're really damn stubborn, you know that?"

"Yep, heard it plenty of times before," I replied. I wanted to know why his family was just him and his siblings. What about his parents? Where were they? And what was up with the fear of turtles? He eyed me, that grin still staying upon his lips. I could tell he was waiting for me to talk. As much as I didn't want to, I had to at least say something. He had just spilled a bunch of himself to me, and knowing he wasn't going to let it go until I said something was my only motivation to speak. I sighed, "Like I said, I've got a big family: two parents, four kids, two dogs. I'm from a really small town in the Northern suburbs of Chicago. I've danced for basically my entire life, which is why I'm a business major and dance minor, because I wanna open my own dance studio after school. I love scary movies and I hate when other people drive. It freaks me out." I took a sip of my drink.

Axel pulled his eyebrows in a little bit. "But you seemed fine in the car earlier when I was driving."

I hadn't put those two things together. He was right. I would usually freak out if other people drove. There was something about my life being put in the hands and control of someone else that scared me. The only other person I had ever let drive me anywhere was *him,* and I don't know why, considering the fact that *he* drove like a maniac. I guess even with *his* insane driving, I still trusted *him* with my life, in more ways than I should have.

I didn't want to give Axel the satisfaction of knowing, that for some reason, I felt kind of safe around him. I didn't know if it was his wild reputation or just him, but either way, it felt too familiar and as comforting as that was, it also scared the shit out of me.

"Out of all of that, that's the only part you caught?" I said, mirroring his response from a few minutes before. Axel licked his lips subtly, his grin still staying in place. My only way to get out of answering his relentless questions was to answer them with another question. It was the one way I could get through a conversation without having to entirely explain myself.

Before he could respond, I noticed a pretty red headed girl across the room from us. Her eyes lingered on Axel and I. She may have had a small frame, but I could feel the insane amount of tension she sent from twenty feet away. Bingo. A perfect way to change the subject.

Axel opened his mouth to speak, but I cut him off. "Who's the redhead?" He glanced over at her quickly before alerting his attention back to me. His eyes grew wide. It was clear that he didn't want her to notice that he was aware of her presence. "C'mon, you totally know her. She's been staring for a while."

"Well," he started, not knowing if he should say what he was about to, "she's just some girl I slept with and then never called again after..." Axel ignored eye contact as he spoke, clearly embarrassed.

"Oh, great, how gentleman-like of you."

He winced at my answer. "Hey, in my defense, she was crazy."

I rolled my eyes. "Okay, how so?"

He shifted around in his seat, the situation making him evidently uncomfortable. Perfect. The tables were finally turned and it felt great.

"She kept calling me every day and I wouldn't answer her calls. Then she showed up at my apartment one day and when I told her I didn't want a relationship or to even continue sleeping with her, she threw her coffee at me and left."

I raised my eyebrows, impressed with the redhead's coffee throwing performance story. What an icon. I wished I would've been there to watch it happen. "Well I mean, you could've just either one, answered her calls and told her right then that you weren't looking for a relationship instead of leading her on. Or two, you could've just not slept with her in the first place," I bounced back. I could tell that all throughout the night, Axel had been trying to be kind, but knowing his reputation and how he was when we first met, I knew better. His kindness was just a ploy for reasons that I didn't know yet, and I sure as hell didn't want to stick around to find out.

"I mean, technically you're right, but why wouldn't I sleep with someone if I had the opportunity to?"

His douchey side was starting to come out again and as much as that side of him annoyed me, I was grateful that it was there, because it meant that it was easier for me to hate him.

"Um, out of respect?" I shot back. Axel's face fell. He could tell I was getting pissed off. Without thinking, my mouth started talking. "What's your body count now anyways? Like thirty?"

"I don't know. I don't keep count," he gently shrugged. His tone didn't sound as bothered as I would've liked. As far as I knew, Axel slept with any and every girl he could. And when you were as good looking as he was, the opportunities were endless.

"Well maybe you should," I crossed my arms. His smirk slowly reappeared, amused with the way I was acting. "Surprised you haven't asked me by now to go back to your apartment with you after this."

He shrugged again. "I promised you that I wouldn't... unless you want me to."

I laughed, "Um, no."

Even with how mad he had made me a few moments prior, I was content knowing that he could at least stick to his word.

Our waitress returned, this time with our food. We both ate quickly, which I was thankful for because it meant I would get the hell out of there faster. When our waitress brought the check, she set it down in front of Axel. There was a number scribbled across it.

"Feel free to call whenever," she said with a wink.

You've got to be kidding me. Did she really have the audacity to give Axel her number when I was sitting right there? He didn't need another confidence boost. He was cocky enough already.

Axel flashed his most charming smile at her, a dimple sinking in as he did. I rolled my eyes at the sight.

He slid the check over to me. I gave him a confused look, pulling my eyebrows in. "Well aren't you gonna pay?" he asked. My mouth parted, amazed at his shady remark. He laughed, "I'm fuckin' messing with you," he said, pulling the check back over to his side of the table.

I was relieved by his answer. I hadn't brought any money with me and even if I had, there was no way I was paying for his shit. Axel paid and then pulled a twenty out of his wallet and left it on the table. Was he tipping her so much because she was hitting on him or because he just simply had a lot of cash?

I could feel the redhead's eyes on us as we walked out. I didn't want her to think that Axel and I were dating. That rumor would spread fast and if people thought I was dating Western's biggest douchebag, I'd be judged and chided extremely. And above all, I didn't want Claire to somehow find out. She'd be pissed.

I opened my car door to get out when Axel pulled up to Stanley. "Thanks for dinner," I said.

"Yeah, of course. And if you ever want to hang out or anything, just shoot me a text."

"Will do," I vaguely replied, with both of us knowing that I wouldn't.

22

Right before I shut the door behind me, Axel spoke again. "And Tate?"

I sighed, "Yes?"

He looked me dead in the eyes. "That whole fake bitch thing you've got going on? I see right through it." He grinned cheekily. "Later," he winked as I shut the door.

In a quick second, his car was gone.

Fuck.

Chapter Three
The White Pick-Up Truck

I hadn't heard from Axel since he dropped me off after dinner a few days prior, but I had a gut feeling that it wasn't the last I would see of him. I still hadn't told Claire about the whole ordeal, and I was hoping that Axel would stay away so that I wouldn't have to.

I knocked on Claire and Gianna's door, ready to go get lunch before I had to head to math. Gianna's flustered face opened the door.

"Ready for lunch?" I asked, making my way inside. "Where's Claire at?"

Gianna frantically shoved her things into her backpack. "I really have to hit the library to study before my bio test later, so I have to take a raincheck. And Claire went out to eat with Jason," she finished with an eye roll.

Of course, Claire was with Jason. I wasn't surprised, but disappointment did flood over me. I hated eating alone and Penelope was at class, so it's not like I could've gone with her either. My shoulders fell and I tipped my head back. "Ugh."

"I'm really sorry, Tate."

"It's fine," I sighed.

Gianna threw her backpack over her shoulder. "But we can all hang out later?"

I nodded, following her out of the room. I retreated back to my own room, briskly picking up my bag, so that I could get some homework done while I ate.

After getting my plate at the dining center, I chose a table in the back, hoping that no one would notice me. Sitting down with a huff, I pulled out my laptop and textbooks.

I slumped back in my seat and typed away on my computer, taking a bite of my food every minute or so. I felt eyes on me, so I slowly peered my chin up, noticing Lucas sitting at the table across from mine. He turned away when he realized I had caught him staring. Knowing he was watching me made me uncomfortable and I wanted to switch tables, but having to pack up all my stuff, grab my food and drink, and move it all was too big of a hassle.

I noticed him looking again using my peripherals as I silently sat, hoping that he wouldn't come over to my table and try to start talking to me. I sank down into my seat as my focus remained on my laptop and food, trying to finish eating as fast as I possibly could. Dread overcame me when I saw Lucas stand up and head towards my table. But just as he was approaching, Axel slid into the seat next to me.

"Hey," he said. He eyed Lucas, unhappily. Lucas stopped in his tracks. The sight of Axel made him uneasy. I could tell he was silently deciding if he should still come by or not.

Lucas glanced at me again, then to Axel. His shoulders went up and dropped down with a sigh as he shook his head, walking past our table and leaving the dining hall. Thank God. I had never been happy to see Axel before that moment. He just saved my ass big time.

"Thanks for saving me right there. I did not want to be stuck here listening to him hit on me every two seconds."

Axel twisted his face in disgust at the second part of my explanation. "Yeah, no problem. I could tell you were uncomfortable, and I hate that kid, so I figured I should step in."

"You know him?"

"Yeah," he looked up at me with those pretty green emeralds of his. "He's in my physics class. He's a little, preppy bitch." I nodded, taking another bite of my lunch. "So, he hits on you a lot?" Axel's tone sounded bothered, almost upset at the thought. He looked down and used his fork to play around with the food on his plate. I wondered why the idea of Lucas and I bugged him so much. It's not like Axel Burne was the type of guy to care enough to be jealous, so that possible explanation was off the list.

I debated answering with a bitchy response like I usually would when I talked to Axel, but then I remembered his comment as I got out of his car. He knew that I had been pretending to be a bitch the whole time. I had only been that way towards him because his aura made me afraid. His personality was recognizable, and his reputation was terrible. He made me feel the need to put my guard up higher.

"Yep, every time I see him, he's offering dates left and right," I said in between bites.

"And you never go?"

I shook my head. "Hell no. I don't go on dates, and I especially wouldn't go with him." Axel beamed at my response. "What are you smiling at?"

He bit his lip, making butterflies flood my stomach at the sight. The thought of kissing him popped into my head for a second, but I pushed it away, knowing damn well that could never happen.

"You went on a date with me though," he answered.

I gave out a short laugh. "I told you when I agreed to it that it was not a date. It was your apology to me for being a dick before."

"Well where's my apology for when *you* were a bitch?" he said only half-jokingly. I peeked over at him, lifting a single eyebrow. Axel lifted both of his, waiting for me to respond.

"Okay, I'm sorry for being a bitch. There's your apology," I turned back towards my laptop, trying to do more of my homework, but lacking the ability to focus.

"Hmm," he started, pushing his lips together, "well you *could* make it up to me by hanging out with me later."

"Interesting... Is this your way of asking me to sleep with you?" I glared at him, suspicious of his intentions.

"I just asked for a hang out, not a porno session," he laughed. "I'll sit all the way across the room from you if that makes you feel better. And you could even bring a friend with you if you want."

"You, me, and one of my friends? Wow, sounds like such a blast. I'm sure whichever friend I bring would feel absolutely not like a third wheel at all," my sarcasm called out.

His perfect teeth showed, revealing his infectious smile. It seemed as if he was constantly entertained by my resistance to him. "My brother will be there too, since you know, I live with him."

I broke eye contact, looking back to my laptop. "I'll consider it."

26

"I'll text you my address later." He stood up, taking his plate with him. "I better see your fine ass at my place tonight to hang," he said, walking backwards, never taking his eyes or smiling face off of me as he did.

If Axel wasn't trying to sleep with me, then why did he want me to come over so badly? It's not like he was the type that had a lot of friends who were girls, and even if friendship was the only thing he wanted from me, the thought made me a little upset. I didn't want to be in a relationship with Axel, but I also didn't want to be just friends. I needed there to be nothing between us. Staying away from Axel was the safest thing I could do for myself, and knowing that there was a slight fascination he sparked inside of me, made me frightened.

I walked back to Stanley after math, with the shitty realization that I had originally made plans tonight with Claire and Gianna. Axel had said I could bring a friend, but I didn't want to overstep my boundaries by bringing two and even if I could, there was absolutely no way that I was taking Claire over there. I would eventually have to text Axel and tell him that I couldn't come over, which was both a blessing and a curse within itself.

Gianna was sitting at her desk, doing homework when I walked in. Their beds were lofted, with a small futon sitting under one, so I gladly laid down, exhausted from my hell of a math class.

Knowing that Claire wasn't in the room gave me some leeway to be honest. "I ran into Axel earlier at lunch and he asked me to hang out tonight."

Gianna's eyesight didn't stray away from her textbook. "Thought hanging out with him was a one-time thing?"

"I mean, it was. I mean... he promised he wouldn't try to hook-up with me and he told me I could bring a friend tonight." I felt the need to tell someone what was going on, and obviously, I couldn't tell Claire. Gianna had always been a little easier to talk to.

"Tate," she finally looked over at me, a look of worry resting on her face, "you know he's a bad idea."

"I know, I know. I didn't say I was gonna go over there, and even if I did, it's only as friends." But as soon as the words left my mouth, I didn't believe any of them myself. "Don't worry, Gi. I have plans with you guys anyways. So, what are we doin' tonight?" I wondered, eager to change the subject.

She shook off the previous topic. "Uh, I honestly have no idea. Claire still hasn't come back from Jason's."

My eyebrows shot up at her response. "She hasn't come back all day?"

Gianna shook her head disappointingly. "Should I text in the group chat?"

"Yes, most definitely. She's been gone since this morning."

Gi took her phone out and typed away.

Claire, where are u?

It was unlike her to be AWOL all day, and we were both worried and annoyed at her behavior. We knew that Claire hadn't had an actual love interest in a few years, and as much as we wanted to cut her some slack, she was making it hard to. We had already sucked it up numerous times to go to Jason's frat just so that Claire could see him, and now, she was spending all day, every day with him.

Oh shit, sorry guys, I totally forgot we had plans. I prob won't be able to make it tonight. I think I'm gonna spend the night at Jason's!

"Is she for real?" Gianna didn't usually get angry with her cousin, but right now, she was pissed. Gi looked up at me after a minute, deep in thought, her brows furrowing. "So, Axel really said you could bring a friend?" I nodded, taking a deep breath. She looked down for a second at the text from Claire again, slamming her phone down on the desk in frustration. "Fuck it. Let's go."

Gianna and I carpooled in her car over to the apartment. We would've taken my car, but I was nearly out of gas. Gianna was fully aware of my fear of other people driving, so she allowed me to drive us there in her car.

I didn't want to overdress to simply go hangout with Axel, but I didn't want to underdress either. I decided on a plum sweater with buttons down the center, tied at the bottom, showing off the tiniest bit of my tummy between the sweater and my jeans. The sweater dropped low on one side, exposing my small shoulder and collarbone.

Nerves took over my body as the door to the apartment opened. A man who mirrored Axel stood in the doorway. Unlike Axel, his brown hair was short, quaffed in the front. He didn't have as many tattoos, but his facial features greatly resembled Axel's, other than the fact that this guy had brown eyes instead of green ones.

"Come on in," he said to us, cocking his head towards the inside. "I'm Ashton, Axel's brother," he stated, matter-of-factly, while shaking both of our hands.

"I'm Gianna."

"And I'm Tatum," I flashed a friendly smile.

A lightbulb went off in his head. "Oh, so you're the girl he won't stop talking about."

Crimson flooded my cheeks. I was thankful that the lighting in the front room was dark enough to hide it. The girl he wouldn't stop talking about? What the hell did that mean?

Ashton smirked. "Axe is currently in the shower, because he's a dumb fuck and can't plan things accordingly. He should be out soon though." He glanced at Gianna and then back towards me. "So, are you both freshmen?"

I licked my lips, still unsettled by his earlier comment. "Yeah, both freshmen. How 'bout you?"

"I'm a year older than Axe, so I'm a junior." Ashton may have looked very similar to Axel, but he didn't give off douche vibes like Axel did. He seemed very put together and polite.

Gianna was just as shy as I was at the moment. I didn't want to say the wrong thing, feeling a weird urge to be approved of by Ashton.

I took a look around. The apartment was surprisingly clean for somewhere that two boys lived. It had a long hallway in one direction, which is where I assumed the bathroom and bedrooms were. In the other direction, there was a living room, then a kitchen across from it.

I noticed a framed photo hung on the wall. Curiosity took over as I walked closer to get a better look. Two young boys, a teenage girl, and an older woman, who looked to be in her late thirties or so, all hung onto each other happily. The joy in their faces was remarkably visible.

"Is this all of you guys?" I questioned, with a light smile.

"Yeah," Ashton walked over to where I stood. He pointed to each person in the photo as he spoke, "That's us, our older sister

Amberly, and our mom." He had a specific longing in his eyes, one that made me feel sad as well.

"You guys look so young."

"Yeah, I think we were about twelve and thirteen when this was taken. It was shortly before our mom passed." He didn't take his eyes off the frame.

I was surprised by Ashton's answer. Axel hadn't brought up his mom's passing. It reminded me of how he had said at the restaurant that it was just him and his siblings, but it didn't explain anything about his father. That puzzle piece was still missing. His father wasn't even in the photo.

I wanted to ask what happened with their parents, or at least with their mother, but I didn't want to push the topic. I had just met Ashton five minutes prior, and I didn't want to be the person that pried into his personal business.

"I'm so sorry."

"It's alright," he said openly, trying to seem as if the subject didn't faze him.

I wondered why Axe had left such a big part of his life out. But then it dawned on me that I had done the same thing.

Just then, the bathroom door opened, and a small amount of steam spiraled out, along with Axel. He had a towel tied around his waist, revealing more tattoos on his chest that I hadn't yet seen, and as I had guessed on the night we met, his chiseled abs were the perfect addition to his muscular upper torso. I tried to force myself to look away, afraid that I would be caught staring. A bedroom door shut, making me grieve the missing sight of his beauty.

Within a couple minutes, Axel reappeared from his bedroom, dressed in a vintage Rolling Stones t-shirt and black jeans. He walked down the hall, running his hand through his hair, grinning the second we made eye contact. "You're here."

"I'm here," I said. "Oh, um," I gestured to Gi, "Axel, this is Gianna. Gianna, Axel."

They shook hands and then the boys led us over to the living room. Ashton made his way to the kitchen, taking bottles of whiskey and vodka out. "You guys want a drink?"

Gianna and I looked at each other. "Yeah, alright," she said to Ashton with a shrug.

His smile looked similar to Axel's, but I liked Axel's more. "Shots?"

"Fuck, yeah," Axel answered in everyone's honor, making his way off the couch and towards the kitchen. We followed him over. Gi and I each took a seat on the stools at the granite countertop.

Ashton poured four shots of vodka and took juice out of the fridge. "Chasers for the ladies."

I glared at him. "Woah, woah, woah, you think I need a chaser?"

"I mean... most girls take chasers," he shrugged a shoulder.

I had one hand on my full shot glass and gestured my open hand towards Ashton with the other. "Pour me one of whiskey. I'll chase the vodka with the whiskey."

His eyebrows shot up, clearly doubting me. He abided to my request, then looked over at Gianna.

She dropped her chin a little. "Yeah, well, I'm gonna need the chaser." Ashton smirked and quickly winked in Gi's direction, causing her to blush.

When I looked over at Axel, his green eyes were softly eyeing me. I could tell he also doubted my drinking skills. I was only ninety-something pounds, but I sure as hell wasn't a lightweight. The drinking genes ran in my family. I was constantly careful to make sure I didn't drink too often, so that I avoided the alcoholic I was made to be. But even so, when I did drink, I could drink a shit load.

We tapped our shot glasses together. I threw my vodka down, then immediately followed with the whiskey. Both boys looked at me intensely, impressed.

"She really just shot those both down," Axel announced, almost with a hint of pride in his voice.

I looked directly at him, parting my glossed lips. "Wanna see me do it again?"

He bit his lip for a quick second before releasing it. The sight sent a shiver down my spine, making me want to jump across the counter and plant a kiss right on his lips.

Ashton poured me two more, and I downed them just as fast as the first two. "Damn Axe," Ashton started, "your girl's a badass."

For the first time, Axel was the one with the crimson in his cheeks. "Uh, not his girl," I budded in, pushing my lips into a straight line.

"But you wish you were," Gianna muttered under her breath, so quietly that if I wasn't sitting next to her, I most definitely wouldn't have heard. I shot her a look. She was lucky that the boys didn't hear her comment. I would've ripped her head off.

Within the next hour and forty-five minutes, I had taken four more shots. I was already at eight, which is what I usually forced myself to max out at. I could still stand up without falling over, but my body felt a satisfying numbness. My drunken self tended to be overly flirty and touchy, but since I was still trying to limit myself to friendship with Axel, I did everything in my power to control myself.

Gianna and Ashton were in the kitchen, laughing and flirting their brains out. They had been that way all night, being overly touchy and never leaving each other's sides. She may have been drunk, but she beamed around him in a way that I had never seen her beam before. It was clear that they were interested in each other, but from knowing Axel's fucked up lifestyle and his lack of commitment, I had no idea if Ashton was the same way.

"Is that a balcony?" I asked, pointing to the blinds.

"Yeah." Axe's head was resting on my shoulder as we sat on the couch. We had both been drinking, so I didn't really think anything of it. I saw it as a meaningless and harmless, friendly gesture. "You can go look out there if you want."

I got up and opened the balcony door, stepping out. The wooden balcony was small, but their apartment was on the fourth floor, the highest floor of the building, so it overlooked the parking lot and part of Kalamazoo. It was already past eleven, so the lights of the city were all on, shining brightly.

There was movement in the parking lot, so my drunken eyes tried to focus on the dark figure I saw walking around. The figure made its way into the light of a street lamp. Lucas? I furrowed my brows, confused. He didn't live in this apartment building. What was he doing here? I watched him, trying to make sure my drunken self was identifying the mysterious person correctly. I could make out the shadow turn their head towards me for a moment, before turning the other way and walking rapidly out of the lot, disappearing into the dark of the night.

I heard the balcony door open and disregarded the sketchy person as Axel stepped beside me. He stood so close that I could feel his warmth radiating off of him.

"It's really pretty out here," I said, referring to the lights.

"Yeah, it is," he gazed at me before looking back out. "I'm really glad you came." Axel got slightly closer, close enough to where I could smell the alcohol on his breath. My eyes dropped to his lips and I wanted so badly to connect them to mine, but I still tried to resist with everything inside of me. I thought about how it felt when he held me against him and kissed my neck the night we first danced. I secretly longed for that closeness again. There was no way I would initiate it, but if he had, then I didn't think I would've had the self-control to stop him.

"Me too."

He licked his lips lightly, beginning to move his mouth towards mine. He lingered closer and closer, slowly making his way towards my mouth. My eyes shut as Axel neared my lips, but before he could connect them, an engine roared. I jumped at the sound and peeked over, catching the sight of a white pick-up truck parked under one of the street lamps. The sight of the truck caused me to freeze. Oh no. *He* was here. The car looked nearly identical to *his*. *He* came back to ruin my life once again. *He* came back to rub *his* wedding ring in my face and to make me feel worthless, yet again. I couldn't look away, no matter how much I wanted or needed to. My heart started to pound as my hands shook, all normal signs of a panic attack.

Everything flashed through my mind once again. My body felt as it did during each moment that *he* degraded me, left me, and blamed me.

I heard *his* voice. I saw *his* face.

But only in my own head.

I started to back up away from the balcony, tears filling my eyes.

I had been emotionally abused and ruined. No, he never physically hit me, but with the amount of emotional, mental, and psychological damage that he caused, he might as well have. Other abuse victims had scars and bruises on their bodies, whereas mine were all mental. And I had all the ongoing symptoms to prove it.

My chest expanded in unhealthy amounts, causing it to become hard to breathe. I didn't know what to do. My mind wasn't in my body. It was elsewhere.

I felt Axel's hand grab mine and immediately, I snapped out of it. "Tate," he said, with a genuinely worried sounding tone, "are you okay?"

I glanced back at the parking lot. The truck was gone. "Yeah… yeah I'm okay." My breathing was still heavy, but Axel's eyes on mine caused each breath to become easier.

"Are you sure?"

I nodded, swallowing, "Yeah, I'm, um, I'm… I'm okay." A small tear escaped my eye, rushing down my cheek.

He pulled me into him, hugging me tight. I nuzzled my cheek against his chest, feeling his warmth as he rested his chin on top of my head.

"You wanna go take another shot?" Axel offered.

I nodded against his chest, and he led me inside, never letting go of my hand.

Chapter Four
The Hangover

When I awoke the next morning, I was wrapped up in blankets. I observed the posters of old rock bands that were scattered across the gray walls of the room, until it dawned on me that I was in Axel's bed.

Oh, fuck.

Hysteria rushed through me as I tried to remember the ending of the night before. I couldn't remember much after Axel and I had come back inside from our almost kiss on the balcony. I immediately flipped over, relieved to see that the other half of the bed was empty. My hands rubbed over my eyes as I could feel a massive headache beginning to come on. My stomach pulsed with tightness. Hangovers sucked.

I slowly climbed out of the bed, as fast as my hungover body would let me. I was in one of Axel's t-shirts that glided all the way down to above my knees, but I was only wearing a thong underneath, no pants. I skimmed the room for my clothes, but when I couldn't find them, I slowly made my way out of the room and tiptoed down the hall. The apartment was silent. Where was everybody?

Axel was laying on the couch, sound asleep. I stood there for a minute, studying the way his bare chest peacefully rose and fell. The large dragonfly tattoo on his stomach expanded with each breath, and as much as I hated to admit it, I wished I was lying next to him.

His eyes fluttered open. "Watching me sleep, weirdo?" he said playfully. His groggy, raspy morning voice wasn't helping my urge to go cuddle up next to him.

I was embarrassed that I had been caught admiring him. "No, I—I just got up," I responded with my head down, trying to cover up what we both already knew. As I looked down at the t-shirt, sudden realization washed over me that someone had to have undressed me in order to redress me. I got kind of mad at the thought of Axel undressing me without my conscious permission. "Did you put this on me?" I sounded a little meaner than intended, but it was for good reason.

Axel sat up, stretching his arms above his head as he did. He inspected me for a quick second before answering my question. "Nah, Gianna did."

My anger subsided with his response, allowing me to relax. "So... we didn't..."

"No," he pulled his eyebrows together, "of course not. I would never do anything with you if you weren't in the right state of mind."

I was happy to hear that at least he was respectful. I had worried that Axel had taken advantage of me while I was blackout drunk, but the more I was around him, the less of an asshole he seemed to be, which made him even more dangerous.

"Okay, good. Where's Gianna and Ash?" I crossed my arms from the cold of the living room. Slight embarrassment overcame me as I realized I was standing in Axel's living room, talking to him with no pants on.

"They each had class, so I'm pretty sure they both left."

"Left?" My eyes widened for two different reasons. The first being the fact that Gianna had left me here unannounced and the second being that I had class today too. Shit. I forgot.

I picked up my phone that was on the kitchen counter. My eyes bulged as I checked the time. It was already half passed noon.

"I have class in an hour."

"I can drive you if you want."

I slowly nodded, closing my eyes and bringing my hand back up to my throbbing head. I winced at the feeling, my body so tired from the amount of alcohol I had doused myself in the night before.

Axe noticed I was in pain and clearly knew why. He treaded to the fridge, taking out a bottle of water and handing it to me. "Thank you," I said as I gladly took it.

"You should eat too. Do you want me to make you some breakfast?"

36

His offer took me by surprise. As far as I was aware, Axel Burne did not make breakfast for girls that slept at his house, whether they slept *with* him or not. He was the douchebag that would kick them out the second they woke up, or even worse, the second they were done doing their deed.

"That's okay, I can just get something after class."

He stood on the opposite side of the counter from me and pressed his palms into the countertop. His muscles bulged as he did. It was nearly impossible not to examine every inch of his bare torso, but I somehow managed the strength to not stare. No wonder why girls were constantly all over him. If I wasn't so fucked up in the head and afraid of everything the world threw at me, *I* would be all over him too. But I didn't have a healthy state of mind to go for each and every guy my eyes were interested in. That's what I had done before, and that's exactly how I had ended up where I had.

"No, really, it's okay. What do you want? Pancakes?" He pulled out a pan from one of the cabinets, glancing at me as he did.

My mouth turned up a tiny bit on one side. "Could you put chocolate chips in them?"

A grin came across his face as he winked. "Hell yeah, I can."

After eating some of the best chocolate chip pancakes of my life, I dreaded going to class. I felt better than I had when I first woke up, but I still didn't feel good enough to go. After changing back into my clothes, I walked out of Axel's room, still a little pissed about Gianna leaving me here, especially when she knew that I had class today too. But on the bright side, I got pancakes and she didn't, so I guess it was alright.

"Are you really sure you wanna go to class?" Axel asked, grabbing his keys off the counter.

The truth was that I didn't want to go. And I could tell he didn't want me to go either.

"Well, what are we gonna do if I don't?"

He stood there thinking for a moment, then a smile crept onto his face. "I know the perfect place to cure a hangover. C'mon, let's go."

The second I heard coins, children's laughter, and video games, I was immediately confused. I followed Axe through the front as my eyebrows pulled all the way in.

"An arcade?" I asked, eyeing him.

"Hell yeah," he responded.

"You think an arcade is going to fix my hangover?"

Axe shrugged. "Fixes mine."

I looked away as I rolled my eyes, wondering how on earth an arcade could fix a hangover. I brought my hands up and smacked them down by my sides. "Axe, I don't have money to be spending here."

"I'll pay for you."

"No."

"It's fine," he insisted. "After all, I'm the one who encouraged you to get so drunk last night."

I crossed my arms, throwing a small tantrum that this was what I was missing class for, but at the same time, I guess I didn't mind.

Axe led me over to a machine to get tokens to use. He pulled out his wallet, revealing a wad of cash and slipped two twenties into the machine. I hadn't known Axe long, but it seemed like he always had money.

I kept messing with my hair, moving it from one side to the other. I contemplated throwing it up into a messy bun or ponytail, but I was too indecisive to choose. I was tired and hungover, and by the look of my face and messy hair, it showed.

Axe studied me, lifting an eyebrow. "Stop it. You look fine."

"Yeah, if you think circus clowns look fine."

"Maybe I like circus clowns."

"Says the one afraid of turtles."

"Only the ones that bite you," he smirked as he handed me a dixie cup filled with coins. "I'll play you in skee-ball," he said.

"You're on."

We treaded past a small group of kids, making me feel slightly out of place as we made our way over to skee-ball. I placed my cup of coins on the ledge, my eyes trailing up to meet Axe's, which were already looking at me. He raised a brow, waiting for me to speak first.

"You first, princess," I said, motioning to the machine.

He rubbed his chin as he chuckled, picking up a token and sliding it in to the coin slot.

I took a step back so that he had room to play, furrowing my brows as he missed his target, time and time again.

"You suck," I said with my arms crossed.

He threw his last ball, before turning his curly-haired head to me. "Think you could do better?"

"Yes. One-hundred percent."

"Alright, Miss. Know-It-All. Prove it then."

"Step aside," I said as I placed my small hand on his bicep and playfully pushed him out of the way, pretending that the bulge of his muscle didn't faze me.

I rolled each ball carefully, trying my best to make it into the holes with the higher points, considering how shitty my aim was. But even with my bad aim, I still managed to beat Axe's score.

I happily raised a brow at him, delighted by my own performance.

"Whatever. I let you win," he said.

"You let me?" I stifled a laugh. "Yeah, right." Axe smirked, amused by my reaction. "You want a rematch?" I offered.

"I'm good."

"Yeah, that's what I thought."

I bent down to pick up my cup of tokens, my heart pausing as Axe began to speak again.

"There's something about you that I like," he said.

I paused for a quick second before reminding myself not to let him or anything he said faze me.

"Thanks," I responded, trying to avoid eye-contact with him.

He shook his head, a perfect smirk still resting upon his face. "So damn stubborn."

"I prefer to be stubborn."

"I can tell."

I shrugged, trying to end the conversation there. I didn't know what to make of his comment. Was it a compliment? I couldn't even tell.

"You know you don't have to pretend be a bitch around me, right?" he asked.

"Maybe I'm not pretending."

Axe tilted his head, refusing to believe my words. "Oh, c'mon. I see right through it."

"What makes you so sure?"

"I just know," he softly said.

"You don't know anything," I shook my head, unable to hide the tiny grin upon my lips.

After spending the entire day with Axel, I was just as confused as ever. We went everywhere from the arcade to the mall to a pizza joint.

I laid in my bed, staring at the ceiling, deep in thought. The image of Axel's beautiful and lively smile kept finding its way into my mind, and every time I pushed it away, it only came back. This was the exact thing that I was afraid of. Vulnerability to feelings. Not knowing what was going on in his head. And the worst, the lack of control of the situation itself.

I couldn't stop thinking about my flashback from the previous night. Axel had been there to stop it, and that was exactly what I didn't need. I was thankful that he had snapped me out of it, but I didn't want to have to rely on someone to take away or control my flashbacks for me. I wanted to be able to do that on my own.

He floated around in my thoughts. The memory of *his* departure fresh in my mind, even though it happened over a year ago. All the moments I had with *him* and all the distraught tears that had fallen because of *him*, were engrained in my memory. Every move *he* had made had wrecked my independence, my trust, and my confidence, and *he* never cared that he was doing so. What *he* did to me wasn't fair and I often wondered why nobody else I knew ever had to go through anything remotely close to that situation. And even after all this time of *him* being gone, *his* presence stayed to haunt me.

I tossed and turned, trying to shake away the thoughts, until I finally fell asleep.

Four years ago, I sat on the edge of my bed, crying at the realization that my first real relationship was ending. After an entire year of being with Connor, he sat across the bed from me, unfazed by the situation.

"I just feel like you don't love me anymore," I managed to get out, holding my teddy bear tightly.

Connor looked me dead in the eyes for a second, before looking away. "I don't know what you want me to say."

My heart shook, devastated by his response. How could he say that to me? Did I really mean nothing to him after an entire year of being together?

He checked the time on his phone. "I, um, I have to go now. I have plans," he stated, giving me a gentle hug, and then walking out. After a minute, I slugged out of my room and stood at the top of the stairs. I watched from the banister as he slipped his shoes on by the front door. *Please turn around*, I thought. *Please look at me. Please don't go.*

Connor opened the front door, letting himself out, but not looking back.

Within the next week, rumors sparked of his new relationship with Nicole, his coworker. But unfortunately for me, the rumors turned out to be true. He had been cheating on me for months. I was so blinded by the way I felt for him, that I hadn't even noticed the signs. He would ignore me for hours on end, refused to make plans with me, and picked up extra shifts at work. How could I be so incredibly blind?

Throughout the summer and next school year, I watched from afar as Connor and Nicole fell in love. He showered her with attention and affection, giving her the perfect relationship that he never gave me. She gave me dirty looks every chance she could, and he did his absolute best to make his hatred for me known. I compared myself to her, wondering why I wasn't good enough. She was beautiful, but everyone who knew her personally said she was a bitch.

I often found myself crying in the bathrooms at school, distraught by not only the sight of them together, but also by the way they were carelessly treating me.

When Connor and I were put in the same Chemistry class, he made dick comments to me from across the room, embarrassing me every chance he got. And each time I ignored him, the comments only became more persistent. Eventually he dropped the class, but it didn't take away the bad taste that chemistry left in my mouth.

When the next summer rolled around, marking the one-year anniversary of our breakup, my phone buzzed with a text. And so, it began. The apologies poured out of Connor's mouth as he tried his best to win me back. But the truth was that I didn't want him back. I didn't feel like dealing with his nonsense, but the more relentless he became, the more I started to give in.

Connor promised up and down that if I ever forgave him, he would never leave again. He told me that he wished he had chosen me instead of Nicole and even when he recited over and over again how much he regretted leaving me, he still found a way to turn the tables on me. He put the blame on me.

"I might have been the one that left, but you're the one who let me leave! You let me walk out the door that day and she never let me do that, even when I tried to! So, this is your fault too!" he threw in my face. "She cares about me more than you do. She fights for me."

"I fight for you too," I'd quietly argue back.

"No, you don't. All you do is walk away. That's all you know how to do. You never know how to solve or fix anything!"

The more he said it, the more I started to believe it and the more I compared myself to Nicole. I began to blame myself.

I would cry to myself silently, disappointed that I had let him back into my life in the first place. I was too embarrassed to talk to other people about it. And not only that, but I never wanted to bother people with my own problems, so I kept it all in.

The pain was drilled so deep within me that I started a war with myself. Every day was a different battle between forgiving him and walking away. And every time I communicated my feelings to Connor, his reaction would be different. If he wasn't yelling at my indecisiveness, then he was soft, comforting me and affirming me that everything would be okay. The manipulation was hidden behind kind eyes, narcissism hidden behind a beautiful smile. Each day I changed my mind, going back and forth between what I wanted. Exhaustion began to take its form under my eyes.

But Nicole wasn't gone. She begged for Connor and as much as he told me he didn't want to be with her, I absolutely had my doubts. The second Connor would leave my house, he was at hers. And the worst part was that I knew it. He was playing us both, telling us the same things as he kissed our skin within hours apart of each other. But even though I knew it, part of me still hoped I was wrong.

"It's over between me and her," he said, reaching for my hand as we sat on the couch. "I only want you."

"Then please just block her and delete her number and stop hanging out with her," I requested.

He dropped my hand. "I can't do that," he shook his head.

"Why not?"

"Because..." he glanced around, "I still need to make sure that she's okay."

"You didn't make sure I was okay when you left me," I said.

He zipped around to face me. "Well that's in the past. I can't fix that. What do you want me to do about it?"

I already hardly trusted Connor after what he had put me through the year prior, and I wasn't about to be cheated on again. "Well, if she's going to be around still, then I don't know if I could be with you."

He shook his head. "You're overthinking."

"I'm not overthinking," I said.

"Yes, you are. You're making everything about her. How do you expect us to move on if you're making everything about her?" he snapped.

I looked down for a second, wondering if it truly was my fault. Was I overthinking? Was I the reason why we kept arguing every damn day? I couldn't be. Right?

"You're not really giving me any choice..." I said in my small, frail voice.

Connor angrily stood up. He stomped over to the front door and opened it, stepping to the side of it. He turned back to me. "Fine. Then leave. Like you always do. That's the only thing you're good at."

I studied my lap as a single tear started to fall down my cheek, but I caught it and wiped it away before Connor could notice. I took a deep breath as I stood up and walked past Connor out the door.

I hopped in my car and started to drive home, trying to keep myself as calm as possible. I loved him, but I needed to do what was best for me. Right? Or was he what was best for me? I couldn't even tell at this point.

My phone started pinging over and over again in my lap and after a few minutes, curiosity got the best of me. I pulled over to read the text messages that had been flooding my phone, stress overwhelming me as more rolled in.

Connor could see that I was reading them and not responding. My silence only caused more of a reaction from him. But what I didn't understand was why he was texting me so much when he just told me to get out of his house? In my mind, it was because he loved me. At least, that's what I wanted to believe.

Can we talk?
Tate?
I'm sorry, okay?
Come back
Tate, answer me
I said I was sorry
So, that's it? You're really just gonna walk away again?
Like you always do?
I don't feel bad for saying what I did
You've changed
Why don't you love me?
Can you say something?
This is why it's your fault. You don't even try
Tate? C'mon, let's talk. Come back
You're going to regret this.

I didn't want to be the reason why things didn't work out between us. I wished I could go back and stop Connor from walking out the door that day. Stop him from ever being with Nicole. But I kept trying to remind myself that it was his choice to go. I wasn't going to hold him against his will back then if he didn't want to be with me. But that's the part that sucked the most. He wanted to be with me *now*. And deep in my heart, I wanted to be with him, because I had hopes of things going back to how they were before any of this bullshit ever happened.

My phone pinged again with one more text.

I'm sorry. Please come back. I love you. Let's fix this.

I threw my head back, my heart aching. I knew I should walk away and not look back, but for some reason, I didn't. I felt like staying and waiting it out would be better than running. I wanted to fight. I wanted a happy ending.

I turned the car around and went back.

At that point, the battle within me was less important and the war against Nicole, ignited. I fought tooth and nail for Connor's love. I wanted to be the only one, but so did she. Once he noticed my weaknesses and my fears of the situation, he started to use them against me. Connor would threaten to go back to her, knowing that it would get me to stop doing anything he didn't approve of. It was his own way of controlling me. He put himself first and put me last. He was the true definition of a narcissist. In his mind, nobody in the world was perfect besides him and everyone should feel blessed to be in his presence. He required constant, excessive admiration, believing that he was superior to everyone else. He made me feel like I didn't deserve him, made me feel like I was never going to be good enough for him.

As time went on, the pressure began to rise. Because ironically, the one thing we didn't have was time. It had been an exhausting six months since Connor initially came back for me, and time was running out until he would be leaving to join the Marine Corps.

One day, I walked into Connor's room, immediately pained at the sight. On each wall, three hundred and sixty degrees, were pictures of Connor and Nicole. There was not a single square inch of me, reminding me of just how much I truly meant to him. Tears gushed out of my eyes at the sight, but I couldn't bid myself to look away.

"C'mon, let's go eat." Connor stood in the doorway with crossed arms. He hadn't said anything about my crying eyes, completely disregarding them. His eyebrows raised, waiting for me to get up and follow him.

"You put all of these back up?" I quietly asked.

He shrugged once. "It's how I like to decorate my room."

"But—"

"I'm not changing it just because you want me to," he said. "Let's go eat," he repeated.

I looked up at him with my stinging eyes, dumbfounded by how he still hadn't said a single thing about them. "How come you only care when she's sad?"

He sighed, shaking his head. "Because it's different. My relationship with her was better."

My jaw dropped, shocked at his response. I couldn't believe that this was what I was fighting for. I gained the courage to walk out of the house without saying anything else to him. I walked home by myself that day, with blurred vision from unstoppable tears.

The next day, I sat in the car next to Nicole, a day that would go down in history. We had joined forces for the night, for the first and only time ever. Each of us had had enough of Connor's games and lies, and for once, we were overtaken by anger instead of sadness. Don't get me wrong, I still wasn't the biggest fan of Nicole, but it felt good to have the upper-hand on Connor, who still hadn't tried contacting me since I left his house bawling the day prior.

When Connor found out Nicole and I were together, he wasn't happy. Our mutual friend Bianca drove the car, pushing hard on the gas as Connor followed behind us in his white pick-up truck.

"I need to stop," Bianca called to us.

"Don't stop," I pleaded, scared of what would happen if she would. Nicole's phone was ringing nonstop, full of missed calls and texts from Connor. But why wasn't he trying to call me?

Bianca pulled into a shopping mall and the three of us got out, trying to run inside as quickly as we could before Connor could catch us. We figured that if we were inside and surrounded by people, then he couldn't do anything. We were still on the sidewalk when the pick-up truck pulled up to the curb. Connor leaned over and the passenger door flew open.

"Nicole, get in the car," he demanded. The three of us stood, afraid. I had never seen so much anger in his eyes. And even as scared as I was, I still wondered why he wanted Nicole to get in the car instead of me.

He began to shout at both Nicole and Bianca, who didn't want to let Nicole leave with Connor. The three of them got into it, screaming into the night air. I stood back, silently. Watching the ordeal was my only option. I was too afraid to add into the chaos and before I knew it, I had been standing on the sidewalk, listening to a vicious argument for more than thirty minutes. It was as if I wasn't there. Connor neglected the fact that I was even there, careless as to how I felt at the moment. Only concerned with his own wants and needs.

Nicole started to move towards the truck, and I grabbed her by the wrist. "Nicole, please... don't," the desperation in my voice echoed off the buildings surrounding us.

She looked at me for a second, then looked at Connor. I gently released my shaking hand from her wrist as she slowly got into the car. They drove off into the night, leaving Bianca and I to sit in silence for the whole car ride home.

Within a month, Connor was back at my door and the cycle had restarted. I would awake each morning, and the first thing I would wonder was which side of Connor I was going to get that day. Would I get the side that was full of kindness and affection? Would I get the side that blamed me for all his issues and made me feel like I didn't deserve anything? Or would I get the side of him that was silent—the one that pretended I didn't exist?

I had finally had enough. I wasn't going to buy into his games anymore. And I wouldn't give in this time.

"Connor..." I started, absolute, utter exhaustion draping every inch of me from the pain and stress of the past few years. "I'm done."

"You're done?"

I nodded. "I'm done. I can't keep doing this," I said. He looked at me as if he didn't understand what I meant. "I can't keep being just an option to you."

"So, after everything, you're just gonna throw this all away?"

"You can't decide between us. You've been back and forth between her and I for all this time now. I told you that you had to choose and you still haven't. It'd be easier on you anyways if I just removed myself from the situation."

"She wouldn't ever do that."

"Okay, then go be with her!" I called out, covering my face with my hands, frustration overbearing me. "If she's so perfect and so much better than me, then go be with her."

Connor rolled his eyes. "I never said that. You're putting words in my mouth." He shook his head, jaw twitching. "I'm just saying. But whatever. I'm done putting in extra effort. If you're leaving, then that's on you. Don't try to come back to me after you realize that this was your fault, because I'm not trying again," he shook his head.

"Okay," I shyly replied, unwilling to meet his gaze.

"And Tate?" he said, all seriousness resting in his tone.

I finally turned to look at him. "Yeah?"

"Just remember," he paused, anger glowing in his eyes as he leaned in, "this one's on you."

I tugged at my hair as I watched him walk away, both relief and guilt washing over me. But at the same time, I wasn't worried. Because I knew he'd be back.

Connor and Nicole got back together almost instantly and within a few weeks, I awoke to my phone buzzing on my nightstand. I groggily answered, holding the phone up to my ear.

"Hello?"

"Tate?"

The voice caused my eyes to immediately open, overtaken by a million feelings hijacking my conscience. "What do you want, Connor?"

"Just wanted to talk."

"You shouldn't be calling me."

"You should be happy that I am."

"You have a girlfriend."

"I haven't talked to her in a couple of days."

"Why?" I asked.

"She was annoying me," he shortly responded.

"If she annoys you so much, then why are you with her?"

"Because I love her."

His answer caused a little twinge of pain inside my chest. I scrunched my eyes shut. "Then why are you calling me?"

"Because I can."

I rubbed my forehead, too tired to be getting into this conversation. I sighed, "I'm going to bed. Goodnight." I hung up the phone and laid back down, but once my eyes shut, the phone rang again. I grabbed at it, annoyed, knowing who it was. "What?" I answered.

"Why'd you hang up on me?"

"Call your girlfriend instead," I snapped, hanging up again. But the second I placed my phone back on the nightstand, it was immediately buzzing again. I sighed loudly. "Stop calling me!" I said, irritated.

"You wanna know why I'm with Nicole?" he asked, before I had the chance to hang up again. I stayed silent, my tired mind unable to keep up with the conversation. "Because you fucked things up."

His words drilled into me, plunging at my heart. "I didn't..." I sadly said.

"Yes, you did. You gave up. You left."

A single tear fell down my cheek. "I'm sorry... I didn't have a choice."

"You didn't fight for me."

"I tried..."

"Well, you could've tried harder."

I wiped my tear away, taking a deep breath. "I'm going to bed," I repeated. "Goodnight."

I hung up again, turning my phone off this time to ensure that I would not be receiving any more calls. But even though my phone had stopped ringing, my mind was still on a loop, unable to stop thinking over the situation.

Each night from then on, between the hours of midnight and three in the morning, my phone would be buzzing. Nonstop. He would keep me on the phone for hours to tell me about his love for Nicole and how he only felt that way because I had fucked up. And if I hung up the phone, he would just keep calling until I answered. If I blocked his number, then he would use someone else's phone.

On top of calling anytime he was bored, he called me any and every time he needed a favor, guilting me into doing it for him. And if I didn't, then I would be accused of never truly loving him and that that was why things never worked out between us.

On the last night that I saw Connor, I went to his house to say goodbye to him. He gave me a quick hug and I pulled away before asking, "So are you really never coming back to Wilmot?"

Connor glared at me with no feeling or guilt in his eyes. "No, I'll be back. Only for her though." His straight face as he spoke shattered my heart, leaving me breathless. Why didn't he want to come back to see me? Did she really mean that much more to him than I did?

On the night before Connor left for the Marines, he gave me one last phone call. I sadly answered the phone, knowing that it would be the last time I talked to him for a while. We casually talked for twenty or so minutes and I began to tear up when I knew the conversation was coming to a close.

"I have to go..." he said. "Goodbye, I love you."

"I love you too," I said, before hanging up the phone, tears immediately running down my cheeks.

The phone call haunted me. I didn't go to school for over a week, my mind too disrupted to focus. The only thing I could do was sit in bed and cry, lost in my own thoughts. And the worst part was even after everything he put me through, I still missed him.

I wrote a letter to him each week, desperate to get a response, but I never did. Within six months of his departure, there was a ring on Nicole's finger, and I hadn't heard from or seen either of them since. That phone call was the last time Connor had ever spoken to me.

I had spent over three years as Connor's property. I was his puppet. And he pulled the strings.

After their wedding, I was never the same. I shied away from everyone, and even when other guys started to take interest in me, I refused to get involved. The constant hurt and feeling of emptiness lead to the beginning of my symptoms. The shaming, lying, manipulating, gaslighting, threatening, belittling, ignoring, criticizing, blaming, controlling and the pressure of the situation itself all caused permanent damage.

I had to start seeing a therapist when the flashbacks started to get out of control. She informed me that I had foregone a lot of emotional trauma, explaining that trauma chemically changes the brain, and that it didn't help that it all happened at a vulnerable point in my life. My early teen years were ruined by emotional, narcissistic, and psychological abuse. A psychologist diagnosed me with Complex-Post Traumatic Stress Disorder, which was similar to regular PTSD, but had more symptoms and occurred from ongoing stress or trauma, rather than just one single event.

Over time, I learned coping methods for better controlling my flashbacks and breakdowns, but that didn't mean they fully went away.

The scars would always stay.

Chapter Five
The Guitar

I had nightmares regarding Connor and Nicole for the next few nights, which was sadly normal for me. Axel had been texting me numerous times a day, trying to make small talk and asking if I wanted to hang out, but I had been ignoring all his texts since the last time I saw him.

Cutting Axel off wasn't necessarily what I wanted to do, but I knew that it was what I needed to do. I barely trusted myself as it was, so I sure as hell couldn't trust anyone else.

Claire, Gianna, and I were sitting in their room, doing homework. I was sprawled out on the couch, glancing over at Gianna every few minutes to see the sight of her gushing at her phone. Her and Ash were still talking, seeing each other almost every day. As happy as I was for Gi, I was also kind of upset by it. The thought of Ashton obviously made me think of Axel.

Gianna stood up from her desk. "Where are you going?" Claire asked. She still had no idea about Axel and I, nor Ashton and Gianna.

Gianna and I had made a deal that we would cover for each other if anything regarding either of the boys popped up. She gave me a concerned look, begging for me to help her out.

"Um," Gianna started, pulling excuses straight out of her ass, "I told my friend Ashley that I would go study with her."

"Who's Ashley?" Claire innocently asked.

"She's... from my bio class," Gi said.

"Oh, yeah, I... know Ashley," I budded in, trying my best to help cover for her.

"You know her too?" Claire asked, turning in her desk chair to face me.

I nodded briefly, trying not to make eye contact with her so that she wouldn't be able to sense my bullshit.

"Oh, okay," Claire said, not thinking anything of it. "Well when will you be back?"

Gi glimpsed over at me, unsure of herself and cringing at the fact that she was lying straight to her cousin's face. "I'm not really sure."

"Okay, well if you're leaving, then maybe I'll go hang out with Jason for a while." Claire turned towards me, "But only if you don't mind us both leaving."

The truth was that I did mind, but I wouldn't admit that. I didn't want to stop either of them from seeing people they genuinely enjoyed spending time with, even if that meant that I would be alone.

"No, that's okay. You guys can go."

They both seemed relieved as they thanked me, letting me know that I was welcome to stay in their room and do more homework for as long as I wanted.

Shortly after they left, I went back into my own room. Within minutes of plopping into bed, there was a knock at my door. I grumbled as I climbed down from my lofted bed, curious as to who would be knocking on my door on a Friday afternoon. When I opened the door, Axel stood in front of me.

"Hey," his glowing eyes rested delicately on me.

"Hi," I responded, puzzled by his random appearance.

"Can I come in?"

I pushed the door fully open and moved out of the way so that Axel could come inside. This was one of the many moments that I was glad Penelope took so many classes. It would've been extremely awkward if she was here right now and she would've wondered what the hell was going on.

"How did you get into the building?" I wondered.

He looked down at the floor and then up at me. "I waited for someone to go in before me and then I snuck in behind them," a small, embarrassed grin came upon him, making me want to grin too, but I didn't. "But um," his grin fell as he continued to speak, "I just wanted to come here and make sure you were okay, since you haven't really been answering my texts for the past few days."

I was taken off guard by his reasoning for coming here. Why did he care enough to take time out of his day to come make sure I was alright? Axel usually got bored easily with the girls he messed around with and the fact that we were never messing around with each other made me even more confused as to why his efforts were still high.

"Oh, yeah, I'm okay," I shyly uttered. I could tell he didn't believe me, and I didn't blame him. I didn't believe me either.

His eyes softened, "Are you sure? Tate, you can tell me if something's wrong."

I was astounded by how caring and gentle he was being. When I first met Axel, he was a douche, and now he was acting as if he truly cared about me. Of course, I wanted to believe that he did, but I couldn't allow myself to fall back into old habits. And on top of my lack of trust, I was too scared to tell him the truth.

"I'm fine."

"Then come hang out at the apartment tonight," he pleaded.

Since Claire and Gianna had left to hang out with their boy toys, I had no idea what I would be doing tonight. I debated waiting around for Penelope to get back so that I could ask her if she wanted to go to the frats tonight, but knowing her, she wouldn't want to.

"Well, I was gonna go to the frats tonight," I lied, knowing that I currently had no solid plans.

"Then we can pregame at the apartment with Gianna and Ash and then the four of us could all go to ATA for the night," he offered eagerly.

I was scared to go, afraid that another night drinking would cause me to give in to Axel. But I also didn't want to be stuck in my dorm on a Friday night. Either way was a loss.

"Okay, fine," I gave in. "I'm gonna take a shower and get ready and then I'll meet you over there."

He tilted his head down. "Promise?" He doubted that I would actually show up. I hated the fact that I seemed so wishy-washy to him, but I couldn't help it. My mind was a clusterfuck and it was stressing me out. I had tried numerous times now to stay away from Axel, but every time I did, he just kept reappearing.

"Yes, I promise," I replied, reluctantly.

After my shower, I threw some makeup on to hide the bags of stress that had been forming under my eyes and got dressed.

Although a big part of me didn't want to go over to the apartment, I knew that I had to. I made a promise to Axel that I would and even though tons of people had broken promises to me throughout my past, I had never broken any of mine.

I sighed as I opened my door, about to leave to go to the apartment.

"Oh, Lucas," I jumped.

"Hey," he rubbed the back of his head, "I was just about to knock."

I did another one of my shy, meaningless smiles that I always put on when around Lucas. I assumed that he had done what Axel did and snuck into the building behind someone.

"I, um, just wanted to come by and ask if you had plans tonight? Pi Rho is throwing so I was wondering if you wanted to come to the party with me."

Even though I initially dreaded going to the apartment, now I had never been so happy to have plans with Axel. At least I had an excuse to turn Lucas down.

"I'm so sorry, but I already have plans tonight," I explained.

His face contorted. "With Axel?"

I was surprised by his angry tone. "Would it matter if it was?" I snapped back, annoyed that Lucas was prying into my personal business.

"Yeah, it would actually. Axel is a complete dick and you shouldn't be hanging around him. Did you know he's gotten in trouble with the law *twice* this year alone?"

I was slightly concerned by the new information that was thrown at me, but my concern still wasn't enough to overtake my feelings of annoyance.

"Well, I'm sorry, but I have to go," I said, quickly locking my door behind me and walking away.

After a couple drinks and a few shots, I sat on the other side of the couch from Axel, trying to keep as much distance between us as

54

possible. There was an acoustic guitar sitting in the corner next to the tv, something I hadn't noticed the last time I was over. I stood up and walked towards to it.

"Do you play?"

Axel cringed as I picked the guitar up, clearly not wanting to answer the question. "No, not really."

"Hell yeah, he plays," Ash chimed in, "and he can sing too."

Axel shot him a look, annoyed that Ash had said anything.

"Can you play us something?" I asked in my small, frail voice.

Axe studied me as I gave an innocent smile. His chest rose and fell with a heavy breath. "Um, yeah, I guess so."

I brought the guitar over to him, prepared to hear what he had in mind. Axe rested the guitar on his knee, holding the neck of it with his left hand. He shifted around in his seat nervously.

Ash, Gianna, and I all gathered around in a state of excitement, the absolute opposite of Axel's current feelings. His shaking hands slowly began to strum the guitar, creating a beautiful harmony as he began to sing Ed Sheeran's "Perfect."

I examined the tense and release of the muscles in his right arm as his hands glided across the strings. I didn't know what I was originally expecting, but his voice was more beautiful than I could've imagined. Every so often, he looked up at me, sending butterflies to circle around in my stomach. His song choice was delicate, yet perfect, and it was refreshing to know that he had a soft side. Axe's tattooed arms and bad reputation didn't match his gentle voice, but I kind of liked it.

When he was done, I couldn't wipe the smile off my face, even when I tried my hardest to. The fear of the way he made me feel caused me to tense up. It was clear that no matter how much I tried to ignore or avoid Axel, he just kept coming around. The only option left was to friendzone him before he could actually try to make a move.

Within the next hour, we were already at ATA. The lights were bright, and the music was loud, creating the perfect party scene. I was surprised to find that even after twenty minutes of being there, Axel was still by my side.

I nudged him, "Surprised you're not standing in your usual hunting corner."

His eyebrows shot up as his smile rose. "My what?"

"You heard me."

"My hunting corner?" he asked with a chuckle.

"Mhmm."

He turned directly towards me, his chest less than a foot away from mine. He inspected every inch of my face. "Why spend the night over there when I can be here?" he asked, gently bringing his hand up to my head and moving a single one of my curls that had been out of place.

Butterflies swirled within me, breath faltering as I wondered what his next move was about to be.

"Hey, Axel!" a voiced called.

Axel turned, his charming smile reappearing at the sight of his frat brothers. "I'll be right back," he said.

"Don't feel obligated to," I joked.

He grinned and rolled his eyes as he walked away, leaving me with a feeling of almost missing him.

"I'll be right back too," Ash said to Gi. She nodded before he walked off, following in the direction of his brother.

Gianna and I were living it up on the dance floor as the boys talked to their frat brothers on the other side of the room. I figured that Axel would try to dance with me again tonight at some point, and I was conflicted as to how I felt about it. My drunken self wanted to let loose and have fun, but the growth of my feelings towards Axe were making me paranoid. My best bet was to simply find someone random to dance with. That way, no feelings whatsoever would be involved.

As the party began to fill with even more people, I scouted the crowd, becoming sidetracked by the disappointed look on Gi's face.

"What's wrong?" I yelled over the music.

"I miss Ash!"

I rolled my eyes. "You've been away from him for twenty minutes, calm down!"

"I just really like him, Tate!"

Before I could respond, I felt someone grab my waist from behind. I assumed that it was Axel and just as I was about to give in to his touch and push up against him, I noticed the frightened look on Gianna's face, causing me to turn around. Lucas was behind me, clearly intoxicated.

"Hey," he said, sluggish, "you look hot."

"What are you doing here, Lucas? You're not even in this frat."

"I came to see you," he leaned closer.

The smell of alcohol spilled out of his mouth each time he spoke. His eyes trailed down my body, and he bit his lip at the sight. When I first met Lucas, he made me uncomfortable by being overly sweet. And now, he made me uncomfortable by his impoliteness.

I backed away from him, but his grip on my waist tightened. I was starting to get furious by the way he was acting. I wanted his hands off of me.

"Let me go," I warned, struggling to undo his grip. "Lucas, stop! Let me go!"

"Let's dance," he smugly said. He pulled me closer to him, slowly moving his hand down my backside as I pushed against his chest, trying my hardest to shove him away.

Lucas's focus shifted to beyond my shoulder. His grin fell as his demeanor went rigid, causing him to release his grip on me. Axel stepped between us, a look of pure anger in his eyes. His hands were in fists at his sides and it was impossible not to notice his heavy breathing.

Lucas tried his best to hide his fear, but he wasn't doing a very good job. You could see by the look on his face that he was terrified of Axel. Were people really that afraid of him? Why? After hearing and seeing his softer side earlier, I couldn't even imagine Axe hurting anyone at all.

People around us stopped dancing, turning their attention towards the encounter. It was obvious that the spectators were hoping there would be a fight. I backed up until Gianna grabbed me, holding me next to her.

"I suggest you leave, Lucas," Axel's tone was venomous. I could see his jaw working under his skin in anger as Lucas continued to stand there, glaring at Axe. "*Now*," he added.

Lucas hesitated for a second before slowly backing up and walking away. As his drunken steps made their way towards the door, Ash pushed through a crowd of people that had been observing the confrontation. He ran up to Axe and they began to start talking too quietly for us to hear over the music.

Axe's anger still radiated off of him, but Ash didn't budge at the sight, looking displeased at what Axe was saying to him. It was clear that they were arguing. After a couple minutes of watching the two go at it, Axe turned on his heels, shaking his head as he exited out of the room through the back doors.

"I'll be right back," I told Gianna, following in Axe's footsteps out the back.

Axel's back rested against the brick building, standing under a single light. He brought a lit cigarette up to his mouth. My nose wrinkled at the smell, but I kept walking towards him anyways.

"You smoke cigs?" I raised an eyebrow, slightly disgusted.

He shook his head, avoiding eye contact with me. "Only when I'm pissed."

I took a deep breath as I wrapped my arms around his middle, resting the side of my cheek against his chest. His big frame went from rigid to relaxed at my touch. He switched the cigarette to his left hand to make sure it didn't get too near to me as his free arm went around my shoulder, pulling me close. His body heat warmed me up in the cool mid-October air. I could hear his heartbeat through his black t-shirt and even though I loved that it was the only sound in the air, I spoke anyways.

"Thanks for defending me," I looked up at him.

Axe dropped the cigarette on the ground, stepping on it quickly before retreating his attention back to me. His sparkling emerald eyes trailed down to my lips the same way they had when we were on the balcony. "You don't have to thank me," he whispered.

Axel's green irises didn't stray away from me as his mouth slowly started to make its way towards mine. As bad of an idea as it was, I couldn't resist. His soft lips lingered on mine for a moment, planting a fragile kiss.

The back door opened. Gi and Ash emerged, hand in hand. I dropped my arms from Axe's middle, hoping that neither of them saw our kiss.

"Are you guys ready to go?" Ash called out.

"We're leaving already?" I glanced at Axe, then Ash, whose eyes were fixated on Axel.

"Yeah," Ashton responded, "you guys can come hang out still at the apartment if you want." His eyes didn't turn away from Axel as his smirk slowly rose.

"I think I'm just gonna go back to my dorm and go to bed." I was only a little tired, but a lot of feelings were swirling around in my head. The desire to spend more time with Axel was stronger than ever, but so was the desire to run.

Gianna's frown appeared at my response, but she definitely knew what was going through my mind. "I'll go with you," she cheerlessly offered.

Chapter Six
The Savior

Over the next week, I dodged hanging out with Axel, but I made sure to respond to his texts this time to ensure that he wouldn't show up at my door again.

It was impossible to deny the sparks that flew between us during our kiss, but the issue was that I had no idea what those sparks meant. My feelings towards Axel were so complicated at this point that my mind was foggy. The battle between wanting to be around him and wanting to stay away was becoming overwhelming. All I knew for sure was that at the end of the day, I did enjoy spending time with him. He had shown me numerous different sides of him, including his soft side, and I felt special knowing that I was probably the only girl he's ever done that for. But I also didn't want to assume anything. I was more than okay with the idea of being just his friend, knowing that with the way my mind worked, we couldn't be anything more. But I still didn't even know how he felt. He hadn't talked about his feelings at all since the second I met him, and it was both infuriating and relieving.

Claire knocked on my door, opening it up to showcase her pretty smile. "Hey, you!"

I giggled from my lofted bed. "Hi!" I hadn't seen Claire in days. She had been spending every living, breathing moment with Jason. "What's up?"

"Well I haven't seen you in a while, so I was wondering if you wanted to go grab pizza in town?"

"Yeah, sure! I'm starving," I responded, climbing down.

I brushed my long hair as Claire sat on the futon, going on and on about how great Jason was. After a few minutes of her rambling, I stopped listening. Of course, I wanted her to update me on the things going on in her life, but I couldn't handle hearing Jason's name one more time. After all, Gi was starting to really like Ash, but she wasn't mentioning him fifteen-hundred times a day.

"Is Gi coming?" I asked as I ran the mascara wand over my lashes.

"No, she said she's at some study group or something." She rolled her eyes. "She's been studying so much lately. I don't think she's ever studied this much, like, ever."

I slowly nodded, pretending not to know about Gianna's true whereabouts.

I skimmed my menu when we got to the pizza parlor, trying to decide which personal pizza I wanted. Claire kept looking up at the door every ten seconds, and since my back was to the door, I couldn't see why, but within a few minutes, I *heard* why.

"Hey!" a voice called behind me. My eyes widened at the sound, spinning around to reveal Jason and Lucas striding over to our table. Jason leaned down, planting a kiss on Claire's cheek before sitting beside her. "Hello, my beautiful."

I cringed watching, but cringed even more as Lucas slid into the seat next to me. I shifted my chair over a little, trying to get as much space between us as possible. Claire and Jason immediately zoned us out, only devoting their attention to each other, and leaving me to sit in awkward silence with Lucas.

After what happened last weekend, seeing Lucas anywhere was the last thing I wanted to do. Gianna and I hadn't told Claire about the whole ordeal due to the fact that it involved Axe and Ash, but I was still pissed that Claire invited them without asking. She didn't need to know what recently happened in order to know that I didn't like Lucas. I had expressed that to her numerous times.

I pulled out my phone and held it under the table, making sure the brightness was low, before sending a text to Gianna.

SOS, went out to get pizza with Claire and she invited Jason and Lucas without telling me.

I sat there silently, hating my life, scanning everything in the room other than Lucas. I stared down at my lap, creating a curtain of my hair between the two of us. My phone buzzed in less than a minute.

Oh, hellllll nahhhh, wtf! Can't believe she would do that to u.

"Tatum," his voice caused me to jump, "I just wanted to say I'm really sorry for what happened last weekend." When I didn't respond and only looked down at my lap, he continued. "I don't know what came over me, I—I guess I just got too drunk and you looked so pretty, and I acted out. I disrespected you and I'm sorry."

I didn't want to accept his apology, but I still did anyways. "It's fine."

But even though I accepted his apology, I still didn't like him. I simply didn't want to cause more drama than there had to be.

"No, it's not. I'm really sorry," he said again.

"It's *fine*."

"Let me make it up to you," he offered. "Let me take you out to dinner."

I ran my fingers through my hair, uncomfortably. I took a deep breath before pressing my lips into a hard line.

"Tate?" Lucas quietly added.

The door chimed as it opened, and I didn't think anything of it until two hands smacked down on the table. Axel leaned into his hands. His white tee and leather jacket spelled trouble, but the look on his face spelled pissed. He eyed Lucas closely, his jaw twitching in anger.

Everyone at the table watched carefully in silence, afraid of what Axel's next move was going to be. His focus broke from Lucas, anger melting away as he gazed at me.

"You wanna leave, Tate? I'll drive you home," he spoke softly, almost in a whisper.

I inspected everyone at the table, noting their rattled faces. Turning to Axel, I nodded and stood up.

"Dude, what's your problem?" Lucas shouted.

The look of outrage reignited in Axel's eyes and the table shook as he leaned in, until he was directly in Lucas's face. "You're my problem," he hissed through his teeth.

The petrified look in Lucas's eyes didn't stop him this time. "What are you gonna do about it? Beat me? So that you go to jail again?"

I lightly touched Axel's shoulder. His tense muscles faded under my touch. "Axe," I quietly talked, "let's just go."

He stayed an inch from Lucas's face for a second, breathing heavily, then gripped my hand and led me out of the pizza parlor to the Mustang.

Now I really couldn't cut him off. He had saved me from Lucas more times than I could even count. At this point, I owed him.

I sat in the passenger seat of the Mustang as Axel drove, blowing off his steam.

"How did you know I was—"

"Gianna told me," he stated, not taking his eyes off the road.

I gave a small nod, sitting in deafening silence for a moment before I got the courage to speak again.

"Axe?"

I could tell he was trying his hardest to drop his temper so that he didn't take any of it out on me. "Yeah?"

"Have you really been arrested?" It was a question that I had been wondering since Lucas originally mentioned it, but I didn't have a good time to bring it up until now.

He sighed. "Yeah."

I didn't like being nosy towards him since I hated when people were nosy towards me, but I couldn't resist. I needed to know why. "What happened?"

Axe glanced at me with compassion in his eyes for a second, switching his attention back to the road. He shifted around in the driver's seat, his grip on the wheel tightening and releasing in anxiousness. "There have just been a couple of times in the past where I got into arguments with some people and... just lost my temper for a second. But the charges have always gotten dropped." His eyes peeked over at me again. "Tate, I don't want you to be afraid of me. I've never, ever hit a woman and I never would."

"I'm not scared of you," I delicately responded. But the truth was that I was scared of him, not physically, but emotionally. Every second he was around made my already reluctant feelings grow, and I was terrified of what the end would become. That was one of my worst habits. I always anticipated disaster.

"Good, because I promise you have no reason to be scared of me. I wouldn't ever lay a hand on you." His hands gripped the wheel tightly, but his lips spoke softly.

"I know."

"Good," he repeated. His smirk appeared, along with his dimples. "I'm sorry I pulled you out of there before you could eat. You're probably starving. Do you want me to stop and pick something up? Or if you want, you could come back to the apartment and I could make you something?"

"Chocolate chip pancakes?"

He revealed his perfect, pearly whites again. "You've got it."

A little while later, I picked at my fingernails as Axel flipped our pancakes. He peeked over at me every few minutes, but I kept my eyes on my nails, refusing to meet his gaze. Every time we locked eyes, butterflies swelled within me. He gave me a warm, fuzzy feeling and as nice as it was, I also hated it. Because it meant I had feelings, which was exactly what I didn't want.

"Can you flip these for a few minutes for me?" Axe asked.

"Uh, sure," I agreed, taking his place in front of the stove. I flipped away as Axe went over to the living room and turned on the tv, flipping through the channels until he found one that he liked.

I bit my lip as I focused on the pancakes, jumping as I felt a hand graze mine. Axe's hand rested on mine, guiding me as I flipped the next pancake. He stood so close that I could feel his chest against my back.

"I can do it myself, you know," I quietly said.

"I know. Just figured I'd help you out."

I stood up taller, fidgeting a little from his touch. "How thoughtful," I sarcastically said as I threw the final pancake onto a separate plate.

Axe turned the stove off before tossing the pan into the sink. "You wanna watch a movie?"

"Is that usually what you ask a girl before you make a move?"

He chuckled, rinsing the pan off with cold water. "Tate, if I was just trying to sleep with you, I would've done it by now."

"I like how you're so confident that I'd give into that."

His eyes scanned me, amused. "There you go again with that whole fake bitch thing."

"And?"

"And you wanna know how I know it's fake?"

I sighed, rolling my eyes. "How?"

He turned his back against the counter, leaning against it as he studied me. "Because if you really hated me, you wouldn't hang out with me. And you most definitely wouldn't have cared enough to calm me down earlier at the pizza parlor."

"Just because I don't hate you doesn't mean I wanna sleep with you."

"Didn't say you did," he smiled.

"Glad we're on the same page, then."

Axe tried to hold in laughter, but failed.

"What?" I shot at him.

"You're cute when you're defensive."

I looked down as my cheeks flushed, not wanting Axel to know how he truly made me feel.

I laid in my bed after getting back from the apartment, drowning myself in thoughts about how pissed I still was at Claire. She knew that I didn't like Lucas and the fact that she invited him to our dinner without asking for my permission didn't just bother me, it infuriated me. The one and only thing she's asked me to do with her in so long, she ruined. I had been excited to see her after she'd been up Jason's ass for weeks on end, but now I didn't want to see her at all. She hadn't even bothered texting me since I left the pizza parlor, which only made me angrier.

"Alright, what's up? You've been silent since you've gotten back," Penelope said from her desk.

"I'm just... really fucking mad."

"Why? What happened?"

I sat up in bed, sighing, "Claire asked me to get pizza with her earlier and invited Lucas without asking me and then Axel had to come to my rescue, once again."

"Lucas? Like, creepy Lucas? The one whose been hitting on you all year?"

I nodded, pushing my lips together into a hard line.

"Yikes, sounds like a nightmare."

There was a small knock on the door. As Penelope opened it to reveal Claire on the other side, her face twisted. "Oh... Claire," Penelope awkwardly started, "hey."

"Hi," she said happily towards Penelope before dropping her smile into a frown at me. It was as if the tension in the air had taken a physical form, and all three of us felt it.

"I'll just go outside for a few minutes," Penelope nervously walked out, leaving me to deal with the unnecessary wrath that I knew Claire was about to give me. She waited until Penelope was gone before she started.

"What the hell, Tate! Axel? Really? Even after I specifically told you to stay away—"

"I don't give a shit right now what you told me, Claire! I really don't!"

"Well, you should, considering the fact that he's a dick!"

For some reason, her comment bothered me. A strange urge to defend Axe was swelling up inside of me.

"You wanna know who's a real dick?"

She stifled a laugh as she gazed off. "Who?"

"Lucas!"

"Mhmm, okay, yeah, sure. And why the hell would you think that? He's only ever been nice to you!"

I raised my brows. "Yeah, that's what *you* think. Little do you know his drunken ass showed up at ATA last weekend where he groped me against my will and Axel had to come to my rescue, once again!"

"Oh, so now what? Axel is your knight in shining armor?"

"Well, he keeps saving my ass from Lucas, so apparently, yeah! Me being friends with him has nothing to do with you, anyways. He's been a better friend to me than you've been lately!" I yelled, still on top of my bed.

She crossed her arms with a stunned look on her face. "What is that supposed to mean?"

"It means that you've been with Jason every damn second of every damn day! Ditching Gi and I. Ignoring our texts. And now today, you invite him and Lucas to dinner with us after it being the first time you asked me to do anything with you in weeks? And even when you know that I do *not* fucking like Lucas at all?" I snapped. I wasn't really the type to get super angry, but after bottling up my saltiness with Claire for a couple weeks now, I couldn't help myself.

Claire was taken off guard at my rant. Her facial expression turned from anger to sadness, realizing that I was right. Her eyes glared down at her shoes, but I couldn't tell if she was upset with me or if she was upset with herself.

"I'm sorry," her small mouth muttered into the stiff air. "I guess I have been spending a lot of time with Jason instead of you guys."

My anger subsided a little. "I mean, it's fine. I get it. You like him a lot. But c'mon... inviting them to everything?"

"You're right. I'm sorry. I should've asked you first."

I slowly nodded, biting the inside of my cheek as Claire climbed up my bedside ladder, falling onto me with a hug.

"Forgive me, bestie?"

I sighed. "You're forgiven. Just don't pull that shit again."

"Got it," Claire nodded. "You really are the best," she expressed through her smile.

I laughed, "I know."

"Did Lucas really grope you?"

"Yep," I responded, cringing at the thought.

"And Axel helped you? Interesting."

"Very."

"Well, as long as you're just friends, then I guess there's nothing to worry about."

"Yeah," I quietly responded, attempting to believe myself. "Nothing to worry about."

Chapter Seven
The Rose & The Cigarette

After Claire found out about Axel, Gianna felt that it was a good opportunity to tell Claire about Ashton too. We were both relieved that Claire finally knew about the boys, so that we wouldn't have to keep sneaking behind her back anytime we went to go hang out with them. Claire was most definitely unhappy that we had been lying to her, but she contained her anger and brushed it off, which we were beyond grateful for.

As Halloween rolled around, I contemplated how this year would go. On top of the stress of finding a perfect costume, the three of us hadn't spent a Halloween apart in years and with our new, different friend groups, we didn't know how to handle it. Jason would absolutely not leave behind Lucas, but we all knew that if him and Axe were in the same room together, it would be a blood bath.

The three of us roamed around the Halloween store, looking for good costumes. I wanted something that made me stand out from everyone else. The typical "sexy cat" or Playboy bunny was not up my alley.

After a seemingly failed mission, I came across an overly sparkly yellow top. It was very cropped, almost looking like a bra. The jewels nearly blinded me, but it sure as hell was pretty. I took it off the hanger and held it up to my body in the mirror that was set up in the corner of the store.

"That's cute. What would you be with it though?" Claire stood behind me, scrunching her face deeply in thought.

I studied myself in the mirror for a minute, taking in my long, brown hair with the yellow top.

"What if I wore black spandex with it and did my hair half up, half down and was Belle?"

"Oh my God, yes! And then you can have a rose too," Gianna voiced.

I pushed my lips over to one side. "Do you think Axel would like it though?"

I could see Gi and Claire look at each other in the mirror. "Tate," Gianna started.

"What?"

"Just date him already," she tilted her head to the side.

I eyed her in the mirror. "No way!"

"Why not!" she bounced back.

I dropped the yellow top by my side, taking a deep breath. "Because I don't have feelings for him like that." Lie. Total lie. Absolute. Complete. Utter lie. We all knew I had some feelings for Axe, but the feeling that controlled me the most was fear.

They both shook their heads at me, identifying my bullshit. "Yes, you do. You're just trying to convince yourself that you don't because you're afraid he's going to end up being like Connor." I winced at the name. "Sorry," she added.

Even though in the back of my mind, I knew she was completely right, there was no way I would accept it.

I continued to stare in the mirror, avoiding answering.

"Well to answer your question, I think he'd love it!" Claire joined in smiling, trying to clear the awkward silence in the air.

Her reaction gave me a tiny grin, and after looking at the top one more time in the mirror, I was sold.

I finished curling my hair, throwing half of it up to create Belle's hairstyle. My long, curly brown locks rested against my back, matching perfectly with my sparkly yellow top. The black spandex and the short, black heels that I wore made my legs look even longer.

"Oh! I love it!" Claire said, opening my door. Her enthusiasm made me excited. I was pumped knowing that I looked good in the costume I decided to wear. It gave me a bit of confidence, which was huge for me, because Connor had taken all of mine. I had worked hard over the last year and a half to gain my confidence back and the longer I was out of Wilmot, the more I had.

Claire's devil horns rested easily on top of her straightened hair. Gianna walked in behind her, dressed as an angel. They usually wore matching costumes each year, so this year was no different. The only difference was that we would be attending divergent parties.

"So, are you ready to go meet the boys at the apartment?" Gi asked.

I held up a finger, signaling her to give me a second, before painting my lips with a light pink to complete my costume. I usually did red on my lips, so doing a light pink was a good change for the night. I glanced at myself in the mirror again, then nodded.

Gi offered to drive us in her car, which I was thankful for, because my nerves were too distracting. I had felt more confident than I had in a long time, which sadly, made me nervous. I didn't know if it was the fear of being wrong about the way I looked tonight or if it was simply the fear that my confidence would once again be wrecked.

I sat in the passenger seat, not only nervous about seeing Axel, but also nervous about Gianna driving, but I wasn't in the mindset to be driving myself.

After dropping Claire off at Jason's, we started to head towards the apartment. I bobbed my leg up and down in the passenger seat, staring out the window.

"Stop that. Your nerves are making *me* nervous," Gi laughed.

"Sorry," I quietly apologized.

"You really have nothing to be nervous about, Tate."

I kept my eyes out the window, watching the buildings and other cars pass by. "I know," I sighed. "I just... can't figure myself out."

"Well stop rushing yourself. You always feel the need to know exactly what's going to happen and when it's going to happen. Just breathe and let fate take its course," she assured me.

But that's exactly what I was afraid of. After everything that I'd been through, I couldn't even trust fate. I could not trust the world for shit. The world was out to get me, and I knew it. I felt emotionally unsafe, as if any and every guy was out to ruin me. It was a normal way to feel when you had C-PTSD. I didn't want those thought processes to

70

brand me forever, but my mind couldn't wrap its way around how to successfully get past it without getting hurt in the process.

Ashton opened the apartment door for us, as usual.

"What do you guys think?" he stood, flexing his muscles in his police officer costume.

"The shades are a nice touch," I giggled as he nodded in a dorky way. I knew that Axel wasn't out of his room yet, but the second I stepped inside, all I wanted was for him to be.

Ash gave me a friendly hug before wrapping his arms tightly around Gi, lifting her feet off the ground. A modest grin found its way onto my face, but a little hint of jealously peeked up too at how perfect they seemed to be. Don't get me wrong, I was overjoyed by how happy Claire and Gi both were in Jason and Ashton's presence, but I was jealous by how easily they could put themselves out there. A lot of people in the world had trust issues, but for some reason, they could get past theirs and I couldn't. Was something wrong with me?

Axel emerged from his bedroom. The sight of him caused my heart to skip a beat. He was wearing black from head to toe. I had never seen his hair slicked back until now, but it sure as hell looked good on him. Black shades covered his eyes, a superb addition to the unlit cigarette in between his lips. The black t-shirt he wore hugged him tight enough to highlight every muscle on his body. It made me think about the dragonfly tattoo on his abs that was hidden underneath the shirt.

"What are you supposed to be?" I crossed my arms, inspecting him up and down one more time.

He spun around to show off his whole costume. "A greaser, baby," he responded, dropping his black sunglasses down to look at me. "Duh." I eyed him carefully as a smirk rose onto his face. "And what are *you* supposed to be?" He lifted an eyebrow, the unlit cigarette moving in his mouth to each word.

I lifted the fake rose in my hand. "Princess Belle, duh."

His full smile appeared as he made his way over to me, wrapping me up in a hug. "You look great by the way," he played with my hair, still maintaining a massive smile on his face.

"Thank you." I could feel the butterflies bursting in my stomach as he leaned his head down and placed a precise kiss on my forehead.

"Surprised you're not wearing red lipstick."

I rolled my eyes. "It wouldn't have gone as well with my costume."

Axe chuckled, shaking his head as he made his way over to the kitchen counter to take the liquor out.

After only a few shots, I was slightly buzzed, but nowhere near entirely drunk. I felt good though, satisfied. We danced our way around ATA, laughing our asses off. Axe spun me around and playfully tickled me as he hugged me to him, which surprised me. I had only seen his misbehaved side on the dance floor before tonight.

Last time we were here, Lucas wouldn't get his hands off of me. But right now, being here with Axel, I felt safe. I knew that he wasn't going to let anything happen to me.

More people started to enter the party and the costume contest became fierce. There were costumes ranging from the Mystery Gang from Scooby Doo to sexy witches and wizards.

A small group of girls dressed as Playboy bunnies watched us from the corner, whispering to each other. They gave smug smiles at the sight of Axel, overtaken by his charm.

I nudged him. "Those girls over there are staring at you." He took a quick glance, then shrugged. "Why don't you go talk to them?"

His nose wrinkled. "Nah," he said, leaning in. "Maybe they're not staring at me. Maybe they're staring at you."

I brought my brows in. "And why would they do that?"

"Because... maybe they're trying to figure out if you're beauty or if you're beast."

I playfully pushed him over, trying to hide back my stupid smirk. Axel laughed, "Kidding!" He cocked his head to the side to signal for me to follow him.

We walked out the back doors, revealing the same brick wall that we had our first kiss against.

"Alright, why'd you drag me out here?"

"It was hot in there. I needed a breather," Axe said, resting his back against the wall.

I kicked at the pebbles underneath my feet. "How late did you want to stay until?"

"I'm fine with whatever."

"Okay. I just told Penelope I'd text her when I was on my way home."

72

Axe tilted his head. "You know you're welcome to stay at the apartment."

I scrunched my face together. "Eh, probably not."

"Why not? You've slept there before."

"Yeah, but that was also when I was hammered, so I didn't have a choice. For all I know, you could be secretly plotting to kill me this time," I joked.

"Yep, how'd you know?"

"I can read minds."

"Yeah? Then what am I thinking of right now?"

I squinted my eyes at Axe, deep in thought. "Probably sex."

Axe gazed off for a second, doing one-shoulder shrug. "Not a bad guess, but no."

"Then I'm out of guesses."

"Sex was your only guess?"

"Pretty much," I said, crossing my arms in the chilly air.

"I don't think about sex twenty-four-seven," he said. I lifted a brow, questioning him. "C'mon. I think you know by now that I'm not as bad as you initially thought I was."

"Debatable," I teased.

Axe smirked charmingly. "And just for the record, I was thinking about how pretty you look tonight." A tiny grin came about my lips. Axe caught sight of it, stepping closer. "Ah, there's a smile!"

"I'm going back inside," I insisted, trying to hide my grin as I turned on my heels and retreated back to the party.

I jumped around in the sea of people, enjoying being the perfect in-between of sober and drunk. My smile faded as more people walked in, with one catching my eye in particular. A guy in a Marines costume caught my eye immediately, sending shivers down my spine. The sight made my eyes water, but I couldn't look away. My mind replayed every second spent with Connor, both forwards and backwards, both good and bad. I stood, staring, frozen.

"Tate?" I could hear Axel calling my name.

"Oh shit. She's having a flashback," Gi noted.

"A what?" Axel asked.

"Just get her out of here!"

I could hear them talking, but I didn't have the mental capacity to snap out of my trance. All I could see was Connor's face, disgusted and disappointed with me. Nicole had walked down an aisle to Connor at the end of it while he wore the exact same uniform as the one at the party, yet I never got to see him wear it in person. And at this point, I wouldn't want to. But just because I didn't want to, didn't mean his grip on me loosened any bit. Feelings for Connor were long gone, but the grief still stayed.

Axel picked me up and carried me outside as a few tears fell down my cheek. He carried me the three blocks back to the apartment. I didn't really remember the walk. I was still too dissociated.

"Are you okay?" he asked, rubbing my arm when we got inside. I slowly nodded, finally returning to reality. He moved his body closer to mine, until I could feel his heat. "Tate, are you sure?"

"Yes..." I managed to get out.

His hand softly touched mine. "What happened?" he asked.

"I'm fine," I assured him.

"Tate..."

"It was nothing."

"You can tell me if something is wrong."

"Axe, I'm okay."

His green eyes gazed into mine intensely. I pushed my lips together, listening to nothing but the sound of our breaths. The energy in the air told me he wanted to kiss me, but instead of just going for it, he brought his hand up to my cheek. Axe slowly moved his thumb over my cheekbone, eyes traveling down to my lips.

I couldn't take it any longer. I connected my lips to his and he immediately moved his hands to my hips. My mouth parted, allowing him to slip his tongue inside. I wrapped my legs around his middle as he picked me up and brought me into his room, his lips never leaving mine. Axe set my feet down as soon as we got inside, backing me up against the wall. He gripped his shirt from behind his neck and tugged it over his head, exposing the dragonfly tattoo that I had been missing earlier in the night. I ran my hands over his skin, taking in every inch of it. His soft lips left my mouth and began to carefully trace my neck. I hummed at the feeling, grasping the waistband of his boxers that were peering out of his black jeans.

Axe's lips met mine again. His hands slowly moved to undo the clasp of my top, but just before he popped it off, I turned my head.

"Wait," I muttered, "I don't want to do this unless we were actually... together."

Even in the dim light from the moon shining through the window, I could still see the corners of his mouth turn up. "Okay," he started, "then let's be together. I want to be together."

"No."

His face fell. "No? Why?"

I wasn't ready to be with him, let alone anyone. And I wished I could've explained it to him, but I didn't have enough confidence to. I was still shameful about my past, shameful about my disorder.

My eyes didn't leave his. "I just... I just can't."

Axe's hands fell to his sides, along with his smile. The smile that I adored so much.

"I care about you, you know," he said.

"Just like you care about every other girl you've ever hung out with?"

His frown lengthened, upset with my response. I hadn't meant to hurt him, but the words had just come out. I guess my defensive wall was still up too high.

"C'mon, Tate. Don't be like that," Axe quietly said, turning his head away. After a few moments, he turned back towards me, reaching for my hand, but I pulled it away.

Axe looked me directly in the eyes for a second, realizing that I wasn't planning on responding. He spun around and walked over to his closet, pulling out a t-shirt and setting it on the bed.

"Goodnight, then," he said dryly, walking out and shutting the door behind him.

Damn it. I just fucked him over and fucked myself over all at once.

Chapter Eight
The Truth

My nightmares are what caused me to wake up early. I changed out of Axe's t-shirt that he had laid out for me the night prior and threw my own clothes back on. I felt bad for waking Gi up so early, but there was absolutely no way I could be there when Axe woke up.

After falling asleep with guilt surrounding me, I didn't have the nerve to confront him in the morning. The look on his face when I told him I couldn't be with him was engrained into my mind. Not to mention the embarrassment I felt after having another flashback in front of him.

Gi yawned as she drove us back to the dorms. "So, are you going to tell me why the hell we had to leave so early?"

I breathed heavily, my eyes glossing over. "Last night," I paused, playing with my own hands, "Axe told me he wanted to be together."

Gi's mouth dropped open. "No fucking way! Really? What did you say?"

"I said no."

Her eyes widened, mouth still open. "Tatum Dianne Everley! Why? I mean, I know *why*, but like..." she trailed off.

My head shook back and forth. I bit my lip at the pain of the thought. "I—I don't know. My mind just isn't ready and it's not like he's the best idea."

"Tate, c'mon, are you kidding right now? He has done like a complete one-eighty for you. He hasn't been sleeping around or fighting anyone. He's shown you sides of him that no one else has seen. And he defends you any and every time you need him to. Just for *once*, stop overthinking."

She was right. I did always overthink everything. Because following my heart instead of my head in the past had only led me to a world of pain and shame. And now, to overcompensate for jumping into shitty situations, my mind tried to take every detail into account before jumping into anything at all. But it seemed like now, it was only hurting me instead of saving me.

"Well either way, it's too late Gi. I already told him no. I can't fix that now," I glanced back down.

I could feel her eyes study me for a second before she sighed. "When we get back to the dorms, we are both going to shower, change, maybe eat a little breakfast cause I'm hungry as shit, and then we are going back to the apartment and you're talking to him," she insisted.

"Gi, I really don't know—"

"I'm serious, Tatum," she interrupted me. "You've been beating yourself up over the situation for weeks. Stop letting Connor continue to control your life. Just *talk* to Axel about things. That's all I'm asking."

The anxiety building up inside of me was overwhelming, but if I didn't take control of it now, it would just keep controlling me.

"Okay," I finally agreed.

I had taken a long shower to wash off my stress and nerves, trying to convince myself to just trust myself and to trust Axel. I took all the time in the world getting ready, slowly preparing myself to go talk to Axe. We hadn't told the boys we were coming over, but we knew they would be home. And plus, texting Axe before going there would only add to my anxiety about it, which would make me start to overthink again.

By the time we stopped at the dining center to eat, it was already lunchtime. A little under four hours had passed since we left the apartment and as much as I hated that Gi was dragging me back there to talk to Axe, I knew it was the right thing to do.

I could barely eat with the amount of nerves that were circulating around in my body and the drive there only made it worse.

For the first time, the door was unlocked. The familiarity of the apartment as we walked in somehow caused my nerves to calm down a bit.

Ash was sitting on the couch watching tv. He turned his head towards us. "Gianna! Hi, baby!" His face dropped when he saw me. "Tate," he smiled nervously, his eyes going back and forth between Gi and I, "you're back."

"Yeah, I just figured I—"

The sound of bed springs caught my attention. The moans coming from Axel's room were too loud to be mistaken. My eyes glossed over, embarrassment running through my veins that this was what I came back for.

The noises ceased and within a few minutes, a woman came out of the room, fully dressed, her long, black hair in slight disarray. She walked past Ash and Gi, coming to a halt when she recognized me. "Oh, hey," she smiled. It was impossible not to identify her as our waitress from the night Axel took me out to dinner.

I looked away from her, saying nothing. Our waitress kept walking, stopping at the door. "Just call me whenever, Axel!" She yelled before exiting.

"Alright, Brooke!" he shouted from his bedroom.

Gianna turned to me. "Tate," she whispered, "I am so sorry. Let's just leave right now."

My eyes stayed on the floor, disappointed with myself, once again, for being stupid enough to believe that the world had been trying to help me.

"Hey Ash, would you want to—" Axel emerged out of his room in nothing but his boxers, stopping midsentence as he saw me. "Tate," he started, "you... you came back."

I wanted to both cry and to punch him in the face. But I just stood there, in silence and disgust. Not saying a word.

"Yeah, she came back! She came back to talk about you two being together, and then she walks in on this shit!" Gianna screamed.

"Gi..." Ash whispered, reaching towards Gianna.

"No!" she shouted, resisting his touch. "Don't even try to defend him. What he just did was beyond shitty."

Axel didn't break eye contact with me, even with Gianna's screams.

"Tate, I—"

"Don't," I finally spit out, making my way out of the apartment. I ran down the stairs and walked through the parking lot, heading straight towards Gianna's car.

"Tate, please, stop!" Axel shouted, running after me.

He looked ridiculous following me outside in nothing but his boxers, but still not as ridiculous as I looked for falling for his bullshit.

I wiped my tears away quickly, tugging at the car door. "Shit," I uttered to myself. It was locked.

Axel's hand lightly grabbed my wrist, swinging me around to face him. "Tate, please. I'm so sorry. Please don't leave."

"And why would I stay?"

He could hear the hurt in my tone, but I couldn't change the way the words were coming out. Axel's eyes slightly glossed over too, not giving a single fuck that he was standing in public, basically naked. He locked his fingers together, placing them on top of his head. His weight rocked back and forth, breathing heavily with grief instead of anger this time.

"It's just... last night fucking hurt. I've never wanted to be anything with anyone ever, but you're the only one I've ever felt this way about. And when I woke up and you had left, I—I just... needed to not feel alone," his lips quivered. "I mean, you said last night that you didn't want to be with me and I—"

"No," I cut him off, "I said I *couldn't* be with you, not that I didn't *want* to be with you."

Axe's hands fell back to his sides, glossy green irises staying on me. He took a step closer to me, setting his bare chest against mine.

"Do you want to be with me?" he slowly asked.

"Yes." A smile came across his face. "But I can't," I finished, causing his smile to fall.

His shaking hands carefully moved my hair out of my face. "But why?"

My eyes drifted down to the ground. "It's hard to explain. I just need to leave," I turned away.

"Tate, please stay."

His voice made my stomach drop. I had never heard such a desperate tone come out of his mouth, or anyone else for that matter.

Gianna made her way to the car, unlocking it quickly. I reached for the door handle. More tears burned my eyes, preparing to fall.

"Tate?"

I turned. Axe pulled his eyebrows in, hoping that I would give in. But because of Connor, I had learned my lesson.

"I can't be with you," I quietly said, opening the door.

"Okay... okay if that's how you feel, then you don't have to be. Just please... please don't leave right now," he pleaded.

I took one last look at Axe before getting into the car.

"Just drive, Gi," I stated, my tears finally making their way down my cheeks.

Axe banged on the window, reluctant to let me leave. "Tate, please! I'm begging you! Please stay!"

As she drove away, I glanced in the side mirror.

Axe stood in the parking lot with his head tilted back, covering his face with his hands. I sat in the car with an intolerable pain in my chest.

Great. The exact feeling that I was trying to avoid.

My phone hadn't stopped buzzing since the second I left the apartment. Texts, calls, and voicemails were flooding my phone, but I ignored all of them.

My brain was fuzzy, overwhelmed with a million emotions. Sadness and disappointment were inevitable, but anger made its way around too. I was pissed at Axel for not only sleeping with Brooke, but for even thinking to call her in the first place. And on top of being pissed at him, I was pissed at myself too. Because if it wasn't for me denying him last night, he wouldn't have felt the need to call Brooke. I knew that I shouldn't be blaming myself, but I couldn't help it. That's just the way my mind worked.

Claire, Penelope, and I all sat in my room. They tried their best to comfort me and get my mind off of it, but all I really wanted was to be alone. I couldn't get the idea of Axel and Brooke out of my head, no matter how sick the image made me feel. It was a feeling I hadn't felt since the day Connor and Nicole got married.

"Hey," Gianna gently said as she walked in. "I just got off the phone with Ash. Apparently, Axe is driving himself crazy and Ash couldn't stop him from leaving. He's coming here."

I smacked myself in the head with the palm of my hand. Awesome. More confrontation. Exactly the opposite of what I needed right now.

"I just wanted to warn you before he showed up," Gi added.

I took a deep breath, sighing. My dry eyes searched the room for what to do. Should I leave before Axe got here? Or should I stay and bear the pain of talking to him?

Before I could even weigh the options, there was a sudden knock on the door, and everyone eyed me, waiting for my next move.

"Tate? I know you're in there. Please open up. I really need to talk to you," Axe spoke through the door.

I carefully climbed out of bed and slowly strode over to the door. My shaking hand lingered on the doorknob for a second before pulling it open.

Axel's red, splotchy eyes gazed into mine, a clear sign that he was also in distress.

"We'll all just... let you guys have some privacy," Claire awkwardly stood, motioning for Penelope and Gi to follow.

Gi stopped before walking out, glancing back at me. 'I'm sorry,' she mouthed to me.

She had concluded that some of it was her fault since she had insisted on bringing me back to the apartment. But I didn't want her to put any blame on herself, knowing how terrible carrying guilt felt.

"Can I come in?" Axe kindly asked. I nodded, unprepared to hear what he had to say. "I can't even tell you how sorry I am," his voice rattled.

"You don't have to, Axe. It's fine," I said, even though we all knew it wasn't.

"No, it's not fine. You shouldn't have had to see or hear what happened," he shook his head, closing his eyes. "When I woke up this morning and you were gone," his voice trembled, "that was the closest I've felt to the day my dad left when I was a kid." He looked away. "And when my mom died, that's when I started having a temper and fighting and eventually sleeping around because the guilt was too much, so I had to distract myself somehow. But you make me feel like I don't need to do that stuff. I guess this morning, I just... fell back into old habits from the thought of not being with you," his eyes trailed back up to me. Even glossy and splotchy, those green eyes were still beautiful.

My gaze fell to the floor, unsure of how to respond.

"Tate, I feel like shit. I haven't felt this much guilt since my mom died."

"What happened?" I quietly asked before thinking. I had been wondering what happened with Axe's parents since we went out to dinner for the first time, but there had never been a good time to ask. The subject had never been brought up before now. I finally placed the piece of his father into the puzzle, understanding that Axe's father had abandoned his three children.

Axe blinked an abnormal amount of times, fidgeting. I felt bad for putting him on the spot. He clearly didn't want to talk about the issue, which made me feel bad for asking.

"You don't have to tell me," I said.

Axe nervously looked around, taking a deep breath before speaking, but even as he did, his eyes stayed locked with the floor. "I was eight when my dad left. My mom remarried a few years later, to this guy Paul, but he was an asshole. Got shitfaced drunk every day. Violent. Abusive," he paused, scratching the back of his neck. "Then one night when I was twelve, Amberly and Ash weren't home, but I was in my room, about to go to bed. I started to hear shouting coming from downstairs after he'd been drinking. They had gotten into an argument and he lost his temper and..." he swallowed hard, "killed her."

My heart dropped in my chest, absolutely sickened at the thought. Ash had told me previously that their mom had passed, but I never could've guessed that it would have been from such a violent, tragic way. I couldn't imagine how Axe must have felt.

No wonder why Axel had put all his energy into sex and fighting. He had the worst childhood possible. It explained why he was constantly getting in trouble. I started to feel bad for him, almost guilty from the way I treated him. But even though his current lifestyle had finally made sense to me, his intentions towards me still didn't.

"Axe, I'm so sorry. That's... absolutely terrible," my voice shook.

When Connor used to give me excuses as to why he would act a certain way or do certain things, he would always tell me exactly what I wanted to hear, whether it was true or not. And every time he would lie,

I would easily be able to tell, but I would let him get away with it anyways because I *wanted* to believe he was telling the truth. But standing here now, listening to Axe talk, there was absolutely no way he was lying to me. His eyes told me everything. When I first met Axe, he seemed like the type of guy who never wanted to show his weakness. He kept everything bottled up inside, putting on a show for everyone else. And now, here he was, breaking down in front of me.

The thought of being with Axe scared the absolute shit out of me, but the thought of losing him entirely was even worse. I wanted to kiss him. I longed to feel his arms hug tightly around me. But first, I needed to tell him the truth. This was the first time Axel had mentioned his parents to me. Talking about them clearly made him upset and uncomfortable, but he was honest, and I knew I needed to be the same.

"Axe, the real reason why I said I couldn't be with you has really nothing to *actually* do with you." I grabbed his hand and tugged him over to the futon, sitting down next to him. Starting from the beginning, I explained everything that happened with Connor and Nicole, shivering the entire time I spoke. I had rarely ever said either of their names aloud since their engagement and I dreaded any time I had to talk about the situation, but even with my racing heart, I knew it was necessary.

Axel's hand covered my shaking one. "So, when Gianna said flashbacks?"

I nodded. "Yeah, that's the C-PTSD kicking in."

His thumb caressed the top of my hand. "They diagnosed me with acute PTSD after what happened with my mom, which is when symptoms last about three months after the trauma. So even though I don't have those symptoms anymore, I know what it feels like to carry emotional baggage."

I was amazed with how understanding he was being. Knowing that Axe knew what my symptoms felt like made me feel comforted. Axe was a great listener, which made me happy, since I had never gotten that before.

My eyes peered into his. Emerald eyes shone exquisitely in the light. My new favorite sight.

Axe leaned in, connecting his mouth to mine and I immediately reciprocated. His hand lightly cupped my cheek as mine moved to the back of his neck. I pulled away, a smile covering my face.

His green irises lit up. "I wanna make all of this up to you."

"How?" I grinned.

"Anything you want. We can go eat if you're hungry or go to the mall or something," he winked, standing up and guiding me up with him. Butterflies swirled in my stomach at the sight of his charming smile.

But in reality, I didn't need him to do anything for me. I didn't need him to take me anywhere or spend money on me. All I needed was to spend the day with him.

"I don't need anything," I shook my head, laughing.

"Well we're going to the mall anyways," he said, tugging on my hand.

When he opened the door, Claire, Gi, and Penelope fell into the room. "Were you guys listening through the door?" I asked.

Claire shrugged her shoulders. "We needed to hear the tea."

I rolled my eyes, stepping over all of them. "You guys are ridiculous."

"Don't do anything that we wouldn't do!" Penelope yelled as Axel and I made our way down the hall.

After our entire conversation, I felt the ability to be a lot more open with Axe. We hadn't talked about what we were or being official, which I was fine with, because I needed things to be taken slow and he knew it too. Axe knew my whole past now and knew about my ongoing struggle with my disorder, but just because he knew, didn't mean I was prepared to jump into a relationship. I'd be lying if I continued to say I didn't have feelings for Axe, but I didn't fully trust him. After all, he still slept with someone else this morning.

Axe and I adventured through the mall, never dropping our smiling faces. My left hand was entwined with his, my right hand cupped his forearm as I leaned into him.

We came across a jewelry store and I peeked through the glass as we walked by.

"Do you wanna go in there?" Axe asked, noticing that I was looking.

I turned to him, bringing my brows in. "No, that store is too expensive," I replied, continuing to stride passed it.

He stopped in his tracks, his grip on my hand causing me to come to a sudden halt as well. I tugged, motioning for him to keep moving. "Let's go in," he insisted, cocking his head over to the jewelry store.

I shook my head, still yanking on his hand. He wrapped his arms around me from behind, beginning to guide me over to the store. I laughed as I struggled to stop him, but it was useless. He was too strong. It was impossible to get out of his tattooed grip.

I was grateful to see that the woman working the store was slightly older, so no flirtation towards Axel would be performed. At least I hoped not.

"Hello," she welcomed us, "are you looking for anything specific today?"

"We're just looking around, but thank you," I responded kindly, knowing that I was not buying anything from this store. Everything was too expensive, and I was a broke ass college student.

All the jewelry sparkled brightly in their cases, a clear sign that they were made from precious stones. I eyed the case of beautiful, gold and silver rings before moving onto the bracelets, and eventually the necklaces. A stunning pendant caught my eye. Made from pure silver and diamonds, the pendant glistened in the light, the same way Axel's eyes always did. The two hearts on the pendant were connected, tiny diamond studs making up the shape of each one.

I could feel Axe's eyes on me as I studied the pendant. "Ready to go?" I asked, finally turning back to him.

He narrowed his eyes at me. "Hmm, no." He waved the worker lady over, pointing to the necklace as soon as she got there. "How much for this one?"

She checked the price. "That one would be two-hundred and fifty."

Axe nodded. "We'll take it," he said, pulling his wallet out of his pocket.

I widened my eyes at him. "Are you insane? No, I'm not letting you buy this."

"Would buying you this necklace categorize me as insane?"

"Uh, yes!" I declared.

His shoulders shrugged up and down. "Then I guess I'm crazy." His grin appeared as he went over to the check-out counter.

He leaned against the counter, winking as he looked back at me. I crossed my arms and shook my head, trying to convince him to stop making a mistake.

"That's too much money," I sighed, making my way to where he stood as he handed money to the woman.

"Nothing's too much money if it's for you."

"He's a good one," the white-haired woman stated. "Make sure you keep him."

I smiled at her, heat rushing to my cheeks. We thanked her as we exited.

Axe pulled me aside as soon as we were out of the store.

"Come here." His wide frame towered over me as I stood in front of him. "Turn around," he gently insisted.

Once my back was facing him, I could feel his fingers graze the back of my neck as he moved my hair over to one side. The necklace rested on my chest as Axel guided it around my neck, securing the clasp. I glanced down at the beautiful piece of precious metal, smiling, in shock that Axe just spent over two-hundred dollars on me for no reason. I knew he had said he wanted to 'make it up to me,' but I didn't need material things in order for him to do that. All I needed was his time and affection. I wasn't used to people buying things for me randomly and it felt good to know I was cared about enough to do so, but I also felt guilty. The necklace was too much.

I wrapped my arms around the back of his neck, standing on my tippy toes to hug him. Axe rested his chin on my shoulder, holding me tight. He didn't let go until I did.

"I feel bad." I twisted the pendant around in between my fingers, examining it.

Axe lifted my chin with the tips of his fingers. "Don't. It's the least I could do." I tilted my head over and pushed my lips to one side. "Seriously, stop feeling bad," he chuckled. "Now do you wanna keep shopping or do you wanna go get dinner?"

I raised my eyebrows at him. "Neither! You just spent so much money on me unnecessarily. You are not buying me anything else ever." His dimples appeared at my reluctance. "I'm serious!"

He bit his bottom lip before giving me a quick kiss. "Alright fine, then we can go back to the apartment and I'll make something there."

"Fine," I agreed.

He observed the area around us. "I'm gonna go to the bathroom real quick before we go. I'll go to the one right down there. Be right back, okay? Just stay right here," he placed one hand on my hip and kissed my forehead before making his way down a side hallway.

I remained in the same spot, waiting for Axe, but I felt like I was being watched. I glanced around, trying to pinpoint where my worry was coming from. The mall was fairly empty, since most people were currently in the process of getting ready to go out tonight. But I couldn't shake the feeling that someone was lingering around.

"You okay?"

I jumped at Axe's voice coming from behind me.

"Yeah, I'm fine," I scratched my head, still glancing around.

Axe's thumb rubbed the back of my hand. "Okay, let's go."

I took a deep breath as Axe led the way out, trying to shake off the uneasiness of feeling watched.

But I knew I had nothing to worry about. Axel was with me, which meant I was safe.

Chapter Nine
The Doubt

I played with Axe's hair as we laid on the couch, watching a movie. We had spent the whole day together, being lazy. I dreaded the fact that tomorrow was Monday, because we each had class, which meant I wouldn't be able to see Axe until tomorrow night.

Axe rested up on his elbow, looking down at me. His green eyes lingered on me, seeming as if he wanted to speak, but still not saying a single word.

"What?" I asked.

His grin came into view, along with his adorable dimples. "You're beautiful."

I snickered at his remark. My messy bun and smudged mascara was definitely not a sexy look. I covered my face with my hands, embarrassed.

He laughed, trying to move my hands out of my face. "Stop that. Let me see your pretty face." He tickled my sides, causing me to kick the air.

My hands moved from my face to my sides, trying my best to swat away the tickling. I was laughing hysterically, shifting around.

I stopped whipping my head back and forth when Axe began to kiss every part of my face. He started at my forehead, slowly pecking his way all the way down to the corner of my mouth. I turned, joining our lips together.

Axel's hands stopped tickling me and instead, they started to glide up and down my sides. My palm drifted across the stubble on his face, eventually resting behind his neck. His lips parted as one hand traveled up my shirt, fiddling at my bra clasp.

It only took him a couple seconds to unclip it. Axe lifted my shirt up and over my head, then slid my unhooked bra off directly after. I tugged at the hem of his white t-shirt, signaling that I wanted it off. I lifted it a little until Axe did the rest, smoothly pulling it off and dropping it onto the ground, where he had placed my shirt as well.

His lips trailed down my jawline, delicately placing kisses onto my neck. I was once again surprised by how gentle he was with me. When people heard the name Axel Burne, they imagined someone who was wild, especially with the women he hooked up with. And even though I didn't know if he was this loving with anyone or just me, his softness made me more attracted to him.

I hummed as his mouth made its way down to my chest. I wondered if he could feel my heart starting to beat faster from his touch. His left hand grabbed at my ass while his right kept him in position. Lips stayed against my skin, finding a home on my left breast. I sighed as he began to suck. A love bite formed, marking his territory upon my skin. His free hand slowly slipped into my pants as his mouth connected back onto mine.

Axel launched himself on top of me as the apartment door jiggled open, trying his best to hide my bare chest as Ash trotted in. I giggled at the fact that we had just been caught like two young teenagers, even if we hadn't been actually having sex.

Axe's chest rubbed against mine, vibrating as he quietly laughed too.

"What's goin' on over here?" Ash chuckled, raising an eyebrow.

"Get the hell outta here Ash," Axe ordered.

"Alright, alright, fine. But if it was some random bitch and not Tate, I'd so cock block your ass."

Axe waited until Ash was all the way in his room to get off of me.

"Do you wanna move into my room?" he asked, one hand placed calmly on my stomach.

I started to get slightly nervous, not knowing how Axel would react to me not wanting to go to his room with him. Like I had told him on Halloween night, I wanted to be in an official relationship before I slept with him, but I wasn't ready for an official relationship yet. Things needed to be taken slow in order for my brain to process what was happening around me. C-PTSD didn't just simply make it difficult to trust people, but it made my brain perceive everything as an emotional threat. The more time I spent with Axe and the more he went out of his way to show he cared, the easier it was becoming to open up to him. But those were just baby steps. I was making progress, but I wasn't at the finish line yet.

"Axe... I want to, but I'm not ready to."

"Don't worry. I can wait," he said, before leaning down and kissing my forehead.

I walked through Perry Hall after finishing my last class of the day. My fingers twirled around my necklace, music blasting through my headphones.

A hand tapped my shoulder. I took a headphone out of one ear as I spun around at the feeling, utterly and hopelessly disappointed at the sight of Lucas. I was unsure as to why he was still bothering trying to talk to me. I had denied him more times than I could count at this point and even he knew that I was hanging out with Axel, so I didn't know why he had motivation left.

"Hey," he smiled, as if no bad blood had ever been shed between us before.

"Hello," I said uncomfortably as I continued to walk.

"You look really good today, by the way." The compliment coming from his mouth made me shiver. He struggled to keep up with my quickening pace. "I mean, you look good every day," he added with a nervous chuckle, scratching the back of his neck.

"Thanks."

"So, listen, I know things between us have been kinda rocky lately and I just want things to go back to how they were before."

As annoying as he was, his best friend was still dating one of mine and the last thing I wanted was for Jason to take things out on Claire because I was being a bitch to his friend. On top of that, I wasn't usually the type of person that hated anyone. Sure, I disliked certain people, but the only people I could genuinely say I hated were Connor and Nicole.

"Yeah, sure, same," I aimlessly replied.

"Alright, cool," he said, "so maybe we can grab lunch or something then?"

I abruptly stopped, pulling him over to the side to make sure we weren't standing in anyone's walkway. "Listen, Lucas, you're a sweet guy and all, but I just want to make it clear that we can *only* be friends."

He slowly nodded his head, trying to make it seem like he was understanding everything I was saying. "Okay, yeah, um, no worries."

"Thanks for understanding," I adjusted my backpack. "I'll see you around then." I timidly smiled, retreating to the exit doors.

As I made the journey to the dining center to meet Axe for lunch, a peculiar set of bright blue eyes caught mine. The same set of eyes that I saw on the night I met Axe. The same set that belonged to the guy who groaned and sighed when his friend group wasn't allowed into Sig Omega's party. He stopped when we made eye contact and I quickly looked away, trying to brush off the fact that I had been caught staring at him. He was attractive for sure, but I already had a guy waiting for me. One whom I genuinely enjoyed being around. One whom made me feel almost whole again.

"Hey," the kid called out in my direction.

Damnit. He caught me.

"Hi," I turned, trying to nonchalantly keep walking as I brought my red lips into a hard line.

"I feel like I've seen you before," he furrowed his brows, beginning to walk beside me.

"Oh, really?" I tried playing it off as if I had never seen him, but I was a terrible liar.

"Yeah," he grinned, "maybe it's the red lipstick that made you memorable."

He was clearly flirting, but he was lucky that Axel wasn't around to hear it. He would've ripped the kids head off.

I kept my gaze ahead, making it evident that I didn't feel like talking to him.

"So, um, what's your name?"

"Tatum," I responded shortly.

"Oh, that's a cool name. I'm Nick."

I didn't want to be rude, but if this kid followed me all the way to the dining center, Axe would probably have a heart attack before nearly kicking the shit out of him.

"Nick, um, I don't mean to be rude or anything, but I'm supposed to be meeting my boyfriend for lunch right now, so I have to go."

Was Axel actually my boyfriend? No. But was I hoping that saying he was would make this kid go away? Hell yeah.

"Boyfriend?"

I nodded, not stopping my stroll.

"Oh, okay. Sorry if I overstepped any boundaries, but I'll see you around then," he innocently said, pivoting around and continuing to walk in the direction he was originally going in.

I was relieved by how polite and understanding Nick was. It kind of pissed me off that Lucas couldn't be that way. I would have absolutely no problem with Lucas if he just kept his distance and understood my denial for what it actually was.

Axe was waiting outside the dining center for me, leaning against the brick wall. A grin extended across his face as I approached.

"Hello, gorgeous," he wrapped his arms around me, picking my feet up off the ground. "I've missed you all day," he said, playing with my French braid.

"I missed you too."

We found an open table and sat down with our food. I carefully took each bite, doing my best to keep my lipstick intact.

"Why are you eating like that?" Axe laughed.

"Cause I can't mess up my lipstick, duh."

"Well can *I* mess it up later?" he winked.

I playfully hit his arm, taking another bite of my food.

"Why do you always wear that lipstick anyways?"

"Because it's my look. So, pop off."

Axe brought his hands up in front of him in a defensive manner. "I didn't say I didn't like it," he laughed. "I'm gonna go refill my root beer. Do you need anything?"

I took a glance at my empty glass. "Could you get me some more lemonade please?"

He nodded, planting a quick kiss on my forehead before grabbing both glasses and heading over to refill them.

I continued to eat, becoming uneasy when I noticed a group of girls staring at me from a table across the cafeteria. I didn't know how long they had been watching, but it made me shift around in my seat. Any time eyes were on me for unknown reasons made me nervous. They talked amongst themselves after each glance in my direction, which only ensured my suspicions that they were talking about me.

"What's wrong?" Axel asked as he sat back down.

I pressed my lips over to one side. "Those girls over there have been staring at me the whole time you were gone."

Axe turned to look, but immediately zipped back around to face me.

"What?" I wondered.

He stared down at his plate, thinking of how to answer. He nervously chuckled. "Funny story, actually."

"What?" I asked again, this time firmer.

"Well," he scratched the back of his head, "I've kind of, sort of... slept with all of them before."

My eyes widened. I scanned the table again. "Axel! There's *five* of them over there. You've slept with all five?"

He winced at my reaction, nodding. Knowing that Axel's hands have been on those girls made me cringe. No wonder why they were watching me. They all assumed I was next on Axel's hit list.

"They were all before I met you though," Axe commented.

"There was one that was after you met me," I raised my brows, referring to Brooke as I took a sip of my refilled lemonade.

Axe winced again. "If it makes you feel better," he said, stabbing his fork into his food, "I was thinking of you the whole time."

Axe's comment did make me feel slightly more reassured, but my eyes were still peeled.

Chapter Ten
The Redhead

I had spent a lot of time with Axel over the past few weeks. Each day, I found that my feelings for him were growing. And each day, my fear grew with it. I had been trying my absolute best to ignore the anxiety bubbling up inside of me, but it was hard to shake the thoughts that were engrained within my head. I was used to being used and accustomed to being left. I was waiting for the moment that Axel would leave.

Every couple of days or so, when I would be out with Axel, girls glanced in our direction, only making me more concerned about the situation. The girls would eye me curiously, disapproving me, making me feel self-conscious. It reminded me of the way Nicole used to study me in disgust.

On top of my anxiety regarding Axel and my complicated chemistry, I was even more anxious with the fact that Thanksgiving was right around the corner. My family celebrated every year, usually inviting all of our relatives over for dinner. I missed my family dearly, but the idea of going back to Wilmot was unsettling. I wasn't ready. Every single thing in that town reminded me of Connor and Nicole. Since it was such a small town, each specific place held a tainted memory of them, a nightmare. I hadn't had a flashback since Halloween night, but I knew that going to Wilmot would cause me to have plenty.

I planned on calling my mom later that night to get her advice about the situation. But I worried that she would guilt trip me into going home.

While Axel was in class, I decided to get some homework done at the library. I sat at a table all the way in the back, doing my best to avoid people, as usual.

I jumped, glancing up when a textbook slammed down on the table. A redhead sat in the seat across from me, accompanied by two blondes standing behind her. I recognized the redhead as the one from the fancy restaurant that Axel and I had eaten at the first night we went out. The same restaurant that Brooke worked at. Fuck Brooke.

"Hey," the redhead spoke.

"Hey," I slowly said with furrowed brows.

"I'm Olivia, and this is Emma and Ryleigh," she gestured to the blondes.

"I'm Tatum," I responded, disoriented.

Olivia smirked a bitchy smirk. "So, *Tatum*, is it true that you're dating Axel Burne?"

I brought my chin down as I glared at her, shifting around in my seat. Why were these girls so interested to know about Axel and me? And how did they have the nerve to ask me about it when they've never talked to me before?

"Um," I got defensive, "well I wouldn't really necessarily say dating, but why is it any of your business anyways?"

"Oh, so you're just fuck buddies then?"

"No. We haven't even—"

"Wait... you haven't slept with Axel yet?"

I wanted to pull the redhead's hair out. I didn't want to keep discussing this with them, but all my shit was scattered across the table and I wasn't about to pack up all my things and leave just for the sake of escaping them.

I moved my attention back towards my homework, hoping that if I ignored them long enough, they'd just leave.

"Well we just want you to know," Olivia began again, throwing her long, white painted fingernails on the table, "that Axel did to all of us the same thing he's currently doing to you. And the same thing he has done to half of the female population at Western, which is use you and then dump you. He likes the chase, but once he gets what he wants, he leaves."

"Well thanks for the concern, but I think I can handle myself."

The blondes glanced at each other before looking back at me. They hadn't spoken the entire time they were here. What was the point of them even being here if they weren't going to say anything?

There was something about Olivia that I didn't quite like, but I couldn't entirely put my finger on it. I wasn't sure if she was genuinely concerned for me or if she had other motives.

Olivia shrugged. "Suit yourself. But once he's screwed you over, let me know. I'll add you to the group chat," she said, standing up.

"Group chat?" I asked, curiously. All three of them nodded. "And...how many girls are in the group chat? If you don't mind me asking."

Olivia picked up the textbook that she had thrown on the table. "Eighteen, but those are just the girls in our grade alone. See ya around."

The three of them walked away, leaving me left with nothing but my sky-rocketing anxiety.

I tried to forget about my encounter with Olivia and the blondes. As concerned as I actually was about it, I had bigger, current issues to deal with first. A phone call with my mother.

I dialed her number, pacing slowly back and forth in my room.

"Hi Tate!" My mom cried out.

"Hi Mom," I responded.

"How are you, sweetie?"

"I'm good. How's everything at home?" I tried to play it off as if the semester had been uneventful so far, when everyone here knew that it absolutely was not. But my mom didn't need to know that.

"Everything is good. We're excited to see you over break!"

I cowered at her reply. I didn't know how to break it to her that I didn't want to go home.

"Mom, about that... I don't know if going home right now is the best option for me. I've been doing better over the past few weeks

96

controlling my flashbacks and I'm afraid that going home will make them come back stronger."

She sighed on the other end of the phone. "Tatum, honey, listen. I know that you're still a little hung up on Connor or whatever—"

"What?" I snapped. "Hung up on him? Are you serious?"

"Well, honey, I just think—"

"No," I cut her off again, "you think I *choose* to live like this? You think I want this to still control my life? You and Dad have never fully understood any of it and I hate that I keep having this same conversation with you guys over and over again."

Her voice remained calm, but it wasn't enough to keep my tears from falling down my cheeks. "Tatum, I just think you may be overreacting just a little bit. C'mon honey, just come home for Thanksgiving."

I pulled at my hair, frustrated that my family didn't understand. My sisters were the only ones that sympathized, but even they didn't fully understand either.

"I'm staying here," my voice quivered. "Sorry, Mom." I hung up the phone, setting it down on my desk.

The worst part wasn't that my family didn't understand my disorder, but it was the fact that they didn't even *try* to understand it. People in general just didn't understand, which was why I never talked about it.

Not only was the emotional abuse a major factor in the development of my disorder, but the situation had been unexpected. I was unprepared to be caught in the middle of Connor and Nicole, unprepared to be an option to him, unprepared to be his personal puppet, and especially unprepared for the way things ended. I couldn't prevent his narcissism. I couldn't prevent his actions. I couldn't prevent their marriage. Everything had been out of my control.

Trauma wasn't just classified as physical situations where your life was at risk. Trauma was simply stress run amuck, stress out of control, whether if that stress was physical, psychological, or emotional. Whether if that stress was within one situation, or a long-term one. People were put under stress all the time, but the difference was that their brains went back to normal after a while, whereas mine never did. My brain had been scientifically and chemically changed after the stress and emotional trauma. Damaged. Maybe it would've gone back to normal if I had had a solid support system after the damage, but I had been on my own. I had people around me that did care about me, but nobody took into account the severity of the situation. Everyone overlooked it, completely unaware of the damage it caused and was continuing to cause. All everyone else saw was a sad breakup, nothing more.

I climbed into bed and cried for a while, upset that my family didn't understand what I was struggling with, but also saddened with the reality that I wouldn't be spending Thanksgiving with my family.

Once again, I was shedding more tears. And once again, it was all Connor's fault.

I awoke several hours later to a knocking on my door. I pulled myself out of bed, groaning as I shuffled across the floor.

Axe stood, looking concerned.

"Hey," I yawned.

"Hey," he walked in. "Are you okay? I've been worried."

I checked the clock on my desk, realizing that I had missed my dinner plans with Axel.

I rubbed my forehead, my tired eyes fighting to stay open. "Oh, damnit, I'm so sorry Axe. I guess I was just so upset after getting off the phone with my Mom that I fell asleep."

He pulled his eyebrows in. "Why were you upset?" he worried.

I pushed my hair onto one side, sighing. "She just... doesn't really understand anything. My dad doesn't either. So, I don't really think I'll be going home for Thanksgiving." I gazed down, inspecting the floor.

He placed his hands gently on my hips. "Hey, don't worry. Ash and I go to my sister's every year for Thanksgiving. You're more than welcome to come with. I'd be happy if you came."

I looked up at him and gave a small smile, falling into his arms for a hug as he buried his head into my messy hair.

I pulled away after a minute. "I'm sorry I missed our plans," I said, rubbing my eyes.

Axe moved my hair out of my face. "It's okay, babe." That was the first time Axe had called me anything other than Tate. Butterflies floated throughout me at the sound. "I was just worried when you weren't answering."

I packed my bag, preparing to go to Axel's sister's house for Thanksgiving. Penelope had already left to go home for break, and Gianna and Claire were about to leave as well.

"Hey, girl!" Claire strode in, followed by Gi.

"Hey," I threw more clothes into the bag.

"Honestly Tate, I'm freaking jealous that you're spending break with the boys and Amberly. I wanna meet her!"

I was truly excited to meet Amberly, but at the same time that Gi was jealous of me, I was jealous of her. They were going home to spend Thanksgiving with their own families and although it was technically my own choice not to, I only did it because it was what I needed, not wanted. If Wilmot wasn't full of such negatively unforgettable memories, I would be back there in a heartbeat. I dreaded seeing all the pictures that Claire and Gi would post over the break, a little spike of both anguish and envy in my veins.

"I'm sure you'll meet her eventually," I said.

Gi sighed. "Yeah, I know, but still."

"So, Tate, how are you feeling?" Claire asked.

"About meeting Amberly? Kind of nervous, not gonna lie."

"I meant about Axel," she said, sitting down in Penelope's desk chair.

"We all know she's got a fat crush on him, Claire. No point in even asking," Gi chimed in.

My mouth fell open. "I do not."

"Yes, you do," they said in unison.

"Do not," I repeated, stuffing more clothes into my bag.

"She's still in denial," Gianna said.

"I mean," Claire started, "I'm still not a big fan of him, but I'll give it to you, he is hot as shit."

"Claire! You have your own boyfriend," Gi shamed her.

Claire shrugged. "You want me to lie?" she said to her cousin, before shifting her attention back to me. "Well, are you gonna seal the deal and sleep with him over break or what?" Claire eagerly asked.

I shot her a disapproving look. "Really?"

"It was just a question. No need for attitude," she said. I rolled my eyes. "So, are you gonna or what?"

"Claire," I warned.

"What! I wanna know if he's actually as good as everyone says he is."

I shook my head, turning towards Gianna to change the subject. "Do you remember how much older Amberly is than the boys?"

Gi thought to herself for a moment. "I'm pretty sure Ash said she's four years older than him, so that would make her twenty-four, I believe?"

I nodded, thinking about their troubled childhood again. Axel was around thirteen when their mom was killed, which meant Amberly was eighteen at the time. She had taken care of the boys afterwards, being their primary caregiver. Her youth, independence, and the supposed 'best times of her life' were taken from her, due to the fact that she basically had to become a mother to her younger brothers.

"Okay, well, we just wanted to come stop by to see you before we left," Claire graciously stated. "But if you get some action, you better text us in the chat asap."

I rolled my eyes, going in to hug the both of them. "Drive safe. Let me know when you get home, okay? Love you guys," I said, right before they walked out.

I finished packing and then relaxed on the futon, contemplating how meeting Amberly would go as I waited for Axe to come pick me up. I didn't know what she would think of me and after hearing what Olivia and the blondes said, I was curious as to how many other girls Axel had taken to meet Amberly.

The conversation with the redhead had been stuck in my head for the past few days, eating me alive with fear and curiosity. But no matter how much it was bothering me, I still hadn't mentioned it to Axe yet. There was too much currently going on with Thanksgiving, which was why I didn't want to bring it up. Not only that, but I was also scared to hear what he would say. The thought of him leaving kept recurring and I was unsure if bringing up the redhead would cause him to become annoyed with me and leave as a result.

Ash sat in the back so that I could be in the passenger seat while Axel drove. Amberly lived about a half hour from campus and as we got closer to our destination, my apprehension was rising.

I remained quiet in the car, a million thoughts running through my head. How many girls had Axel actually slept with and was he truly just interested in the chase? What if Amberly didn't like me? And what did it honestly mean that he was taking me here? Was he going to try to sleep with me soon? Was he going to leave if I slept with him? Was he going to leave if I didn't sleep with him?

I picked at my fingernails, breathing heavily. I didn't trust the world. And with each second that passed, I didn't trust Axel more and more. Axe hadn't done anything specific to wreck my trust with him, besides the whole Brooke situation, but other than that, it was just my own paranoia that was pushing me over the edge.

Axe pulled into the parking lot of a gas station. "You brought your fake right?" he turned to Ash.

"Well, no shit," Ash replied.

Axe rolled his eyes, pulling out his wallet. He handed Ash two twenties. "Do you want anything, Tate?" Axe asked.

"I'm okay."

His soft eyes pulled another twenty out. "Here, Ash. Get Tate some of those fruity drinks. She likes those. Amberly probably wants what she usually does. And don't forget my beer."

"Got it," Ash said, opening his door.

I waited until Ash was entirely inside to speak. "Hey, Axe?"

"Yeah, babe?"

More butterflies.

"How come you always have so much money?" I had been wondering about it since the first time he had taken me out. He always paid for everything, from dinner to the arcade to my necklace. As far as I knew, Axe didn't have a job, so I had no idea how his wallet was always full.

"Well, my mom left a lot of money to each of us. And after her trial, the state gave us money too. They gave me the most since I endured the most trauma."

His explanation finally caused everything to make sense. I was saddened each time he brought his mom up, but I was also slightly relieved that the money came from a true source and not from selling illegal drugs or any shit like that.

I nodded, glancing back out the window.

"Are you okay?" Axe asked.

"Hmm?" I turned back towards him.

"Are you okay? You seem a little quiet."

"Oh... yeah, I'm fine."

"You sure? I know when something's brewing up in that noggin of yours. You always get a certain look on your face."

I tilted my head, bringing my brows in. "What look?"

"That look," he identified, pointing to me.

"I'm fine," I giggled.

Axe glanced out the windshield for a second, looking for any sign of Ash, but turned back towards me when he didn't find one. "Look, I know this isn't exactly the ideal Thanksgiving that you wanted, but I want to make sure you're okay and that you still have a good time."

I gave a tiny grin. "I promise, I'm fine," I assured him. "Just a little nervous, that's all."

"Why?"

"I haven't met your sister before."

"Don't be nervous. She'll love you," he waved it off.

I leaned over and kissed his cheek. The second I pulled away, he grabbed my face between his warm hands and planted a kiss directly on my mouth. His lips lingered there until Ash opened the car door.

"No PDA allowed," he joked, holding numerous bags of liquor as he slid into the backseat. I blushed, embarrassed that we had once again been caught by Ash.

Axel sighed. "Shut up, douchebag. Did you get everything?"

"Yes, now drive."

After another five minutes of driving, we pulled into a driveway. The house looked really nice on the outside, with a two-car garage and a stone pathway leading up to the front door. It was an obviously newer and larger house and I wondered if Amberly lived there by herself.

A slim, beautiful woman opened the door. She was only a few inches taller than me, which meant the boys towered over her as well. Her dusty blonde hair fell in waves slightly past her small-framed shoulders and her bright white smile radiated all the way to the sun. I noticed right away that her eyes matched Ashton's brown ones, meaning that Axel was the only one out of the three siblings that had green eyes. I liked that.

"Little brothers!" she called, loud and proud, pulling them each in for a hug. Her attention stopped on me. "And you must be Tatum."

"Yes, hi, it's so nice to meet you," I smiled.

"Same to you." She gave me a light, motherly squeeze. "Come in guys! Come in!"

The inside of the house was even nicer than the outside. The wooden floors were shiny clean, so clean that it was impossible not to notice. I didn't know what Amberly did for a living, but it must've paid well combined with the amount of money their mom left her. The same framed photo of Amberly, the boys, and their mom was hung up on the wall, giving me a disheartened feeling again, but I didn't allow it to show on my face.

We were planning on spending tonight and tomorrow night here, since tomorrow was Thanksgiving. I wasn't sure what exactly I would do for the rest of the weekend when we got back to campus, but I assumed Axel would offer for me to stay with him. My mind tugged back and forth between wanting to spend the entire break with him and wanting to spend the rest alone once we got back.

"Where's Drew at?" Axe asked.

"He went to go pick up the pizza. He should be back any minute." Amberly walked into the living room, signaling for us to follow.

"Pizza? Bet!" Ash called out.

Axe and I sat on the dark brown couch, his hand covering mine. He pulled me closer, until my head was resting on his chest. Axe kissed my forehead, not seeming to even care when Amberly started to take notice of his affection.

The front door opened and closed, revealing a young man carrying three large pizzas. He was tall, around the same height as the boys. His bright blue eyes stood out against his light brown hair.

I assumed that this was Drew. He placed the pizzas down on the granite island in the kitchen, leaning down to plant a quick kiss on Amberly's lips.

"C'mon baby, let's go eat," Axe whispered, dragging me up with him.

Drew smiled at me as we approached. "I'm Drew, Amberly's boyfriend." He held out his hand, and I shook it. So, she didn't live here alone.

"Tatum," I smiled back, leaving it at that because I didn't want to call myself Axel's girlfriend.

Steam rose as Axe opened up the large pizza box.

"How many do you want?" he kindly asked me.

"Just two is fine."

"Toss me a couple slices too," Ash requested.

"Get it yourself, asshole," Axe said, throwing two pieces onto a plate and handing it to me.

Ash groaned, fixing himself a plate of pizza and dropping it on the kitchen table. He turned to Drew, sticking his hands on his hips. "And where the hell have you been, dick? I haven't heard from you in weeks!"

Drew subtly licked his lips, glancing at Amberly, who tipped her chin towards her chest, giving him a warning glare.

"None of your business," Drew jokingly responded with a smug smile.

"Wow, okay."

"Maybe I've been trying to avoid your dumbass," Drew laughed.

"For what!"

Drew's blue eyes zoned in on Ash, the sides of his mouth slowly turning up. "You wanna go right now?"

Ash pointed to his plate. "After I down this... you and me. Living room. Fight night."

Amberly found a seat next to me. "They've got this weird bromance going on," she whispered.

"Are they always like this?"

"Pretty much," she replied. "They're always aimlessly arguing and wrestling. Except now, they don't let Axe wrestle with them anymore," she giggled.

"Why not?"

"He beat the shit outta them too many times," she laughed out loud.

"They asked for it," Axe chimed in.

Amberly narrowed her eyes at Axe. "Giving your brother a tiny black eye is one thing, but nearly breaking his arm is another."

Axe sank down in his seat, embarrassed to be put on the spot.

Nearly broke Ash's arm? From what I knew, it took a lot to break an arm, so Axe must've been pretty pissed at the time in order to go to that extreme. Either that, or he just became overly aggressive easily, but I had known Axe for months now, and I had never seen him reach that point. I couldn't even imagine him reaching that point.

Drew and Amberly were very welcoming and as the night went on, I started to feel more at home. Amberly poured herself a glass of wine. "Would you like some, Tate?"

"Sure, thank you," I grinned, taking a glass.

The boys were messing around in the living room, already drunk off all the shots and beers they had drank. Amberly watched, shaking her head as the boys wrestled each other to the ground. "Follow me," she quietly said.

I followed her to the back door, leading out to a screened in porch. The November, Michigan air was starting to get cooler and although I was wearing a long sleeve, I was still a bit chilly. Amberly noticed, running back inside. She emerged again with two blankets, handing me one kindly.

"Thank you," I gladly took it, taking a seat in one of the rocking chairs. I placed my wine on the side table, too afraid that I would spill it on the blanket.

Amberly sat in the seat on the other side of the small, round table. Her kind eyes peered into me. "Where are you from?" she asked.

"Suburbs of Chicago. And Axe said you guys are from here?"

Amberly nodded. "Born and raised."

"Ah, I see. I do really love Michigan, though."

"Yeah, it's a good state. Other than the arctic winters," she joked. I giggled in agreement, cuddling up against the rocking chair. "So, when did you and Axe meet?"

"Um," I thought, "about mid-September."

"Oh, so you've been dating for a little while," she said, surprised.

My eyebrows shot up, my mouth opening and closing with words that weren't coming out. "Well... we're not like dating, dating."

She dipped her head towards her shoulder. "Really? It seemed as if you two were together." She swished her wine around in its glass. "I'm actually really surprised that Axel brought you here, honestly."

"Oh, why?"

Her comment made me nervous that I was about to hear something that I didn't want to. I gripped the blanket, preparing to hear the possible worst.

"Because he's never brought a girl here before."

I took a deep breath, relieved. I could tell she was just as confused as I was. I had been wondering how many other girls Axel had brought here in order to successfully sleep with whoever his target was at the time, but knowing that he never brought anyone else here both comforted and concerned me. Was I the only one because he genuinely had feelings for me? Or was it because I was simply the toughest target he ever had?

"But thank God he did," Amberly laughed. "I've been the only girl for years."

I giggled at her remark, trying to imagine what it would be like if I had three brothers instead of three sisters.

"He's really never brought another girl here before?"

"Nope," she shook her head. "That's why I was so sure you two were a couple."

"I mean," I nervously started, "he says he wants to be, but I'm just..."

"Worried?"

"Yeah," I admitted.

"Don't blame ya. It's no secret that he doesn't have the best rep."

"Do you think he—"

Axel slowly opened the back door. "Sorry if I'm interrupting your girl talk," he smirked flawlessly, "but it's time for drunk Monopoly!"

I furrowed my eyebrows, confused. Amberly rolled her eyes. "Oh great, not this shit again," she said. I snickered at her sudden annoyance, but I was slightly disappointed that we didn't get to finish our conversation. Amberly turned back towards me. "Ever since I've been dating Drew, which is almost four years now, at every family gathering, all the guys get hammered and force me to play Monopoly with them."

"It's the best part of the night!" Axe chimed in, standing with his arms out.

"It sounds like fun," I expressed.

"Yeah, you'd think that," Amberly adjusted her hair. "Until they all start yelling at each other and not playing by the actual rules, whatsoever! Which pisses me off!"

106

Axe stood against the door frame, arms crossed. "We're all playing. *All* of us." He walked over to me, holding his hand out and helping me stand.

I kept the blanket wrapped around me, too chilly to put it down. Axe grabbed my wine glass for me, putting his free hand gently on my lower back to guide me inside. Amberly sighed, then reluctantly followed.

Axe and Ash set up the game as we gathered around the kitchen table. Drew and Ash kept eyeing each other with smirks on their faces, as if they were preparing to wrestle again.

Amberly took notice, shaking her head. "Sometimes I think Drew would much rather be marrying Ash than me." The room went silent as all heads turned towards her. Her cheeks flushed as she covered her mouth with her hands.

"Amb," Ash started, "what the fuck is that on your finger?"

Amberly dropped her hands, her worried eyes darting over to Drew. "Nice one, babe," he said.

"It just slipped," she sighed.

"Spill," Axe insisted.

"Okay, so," she began, biting her lip, "we were gonna wait to tell you guys until tomorrow... but we're engaged!" She held up her left hand, showing off the beautiful diamond on her ring finger.

"It's about damn time!" Axe yelled.

"Woah," Ash grabbed Amberly's hand to get a closer look. "That thing's pretty fuckin' big. How did none of us notice it all night?"

Amberly burst with excitement. I could tell she had been trying to hold it in all night. Drew was just as excited, maintaining a smile on his face as well.

Ash turned to Drew. "You didn't tell me you were proposing!"

"Out of everyone on Earth, why would I tell you?" Drew joked.

"He'd tell me before he'd tell you," Axe said with a grin as he took out all the Monopoly pieces.

"Yeah, right," Ash said.

"Speaking of you, Ash..." Drew started, "how's it going with your girlfriend?"

"What?" Ash asked.

"Did she dump your sorry ass already?" Drew joked.

"No," Ash said with his eyes narrowed.

I leaned towards Amberly. "Gianna is one of my best friends," I smiled.

Her face lit up. "Oh, I see! Is that how her and Ash met then?"

"Yeah," I said, "it's funny how it all worked out."

"Awe, I love that!" she smiled.

Axe turned back towards his brother. "Yeah, so you're welcome, douchebag."

Ash narrowed his eyes at his brother. "Why would I thank you?"

"Because if I hadn't invited Tate over, you never would've met Gianna."

"Well, you're welcome too, asshole," Ash said.

"For what?" Axe asked. Ash raised his brows and after a second, a bell went off in Axe's head. "Oh, fuck off!"

"Finally, took you two long enough to stop swinging your dicks around and just commit to somebody," Drew said with a laugh.

Both boys shot him a look, anger resting on their faces. The room exploded as the three started bickering.

Amberly sighed as she turned towards me. "See, we haven't even started the game yet and they're already yelling at each other." I laughed as she stood up from her seat. "HEY!" she yelled. The room turned to silence. "All three of you... shut up!"

The three boys complied to Amberly's command, shutting their mouths immediately. After a moment, her mouth slowly turned upwards and she raised her left hand again, her engagement still being the number one thing on her mind.

"That ring is really beautiful, by the way," I said.

"Thank you!" she replied.

"And congratulations!" I happily added.

She leaned across the table, squeezing my hand. "Thank you, Tatum. And I would love for you to come to the wedding." Her response made me happy. I had been worrying all day that Amberly wouldn't like me and knowing that she did and approved of me lifted a weight off of my shoulders. "Which means," she pointed at Axel, "*you* cannot fuck things up with her."

"I'm trying my best," he peeked over at me.

"The wedding will be early next summer. And also, I want the both of you to walk me down the aisle," she gestured towards Axe and Ash. "One of you on each side of me."

108

"Awe, how cute," Ash blabbered.

"We'd love to," Axe said.

Monopoly consisted of a lot of yelling and laughter. All three drunken boys got extremely into the game, leaving Amberly and I to sit back and chuckle at their predicaments. When the game was finally over, it was nearly one in the morning. I yawned, ready for bed.

"So, Ash you take the first guest bedroom and then Axe and Tate, you guys can take the other one," Amberly announced as she collected all the game pieces, throwing them back into the box.

Only two beds? That meant Axe and I would have to share a bed. We hadn't shared a bed together yet, and with the new knowledge that Axe's body count was well over twenty, I didn't know if he would try to pull a move or not. And above all, I was afraid that if he did try, I would give in.

Axe sensed my nerves. "I can sleep on the couch," he faintly spoke to me.

"No, it's okay," I shook my head. As nervous as it actually made me feel, I didn't want to make a big deal out of the situation, especially in front of his family.

I got ready for bed in the bathroom, taking my time during my nighttime routine. I made sure to wash my face well and put plenty of my moisturizer on, scared that I would wake up next to Axel with a breakout. I used to have a fair amount of acne when I was a younger teen and although my skin was clear now, I was always afraid I would breakout at the worst times. My acne was never anything terribly bad, just the normal amount that every teen got, but Connor always used to point it out to me. So, I was self-conscious.

Axe was already in the bed when I climbed in. Usually, I just wore a long shirt and a thong to bed, but tonight, I had shorts on underneath my t-shirt. I was definitely not about to be that exposed when I slept next to Axel.

As soon as I laid down, Axe's arms were already around me, pulling me to him. His warmth fused throughout me, feeling like a big blanket. He wasn't wearing a shirt and for the first time other than on Halloween, I got to see his chest tattoos up close. It was slightly hard to make out exactly what each one was, but within the moonlight shining through the window, I could vaguely piece some of them together. There was the obvious dragonfly tattoo on his abdomen, accompanied by two small swallows that sat near his collarbone, and the name "Anne" over his heart with a date under it. I assumed it was for his mother.

After I finished my quick tattoo inspection, I rested my head on his chest, above his heart, near the tattoo that I had just recently discovered. His heartbeat was so calming to listen to. I could feel his soft lips touch my head as I closed my eyes. I was nervously waiting for him to try to start kissing me or for the moment that his hands would start to wander, but neither of those moments came. I wanted to lean up and kiss him, but I didn't want to start something that we couldn't finish.

"Tate?"

"Mhmm?" I hummed against his chest.

"I'm really happy that you're here."

"Me too," I melted into Axe, falling asleep almost instantly.

Chapter Eleven
The Batter

Axel was still asleep when I awoke. Our legs were tangled up in each other, bringing a tiny smile to my lips. I carefully slipped away from his grip, trying my best not to wake him. Once I was out of his grasp, I sat on the edge of the bed for a moment, admiring him. His beautifully tattooed chest rose and fell with a peaceful rhythm, messy hair sitting perfectly. I wondered what he was dreaming about.

I made my way downstairs after quickly getting dressed and getting my hair under control. Amberly was already in the kitchen, starting to put everything together for the day.

"Good morning," I said. "Do you want some help?"

Amberly smiled brightly. "Oh my God, that would be wonderful. I've always done basically everything by myself each year. Sometimes the boys try to help, but they always fuck everything up, so I don't usually let them do a lot," she laughed.

I smiled, helping her throw the turkey into the oven.

"So, how was your night?" she asked.

"It was good. How was—"

"But how was your *night*?" she asked again, raising a brow with a cheeky smile.

"Oh," I said, finally understanding what she meant. Heat rushed to my cheeks. "We didn't..." I shook my head, trailing off.

Amberly nudged me. "I'm just teasing you. I really don't care if you did or didn't. But if you ever actually do," she said, scrunching her face in disgust, "don't tell me. I don't wanna know about my baby brother getting laid."

I laughed, relieved that she wasn't being serious. "Got it. And nah, I told him I wouldn't unless we were actually dating."

"Good. He needs that type of rejection in his life," she chuckled. "He's so used to girls throwing themselves at him."

I felt a small twinge in my stomach at the thought of other girls with Axe.

We continued to talk and laugh for what seemed like hours until anyone else came downstairs.

"Morning," Drew said, wrapping an arm around Amberly's waist as he kissed her.

"It's almost afternoon," Amberly corrected him as she pulled away, smiling. She sighed. "Ash and Axe still aren't up?"

Drew shrugged.

"I'll go see if Axe is up," I said.

Axe was still laying on his side of the bed when I quietly entered the room. I shut the door behind me and tiptoed over, placing a knee on the bed.

"Axe," I whispered, getting closer. "It's almost noon," I giggled.

He groaned at my words before grabbing my hand and yanking me to him until I was laying on top of him. My hair fell around his face, framing it. Axe's green eyes popped open and his lips reached up, carefully placing themselves on mine. He slipped his tongue inside my mouth, his hands sliding up and down my back, but not going any lower. I yearned for his touch, but I knew it was a bad idea. Each time we touched, there was a spark, and as addictive as that spark was, sometimes, some sparks were deadly. Axe sucked my bottom lip as he pulled away, looking up at me with gentle eyes. I ran my hand through his hair, still on top of him.

"Time to get up," I said, moving to a sitting position on him. He rubbed his eyes and dropped his head to the side, grinning.

I swung my legs around him, getting off the bed. I stood with my hands on my hips, waiting for him to follow my lead. He watched me for a moment, a specific longing in his eyes.

"How 'bout you come back to bed?" he reached for me. I couldn't help but smile.

"How 'bout you stop being a lazy ass and get up?"

He bit his lip, smiling. Dimples appeared. My favorite smile. He groaned again, finally sitting up. "Still so stubborn," he shook his head.

112

"Good," I grinned, still high off of his touch. "Then I will see you downstairs once you're ready." I walked towards the door.

"Wait, Tate."

"Yeah?"

"You look great in those jeans," he winked with a mischievous grin.

I shook my head, not able to contain my smile as I walked out.

After a long day of cooking, eating, drinking, and laughing, I relaxed on the couch with Axel. Drew had put a movie on, and we all sat around, watching. I could tell Axe was thinking about something, but he wasn't coming out and saying it.

I nudged him with my elbow. "What's up?"

He stood, cocking his head. I followed, feeling the anxiety beginning to swell up inside of me. He grabbed a blanket on the way, handing it to me as soon as we got outside on the screened in porch.

I wrapped the blanket around myself, trying to hide my shivering. But I couldn't tell if I was shivering because it was cold or because I was scared as hell of what he was about to say.

Axe rubbed the back of his neck. "I just... can't stop thinking."

"About?"

"You."

I swallowed the lump of tension that was forming in my throat. Axe stepped closer to me, grabbing my hand. His eyes drilled into my soul.

"I want to be with you," he stated.

I didn't know what to feel. I didn't know if I should feel relieved because he didn't say anything bad, or if I should feel even more anxious because I didn't have an answer for him.

I grazed my forehead with my free hand. "Axe... I just still don't know." His face fell, clearly unhappy with my response. "I'm still trying to figure out what's going on in my head and after hearing Olivia last week, I just—"

"Olivia?"

I nodded. Shit. I totally forgot that I still hadn't told him about my run-in with the redhead. "Her and two blondes confronted me at the library."

"Saying what?"

"They asked me a couple questions about you and then warned me about you."

His eyebrows raised. "Warned you about me?"

I gave another, nervous nod.

"Warning you how?" he asked, nervously shifting his weight back and forth.

"They said you only liked the chase and that once you slept with whoever it was you were going for, you would leave. And that that's what you did to all of them," I looked down, not wanting to meet his gaze.

"Tate," he lifted my chin, "I'm not gonna do that to you."

I turned away from his touch. "But you've done that to *at least* twenty other girls. How am I supposed to believe you?"

"I know it's hard to believe, but I'm not going to do that to you," he said again, rubbing the back of my hand with his thumb.

"I just can't figure out what game you're trying to play," I quietly muttered to myself.

"Game?" he dropped my hand, eyeing me in awe. He paused for a second, looking at me with a hurting behind his eyes. "Can't you see it?" he asked, backing away and retreating back inside.

I was stunned. See what? Confusion draped over my face at the fact that defeat just draped over his. Part of me wanted to follow him and finish the conversation, but I didn't. I brought my fingers up to where my necklace lay against my chest. I stayed outside for a little bit, blanket still wrapped around me, hovering in my own thoughts.

When I went back in, I said goodnight to everyone and made my way back upstairs. After getting ready for bed, I laid there, again, stuck inside my own worries. Axe was still downstairs and one by one, footsteps were coming upstairs, but none of them were Axel's.

I could hear voices coming from the kitchen. Curiosity got the best of me as I made my way out of bed and over to the door. I cracked it open, making out the voices of Axe and Amberly.

"I don't know what to do," Axe said.

"Well, what exactly is the problem?"

"She... doesn't trust me. And she has every reason not to, but... I don't know how to fix it."

"Well," Amberly talked, "I mean, you don't exactly have the best track record with girls."

"No shit, Amb, but I've really been trying my best to prove to her that I could be better for her. I mean I know I'm probably the worst guy on the planet and that I don't deserve her whatsoever, but I just want her so bad."

I could hear Amberly sigh. "But Axel, do you want her because of who she is or because she's not yours?"

"Amberly, I honestly think I'm falling in love with this girl. But half the time, I feel like she hates me."

Axe's response made my heart hurt. I didn't hate him at all. Not even close. I didn't want him to feel that way.

"You've just gotta keep proving to her that you could be who she needs," Amberly said. "And eventually, she'll come around. I see the way she looks at you, Axe. There's something there. Don't give up on it just yet."

A couple minutes later, I heard footsteps coming up the stairs. I ran over and squirrel dived into the bed, pretending to be asleep. The door opened and closed, and I nonchalantly peeked my eyes open just enough to see Axel taking his shirt and jeans off. His chiseled abs could still be made out, even though it was dark.

I slammed my eyes shut again as Axe climbed into the bed. I didn't dare make a single move as he wrapped an arm around me, nuzzling his head into the crook of my neck.

Once Axe's breathing evened out and I knew was asleep, I laid in his arms, wide awake, unable to get the events of the night out of my head.

Axe had told Amberly that he was falling in love with me. As sweet as it was and as nice as it was to hear it, it freaked me out. I had been told so many times from Connor that he loved me. He swore up and down that he loved me and told other people the same thing as well. But at the end of the day, he still left. That last phone call with him replayed inside my head, the one where he told me he loved me for the last time. The pain I had felt in that exact moment took over my body, accompanied with the feeling that Axel would do the same thing.

I couldn't sort my feelings out. I knew in my heart that I wanted to be with Axel, but between my already paranoid mind from my past and the extra anxiety that Olivia and the other girls added, I was stuck. It felt like I was in the same war that I had been in when Connor was around. A war between my heart and my head. A war between myself. The absolute, worst, most terrible civil war.

I could not fall asleep. Too many thoughts and moments kept repeating and before I knew it, a few hours had passed.

It was the weirdest thing. Feeling so safe, yet unsafe in someone's arms. I didn't know what would happen when I woke up. Would I have the answer that I needed? Or would I be even more confused?

I was fucking terrified. And the only thing that made sense was to leave before he could.

I had been ignoring Axe's texts since we got back to campus. I knew he would most likely show up at my dorm eventually, but I hoped that with so many people being gone over break, he wouldn't have anyone to sneak in behind. I needed to stay as far away from him as possible until I could figure myself out.

The room was sort of lonely without Penelope there. The constant silence started to kill me after a while, so I turned on a horror movie, hoping that it would help kill my boredom. I wanted more than anything to call Axe and go over to the apartment to hang out with him, but fear prevented me from doing so.

I had only been back in my dorm for five or so hours before I heard a knock. In my heart, I knew it was Axel.

I opened the door and there he stood, guitar in hand.

"Even with this place nearly deserted, you still found a way to sneak in?" I joked.

"Hell yeah," he walked in, taking a seat on the futon. He took a deep breath. "Tate, I know I'm a piece of shit. And that I'm not good enough for you. But," he paused, holding the guitar on his knee. Instead of continuing to talk, he began to play.

I sat next to him as he sang "Can't Help Falling In Love," by Elvis. His beautiful voice echoed throughout the room. I was quiet as he sang, making sure not to make a single noise that would disrupt him. Every so often, he would look up at me, sending butterflies to ripple throughout my entire bloodstream. No matter how much I had tried to ignore or

116

avoid Axel, he always came back. I couldn't escape him, and I especially couldn't escape my feelings.

I knew that I wanted to be with him, but my fear had caused me to fight it this whole time. And in that moment, I realized that that was what Connor wanted. He wanted to still control my life, whether he was in it or not. The only way to escape the past was to create my own future. One where each decision I made would have nothing to do with Connor.

And as he came to the end of the song, I sat there, a faint smile on my lips. Praying to God that I wouldn't regret what I was about to do.

The second he stopped, I threw my lips onto his and he went rigid for just a moment, caught off guard, but then melted into me. He slowly set his guitar on the ground, still managing to keep our lips together. My necklace flopped around as he laid me on my back, positioning himself on top of me. He hummed against my mouth as I pushed my hips up against his. Even though he was wearing his black jeans, I could still feel the hardness through them. He pressed against me harder, making me wish he was closer, but knowing that now was not the time to go down that road.

I pulled away from his mouth. "I wanna be with you."

He smiled from ear to ear. "Finally."

I bit my lip and he leaned back in, kissing me passionately.

Our mouths separated once again. "Took you long enough, with your stubborn, cute ass."

I laughed, covering my mouth with my small hand.

"Come back to the apartment with me. We can watch movies all night and make chocolate chip pancakes."

"Fine," I smiled, "only for the pancakes though."

He rolled his eyes before looking back at me, taking in every inch of me. "So, you're mine now?" he smirked.

"All yours," I said. His smirk turned into a full smile. "And you're mine now?"

"I've been yours this entire time," he said. My heart swelled at his response, happiness overtaking me.

Part of me felt relieved that I had finally given in, as if the weight of my own denial had been lifted off my shoulders. Axel and I were official, but that didn't mean that my guard was entirely down. I still had some doubts in the back of my mind. And until I could deal with my own self-trust and with completely giving my heart to Axel, those doubts would vaguely remain.

We drove over to the apartment. I think it was the first time I had been more excited to hang out with someone than I was to be eating chocolate chip pancakes.

I stirred the pancake batter in a large, glass bowl while Axe grabbed the chocolate chips out of the cabinet. I turned on the sink, rinsing off the batter that got on my hands. As I spun back around towards Axe, my mouth dropped open as a glob of batter was placed on my cheek.

"You didn't," I breathed heavily.

"But I did," he smirked. I scooped a little bit of batter and planted it on his forehead. His smile grew. "You... didn't," he said, wiping the batter off before it reached his eyes.

"But I did," I repeated him, leaning in.

Axe lifted a brow, reaching into the bowl and quickly flicking more batter on me.

"You suck!" I yelled, laughing as I grabbed a handful of batter and launched it towards him.

Axe tried dodging the glob, rushing towards me and wrapping his arms around me from behind. He picked me up and spun me around.

"Axe," I laughed, "I'm getting dizzy!"

He placed me on my feet, hugging me tightly from behind, the both of us still covered in batter.

"I'm so glad you're mine now," he said, resting his chin on my shoulder.

Chapter Twelve
The Dragonfly

Within the next few weeks, finals were upon us. I was relieved to hear that my parents finally agreed to come to Kalamazoo for a few days over winter break, since I still didn't want to go back home. One semester away from Wilmot just wasn't enough. I wasn't ready to go back.

Everything had been going good with Axel ever since we made things official. Everywhere we went together, girls stared, and I tried my best to ignore them, reminding myself that they were all part of Axel's past, not his present. The flashbacks and nightmares had slowly started to go away. The fear was still there, and I was still in my head, but each day made it slightly easier. I was taking baby steps and I was proud of myself for it.

Since winter break would be so much longer than Thanksgiving break, the dorm halls would all be closed, which meant that my only place to go would be the apartment. I looked forward to spending so much time with Axel, and although he still hadn't tried pushing his boundaries, I kept my eyes open. I almost felt bad for making him wait so long to sleep with me, but in my mind, it wasn't a choice. I had to do this for myself. For my own sanity.

I had been studying almost non-stop, trying my best to review everything I had learned over the entire semester. Axel wanted to study with me, but I told him no, knowing that I would be too distracted to get anything done.

I decided to go to the library to study for a change of scenery from my room. The last time I had been there was when Olivia and the blondes confronted me. I screwed my face into disgust at the thought, choosing a completely different table from where I had sat at before.

I took a seat, reaching into my backpack for my textbook. When I placed it on the table, Lucas was standing across from me.

Fabulous.

"Hey Tate, how was your break?"

"Good. How was yours?" I asked, trying to be polite.

"Mine was good, thanks for asking."

I smiled shyly, turning my attention back onto my book. Disappointment dawned over me when I realized that he was still standing there.

"So, um," he started, "I was wondering if you were busy after you were done studying?"

Was he asking me out *again*? I had told him before break that we were just friends, despite the fact that I was only agreeing to be friends in order to keep the peace between Claire and Jason. I didn't have the patience for this bullshit. Not to mention that I had a boyfriend now.

"Well I'm really tired already, so I'm planning on just relaxing and going to bed right when I get back to my room."

"Are you sure? We could go get dinner or ice cream or something? We could invite Claire and Jason?"

"I'm also in a relationship now, so I don't know if that's really the best idea," I said.

His demeanor changed, his face twisting from happy to pissed. "With who? Axel?"

I nodded, suddenly intimidated as his tone shifted.

He slowly nodded, his jaw working under his skin. "Gotcha," he reluctantly said. "Well if you change your mind, let me know," he winked as he walked away and turned around the corner, leaving me with an unsettled feeling.

If Axel knew that Lucas talked to me, or even breathed in my direction, it would've been the end for Lucas. It seemed like Lucas had always gotten lucky, running into me every time I wasn't with Axel.

The sun set early in Michigan during the winter, so by the time I finished studying, it was already dark out. I collected all my things, throwing my grey winter jacket on. The cold air hit my face as I walked back to my dorm.

A sudden feeling came over me again. The same feeling I had when I was at the mall with Axel. The feeling of being watched. I glanced around me, looking for any sign of someone looking in my direction, but there was nobody. I could hear faint footsteps behind me. I held the pepper spray that was on my key chain, gripping it tightly as I whipped my body around, looking behind me. But nobody was there. I took a deep breath, shaking off my paranoia.

I've got to stop watching so many scary movies.

I was relieved when finals were over, marking the official start of winter break.

Axel and I sat next to each other in a booth at a nearby café. My legs bobbed up and down with nerves, waiting for the arrival of my parents.

Axe placed his hand on my knee. "Tate, babe, stop worrying so much. Everything's gonna be fine," his soothing voice spoke.

I rubbed the back of my neck. "I know, I know. I'm just nervous."

I hadn't seen my parents since before I left for school and I had never taken any guy to meet them other than Connor. I didn't know what they would think of Axe, with his intimidatingly wide frame and tattooed arms, but I hoped they would like him. I would be devastated if they didn't.

Ten minutes later, my parents strolled in. Axe and I both stood. I hugged my mom and dad, watching as Axe gave my father a firm handshake. We slid back into the booth, across from my parents.

"How was your drive?" I asked.

"Not too bad. Took us a little under three hours," my mom answered.

Axel's eyes darted back and forth between my mother and I.

"What?" I quietly asked.

"You guys look like twins," he responded.

My mom and I both laughed. "Yeah, we get that a lot," I nodded.

"So, Axel, what's your major?" my father asked.

"Chemical engineering," Axe answered confidently.

"Impressive. Tate's following in her father's footsteps in business."

"Well, she's also following in her mother's footsteps in dance," my mom said.

I rolled my eyes. "Yes, we get it. I take after you two."

"Yes," my father smiled, skimming the menu, "and you're a better person for it," he joked. I rolled my eyes again.

"She's easily the smartest person I know," Axe said, glittering eyes resting on mine, causing me to blush the tiniest bit.

"She's always been super smart," my mom smiled proudly. "Did you know she started reading when she was just three years old?"

"Yeah, she was a smart kid," my dad added. "Except for that one time when she was little where she tried playing hide and seek with her pet hamster and lost it."

My mom giggled. "Or the time when she drew all over herself in Sharpie?"

"Or when she tried giving herself a haircut?"

"Oh my God," my mom laughed loudly, "I forgot about that one!"

"Okay, we get it," I said. "I've had some embarrassing moments. No need to discuss more."

"Sorry, honey," my mom said, still lightly chuckling.

Axe was trying to contain his laughter. "You cut your own hair?" he asked.

I crossed my arms and sank back down into my seat. "I don't like this type of attention."

"I'm sure we have pictures somewhere," my mom said.

"Don't you dare," I warned.

"Alright, alright," she said. "We'll stop embarrassing you."

"Thank you," I gritted through my teeth.

I was relieved when my parents started putting more attention on Axel, asking him questions about himself rather than talking about my most embarrassing moments. I sat back for the rest of lunch, listening to the conversation, only budding in on the important questions.

122

After a big meal, Axel offered to pay for the check, but my father refused. As usual, Mark Everley did not let anyone else pay for his or any of his family's things.

Afterwards, I was relieved. Axe was very open with my parents, telling them all about his major and his hobbies and where he was from. The positive vibes echoed throughout the entire café, leaving me with a sense of fulfillment.

My parents would be in town, staying at a hotel for the next three days, but after that, Axel and I were going to be all alone. With the exception of Ash being around every now and then, of course.

There were a few days left until the dorms were closing for break, so the girls and I were going to have a movie and wine night in their room. After waiting nearly an hour for Claire to get back from Jason's, we ran out of patience and decided to start drinking without her. I sat criss-crossed applesauce on the futon with my wine glass in hand.

"So, how did everything go today with your parents?" Gi asked, sipping out of her wine glass.

"It went really good actually," I smiled, thinking about how well Axe had gotten along with my parents.

Gi smiled. "Good! You know, I'm really proud of you for getting out of your comfort zone and pushing past your fears."

"Thanks, Gi. That means a lot."

"And I'm still hella jealous that you met Amberly and got invited to her wedding!"

I laughed, taking another sip. "She's awesome. You're gonna love her when you meet her."

The door swung open. "You were totally flirting with that guy!" Jason screamed at Claire, following her inside. Gi and I looked at each other, confused as to what was going on.

"No, I wasn't! Why the hell would you even think that I was?"

"Because I saw it!" he yelled, taking a step closer to her.

She took a step back, clearly uncomfortable, but not dropping the anger off of her face.

"Jason, don't yell at my cousin like that," Gianna said, setting her wine glass down.

He shot a look at Gianna, not giving a single fuck about her warning. "Don't get involved," he hissed. His jaw worked under his skin.

"Jason," I added in, "just calm down. There's no need to be screaming over this right now."

He whipped around to face me. "Yeah?"

"Yeah," I shot back. "You're causing unnecessary drama."

"Like you're one to talk! Always leading my best friend on and then dropping him for some hot-headed, criminal freak!"

My eyebrows shot up. Was he for real?

I couldn't contain my laughter, knowing that I would never, not ever, *ever* date Lucas or lead him on in any way. I covered my mouth, trying to silence the laughter that was escaping.

"You think that's funny?" Jason dropped his chin to meet my gaze. He marched over to where I was sitting, getting so close to my face that I jerked back, spilling red wine all over the futon.

Gianna grabbed his shoulder, spinning him around to face her. She lifted her phone. "Don't. Make me. Call people. That would drop-kick your sorry ass out the window," she threatened.

"Who? The Burnes?" he spat back.

She nodded intensely and his anger stayed, but you could tell the threat worried him.

He turned back to Claire. "You gonna let them threaten me like that?"

She was backed up against her desk, leaning on it, staying silent. Her eyes were glossy, a solid sign that she didn't know what to do.

Jason glanced at all three of us again, before walking out of the room, huffing and puffing.

Gianna typed angrily into her phone and within ten minutes, Axe and Ash burst through the door.

"Where is he?" Axe asked as I scrubbed the futon, trying to get the red wine out.

"He left," Gianna answered. Ash wrapped his arms around Gi, holding her as she relaxed into his grip.

Claire sat at her desk, solemnly picking at her fingernails. She hadn't said anything since Jason left.

Axe rushed over to me as I looked up at him. "Are you okay?" he asked.

I nodded. He bent down and kissed my forehead before standing back up and walking over to the window. He inspected outside, watching for any trace of Jason. "I fucking swear if he ever gets near you again, I'll fucking kill him."

Ash accompanied his brother by the window. He placed a hand on Axe's shoulder. "Let me," he said. "You can't get arrested again."

I spent the next couple of days hanging out with my parents, showing them around Kalamazoo. It was nice to be able to see them. So much had happened over the semester that I almost forgot how much I missed them. But even more so, I missed my sisters. Brynn, Kendall, and Macey were my built-in best friends and I wanted them to visit so badly, but with everyone's busy schedules, it was hard. But everyone here at Western had truly become my home away from home.

When I said goodbye to my parents, I was a little upset. I didn't know when the next time I would see them would be. I hoped that soon enough, I would be ready to go home and face the darkness that Wilmot had engrained into me. I needed to be in a good enough place to do so, and Axel was helping me get there.

Claire had been fairly quiet ever since our encounter with Jason. I was worried about her, but I knew that now wasn't a good time to bring it up. I wanted Claire to be happy again, the same way she was when her and Jason originally started dating, but after seeing the rage in Jason's eyes, I was concerned. If Gianna and I hadn't been there to help diffuse his anger off of Claire, I don't know what he would've done.

Gi had been stressing too. She wanted to come back for New Year's Eve to spend it with Ash, Axel, and I, but since her and Claire shared a car, Gi would be stuck at home until Claire worked shit out with Jason.

We all helped Claire and Gi pack up their car, waving goodbye as they drove away, leaving me left with Axe and Ash.

The three of us watched movies and played drinking games for a while and before I knew it, it was already time for bed.

I put on my pajamas and climbed in next to Axel. I faced him, running my hands down his bare chest until I reached his dragonfly tattoo.

"Why a dragonfly?" I asked.

He watched me as I studied the tattoo, tracing it with my finger. "A lot of reasons," he said. "It symbolizes prosperity, self-realization, transformation," he paused, "and my mom used to like them a lot."

A tiny smile formed on my lips at his response. Axe pulled me in, bringing me so close that I could feel his warm breath on my neck, sending a ripple of satisfaction down my spine. I tilted my head up so that he could reach my lips. He kissed me softly and passionately, moving his lips across my jawline and down my neck. I dipped my head over to the side so that he could get a better reach. His hands slipped under the covers and grabbed at my hips, making me want them to linger elsewhere. I clawed at his bare chest, running my hands down his perfect abdomen.

He pulled away from my lips, not letting it go any further. I blinked a few times, staring directly into his eyes as I wondered why he stopped.

Axe pushed the hair out of my face. "I can still wait," he said.

"I know," I looked away for a second, "but I feel bad making you."

He brought his eyebrows together. "Don't."

I dropped my head onto his chest, closing my eyes as Axel held me.

On Christmas morning, I woke up without Axel next to me. I had grown accustomed to being pounded with kisses every morning, so today was off to a bad start.

I tiptoed down the hall. Axel was at the stove in the kitchen, flipping chocolate chip pancakes over.

His eyes brightened when he saw me. "Good morning, gorgeous."

"Good morning," I smiled. My smile quickly faded as I glanced over to the Christmas tree that Axel and I had decorated together, noticing the massive mound of presents sitting under it. "What is all of this? Please tell me that some of these are for Ash."

He chuckled. "Nope. All for you."

126

I scratched my head, not knowing how to react. I had only bought Axe the pair of shoes he wanted and a new leather jacket. If I knew that he was about to buy me the entire mall, I would've gotten a few more things.

"You didn't have to go on a full-on shopping spree for me. I would've bought you more stuff if I knew you were gonna go wild like that," I said.

"Tate, baby, I don't need anything other than you."

I rubbed my arm. "Well I don't need anything other than you too, so you can return some of this stuff."

"Absolutely not," he smirked, finishing up the pancakes. "Amberly helped me pick a bunch of them out." He leaned against the counter, green eyes gazing into my brown ones. "Go ahead. Open them."

It took me over a half hour to unwrap all the clothes, makeup, shoes, and framed photos of us. I thanked Axel a million times, giving him a thousand tiny kisses all over his face.

"And one more thing," he held up his finger. He ran back into his room and reappeared with a small, wrapped up box with a bow on it.

Axel placed it in my hands, signaling for me to open it. I took the bow off and opened the box to reveal a key. My eyes darted up to Axe.

"It's a key to the apartment," he beamed. "I figured since you're gonna be here all break and hopefully like... every day after that, you should have your own key. So that you can come whenever you'd like."

A smile crept onto my face. I wrapped one arm around his neck, hugging him, while still holding the box in the other.

"Thank you. I love it," I said, planting a small kiss on his lips.

Chapter Thirteen
The Afterparty

Six days later, my phone buzzed, and Gianna's name lit up the screen.

"Hello?" I answered.

"Tate! Oh my God, hi! Okay, listen. Claire and I are coming back for New Year's Eve!"

She couldn't see me through the phone, but I was beaming. "For real?" I asked, afraid that she was messing with me.

"Yes! Jason and Claire worked everything out, so we'll be back tonight. We're already on our way."

My excitement carried throughout the entire apartment. I had missed the girls over the past two weeks. We had never been away from each other for that long before.

A couple hours went by and soon enough, Claire was already dropping Gi and I back off at the apartment after dinner.

We had no idea what we were doing tonight, and just as the four of us were about to figure out our plans, Claire called.

"Hello?" I picked up.

"Hey, Tate! A shit load of people came back early from break for New Years, so there's a giant party going down tonight. You guys should all come!"

"A party? I'm assuming Jason and Lucas will be there?"

I could tell she was wincing through the phone. "Yeah."

I looked around at Gi, Ash, and Axe, unsure if going was a good idea.

"Agh, I don't know, Claire."

"C'mon, pretty please? The three of us already didn't get to spend Halloween together. I want to see you guys tonight," she begged.

The truth was that I wanted to see her too. It felt as if the three of us had been slowly growing apart due to our boyfriend's hatred for each other. And I didn't want to let that get in the way of our friendship.

"I'll talk to everyone and let you know, okay?"

"I'm sending you the address. You guys better get your asses there later!" she insisted, then hung up the phone.

I sighed and looked around at everyone, knowing that they heard that whole conversation.

The boys could tell Gianna and I were wallowing in disappointment, wanting to go to the party, but aware that they wouldn't want to.

"You guys wanna go to that party?" Ash asked.

Gi and I glanced at each other, reading each other's minds. We both shrugged and nodded.

Axe and Ash eyed each other for a second and Axe gave him a small nod.

"Alright, fine," Ash spoke, "but if those two dickheads get anywhere near either of you, we're gonna have a problem."

I sat in front of the mirror a few hours later, trying to perfect my makeup. Since it was New Year's Eve, I wanted to look extra dolled up. I took my time doing my makeup and hair, throwing hairspray in after I finished curling it.

I slipped on my skin tight, mini red dress, following it with red lipstick to match, and then putting on a pair of black heels. My necklace was the last thing I added. When I walked into the living room, three pairs of eyes stopped on me.

"Damn, Tate!" Gianna cried out in her royal blue jumpsuit. "You look hot!"

"You look hotter!" I smiled, looking towards Axel for approval.

"Beautiful," he smirked, causing me to do the same. After a few seconds of looking at me, his face fell.

"What's wrong? Do you not like it?" I asked, looking down at my dress.

"No, no! It looks amazing! I just... it's really, really short..." he winced.

I tilted my head, looking at him. "You want me to change?"

He didn't take his eyes off the dress. "Well do you *want* to change?"

"No."

"Then, no," he said, taking another look at my red dress. He shook his head, his smirk starting to reappear.

I wrapped my arms around him, burying my head into his chest, while trying not to get any makeup on him. I was surprised that Axe had been so okay with me still wearing my dress, even though he would've preferred if I had changed. He let me do what I wanted, which was not only refreshing from what I was used to, but it was respectful as well. He wasn't controlling. He let me make me own decisions and be my own person, and although I wasn't used to it, it felt good.

Axe had offered to stay sober for the night, so that he could drive us to the party. He didn't want us to have to walk in the cold.

We could hear the music blasting from the house before we even got inside. Strobe lights were flashing through the windows. People were walking in and out of the house and some were scattered across the front lawn, even though it was freezing.

Axe led me by the hand inside. The massive house was packed, and empty beer bottles were already piling up everywhere. I was surprised by how many people had come back from break early, wondering where half of them would be staying since the dorms didn't open up for a few more days. But then again, everyone's hometowns were boring, so it was no wonder why people wanted to get back to Western as quickly as possible, especially for New Years.

A tall male approached the four of us. His brown hair was carefully gelled. He originally had his focus on me, but once I leaned onto Axel's arm, he clearly got the message.

"Hey!" he yelled to all of us over the music. "I'm one of the guys that lives here, so I'm just going around and meeting everybody!" The guy shook Axel's hand and then went to shake mine. "I'm Connor!"

130

I dropped his hand, taking a step back. My smile fell with it and my heart started to beat a little faster.

I hated that fucking name.

Axel's hand squeezed mine harder. He delicately turned my chin to face him with his free hand.

"It's okay. You're okay. That was then and this is now. He's not here now. He can't hurt you anymore," he whispered.

His soft eyes instantly made me snap out of it. I gave a slow nod. Axe pulled me to him, giving me a bear hug.

"C'mon, let's go in here," he offered. Leading me by my hand, we walked into the next room over, and within minutes, I had already forgotten about my almost flashback and was back into a better mood. Axe had that effect on me. He made my heart flutter. And even more so, he made my heart want to heal.

The house was very much alive, filled with some familiar faces, but we didn't know most of the people that were there. Guys that I didn't know kept glancing at me and I could tell it was not making Axel very happy. His eyes scanned the room for any guys that may have been staring for too long.

Claire ran up to me, and I immediately wrapped my arms around her, hugging her as if I hadn't seen her a few hours prior. She looked stunning with her long blonde hair in a side braid, perfectly accompanying her deep purple dress.

"You look great, bestie," I said.

"Right back at you," she winked as she swayed slightly.

"Where's Lucas and Jason?" I asked, noticing that she had approached me by herself. She was clearly a little tipsy already, and I didn't want her to be walking around alone.

"I told them to stay in the other room while I came over here. Didn't want any problems, ya know?"

"Good idea," Gianna walked up to us.

Claire's face brightened as she reached for Gianna. "My dear cousin!"

"You're drunk," Gi said.

"Drunk?" Claire's face twisted in confusion for a split second before her smile reappeared. "Oh my gosh, guys! Let's go get a drink!"

I giggled at her drunken excitement. "How many have you had already?" I asked.

"Probably too much," Gi said.

Claire thought to herself for a moment. "A good amount, but I'm trying to get plastered tonight!"

I shook my head, laughing. "We're gonna go get a drink, okay? We'll be right back," I said to Axe, rubbing the top of his hand with my thumb.

He cringed, looking around. "I don't know if I really trust any of the guys here. I should probably go with you."

"Axe, I'll be fine. We'll just be right over there."

"Okay... just please be careful and don't take drinks from any guys please. I'll end up killing someone if your drink gets spiked. Just yell if you need anything, okay?"

I could tell Axe was trying not to be the overbearing or controlling boyfriend, which I appreciated. He just genuinely cared and wanted me to be safe.

I nodded to Axe, then walked off with Gi and Claire towards the drink station.

"So, I see you and Axel are still together?"

I twisted around to face a skeptical Olivia. Her red hair was straightened, sitting directly on top of the cleavage that was sticking out of her black dress. She looked pretty, but her pink lips didn't compare to my red ones.

"So, I see you're still nosy?" I seethed back.

Olivia placed a hand on her hip, unhappy with my response. She swung around and stomped off, leaving me satisfied.

"Here, Tate," Gi said, handing me a drink.

"What is it?"

"Seltzer," she shrugged. I scrunched up my face for a moment, disappointed. Gi rolled her eyes. "Just drink it."

Everyone knew I preferred the hard stuff. It made me get drunk a hell of a lot faster than a goddamn seltzer. I popped the can open without complaining anymore, knowing that taking a closed seltzer would be better than taking an open drink that could have potentially been spiked.

I scanned the party, spotting Olivia next to Axel. Her fingers ran through his hair and he swatted them away. She slid her hands down his chest, but he put his hands up, creating space between them, signaling for her to back off. Olivia took a step back. Her facial expression turned from seduction to anger. I obviously couldn't hear what she was saying from so far away, especially with the loud music, but once she pointed in my direction, I had a pretty good idea that the subject was me. Axe crossed his arms, not budging. Whatever his response was, it was enough to make her turn on her heels and prance off.

Happiness and confidence swelled inside of me. Accompanied with a sense of pride as well. Axe had just denied a girl because he was with me. I had been worrying for so long how loyal he could possibly be and if he was just trying to use me, but each day, he kept proving himself more and more.

Gianna nudged me, diverting my attention back to her. "What?" I asked, a little snippier than intended.

"Creep alert. Nine o'clock."

"My clock or your clock?"

"Your clock," she said, sipping her drink.

I casually glanced over to my left, noticing Lucas staring from across the room. I should've known he was going to be the creep she was referring to.

"What are you guys looking at?" Claire drunkenly asked, tipping over. When she realized it was Lucas, she looked back at us, pushing her lips together into a straight line. "Bro, he's crazy about you," she said, touching my arm.

"Yeah, well, I'm crazy about someone else."

Lucas stood talking to two guys that I didn't recognize, his eyes darting over to me every few seconds. He nodded to the guys before starting to walk in our direction, a determined glow in his eye. I stepped back, preparing to go back by Axel before Lucas had the chance to trap me in a conversation.

"Tate—" Lucas began.

"Don't even try," Axel hissed, appearing by my side.

Lucas glared at him. "Oh, so now I can't even talk to her?"

"No," Axe shot back.

Lucas crossed his arms, making me surprised by how he was suddenly so focused on standing his ground. I had a feeling it was only because he felt Axel wouldn't do anything with so many people around. Lucas felt safe, but he shouldn't have.

"Interesting how controlling you are," Lucas said.

Axe's eyes narrowed. "What?"

"Just saying. With your anger and all, makes me wonder what happens behind closed doors."

"What are you trying to say?" Axe gritted through his teeth. Lucas shrugged, raising his brows. "Are you saying I hit her?"

"Well, I wouldn't put it past you."

I could feel Axe's heat radiating off of him. I had never seen him fully explode, and I sure as hell didn't want him to now. I glanced back and forth between the two before stepping in front of Axe.

"He would never," I said to Lucas, before turning back to Axe. I gripped his hand and squeezed as hard as I could, causing his eyes to meet mine, softening. "Let's just go have fun."

I was relieved to feel Axel's hand entwined with mine, a reminder that he would protect me at all costs. He took a deep breath as we walked away from Lucas, finding our own space on the opposite side of the room.

Gi found my side again, widening her eyes. "Damn," she quietly spoke, "he really hates Lucas's guts."

"I know," I agreed.

"Good thing you were there. Things could've gotten real ugly, real fast."

"What'd I miss?" Ash asked, walking up with a beer in his hand.

"Axe almost beating the shit out of Lucas... again," Gianna said.

"What?" Ash firmly asked, brows lifted. He turned to his brother. "I told you to let me handle shit from now on. I don't want you getting in trouble again."

Axe rolled his eyes, pushing his hands into his pockets. His agitation was showing. He was over the situation.

"He didn't. Everything's fine," I budded in.

Ash leaned into Gi and I. "That little fucker. If he gets into one more fight and gets arrested one more fucking time."

Axe loudly sighed. "Dude, I can fucking hear you."

Ash tilted his head. "Good, I'm glad," he scolded his brother.

"Let's all chill," Gianna said.

"Please. Countdown is starting soon," I said.

Both boys reluctantly agreed to quit bickering.

"Claire's fine, right?" I asked, looking around. "She's with Jason?"

"Yeah, she's drunk, but she's fine."

134

I nodded, relieved. I didn't want Claire to be lost or alone when the countdown began. I took one last chug of my seltzer, finishing it within fifteen minutes of opening it. I crushed the can and threw it on the ground, allowing it to accompany the other cans piling up around the house.

Within a few more minutes, the countdown started, and everyone began to yell, "5...4...3...2...1... Happy New Year!"

Axel immediately connected his lips to mine, delicately, to make sure he didn't ruin my lipstick. I smiled as he pulled away, suddenly getting the urge to get closer to him.

"Let's go back," I said.

"You don't wanna stay?" he asked, pulling his eyebrows together.

My head shook back and forth. I pulled my lips to the side as I tilted my head, and he immediately knew what I meant.

"I think we're gonna go back," he voiced to Ash.

Ash eyed Axe, then me, the sides of his mouth turning upwards, knowing why. "Alright," Ash said. "I'll just give Gi my jacket and we can walk back. It's not that far. Is that okay with you, babe?" he asked, turning to Gi.

"Oh, uh, yeah that's fine. I don't mind," she shrugged.

I winked to her as Axe and I strode out. I took a makeup wipe out of my purse and removed my lipstick in the car, thinking one step ahead. I didn't want to have to deal with that mess later.

The second we walked through the door, Axe's lips were smashed onto mine. I ran my hand down his stomach, feeling his six-pack through his shirt. Axe picked me up and led me into his bedroom, gently lying me down on the bed. He laid on top of me after stepping out of his jeans, his lips traveling all the way down from my jaw to my collarbone. His hand slid up my dress, feeling the inside of my thigh, fingertips stopping at the hem of my thong.

"Are you sure?" he asked, pulling away from my lips.

I gazed into his sparkling eyes. They made me feel at home. He had met my parents and they loved him. He showered me with presents on Christmas morning. He turned down Olivia in front of me. He showed me sides of him that no one else had ever seen before. He took all my symptoms away and protected me when I needed to be protected. Axe made me feel safe, wanted, and loved. He didn't lie to me or try to manipulate me. He didn't make me feel at competition with another girl or make me feel like I wasn't good enough. Axe was the person I needed, and in that moment, I had never felt so grateful.

I gave him a small nod. "I love you," I said.

His smile grew wider than I'd ever seen it, dimples showing. "You love me?" he asked. I gave him a firm nod, happy that I was finally getting the words out. "I fucking love you," he said, throwing his lips onto mine.

Axe carefully slipped the straps of my red dress off, allowing the fabric to glide down the rest of my body. My strapless bra was popped open and thrown on the floor. I lifted his shirt above his head and tossed it over by my bra. The only fabric left between us were his boxers and my thong. I grabbed at the hem of his boxers, slowly tugging them down. He guided my thong off of me, reaching over to grab a condom out of the nightstand.

He slowly and carefully slid inside, taking his time as he began moving into me rhythmically. It was a little uncomfortable at first, but after a few minutes, I relaxed and moved my hips up towards him. I sighed as he went deeper, feeling the bed rocking underneath us.

I buried my fingertips deep into his back, feeling his muscles bulge. Each thrust was firm, but gentle. I quietly cried out his name and he moaned in reaction.

It lasted a while, and eventually his body went rigid for a second as he drove himself into me one last time, groaning. Axe collapsed next to me, both of us out of breath, drenched in sweat.

Axe moved my damp hair out of my face, pulling me in closer to his sweaty, yet perfect body. His arms wrapped around me.

"I love you," he said. "God, it feels so good to finally say it out loud."

I looked up at him, grinning. "I love you more."

"Not possible," he stated, hugging me tighter until we eventually fell asleep in each other's arms.

Chapter Fourteen
The Visit(s)

The first few weeks of January flew by, fairly uneventful. Axe and I spent most of our time together, doing the most mundane things like grocery shopping and cleaning the apartment. Axe was upset once winter break was over, marking the end of me staying with him, but I was still hanging out at the apartment almost every day anyways.

I carried the bag of snacks out of my car that Axe had just bought me from the grocery store. I opened the door to my dorm room. Claire, Jason, Penelope, and Lucas were all sitting around, talking. I glanced around, both confused and uncomfortable as to why they were in my room.

"Hey, Tate!" Claire smiled.

"Hi," I said.

"Do you mind if we all hang out in here for a little bit?" Penelope asked.

I wanted to say that I did mind, but I was put on the spot, and it would be a big bitch move if I denied her request in front of everyone. In addition, Penelope let me have Axel over whenever I wanted, so I felt that it was only fair to allow her to have people over too.

"Sure, I don't mind," I gave a wry smile.

They hung out in our room for another hour or so, talking and laughing, but I never inserted myself into the conversations. I didn't want to.

Lucas, Jason, and Claire all stood, and I watched Lucas walk over to Penelope and kiss her on the cheek. She blushed from his affection and batted her eyelashes as they all walked out.

"What was that all about?" I lifted an eyebrow, hanging up my clean laundry.

"I don't even really know," she smiled. "We've been talking a lot lately and I actually think I might like him."

"Well, it seems like he likes you too."

Relief washed over me. Finally. Lucas had moved onto someone else. And even if that someone was my roommate, someone who was still so close to me, it was better than nothing.

Lucas started coming over more to hang out with Penelope over the next week. Even though it bothered Axel to know that Lucas was near me so often, I kept him calm and assured him that all of Lucas's attention was on Penelope each time he was over.

My phone buzzed and I glanced at it, reading a text message from Claire.

Come over right now!!

I got up from my desk, abandoning my homework and walking over to Claire and Gi's room, unsure of what the urgency was about. When I walked in, Kendall and Macey stood in the center of the room, smiling like kids on Christmas morning. My jaw dropped and I immediately jumped into their arms.

"Oh my God! What are you guys doing here?" I shrieked.

"We wanted to surprise you! So, we asked Claire and Gianna to let us into your building," Kendall giggled.

"How long are you guys staying for?"

"Just the weekend," Kendall answered.

"And Brynn?" I asked.

Macey shook her head. "She couldn't make it, but she wanted so badly to come."

138

I was overly excited. I hadn't seen my sisters since before school started and even though I was disappointed that Brynn couldn't come, I was still happy that Kendall and Macey were here.

I couldn't hold back my smile as I hugged them both again. "I can't believe you guys are here," I said.

"Well when we heard that mom and dad got to meet your boyfriend before we did, we got motivated to drive the three hours," Macey laughed.

I rolled my eyes. "You wanna go meet him?"

Their faces lit up as they both nodded. I said goodbye to Claire and Gi, thanking them, as I motioned for my sisters to follow me into my room so that I could call Axe. The phone rang for a second before he picked up.

"Hey, beautiful. What's up?"

I smiled at his hello. "Hi, so my sisters are in town for the weekend and they wanna come meet you. Is it okay if we come over in a bit?"

"Absolutely. Baby, you don't have to ask to come over. I gave you your own key for a reason."

I bit my lip. "I know, but I wanted to make sure I warned you that company is coming with me this time."

He laughed. "Okay, I'll see you in a bit, Tate. Love you."

"I love you too," I happily responded, hanging up the phone.

Both of my sisters grinned at me, watching my giddiness. All of us greatly resembled each other, four spin-offs of our mother. Kendall was the tallest out of all of us, even though she wasn't the oldest. Brynn was the oldest, eight years older than me. Then Kendall, who was five years older than me and Macey was three years older than me. I was the baby of the family. Even with our age differences, the four of us always stuck together. We were close. We told each other everything and backed each other up, no matter what the situation was.

I was the tiniest bit nervous for my sisters to meet Axel, but I was confident that they would love him just like my parents did. He was kind and compassionate and even when we were around others, he wasn't afraid to show it.

Axel's eyebrows shot up when we walked in.

"You guys look *a lot* alike," he said.

"Yeah, we know," I laughed.

Macey leaned in towards me. "He's fuckin' hot bro. Good job," she whispered.

I stifled a small laugh. "I know." I stood next to Axe, gesturing towards my sisters. "Axe, this is Macey and Kendall. Macey and Kendall, this is Axel." They shook hands, smiling kindly at each other.

An hour later, my sisters and I sat at the stools in the kitchen as Axel made dinner.

I got up, making my way over to Axe. I rubbed his muscular shoulder. "Are you sure you don't want any help?"

"I'm sure. Just go have fun with your sisters. I'm almost done anyways, don't worry."

I went up on my tiptoes, planting a kiss on his cheek before retreating back to my seat.

"Is he in a frat?" Macey asked me quietly.

"Yeah," I nodded.

"Hmm... weird."

"Why?"

"Aren't frat guys supposed to be total dicks?" she asked.

I pushed my mouth into a hard line. "Good point."

Axe walked over and handed each of us our plates with a kind smile.

"So, Axel," Macey started, "how's the frat life?"

"Good," Axe said with a light chuckle.

"You get a lot of girls?"

I smacked my face with my hand, wishing Macey would shut her hole.

"Used to," Axe confidently responded.

"Mace," Kendall warned.

"What? These are solid questions!" Macey said.

Kendall rolled her eyes, taking another bite of chicken. "Anyways," she said after swallowing, "thank you for having us and making dinner."

"Yeah, thanks!" Macey agreed.

"Of course. My pleasure," he replied.

"So, Burne? Is that like Irish or something?" Macey asked.

"It's Scottish, actually," Axe said.

"Hmm... Tatum Burne," Macey muttered to herself, but still loud enough for everyone to hear.

140

"Dude!" I cut in.

"Yeah?" she innocently asked.

"Shut up!"

Axe gave a light chuckle. "I like how it sounds," he shrugged. Heat rushed to my cheeks, but I couldn't hold back the tiny grin on my lips.

"Me too. I think it has a nice ring to it," Macey agreed. "Speaking of rings..."

"Can you not?" I intervened.

Kendall laughed at my annoyance, but when I shot her a look, her face went straight. "It's not funny," she said.

As dinner went on, I spent the rest of it hoping that Macey wouldn't embarrass me anymore.

An hour later, I yawned. "Are you guys ready to go?"

Axe budded in. "Babe, you can't leave. You've been drinking."

I had only had a few drinks throughout the night, and I knew I was perfectly fine and capable to drive, but it was clear that Axel was still concerned. I tilted my head to the side and looked at him.

"You guys can all take my bedroom. I can blow up an air mattress and put it in there to make sure there's extra room for you guys, and I'll sleep on the couch," he offered.

I gave a light smile, but then shook my head. "I'll just sleep on the couch with you and they can take the bed," I said.

His dimples appeared, and he made his way over to his bedroom to make sure everything was ready for my sisters. As he walked away, my sisters started their blabbering.

"Marry him," Kendall spat.

"Marry him, *now*," Macey added.

"Guys," I couldn't contain my happiness, "I'm not getting married for a long while."

"Then I'll marry him," Macey said.

My smile quickly turned to a defensive grimace. "Absolutely not."

Macey raised her brows. "See," she said, "you're *so* in love with him." I rolled my eyes with a smile.

"Tate," Kendall spoke softly, "he's seriously perfect for you."

"You think so?"

"Definitely," she answered, taking another sip of her martini.

141

Macey nodded in agreement. "And he's hot," Macey said. I rolled my eyes again, moving my hair out of my face. "But for real. He's like... everything you've always been looking for." I lightly brought my fingers up to my lips, hiding my smirk.

"I think he's a good guy," Kendall added.

"Do you know how pretty your babies would be?" Macey said. My eyes widened. "One step at a time, Mace."

"Just saying," she said.

Relief washed over me that my sisters approved of Axel. I had suspected that they would, but having the assurance was comforting.

I thought about Axel for a moment. Thinking about the sight of his beautiful green eyes and the dimples that sunk into his cheek when he smiled. The way he constantly made it clear that he loved me and only needed me. I loved him. So much. Being with him made me happy, but now that I was thinking about it, the fear was starting to creep back. I knew that Axel loved me. He showed me and reminded me every day, but what would happen the day that he decided he didn't anymore? The day he decided I wasn't good enough anymore?

My heart raced with the thought, and I fell asleep next to Axel on the couch, praying to be able to stay that way forever.

My sisters and I spent the rest of the weekend together, walking around the mall, getting our nails done, and having a wine night. Saying goodbye to them was hard, but it gave me hope that I would be able to go home to see them soon.

I tried not to worry while they were still here, or even after they left, but worry was all I knew. I didn't express my concerns to Axe, because I knew he would just assure me that he wasn't going to leave and that everything would be okay, but Connor used to do the same thing. Axel had made it clear that he was nothing like Connor, but my brain was still just a little fucked up. Even with my lingering fear, I didn't allow it to affect our relationship.

Axel and I had just gotten back to the apartment from class. We had planned all of our second semester classes together, mirroring each other's schedules as much as possible, so that we could spend even more time together outside of class.

I was laying on my stomach on the couch with my computer in front of me, trying to write my business essay.

"Alright, what do you have so far?" Axe asked, lying next to me as he tried his best to help.

"I have an introduction and my first body paragraph, but I need two more body paragraphs," I sighed.

"Too bad it's not a chemistry paper. I'd kick that paper's ass."

"Gross," I wrinkled my nose. "I hate chemistry."

Axe chuckled, taking another look at my computer. "Well your first paragraph is good."

"I just don't know how to even start the second one," I grumbled. I twirled the little hairs sticking out of my ponytail as I got up and made my way over to the kitchen. As I pulled the orange juice out of the fridge to pour a glass, there was a knock on the door. Axe got up and stretched his arms out, then jogged over and opened it.

Brooke shifted her weight nervously. She glanced around, her mind clearly racing as she stood, looking uneasy.

"Brooke," Axe spoke, "what are you doing here?"

She pressed her lips together into a hard line as she glimpsed beyond Axe, peeking over at me. I held my glass of orange juice tightly in my hand, too confused to even take a sip.

"I, um, I need to talk to you," she said to Axe.

"Okay... what is it?"

She licked her lips. "Can I talk to you in private?"

"Whatever it is, you can say in front of both of us," Axe said, trying to ensure me that he wasn't trying to hide anything.

"Axel, I don't really want—"

"What is it?" he insisted.

Brooke rubbed her arms with her hands and looked down for a second. "Well I was originally going to just call you, but I figured I should talk to you in person instead," she paused, clearly struggling with what she was trying to spit out. "I'm pregnant. And there's a possibility that it's your baby."

I dropped my glass, watching it shatter across the floor. My shaking hands made their way up towards my face, holding them against my mouth.

Axel flinched at the sound, turning towards me to make sure I was okay. I moved my foot slightly, yelping in pain as a piece of glass cut it open.

"Brooke, I'll call you later, okay?" Axel abruptly said, shutting the door and hurriedly making his way over to me. He carefully stepped around the glass, reaching for me. He picked me up and carried me to the couch, slowly setting me down. Axe delicately blotted my bloody wound with a wet towel, then grabbed a bunch of bandages and wrapped them around my foot.

I watched him, my eyes glossing over. "Did you not use a condom that day?" I asked, disregarding my new injury.

Axe took a deep breath. "I've never not used a condom with any of the women I've ever slept with, but... that morning was so fuzzy..." he trailed off.

"Did you? Or did you not?" I seethed through my teeth, waiting for my tears to spill over.

"I—I don't know," he covered his face with his hands.

"Call her," I said, still not caring that I had just sliced my foot open.

"I'll call later," he shook his head, reaching for me.

I backed away. "No, call now," I demanded.

He sighed and reluctantly got up, searching for his phone. He dialed her number and put it on speaker.

"Hello?" Brooke answered.

"Hey," Axe said, unsure of what he was supposed to say.

"Hey, um, so basically... I'm nine weeks, which goes back to the week you and I had... slept together. Um, I'm going to be getting a prenatal paternity test done because there is another guy that might be the father and I don't want to wait until the baby is born to find out."

"Okay," Axe quietly said, his hands shaking.

"So, I'm going to need a blood sample from you," she said. Her nerves were echoing through the phone.

"Okay, no problem. Um, Brooke?"

"Yeah?"

I could tell he was trying to look anywhere other than at me. "Did we not use a condom that day?"

"I feel like we did, but I honestly can't remember."

144

I dropped my head back, wondering how Axel could've been so stupid. I pulled my injured foot closer to me, anger and sadness both bubbling up inside.

Axe could tell I was on edge. He breathed heavily. "How long will the test take?"

"A couple of weeks," Brooke answered.

"Okay, just... keep me updated. I've gotta go," he hung up the phone.

I wiped my tears away, looking down.

"Baby," Axe said, grabbing my hand.

I tugged it away from him, not wanting to feel his touch for the first time since we met. I shook my head as more tears spilled over.

"I'm sorry," he said quietly, rubbing his forehead.

"Just," I sighed, "I'm gonna go."

"Stay," he begged.

"I'm gonna go," I repeated. I went to stand, but pain rippled through my foot when I put weight on it. I winced, closing my eyes. Axe gripped my arm, helping me stabilize myself.

"Tate, you shouldn't drive like this. If you really want to go, then I'll drive you."

I shook my head. "I don't wanna leave my car here."

"I'll pick you back up tomorrow so you can come get it."

"No," I breathed, heavily.

I hobbled out of his grip and hopped over to the door, realizing that I would have to climb down numerous flights of stairs.

Axe raced over to me. "I'll carry you," he sadly said. I knew he wanted me to stay, but I had made it clear that I didn't want to, and Axe wasn't going to hold me against my will.

He grabbed my computer and my bag before picking me up and carrying me all the way to my car. My left foot was the one that had endured the damage, so I was still able to drive with my dominant foot. I'd be fine.

Once I had successfully limped up to my room using the elevator, Penelope stared at me as I stood in the doorway.

"Are you okay?" she asked.

My bottom lip quivered and my tears began to tumble. Penelope came and hugged me tightly, rubbing her hand up and down my back to comfort me.

"What happened?" she asked, still keeping me close. I couldn't get the words out as I put all my weight onto my one, good foot.

It felt like everything was finally collapsing. It wasn't for certain if Axel was the father, but I assumed the worst. And once those results were given, it would tear us apart.

Penelope helped me over to the futon before running out of the room. She reappeared a minute later with Claire and Gianna. They both pulled me in for a comforting hug, and then helped me get my foot situated.

"What happened, Tate?" Gianna calmly asked.

I finally got myself together, breathing deeply to slow down my racing heart.

"Brooke," I said, shaking my head.

"Brooke? Ew, what did that skank do now?" her eyebrows shot up. "Did he sleep with her again?"

I shook my head quickly. "No, worse."

"What could be worse than that?" Claire asked.

I bit the inside of my lip, dreading what I was about to say. "She's pregnant. And the baby might be Axel's."

It was silent for a few moments before anyone spoke again. "Okay, yeah, you're right. That's definitely worse," Claire said.

It felt embarrassing to say it aloud. That my boyfriend may have had knocked up some other chick. At this point, I would've rather had me be the pregnant one.

Everyone's jaw stayed open, clearly just as surprised, confused, and worried as me.

"So, did you break up with him?" Claire asked.

"No," I said, dropping my head into my hands. "I don't know what to do," I cried.

"Do you love him?" Gianna asked.

I looked up at her with splotchy eyes. "Of course, I do."

"Then there's your answer. Don't let this tear you guys apart."

I put my head down again, trying to clear my thoughts. I did love Axe, and even though I felt like I was falling apart, I still wanted to be with him. I had put up a fight with myself for months to get myself to let my guard down and let Axel in. And now that I finally had, now that we were finally happy together, I couldn't let Brooke fuck that up.

146

I had six missed calls from Axel since I left the apartment, and knowing him, he would show up at my room soon. I dialed his number to talk to him before he hopped in his car and made his way over here.

"Hey, baby," he quietly answered.

"Hi," I said in my small, frail voice. "I wanna come talk to you. I'm probably gonna ask Gianna for a ride."

He sighed through the phone. "Okay."

"You okay?"

"I mean..." he trailed off.

"I know... I'll see you in a bit."

I hung up the phone and turned to Gianna. She nodded at me and proceeded to help me limp to the car with my crippled foot.

I didn't know why, but I was a little nervous to talk to Axel. It had only been a few hours since I last saw him, but I had no idea what thoughts had been going through his head for those hours.

When we got there, he immediately picked me up and carried me into his bedroom, trying to make me avoid any walking whatsoever.

"Alright," he looked down, "let's hear it."

I brought my eyebrows together. "Hear what?"

"You telling me you wanna break up."

I eyed him in awe. "Is that why you sounded so upset over the phone? Because you think I wanna breakup?" He nodded, worry still resting in his gaze. "Axe, that's not why I came here to talk to you. That's like, the complete opposite, actually."

Axe's worry fell, and he scooted closer to me. "So, you don't wanna breakup?"

I gave a small smile, shaking my head. "No. I came here to tell you that I still love you and that I want to support you and be with you. Even if you did fuck up," I rolled my eyes at the end.

Axe beamed, his face lighting up. He wrapped his arms around me and pulled me on top of him, repeatedly kissing my face over and over again everywhere.

"Fuck, I love you so much. I was so fucking scared that you were gonna come here and dump my ass. I wouldn't know what to do if you did."

I played with his hair, still unsatisfied with the situation, but satisfied that I was at least in his arms.

"Tate?"

"Yeah?"

"You're the fucking best. And I'm sorry all of this got put on you. I'm gonna make it up to you."

"Last time you said that, you bought me a necklace that was *way* too expensive. So no, you do not need to 'make it up to me,'" I made quotations with my hands at the last part.

"I'm gonna throw you a rager for your birthday in a few weeks."

I laughed. "You're gonna throw me a rager?"

"Hell yeah. Because you deserve one. And your birthday is definitely something to celebrate," he kissed my wrist.

I giggled. "You don't need to throw me a party, Axe."

"Well I'm going to," he said, kissing my face all over again.

Chapter Fifteen
The Ragdoll

Within a few weeks, my foot was completely healed. All that was left of the incident was a small scar. Axe had given his blood sample to Brooke to get the prenatal paternity test done and each day that passed made me more anxious about it. I could tell Axe was trying to keep us both occupied by planning the party and doing other little things to distract us from our real problems, but in reality, it was killing me. I didn't want to wait a few more weeks to find out the results. There was the possibility that Axel wasn't the father, but with my shitty luck, he would be. The thought of Axel having a child that wasn't mine, even though the last thing I would want right now was to be pregnant, was still an unsettling feeling. And if or when those results came back positive, I wouldn't know what to do. I would lose the only sense of security that I had. The only man that ever truly loved me.

Axel had actually planned an entire birthday party for me at the apartment that weekend and I was honestly excited for it. It made me look forward to something other than getting the test results, which was what my mind had been focused on the most lately.

I walked towards my dorm after class, snuggled up in my winter coat. The freezing cold air was drying out my skin, which pissed me off.

"Tate, wait up!"

I turned to reveal a jogging Lucas coming up from behind me.

"Hey," he said, slightly out of breath as he appeared next to me.

"Hey..." I continued to walk. "What are you doing all the way over here? Isn't Jameson Hall across campus?"

"Well yeah, but I'm going up to hang out with Penelope," he pointed to my building.

I nodded, relieved to know that I wasn't the reason for him being on this side of campus.

"So, um," he rubbed the back of his neck, "I heard your birthday party is this weekend?"

Oh no. He wasn't invited for a reason. Ever since Lucas started to hang out with Penelope, he bothered me fairly less than he used to, but Axel was still not a fan of him. I didn't want to be rude about the topic, but I had a gut feeling that giving Lucas an invite would only end in disaster.

I shrugged. "Yeah, um, Axel planned the whole thing," I said, hoping that mentioning Axel's name would scare him off and cause him to drop the topic.

"Oh cool, so what time does it start?"

The fuck? Did he not understand that he couldn't come? I was under enough stress with the possibility that my boyfriend may have impregnated some other girl, so I really did not need him showing up and wrecking the party. On top of that, I was definitely more irritable than usual from the whole situation.

"Lucas, I really, *really* don't wanna be a bitch, but I don't think it's a good idea for you to come. Same goes with Jason."

"Because of Axel?" he asked, frustrated.

"Yeah, I mean, you two clearly don't get along and the party is at his apartment so..." I trailed off, expecting him to get the hint.

"Well if I could guarantee you that there would be no problems, could we come?"

Why was he still pushing it? I didn't understand why he was so butt hurt about not being invited. It's not like him and I were best friends anyways, or any type of friends for that matter. I could feel the annoyance growing inside of me. I took a deep breath, pressing my lips into a hard, straight line.

"It's not my apartment. So, I really don't want to go around inviting whoever," I snapped.

His jaw worked under his skin, obviously unsatisfied with my answer. He made a loud sigh. "Gotcha," he said, trying to hold his anger in as he held the door to Stanley open for me. I gave a tiny smile as a thank you, attempting to brush away the awkwardness that lingered in the air.

As far as I was concerned, Lucas had been treating Penelope really well, probably better than Jason had been treating Claire. But if either of them showed up this weekend, all hell would most likely break loose, and more stress was exactly what I didn't need.

We made our way upstairs, not saying much in the elevator. And when we got to my hallway, I went straight to Gianna and Claire's room. The very last thing I wanted was to be stuck in a room with Penelope and a pissed off Lucas, breathing in the tense air.

"Hey," I opened my eyes wide as I walked in.

"What's up?" Claire asked at her desk.

"Just had to tell Lucas he couldn't come to my birthday party this weekend and now he's not very happy," I whispered, trying to make sure they couldn't hear us in the next room over.

Gianna made a pained expression. "Well at least he won't be showing up."

"Yeah, we'll see about that," I said, sitting down on the futon. "Now he's in my room with Penelope and I do not want to go in there."

Gianna thought to herself for a moment and then her face lit up. "Why don't we just go shopping for your birthday outfit today instead of tomorrow? And then I'm sure Lucas will be gone by the time we get back."

Axel had given me money to go buy myself a new outfit for my birthday, stating that if I didn't spend every penny on myself, he would go out and spend it on me himself. He was really trying to lighten the situation, and I appreciated his effort, but this was a situation that couldn't be lightened easily. We hadn't heard any updates from Brooke in nearly two weeks and I was becoming too impatient to bear. The suspense was killing me. Every day, my mind raced between possibilities of how getting those results could go, and of course I hoped for the best, but I expected the worst.

"Yeah, we can do that," I responded to Gi, yawning with exhaustion.

She stood up from her desk and grabbed her wallet and keys. "Are you gonna come, Claire?"

Claire kept her focus on her textbook. "Um, I actually have a lot to do," she turned around in her seat, glancing at me and then Gi. "You know what? Yeah, I'll come."

"Aye!" Gianna and I both shouted in unison.

I was happy that Claire agreed to come with us. The three of us had been spending more time together recently like we used to, and I wanted to keep it that way. But the more time we spent together, the more I noticed that Claire was acting slightly strange. I couldn't pinpoint why, and with my current anxiety about Brooke's pregnancy, I hadn't gotten around to asking.

We walked around the mall for what seemed like forever, searching for something nice and new for me to wear to my party. I was fairly picky, so we hadn't had any luck finding anything. We entered a new store, on the hunt for the perfect outfit.

The three of us split up, trying to cover as much ground as possible. I rummaged through the racks of hangers, disappointment dawning over me with every piece of clothing that I saw.

"Tate! Come over here!" Claire yelled from the back of the store. I walked over to where Claire was, her eyes scanning the fabric she held between her fingers. She lifted it up as I approached, and immediately, my eyebrows shot up, intrigued by the sight. "Try it on. Now!" she shoved it at me. I gladly accepted it, making my way over to the dressing rooms.

I slipped on the black two-piece and glanced in the mirror. The cami top rested directly at the bottom of my breasts, my strapless bra evidently pushing them up out of the top. My entire stomach was basically exposed between the pieces of fabric. The skirt was skin tight, revealing every detail of my curved hips and backside. My favorite part, the black faux fur that lined the top hem of the top piece, and the bottom hem of the skirt.

I bit my lip as I studied myself, pleased with how the two-piece looked on me. I stepped out of the dressing room, hoping that Claire and Gi would like the two-piece just as much as I did.

"Holy shit!" Claire called out, her jaw dropping.

"That's amazing," Gianna covered her open mouth with her hand.

"You guys like it?" I asked, turning around so they could see the back.

152

"Like it? We love it! Axel is going to piss himself when he sees you!" Claire shouted.

I ran my fingers smoothly over the skirt, a smile forming on my lips.

"And what the hell? Your stomach is so flat," Gi said, irritated. I rolled my eyes.

"And it's black, so I can wear my red lipstick with it," I happily said. "You guys don't think it's too much, do you?"

Gianna laughed, shaking her head. "Definitely not. It's your birthday. You're allowed to be extra."

I giggled, giddy that we finally found an outfit worth looking at twice.

"If you wore black heels with it, your legs would look stellar," Claire added.

Gi nodded, "Seriously, you need to buy that. Like, now."

"I agree with Gi," Claire said. "It's hot."

I pushed my lips together, trying to wipe my stupid smirk off of my face. "Okay," I said, touching my necklace, "I'm sold."

Claire and Gianna exploded in happiness, hyping me up as I took it off and headed to the checkout counter. After making the purchase, we decided to stop at the food court for a bite to eat.

"But really Tate, how are you doing?" Gi asked as we sat down with our burgers and fries. I could hear the worriedness in her voice, truly concerned with my sanity.

"I'm okay," I responded. I shoved a fry in my mouth, refusing to make eye contact with her. Gianna and Claire traded glances.

"Tate, you could tell us how you're actually feeling," Claire said. "It's just the three of us."

I wanted to talk to them about how much stress was intensely building up inside of me, but I didn't want to have a mini breakdown while we were in public.

"I'm fine," I said, finally looking up. But the second I made eye contact with them, they could tell I was lying.

"Tate," Claire warned.

I was known to bottle everything up inside of me, never knowing how to discuss my true thoughts and feelings. When everything had been happening with Connor and Nicole, I rarely ever talked about the situation with anyone, even when it was absolutely and utterly destroying me. Because I was embarrassed. I was embarrassed to admit that I was an option to him and that he treated me like complete trash. I was embarrassed that I felt the way I did about him, regardless of how badly he treated me. And right now, embarrassment was what flooded me again. I was embarrassed that my boyfriend had possibly gotten another woman pregnant. I had been trying to avoid talking about the situation since the day we found out, and now that they were pushing it, I didn't know how to respond.

"I'm *fine*," I said again. I had been wondering and worrying so much about the situation recently that I just wanted to forget about it for a while. My own birthday was this weekend and all I wanted was to go into it with a good attitude. Well, as good of an attitude as possible, at least.

The girls dropped it, sighing heavily, and knowing that I wasn't in the mood for it. We finished eating and hopped back into the car, jamming out to old Taylor Swift and One Direction songs, which made me feel young again, almost stress-free and careless again.

"Do you guys think you could drop me off at Jason's?" Claire asked from the back seat.

Gianna was the one driving, so I glanced over at her, waiting for her to give Claire an answer.

"Would I have to pick you up again later?" Gi wondered.

"No, I'll just have Jason bring me home."

"Then, yes," Gi said, relieved that she wouldn't have to leave the dorms again to drive.

I stared out my window after we dropped off Claire, lost in thought as we drove back to the dorms.

"Look, I know some of the frats are throwing tonight. We could go out to a party or we could stay in and just hang out all night," Gi said.

I turned towards her, messing with my hair. "I don't know, Gi. Not really sure I'm in a party mood."

"Oh, c'mon. It's a Thursday night. Thirsty Thursday!" she shouted, giggling. "Or we could just invite the guys over and drink in my room tonight."

I forced a small smile, knowing that Gi was trying her best to cheer me up. As if it was planned, my phone rang, and a picture of me sitting on Axel's shoulders appeared on the screen.

"Hello?"

"Hey, baby. I was just wondering what you were doing tonight?"

"Is it Axe?" Gianna asked. I nodded to her, still holding the phone up to my ear. "Tell them to come over," she whispered.

I waved her off, ignoring her request. "I'm not really sure," I said to him.

"Babe, are you okay? I can tell you're upset."

I slowly nodded as I closed my eyes, even though he couldn't see. "Yeah, I'm fine."

I was really trying my best to push my fear and stress aside, no matter how badly they were eating me away. At the end of the day, I still loved Axel, and sometimes, you had to endure some pain for the people you loved.

"I miss you. I wanna see you tonight," he said through the phone.

Gi was looking over at me every few seconds, waiting for me to ask them to come over. I shot a glance back at her, annoyed with her silent pressure.

"You and Ash can come over if you want. Gianna and I were just planning on drinking in the dorms."

"I think Ash was originally gonna go to ATA tonight. Would you guys maybe want to go there?"

I made an unsatisfied face. "I don't know if I'm really in a party mood."

"Okay, well we'll come over and we can all figure it out."

"Alright," I quietly said.

"Tate?"

"Yeah?"

"I love you so much. I'll see you in a little bit."

His words caused a true smile to come across my lips, one that has been the most genuine smile I've had in days.

"Love you too," I said, hanging up the phone.

About twenty minutes later, Ash and Axe walked in. Axe's white button down was rolled up to his elbows, the top few buttons undone just enough to see his swallow tattoos. The sight made me want to rip the shirt off.

Axel spun me around in his arms, planting a meaningful kiss on my lips.

"I've fucking missed you all day," he said, kissing my neck. The feeling caused the insides of my thighs to tingle, wanting more, but I tried to ignore the desire, since Ash and Gi were still in the room. I bit the inside of my lip, keeping myself quiet.

Ash rubbed his hands together. "So, what's the plan tonight? We goin' to ATA or what?"

Axe's green eyes darted to me. "I'll do whatever you wanna do."

Everyone looked over at me. I hated when the pressure was on me. I didn't want to be the one to make all the group decisions.

"I don't know if I'm in a party mood," I truthfully said, uncomfortably crossing my arms.

"That's okay, baby," Axe reached to me.

"Boo! C'mon, Tate. Let's go live it up. Don't be such a grandma," Ash joked, playfully pushing me.

I jutted my lips out, giving a single, silent laugh as Axe hugged me from behind.

"Don't talk to her like that, Ash. I'll knock your teeth out," Axe said, only half-joking. Ash rolled his eyes, shoving his hands in his pockets.

I really didn't feel like going out, but I didn't want to be the one to hold everyone else back. It had been a long few weeks with everything going on, and this weekend was definitely going to be an exhausting one.

"Well, Gi, what do you wanna do?" I asked.

"Kinda wanna go out," she answered, shrugging one shoulder.

"You guys can go. Tate and I will just stay here and hang out," Axe spoke, still standing with his arms wrapped around me.

I looked up at him. "You can go too. You don't have to stay back just because of me."

His eyebrows pulled together. "Yes, I do. I'm not leaving you." His lips met my forehead, kissing it gently. Even though I'd known Axel for almost five months, and even though we had been together for a little over two, he still found a way to make butterflies flutter around in my stomach. Axe's thumb rubbed my wrist, which comforted me. My stress had been overbearing, but he somehow had the ability to calm me down.

Ash checked his watch. "Well it's already a little past nine, so we'll pregame here with you guys for a bit and then head out?" he glanced at Gianna for approval. She nodded, grabbing her secret stash of alcohol out of its hiding spot in her closet.

Axe finally let go of me. "Did you find a new outfit for you to wear on Saturday?" he asked as Gianna poured a round of shots.

"Hell yeah, she did," Gi said.

I eyed Axe as his face lit up with excitement. "Can I see?"

"No!" I said. His face fell. "It's a surprise."

He dropped his head back. "That means I have to wait almost forty-eight hours!"

A laugh escaped my mouth. "Yeah, your fine ass is gonna wait forty-eight hours!"

He winked at me, leaning against Gianna's bedframe. The sight nearly brought me to my knees. And suddenly, I couldn't wait for Gianna and Ash to leave.

After a couple rounds of shots, Gi and Ash left. Within seconds of them walking out the door, Axe's lips were on mine. His hands rested on my hips as he backed me up against the wall. He moved my hair out of the way, lightly sucking on my neck as his hands moved to the back pockets of my jeans. His mouth came back up to mine after a few minutes, and when his tongue slipped inside my mouth, I pulled away.

"What's wrong?" he asked, worried.

"I'm not having sex with you in someone else's room," I said, dragging him by the hand.

"Fair enough," he replied.

I opened the door of my own room, thankful that Penelope wasn't there. She was most likely out somewhere with Lucas. The one and only time I was thankful for Lucas's existence.

I locked the door behind us. Axe wrapped his arms around me again from behind, connecting his lips onto my neck. His hands slowly unbuttoned my jeans and pushed them down. I stepped out of them and turned towards him, undoing the rest of the buttons on his shirt. I admired him in the light, the way his v-line perfectly disappeared into his black jeans. His biceps bulged as he pulled me closer.

I looked away for a second, staying still in my red lace thong. I furrowed my brows.

"What?" Axe said, standing shirtless.

"Shh," I silenced him, trying to hear the noise coming from Claire and Gianna's room. It was muffled through the walls, but from what I could make of it, it sounded like sobbing. Either that, or two people trying to silently fuck, but I didn't think that was it.

I slipped on my pair of grey sweatpants. "I'll be right back," I said, kissing Axe on the cheek.

"You want me to come with you?"

"No, it's okay. I'll be back in like two minutes."

I knocked on the door a few times, just in case it really was people hooking up in there. Ash and Gianna hadn't left long ago, so it was possible that they decided to come back. And last time I saw Claire, we were dropping her off at Jason's, so maybe they came here to get some alone time. Who knows.

I put my ear up to the door, but the noises had stopped. I pulled by head back as the door cracked open. Claire's puffy face appeared in the open space.

"Claire? What's wrong? Are you okay?" I pushed the door open all the way and walked in.

A couple more tears streamed down her red cheeks, and she quickly turned away, wiping them. She took a seat at her desk.

"Jason and I got into another fight."

"About what?"

Claire covered her face with her hands. "I don't even know," she wept. "We started arguing and then he told me to leave and I walked back here by myself."

I thought about the day I walked home by myself after Connor sat and watched me cry in front of him, saying nothing. Not comforting me in any way. Looking at me disgusted. I shivered at the thought. That was a terrible fucking day.

"He didn't even drive you?" I asked, anger starting to bubble up inside of me. It was late on a Thursday night in February. Not only was it cold out, but it was dangerous too. No girl should be walking around a college campus by herself at night.

"No," she shook her head, pulling her knees into her chest.

There was a knock on the door, and I assumed it was Axel, wanting to make sure everything was okay. But when I opened the door, a pissed off Jason pushed through. Claire lifted her head out of her knees as he strode over to her.

"I can't believe you actually left," he said heatedly.

"You told me to."

158

Claire's voice was so weak. It made my heart hurt.

"Well I didn't think you actually would."

He sounded exactly like Connor. I wanted to rip his head off right then and there. It took everything in me not to. Connor always used to turn everything around on me, trying to make me feel like it was my fault. And that was what Jason was doing to Claire right now. He was trying to make Claire feel like shit for things that he said and did.

Another tear fell down Claire's cheek and Jason's tense body relaxed. He reached for her, but she turned away. The tenseness that had just drained from his body seconds before, resurfaced.

"Really? You're gonna back away from me like that?"

Claire didn't respond, too afraid to meet his gaze.

"Claire?" he said, his voice slightly more raised than before. "Claire! Fucking answer me!" he shouted.

"Hey! Don't fucking yell at her," I warned.

Jason whipped around to face me, his jaw working under his skin. "Don't. Try. To get. Involved," he breathed.

I narrowed my eyes at him, unfazed. "Well I just did, motherfucker."

He cocked his head to the side and rubbed the corner of his mouth with his thumb. "You know what, Tate? I used to think you were a hot piece of ass, but now, you're kind of just a bitch."

I leaned in. "Fuck you."

His hands started to shake in anger, and before I knew it, he had grabbed me by my hair.

"Jason, let go of her!" Claire yelled, clawing at his back.

"Axel! AXEL!" I screeched at the top of my lungs.

Within seconds, Axel burst through the door. Jason barely had time to react before Axel gripped him by the back of his neck and slid him across the floor like a ragdoll.

"Are you okay?" he rushed over to me, inspecting me for any injuries.

Jason stood and lifted his elbow back, preparing to land a punch to Axel's face, but Axe's reflexes were too fast, catching Jason's flying fist in his hand, rage resting in his eyes.

"I don't think that's a very good idea," Axel hissed.

Jason's fury turned to fear. He slowly dropped his fist from Axel's hand. Axe cocked his elbow back, but before he could even move his punch the slightest bit towards Jason, Jason fell to the ground, covering his face with his arms.

Axe chuckled at his cowardice, then grabbed a handful of Jason's shirt and picked him up by it. "If you *ever* touch my girl *one* more fucking time or even breathe in her direction, I will fucking kill you! Do you understand?"

Jason's fear escalated as he stood in Axel's grip, not responding.

"Do you understand!" Axe screamed in his face. He rapidly nodded, and Axe dropped him. Jason ran out the door without saying another word.

"Wow," Claire quietly spoke, "I didn't know he was such a puss."

Axel laughed out loud. "I did." He diverted his attention back to me. "Baby, are you okay?"

I nodded, bringing my hand up to where Jason had grabbed my hair.

"Claire, are you okay too?" he asked sympathetically.

"Yeah, I'm— I'm okay."

"I should've ripped his fucking throat out," Axe vented, shaking his head.

"Thank you for rushing over here," I said.

His emerald eyes softened as he ran his thumb over my bottom lip. "It's my job to protect you."

I fell into his arms, closing my eyes. His muscles held me, warming me. This was what home felt like. But a small twinge of unsettlement came about me, knowing that there was a very serious conversation I would have to have with Claire.

Chapter Sixteen
The Nineteenth Birthday

The next day, I asked Claire to go get coffee with me. I was concerned about her, hoping that she would take all my advice into consideration.

I messed with my hair as we sat down, nervous to bring up her crumbling relationship.

She sat quietly, her blonde hair framing her tired face and swollen eyes.

"How are you?" I started.

"I'm fine," Claire said, hiding behind her coffee cup.

I tilted my head towards my shoulder, sighing with empathy. "Claire, you're not fine." She sniffled once, holding her warm cup of coffee close to her. "You know you have to break up with him, right?"

Claire looked down. "I know... but part of me doesn't want to." She shuffled around in her seat, unwilling to make eye contact with me.

"I just don't want you to end up where I was." I covered her hand with mine, trying my best to comfort her. "He's toxic. Cutting him off is what's best for you."

"This sucks," she said, her eyes glossing over as she stared down at her cup.

"I know. I'm sorry."

"Is this what it felt like with Connor?" she quietly asked, finally looking up at me. I nodded, swallowing the lump in my throat that formed at the sound of his name. "You dealt with feeling like this for three years?"

"Yeah."

"How? This is terrible."

I drew her in for a hug. "Claire, he sucks. Like, he really sucks. He makes you feel more miserable than happy and that's not okay. You deserve better."

She pulled away, wiping the single tear that escaped down her cheek. "Yeah, you're right."

"End it within the next day or two and then we'll just have fun this weekend, okay?" I said. She gave a small nod, taking another sip of coffee. "And I'm always here for you."

"I love you bestie," Claire said, pulling her mouth over to the side.

I squeezed her hand. "I love you too."

For the first time in what seemed like weeks, I was overcome with pure excitement. I had already done my makeup when Gianna and Claire smuggled me into the apartment to get dressed, making sure Axel didn't see. It felt like prom or a wedding, trying to hide from the date or groom until the "big reveal."

The three of us all piled into the bathroom as I did touch ups on my makeup. People were going to start arriving within the next half hour or so, so I needed to get ready quickly.

"So, Claire, you haven't talked to Jason since the other night, right?" I asked. After hearing what happened, Gianna was pissed that she wasn't there to help. She would've gouged Jason's eyeballs out with her fingernails. But more importantly, after witnessing Jason having Connor-like tendencies and on top of that, getting violent as well, I was more concerned than ever about Claire. I had a first-hand account of how emotional and mental abuse could destroy you and adding physical abuse on top of that would make it a hundred times worse.

I was glad we had our heart to heart at the coffee shop, but knowing how I was during my whole ordeal with Connor, I understood how hard it was to escape a toxic relationship. I wanted to make sure that she wasn't feeding back into his bullshit.

"No," Claire responded, looking down. Her navy-blue mini dress hugged her body, fitting her perfectly, dirty blonde hair cascading elegantly down her back. Claire was stunning. She would have no problem finding a guy who was actually good for her.

Gianna rubbed Claire's back, trying to comfort her.

"Are you lying?" I asked, slightly raising a brow. She rapidly shook her head. "Has he..." I stopped, unsure if my next question was too much for the moment.

"Has he what?" Claire asked.

"Has he ever hit you?"

I watched in the mirror as she crossed her arms, uncomfortably. I didn't think Gianna had ever asked her herself, so the second the bathroom went silent, Gi's concern was raised.

"Claire?" Gi softly spoke.

Claire's eyes were glossy. "No," she shook her head, "he hasn't."

Gianna and I glanced at each other in the mirror, unsure if Claire was being truthful or not.

"Are you sure?" Gi asked.

"Yes," she said, but the glossiness in her eyes didn't fade. I could tell Gi wanted to keep pushing the topic, but I shook my head at her, remembering how cornered I felt the other day at the mall.

I finished applying my red-hot lips and put on my necklace. Then slipped on my black two-piece and completed the outfit with black heels.

"I was so right," Claire said. "Those heels make your legs look stellar."

"Thanks, bestie," I grinned, taking a look at myself in the mirror.

"Ready?" Gi asked. I nodded. She peeked her head out of the bathroom door. "She's ready!" she yelled.

"Okay! We're done out here so you guys can come out now!" Ash called out.

"Where's she at? I wanna see my beautiful girl!" Axe shouted.

I smiled, moving my half up, half down curls in front of my shoulders. I fixed my strapless bra in my black cami top, making sure it wouldn't fall down, and took one more look in the mirror. My red lipstick popped against my black two-piece and I fucking loved it.

I walked out and entered the living room, which was decked out with decorations. Streamers dangled from the ceiling and a giant banner that read "Happy Birthday Tate!" was hung against the wall above the couch.

Axel's special smirk spread across his face, green eyes brightening. "You look incredible," he said, not taking his eyes off of me. I did a little spin, allowing him to see my full outfit. His eyes widened and he took a deep breath, wincing. "Everyone's gonna be checking you out."

Gianna rolled her eyes. "Who cares? At the end of the day, she's still yours, right?"

Axe intertwined our fingers, grinning. "Yeah, I guess you're right."

He clearly didn't want to create an issue, knowing that I would refuse to change if he asked me to. It was refreshing having a boyfriend that didn't try to control you or guilt you into doing the things he wanted you to do. Even when some things worried him, he still let me make my own decisions.

We all began drinking before more people showed up. And in small groups, they arrived. A pile of presents began to grow in the corner of the room. Axel had invited more people than I had even expected, from his frat brothers to friends we knew around campus. Not a single girl was invited that had ever spent the night in Axel's bed, which I was grateful for.

Axe and I stood near the couch, socializing with our guests. He gave me a peculiar look, the one where I knew he was thinking.

"What is it, babe?" I asked. His charming smile appeared. "What?" I asked again.

He stepped up on the couch, still holding onto my hand. "HEY!" Axel shouted. "TURN THE MUSIC DOWN!"

Everyone's heads turned, curious as to what the commotion was about. The room went silent.

Axe licked his lips. "Uh, so as you all know, it's Tate's birthday," he gazed at me. "And I just wanted to give a toast to her," he said, raising his drink. "To the most amazing, most beautiful woman I've ever met. And I'm beyond thankful that she gave me a chance even though I'm probably the biggest asshole on campus. Happy birthday, Tate!"

"Happy birthday!" everyone screamed, before starting to sing happy birthday to me. I smiled the whole time, unable to contain it.

Axe placed a gentle kiss on my cheek, pulling away with a smirk. "Birthday shots?" he asked.

"Absolutely."

Axe led me by the hand over to the kitchen, where all the liquor was lined up on the counter. Three guys were standing in the kitchen, beers in hand.

"Tate, you remember Joey, Owen, and Dylan, right? From my frat?"

"Yeah, of course," I smiled at them. Axe poured himself a shot. "Pour me one too, baby," I said.

"Just one?" he asked.

I had only had two shots and a few sips of Axel's beer within the past hour and a half of the party, trying to steady myself so that I could consciously interact with everyone who had come to celebrate my birthday with me. And already, I could feel those two shots were draining out of my system.

"Um," I thought, "gimme three."

"Three?" Dylan asked. "At once? For you?"

"Hell yeah," I said, leaning against the counter.

Axe poured them with a smile on his face, then pushed them in front of me.

"No chaser, either?" Owen asked.

I shook my head. "Absolutely not. I'm not a 'lil bitch."

Axe chuckled. "Nah," he said, wrapping his arm around my waist, "my girl's a badass."

"Looks like one too," Joey said, eyeing me up and down.

Axe's body stiffened, his eyes targeting Joey. "You checkin' out my girl, Joey?"

Joey shifted nervously as Axel's eyes peered into him. "Uh, no," Joey shook his head, but Axe didn't seem satisfied with his answer.

"You sure?" Axe asked, glaring at Joey.

The last thing I wanted was for Axel to get into a bad mood. "Well I'm about to take these shots," I interrupted, as my attempt to ease the tension between the frat brothers.

Axel's attention turned to me. He knew I was trying to change the topic, but he still let it happen anyways. Axe didn't want to ruin my birthday, so he let it go.

I grinned at him, bobbing up and down on my tippy toes as I pounded down all three shots. A couple people who saw started clapping, impressed by my performance.

Axe leaned down and kissed my cheek, happy to show me off. The feeling was refreshing, because Connor never would. He was constantly reluctant to go in public with me, always afraid that someone would say something to Nicole. He refused to post photos with me, in an attempt to keep the existence of our complicated relationship a secret. He was never proud to be with me, or to even have me in his life at all. I was a burden to Connor, but Axel made me feel like a blessing to him. Axe had a way of making me feel whole. And I fucking loved him for it.

He pulled me into the living room, finding a small open space for us to dance in.

"Are you sure the music's not too loud?" I asked.

He chuckled. "Nah," he shook his head, "the cops aren't gonna do anything."

I didn't know why he was so sure, but I took his word for it. I put my backside towards him, beginning to sway my hips side to side as his hands rested upon them. I reached up and behind me, wrapping my hands around the back of his neck. He leaned in, touching my ear with his mouth.

"I can't wait to take this dress off of you later," he whispered. An impish grin came across my lips. If the apartment wasn't packed with people right now, I would've dragged him into the bedroom right then and there.

I jumped to the sound of a bottle breaking in the kitchen.

"Shit," Axe said. "Don't know what that was, but I gotta go clean it up anyway. Save me a dance still?"

"Of course."

He raised his arms up and dropped them suddenly as he headed into the kitchen. "Damn you, fuckers!"

I shook my head, giggling at his adorable annoyance. I scanned the room, seeing who else was there that I hadn't talked to yet. Penelope came into view.

"Hey!" I approached her.

166

"The birthday bitch! Happy birthday, roomie!" she enveloped me in a hug.

"Thanks," I laughed, flipping my hair around. "I'm so glad you could make it."

"Of course! Wouldn't miss it, Tate. I just can't stay long. I told Lucas I'd hang out with him since he couldn't come."

"Oh, well that's okay," I said, suddenly feeling like the villain for refusing to give Lucas an invitation.

"We'll probably just hang out in our room if that's okay with you."

"Yeah, of course. I'm gonna be spending the night here anyways," I smiled kindly at her. "I'll catch up with you in a little bit," I said, noticing a sappy Claire seated on the couch. "Hey, what's up? Why are you sitting instead of dancing?" I pulled her to her feet, but the second she stood, she sat back down again. I sighed, sitting next to her. "Claire, c'mon. Talk to me. What's bothering you? Is it Jason?"

She slowly nodded. "I just... don't know what to do. He keeps trying to call me and talk to me and fix things, but at the end of the day, he's still toxic and still put his hands on you," she said, shaking her head in disgust. She turned to face me. "I wasn't lying earlier when I said that he's never hit me. He hasn't. But sometimes, he gets so mad that I'm scared he's gonna."

I gave her a hug, her head resting on my shoulder. "Everything will work itself out. And we can talk about this all day tomorrow, but for tonight, stop beating yourself up thinking about it. Just try to have fun, okay?"

"Yeah, Gianna was saying the same thing," she said, pulling away from the hug.

I brought my brows together. "Speaking of Gi," I started, looking around, "where the hell is she?"

Claire raised an eyebrow. "She's been in Ash's room for a while."

I rolled my eyes. "They couldn't have waited until everyone left?"

"Apparently not," she shrugged, still looking miserable.

"Hey," I nudged her, "you see that guy standing near the kitchen? The one with the dusty blonde hair and the beer in his hand?"

Claire nodded. "That's Owen. He's in Axel's frat. He's super cute and super sweet. You should go talk to him."

Claire tilted her head to the side. "I don't know, Tate. I mean he is really cute, but I'm not sure if that's really a good idea."

I stood up from the couch, pulling her up with me. "C'mon. I'll go with you."

"Well... okay."

I smoothed out my skirt before we strolled over to where Owen and Dylan were standing.

"Hey!" they both said, greeting us.

"Hey guys! This is my friend, Claire. Claire, this is Owen and Dylan."

Owen's eyes brightened when he shook Claire's hand, a clear sign that he was interested.

I felt a hand on my ass, happy that Axel had finally finished cleaning up the mess in the kitchen. I smiled as I turned, but my smile automatically fell when Joey's face came into view. I backed away, disgusted.

"Don't touch me," I warned.

"C'mon, Tate. Axel doesn't even have to know," he slurred. He swayed back and forth, clearly intoxicated. There was nothing less attractive than a drunk guy who couldn't handle himself.

"Absolutely not," I called out.

"Just one—"

"Joey," Axel hissed from behind him.

Joey turned, his eyes widening at the sight.

"Axel, I, uh—"

"Just," Axe paused, closing his eyes for a second, his jaw working under his skin, "get the fuck out."

Joey glanced at Owen and Dylan for a second, then to me, then back to Axel. "Yeah, okay," he said, slowly stumbling his way over to the door.

"Sorry about him, Tate," Owen said.

"He's pretty drunk. We should probably go make sure he gets home alright," Dylan said.

"Yeah," Owen agreed, taking a deep breath. "Well, happy birthday, Tate! Thanks for having us Axel," he nodded once in Axe's direction. "And it was nice to meet you, Claire," he winked at her.

She blushed as they walked away. I smirked at her, hopeful that maybe she would finally talk to someone other than dirtbag Jason.

Claire nodded once towards the door, gesturing for me to look. Axel walked out, slamming it behind him. I turned back towards Claire, unsure of why. I could see by the look in her eyes that she knew I was confused.

"Go," she said nodding.

"Okay... be right back."

I made my way out to the parking lot, immediately shivering when the cold, February air hit my bare skin. Axe lit a cigarette, bringing it up to his mouth to take a drag.

He only smoked when he was pissed.

Axe sensed my presence, turning to meet my gaze. "What are you doing out here, Tate? It's freezing. You should go back inside."

I shook my head as I crossed my arms, trying to conserve any warmth that I could. "I'm not going in without you."

He took another drag. He could tell I was shivering, freezing. "Tate, please go back inside. You're in a dress. It's too cold out here."

"No. I'm not going in without you," I repeated.

Axe's eyes glimpsed at the cigarette, then at me. He sighed, dropping the newly lit cigarette to the ground and stepping on it. He wrapped an arm around me, hugging me to his side. "So stubborn," he smirked, shaking his head as he led me back inside, trying to warm me up.

"Why are you pissed?" I quietly asked as we made our way up the stairs.

"Well," he said, rubbing my arm, "for starters, my own frat brother just tried to get with you. And I might be having a kid that isn't yours, so that doesn't really help." We stopped outside the apartment door.

"Fuck Joey," I said, shaking my head. "He's an irrelevant, drunken ass." Axe laughed, looking at the ground. He bit his lip as he looked back up at me. "But when it comes to Brooke... I'm scared," I admitted.

He cupped my face in his hands. "I'm scared too. I'm so fucking afraid that that kid's gonna be mine. But the one thing I'm more afraid of is losing you."

I eyed him, searching his eyes for any hint of a lie, but I couldn't find one. Before meeting Axel, I was used to being lied to. The only times Connor ever said anything like that to me were the times that I was about to walk out the door. Any time I ever tried to leave, he either talked me out of it or made me feel guilty enough to come back. He always knew exactly what I wanted to hear. Always knew exactly how to con me into doing what he wanted.

"You won't," I said, unsure of myself.

"Let's not even talk about this for the rest of the night, okay? It's your birthday. I don't want it to be ruined."

I gave a small nod, and we went back inside, determined to finish the night off in a good mood.

Chapter Seventeen
The Little Things

    Axel had driven me back to my apartment early the next afternoon, and I spent the rest of the day doing basically nothing, too tired and hungover to do anything.

    "You wanna go get dessert?" Penelope asked from her desk. I rolled over in my bed, taking a deep breath as I checked the time on my phone. It was almost seven at night.

    "I still haven't even eaten dinner," I chuckled to myself.

    "Well we can go to the dining center and you can get dinner and I'll get dessert?"

    "Yeah, sure."

    Penelope looked up at me and smiled. "Okay, cool. I'm gonna go see if Gianna and Claire wanna come."

    "Okay," I sat up, "I'll get dressed while you do."

    I climbed out of bed, slipping on leggings and a sweater, then throwing my hair up into a messy bun. I scanned my desk for my keys, but didn't see them. I moved things around, slightly panicking when they still didn't show.

    "Ready?" Penelope asked, peeking her head through the door.

    "Yeah, um, have you seen my keys though? My Western lanyard that has my school ID, room key, and Axel's apartment key on it?"

    "Nope."

"Damnit," I said, rubbing my forehead. "Maybe I left them at Axel's. If they're not there, then I must've lost them. And if so, then I'm fucked."

"I'm sure they'll turn up. Maybe try going over to the apartment after dinner to look?"

"I should, but I still feel like shit. I don't wanna drive." I gave her a worried glance.

"Gianna has a lot of homework to do, so she's not coming. But you could probably ask Claire to run you over to the apartment when we're done eating so that you could look."

I nodded. "Yeah, I'm gonna have to," I reluctantly said, already dreading the fact that I would be a passenger rather than the driver. I grabbed my jacket, following Penelope out the door.

I forced some food down, still a little groggy from my tiny hangover. Claire drove me over to the apartment, but we couldn't find my keys there either. I would have to pay for a new ID, room key, and get a new key to the apartment. Thank God Axel wasn't mad about it, though. He had offered to pay for all three, but I refused. He spoiled me enough already.

On the bright side, I was excited about all the nice things everyone had gotten me for my birthday. I didn't expect anyone to bring me any gifts, considering the fact that we were all broke ass college kids, so it was kind that some people got me anything.

I slept the rest of my hangover off, forcing myself to get up in the morning for class. But as the next few days went on, focusing became harder and harder. Each day that passed felt like ten. My anxiety was rising, counting down the days until we would get the results for Brooke's prenatal paternity test.

Axel had been trying to keep his cool about the situation, but I could tell he was secretly panicking just as much as I was. I loved him, but I didn't know if I would be able to handle it if that baby was his. The idea of sticking around to watch Axel raise a child that wasn't mine was unsettling. And every day, every time I would be around that baby, it would just be a reminder of the morning I walked in to hear the moans of Brooke, the image of Axel's hands on her. It sounded like a nightmare.

A few days after I got a new set of keys, I tucked my red long sleeve into my jean skirt and slipped on my black heeled booties. I put some hairspray into my curls and double checked my outfit in the mirror. Lastly, I threw on my necklace and some lip gloss before there was a knock on the door.

"Happy Valentine's Day, beautiful," Axel said, pulling a large bouquet of roses out from behind his back.

I smiled wide. "Thank you," I said, taking the bouquet from him and setting it on my desk. "I'll put them in a vase when we get back."

"Where's Penelope?" he asked, walking inside.

"Out to dinner with Lucas, I think."

"Weird couple."

"I know," I laughed, throwing my purse over my shoulder. Axe wrapped his arms around me from behind as I stood in front of the mirror. I gladly accepting a kiss on the cheek from him. "Where are we going to eat?"

"You'll see," he smirked.

"Are you taking me to the same restaurant we went to on our first date?"

He lightly chuckled. "Absolutely not," he said, knowing that I was referring to the restaurant that Brooke worked at. A slow smile crept onto his face.

"What?" I asked.

"You just called that night a date."

I rolled my eyes. "I take it back."

He frowned. "You know it was a date."

"Nope," I said, giving him a quick kiss.

He inspected my lips as I pulled away. "No red lips? Shocker."

"Decided to mix it up. I like to keep you guessing."

His dimples lightly appeared. "Ready to go?"

I nodded, following Axe out the door. The second we got into the car, Axel held up a bandana.

"What's that for?" I asked, pulling my brows together.

"I'm gonna blindfold you."

My eyes widened. "Hell no!"

"Uh, hell yeah!" he said with a smile. I pushed my mouth to the side, unsatisfied. He tilted his head and sighed. "C'mon, just let me do it. You can't know where we're going. It's a surprise."

"Do I have to?"

"Yes," he said. I scrunched my face together. "This isn't a horror movie, Tate," he chuckled. "I'm not gonna blindfold you and take you somewhere to kill you. I'm your boyfriend, not Leatherface," he laughed.

"Tell that to Sidney from *Scream*," I said.

His green eyes peered into me as he grinned, dimples never disappearing. "C'mon."

I dropped my head back as I rolled my eyes. "Okay, fine."

I moved my hair over to one side, allowing Axel to securely blindfold me. "That took way longer than it should have. So goddamn stubborn," he laughed.

We drove for less than ten minutes, causing me to become confused by which restaurant we would be attending. Most of the nice ones were at least fifteen minutes away.

The car came to a sudden stop.

"I'll help you get out of the car," Axel said. I couldn't see anything, but I could hear him open his door.

"Why can't I take it off yet?"

"Because you can't see it yet."

He opened my door and helped me out of the Mustang. Axe led me by the hand as we walked, then all of the sudden, he picked me up.

"Axe, what the—"

"It's okay, don't worry. I've got you."

"Are we going up stairs right now?" I asked.

"Maybe, maybe not."

The suspense was killing me. I wanted to know why it was such a big surprise that I had to be blindfolded.

Axe set me down on my feet. A doorknob jiggled and he led me by the hand again a few more steps.

"Okay, stop right here," he said. I stood, still having absolutely no idea where we were. "You can take it off now."

I slowly lifted the blindfold up and over my head, immediately smiling to the sight of lit candles and roses covering the entire apartment. There were rose petals scattered across the small kitchen table, two wine glasses set upon it as well.

"Axe," I beamed, "you didn't have to do all this."

"Yes, I did."

"As if the giant bouquet you already got me wasn't enough?"

He smiled, amused by my reaction. "One bouquet was definitely not enough."

I shook my head, taking another look around. "Thank you. I love it."

He kissed my forehead, closing his eyes for a second. "Anything for you."

I felt like the luckiest girl in the entire world, wondering what I did to deserve all of this. But maybe the world was just building me up strong before it was planning on tearing me apart. Fear of losing Axel was beginning to set in, but I pushed it away. I wasn't going to let it ruin our night.

"So, what are we having for dinner?" I asked, taking a seat.

"Well," he said, standing against the counter, "I figured since this was our first Valentine's Day together, it should be sentimental. So, the handsome chef is preparing chocolate chip pancakes, bacon, and hash-browns." He raised an eyebrow, smirking.

I covered my mouth as I giggled, unable to keep it in. "You're such a dork."

"Well I'm *your* dork, so."

I rolled my eyes, grinning. I couldn't stop looking around at everything. The dim lighting was perfect, the candles illuminating the romantic setting. I had no idea where he had gotten so many roses either, but knowing that Axe spent all this time and money preparing for it made me feel special.

"Is Ash here?" I asked, knowing that he would be with Gianna at some point tonight, but I didn't know when.

"Hell nah," Axe said pouring the pancake batter onto the pan. "I kicked him out for the whole night," he winked.

Butterflies.

"So, you're saying you lit all these candles and then left them unattended when you went to go pick me up?"

Axe scratched his head. "Technically, yeah."

I widened my eyes. "Axe! What if a fire started?"

"That was a risk I was willing to take," he blabbered dramatically.

Once all the food was ready, we sat at the table and ate. I expected wine to be gross with pancakes, bacon, and hash-browns, but surprisingly, it wasn't that bad.

I sat across from Axel, unable to look away from him. I studied his prominent jawline, the way it was sharp enough to cut a diamond. His brown curls were settled perfectly on top of his head, making me want to run my fingers through them. His flawless smile shone brightly even in the dim lighting, dimples sinking into his cheeks. There was no question as to why so many girls had slept with him, thrown themselves at him. Axel was truly the most handsome man on campus, maybe even in the entire world. And studying him now just made me doubt myself more. Why would Axel settle for me?

"Axe?" I asked, while he took another bite.

"Yeah?" he said after swallowing.

"Why me?"

He furrowed his brows. "What do you mean?"

"Like," I paused, "out of all the girls across campus, you could've had any single one. So, why me?"

He was taken off guard by my question, looking confused. "It wasn't anything specific about you. It was everything about you. It was just you," he shrugged.

I still didn't know exactly what he meant. I had spent the past four years believing that I wasn't good enough for anyone.

Connor's constant remarks made me doubt myself and compare myself to everyone around me. He took away my self-worth, my confidence, my sanity, and my identity. And slowly, Axe had helped me start to build it all back.

Axe focused on me. "The real question is, why me?"

"Now what do you mean?" I joked, curious as to how he could be confused by such a silly question.

"Tate," he said, dropping his chin, "I'm not good enough for you. That's not a secret."

"Are you kidding? You spoil the living hell out of me and treat me like some European princess," I gestured around to the room.

"That's because you are one," he laughed. I tilted my head at him, eyeing him with a smirk still resting on my face. Axe stood, helped me out of my seat, and led me over to the living room. He picked up his guitar and sat next to me on the couch, clearing his throat. "I know he hurt you really badly, but I'm not going to do that to you. I'm in love with you and I'm going to be, no matter what."

Before I could respond, he was already strumming his guitar. I instantly recognized the melody as "Little Things" by One Direction.

I wanted to stay in the moment forever, to cherish it, live it. And instead of feeling completely happy, I started to feel almost helpless. Because things like this didn't last long for me. People that I loved always left me. I didn't want to set myself into a panic, but I couldn't help it. Right now, sitting with Axel was amazing, a fantasy come to life, but it made me think about the ending to come. The terrible reality that I didn't have good enough luck to make this last forever.

Axel's mouth on mine was what snapped me out of my thoughts. He kissed me deeply, working his lips against mine. His hands scooped me up and carried me into his room, lowering me down onto the bed. Axe's hands slid up my jean skirt, softly gripping my thigh before resting on my thong. Within a few minutes, all our clothes were off. I sighed as our lips parted, my body longing for his as I ran my hand over his dragonfly tattoo.

"I fucking love you. And I'm never going to leave you. I hope you know that," he said.

"I love you," I responded, crashing my lips back onto his, but not being able to fully believe all of his words.

I typed away at my computer while sitting at my desk, listening to Claire go on and on about both Owen and Jason. After my birthday party, she had asked for Owen's number, so I gladly got it from Axel and sent it her way. She deserved to have someone great, someone who didn't have any violent tendencies or any personality traits of Connor's.

"So, you really think I should hang out with Owen?" she asked, pacing the floor.

"Yeah, definitely," I said, keeping my answers short while I finished my work. I did want to help Claire figure her shit out, but I needed to do all my homework first. And on top of that, I still had shit of my own to figure out too.

"I think I'm gonna," she said, putting her hands on her hips.

"I support it."

"You know what? I think I'm gonna go call him right now and tell him that I would love to hang out with him this weekend."

"Do it," I nodded, still staring at my computer.

My phone buzzed against the desktop. My face brightened seeing Axel's name on the screen.

"Hi," I answered with a smile.

"Hey," Axel said, sounding flustered. "They're here."

My smile dropped. "What is?"

"The results."

I immediately stopped what I was doing and looked at Claire, my heart skipping a beat. By the tone of Axel's voice, it didn't sound like good news.

"Well... what are they?" I swallowed the lump in my throat, my hands shaking while I held the phone. Claire watched me, holding her hands up to her mouth. I could tell she was hoping for the best.

"I haven't opened it yet. I want you here with me when I do."

"Okay... okay, yeah, I'll come now," I said, hanging up the phone.

Claire shook her head. "Good luck," she said, giving me a hug. "Jesus, Tate, you're shaking like crazy."

I looked at her with terror in my eyes, absolutely panicking to find out and face the truth. "I'm freaking the fuck out," I admitted.

"Just breathe," she said. "And call me directly after you find out."

I bit the inside of my lip and nodded. I grabbed my new set of keys and threw on my jacket, then set off for the apartment. The six-minute car ride felt like hours. All the different possibilities ran through my head. What would happen if this baby was his? Would we be able to stick together through it or would we break under the pressure? And what would happen if this baby wasn't his? Would things go back to how they were before, or would we fall apart from the memory of the stress it caused?

I rushed up the stairs and used my key to unlock the door with a shaking hand. Axe stood in the kitchen, staring at the sealed envelope that would determine our fate. His eyes met mine, fear and powerlessness spread across his face.

"Open it," I said weakly.

He took a deep breath as he tore open the envelope, slipping out the piece of paper that was inside. His hands shook as he unfolded the paper and brought it up to his face, eyes skimming the words. My heart was about to physically burst out of my chest, anxiety racing through my bloodstream. I needed him to read it faster. I couldn't wait any longer.

A subtle grin began to appear on his face, green eyes darting over to me. "It's negative."

"It's negative?"

He nodded, a full, beautiful, Axel Burne smile plastered across his face. "It's negative," he said again.

I took a few small steps towards him before full on jumping into his arms, happiness taking the place of fear in my veins. We felt victorious, as if the entire world had just been handed to us on a silver platter.

"Thank God!" I expressed as he set me down on my feet.

"I know. You had no idea how terrified I was that that was going to be positive and that you would leave me for it."

"Well I'm not going anywhere," I said, touching his cheek, trying to assure not only him, but myself as well.

"I don't think I've ever been so relieved in my life."

"Me neither."

A lot had been going through my mind lately and although I was relieved that the results turned out to be in our favor, I was still scared. I was the type of person that overthought every aspect of everything in her life, mostly relationships. I was hypervigilant about the world, hypervigilant about trusting people. My symptoms had been manageable and had even slowed down for the past few months since Axe and I had been together, but I could feel them starting to creep back. I felt helpless, as if no matter what I did, the ghost of Connor and the memory of what he put me through would follow me everywhere.

Axel had been good to me, so good to me that it constantly made me question why. I didn't want to believe that it was difficult for people to love me, but my past had put me in a position where I felt like no one could. Axe was truly amazing, and I wanted more than anything to continue to be with him and to grow with him. He might even be the one for me, but I've thought that about someone else before, and look how that ended.

I swore to myself right then and there that if Axe ever did *anything* that merely resembled Connor, I would leave.

"I need a favor!" Claire voiced with her finger raised, barging through the door.

"What kind of favor?" I asked, swinging around in my desk chair.

"Well," she started, mischievously grinning.

"If you're gonna ask me to loan you money or help you hide a body, then no."

She rolled her eyes. "No, nothing like that! Owen asked me if I wanted to get dinner with him and I said sure."

"Oh, that's great!"

"Yeah, but I'm just really nervous about it. I've never hung out with him before and have only ever talked to him in person at your party, so I was wondering if you and Axel wanted to tag along and do a double date?" she fluttered her eyelashes, doing the best puppy dog eyes she could manage.

"A double date?"

"Yeah," she nodded with a hopeful smile. "Pretty please? I'll owe you big time."

I didn't know why she was trying so hard to convince me. It wasn't a crazy favor that she was asking. I liked Owen, so I didn't mind. On the other hand, if it was Jason that she was asking me to go on a double date with, I would absolutely, positively, without a doubt say no, no matter how much she begged.

"Yeah, sure," I shrugged, retreating back to my laptop.

"Okay, cool, so be ready in an hour."

I widened my eyes as I swung back around to face her. "You meant *tonight*?"

"Yeah," she said in a small voice, twisting her hair.

It was a Thursday night, and although most people would be going out tonight, I had been planning on staying home to finish my economics essay. I was in an oversized t-shirt and running shorts with no makeup on and my hair in a messy bun, but not the cute kind. There was no way I would be finished with my essay and entirely ready in an hour.

I slowly shook my head. "Claire, I was going to finish my essay tonight and there's no way I could throw makeup on and make my hair look half decent in an hour."

"Please?" she begged.

"We can just do another night."

"But what if he never asks again?" she threw her head back.

"He will. Why wouldn't he?"

She intertwined her hands together and brought them up to her chest. "Please?" her bottom lip quivered.

My face remained motionless. "Stop faking it."

She relaxed and rolled her eyes again. "Oh, c'mon, Tate! Your essay isn't even due until Monday!"

"Which is why I want to finish it tonight, so that I can party all weekend."

She crossed her arms, tilting her head. "Please?" she asked again. This time I could hear the desperation in her tone.

I rubbed my neck, sighing. "Fine. I'll call Axe," I grumbled.

Her face lit up. "Ahh! Thank you! Thank you! I love you!" she yelled.

"You better," I said, picking up my phone.

An hour later, I sat next to Claire in the booth, so that we could sit across from the boys. We had ordered our food quickly and even though we had been here for twenty minutes already, I could still feel Claire's nerves radiating off her body.

"So, what are you guys doing this weekend?" I asked, trying to jumpstart a conversation for Claire to join in on.

"I think ATA is throwing, actually," Owen answered. "Are you planning on going?" he turned to Axel.

Axe peeked over at me, waiting for me to respond. I shrugged.

"We'll probably end up going there, yeah," Axe said.

"Okay, cool. Claire, would you want to go with me?"

She beamed. "Yeah, I'd love to."

I glimpsed at Axe and he winked at me, the both of us in agreement that things seemed to be going fairly smooth. I loved when we sent mind messages to each other. We always knew what the other was thinking.

Our waiter hadn't come back since we'd ordered, and Axe was becoming agitated by his empty drink.

"Our waiter sucks," he muttered.

I raised an eyebrow. "I'm just glad it's a guy this time, so at least we know this one won't leave a number for you," I joked while biting my lip, only half-kidding.

"Wouldn't be surprised if he did anyways," Claire added in.

Axe chuckled, amused. "Hey, c'mon. We'll be able to tell our future kids that story and I'm sure they'll laugh about it."

"Future kids?"

"Mhmm," he nodded, moving his straw around in the empty glass.

Owen aimlessly looked around, obviously having no idea what we were referring to, which was fine. I didn't need any extra people knowing that my boyfriend almost knocked up our ex-waitress.

Claire's eyebrows shot up. "Damn, Axel. You're really thinkin' long-term."

"Of course, I am. I love her. I'm gonna marry her one day," he said, gesturing to me.

Claire smiled, but I recoiled. I could hardly handle my thoughts as it was, and Axel talking way into the future wasn't exactly helping. Connor and I used to have dozens of conversations about our wedding and future kids and where we wanted to live when we got older. And obviously, none of those things happened. Don't get me wrong, what Axel said was sweet. Everything he ever said and did was sweet, but I didn't like talking about the far future. It only made me hopeful for things that couldn't be guaranteed.

"Anyways," I said, trying to shake off the subject, "Owen, what's your major again?"

"Well right now, I'm undecided. And I know I have to declare a major by the end of the semester, so I'm leaning towards criminal justice. I've thought about leaving Western and enlisting, but I'm not sure yet."

"Enlisting? Like, into the military?" Claire asked. Owen nodded.

I winced, wishing that I had never asked in the first place. Connor's face flashed through my mind, standing in uniform next to Nicole dressed in white on their wedding day. The thought made my hands shake.

Axel took notice, reaching for them from across the table. When I looked up, his green eyes were already on my brown ones, searching for a sign that I was okay. I gave a tiny smile, ensuring him that I was fine. Owen and Claire hadn't noticed, continuing the conversation as if Axel and I hadn't exited out of it.

As we ate, I couldn't wait to go back to my room and climb into bed. Triggers to my C-PTSD may have become slightly easier to handle, but they were still exhausting, and more so than not, they put me in a bad mood for the rest of my day or night. This time was no exception.

Axel and Owen split the check, covering both mine and Claire's meals. They were true gentlemen and it showed. Claire was super giddy when we got back, inviting herself into my room to discuss how the night went.

Penelope laid on the futon, watching a movie. I hadn't seen much of her the past few days. She had been spending most of her time with Lucas, hanging out with him all day and only coming back to the room to sleep. But as long as Lucas stayed away from me, I didn't mind.

"Where were you guys?" Penelope asked from the futon.

"We just went out to dinner," I explained, throwing my keys on my desk.

"Oh, nice," she sat up and stretched, then walked over to her closet. "I'm gonna jump in the shower."

"Okay. Have fun," I joked.

She grabbed all her shower necessities and went, leaving Claire and I alone to speak freely about the night. It's not that we wanted to hide anything from Penelope, but we were afraid that if she knew Claire was talking to Owen, she might let it slip out in front of Lucas. And we all knew he would go straight to Jason with the information. Jason was still calling Claire every day, trying to get her attention, but she wasn't buying into it. I was proud of her for it.

"So, what do you think of Owen?" Claire smiled broadly.

"He seems like a nice guy," I nodded.

"Yeah, he really does," she glanced off, daydreaming about him. "I'm so excited that he asked me to go to ATA with him this weekend."

"Good! You should be excited! It'll be fun."

She picked the nail polish off her fingernails, still smiling. "You'll have to help me figure out what to wear."

I snickered. "Okay, I will."

"And also," she said, promptly throwing her head back up, "going out with you guys tonight just really had me thinking about Axel."

"What do you mean?"

"Like, I originally thought he was such a dick. And honestly, when you two first got together, I had major doubts. Like who wouldn't though, you know? He was such a douchebag before and now, he's so different."

"Yeah," I furrowed my brows, thinking carefully about what she was saying.

"He's done a complete turn-around after meeting you. Which is so crazy because people don't change, yet here he is, changing all his bad habits because of you," she shook her head, grinning while she spoke. "And don't get me wrong, it's, like, amazing that he has. I just feel like it's so rare that people genuinely change themselves for someone else's sake. Most people are too self-absorbed to do that," she finished, picking at her nail polish again.

My eyes wandered, but so did my thoughts. Claire was right. Axel had changed his entire lifestyle for me, but could anyone truly change that much? Like she had said, people don't change. It takes some people months or sometimes even years to break bad habits, so how did Axe manage to break them so thoroughly, so quickly? Was it possible that I was missing something? That I didn't know something? Because people don't just magically change. And just because someone wants to change, doesn't mean they will. They need to have motivation and support behind them in order to break their bad habits. Axel had repeatedly said that I was the reason he changed, that I was the motivation. But how could I motivate someone to change their entire way of life, just from my presence? Axe treated me like a princess, better than he's ever treated any other girl before, but was it possible that his habits haven't fully been broken?

Chapter Eighteen
The Calm Before The Storm

Claire ripped through her entire closet, leaving a tornado scattered across the room. Maybe's on one side and no's on the other. Gianna was already entirely ready and all I had left to do was my hair.

"Claire, just pick something," Gianna said, her impatience stirring.

Claire shot her a look. "I'm trying to look like a model, okay?"

"You'll look good in whatever you wear. Don't overthink it," I said.

Her eyes softened towards me while she gave a small smile. "You really think so?"

"Absolutely."

"Awe, thanks Tate! Now help me pick something out from my maybe's pile."

I sighed and strode over to the pile, grabbing the first thing I saw. It was a plum crop top that had a cinched drawstring running down the center.

"Wear this with your ripped jeans," I suggested.

Claire studied the shirt as I held it up. She slowly started to nod. "I like it!"

Thank God. I thought we were going to be here all damn night. Gianna let out a deep breath in relief. She had clearly been thinking the same thing.

"Well hurry your ass up and put it on. The guys are gonna be here in like thirty minutes to pre-game," Gianna declared.

Claire got dressed while I did my hair, throwing it up into a tight, high pony before fixing my necklace. My hot pink bodysuit tucked perfectly into my jeans, hugging my skin tightly. I carefully applied lip gloss and smacked my lips together.

A half hour later, there was a knock on the door. Claire's eyes grew wide as she glanced around at the destroyed room, clothes scattered everywhere.

"Shit!" she uttered under her breath.

"Just throw them all back in your closet," Gianna whispered to Claire. "Uh, give us one second!" she yelled.

The three of us grabbed all her clothes and launched them into the closet as quickly as possible. By the time we finished, I was a little out of breath. We let the guys in, and Owen began to pull loads of alcohol out of the backpack that he brought.

"Anyone want shots?" he asked, holding up a bottle of Jack Daniel's whiskey.

"I'll have some," I said.

"Same," Ash and Axe both said in unison.

"I'll have some if I have a chaser with it," Claire stated.

"Same. Whiskey tastes like shit," Gi said.

We all gathered around as Owen poured the shots into double shot glasses, carrying twice the amount of whiskey that a regular shot glass filled. Six shot glasses raised in the air, clinking together. I threw my head back as it went down, the taste of stale whiskey running down my throat.

It was nice that Claire had finally found someone who was okay being around Axe and Ash. I felt like I had gotten closer to Gi this year since we had spent so much time together, which was nice, but it also made me feel like Claire and I had somewhat grown apart. Gi and Claire were cousins, so they didn't have to worry about growing apart. They would be stuck together for the rest of their lives, but I was the one that needed to worry. I didn't want to lose either of them, ever.

Within fifteen minutes, Claire and I had each already downed half of our fruity seltzer, and the boys were preparing to take another shot. I joined in, setting my shot glass down on the desk for Owen to fill.

"I'll have one too!" Claire excitedly said.

186

Gi pulled her mouth to the side. "Are you sure, Claire? They're doubles. So, you've technically already had two and some of your other drink. Maybe you should just wait a little bit?"

"I can handle it," Claire said, setting her glass in front of Owen.

Gi and I traded glances. "Claire," Gi said again, firmer this time, "not every girl is like Tatum. Especially you. You're a lightweight."

"I'm fine," Claire hissed.

Gi sighed. "Whatever. Do what you want, I guess."

I slowed myself down after the second double shot and forced myself to eat a snack before we headed to ATA. I knew that Axel would take care of me no matter how drunk I was, but I still didn't want to be too shit faced.

Claire, on the other hand, didn't bother pacing herself. It seemed as if she was trying to impress Owen with how much she was drinking, but knowing her, it wasn't going to end well. There were dozens of nights where Claire was black out drunk, waking up the next morning not remembering a single thing and having the worst hangover, and it seemed like tonight would be one of those nights.

My genes allowed me to drink a lot for my body size, but I never wanted to take advantage of it. Alcohol was a dangerous game, especially if you had Everley DNA, and I wasn't trying to play.

Soon enough, we were at ATA, surrounded by strobe lights, loud music, and sweaty bodies. I hadn't really bothered going to any of the other frats since Axel and I got together, so a majority of his frat brothers knew who I was by now. It was nice to be able to socialize with them, but ever since Joey tried to make a move, Axel had been on high alert, even at his own frat parties. But other than Joey, none of them had tried anything. They all knew I was Axel's and more importantly, they all knew what would happen if Axel caught them eyeing me inappropriately.

Claire stumbled around and surprisingly enough, Owen didn't seem fazed by it. Most guys would get annoyed if the girl they brought to their frat party was all over the place. Gi and I shoved water down her throat, trying to help her sober up. And although Owen wasn't too bothered by Claire's extreme drunkenness, I didn't want him to get the wrong impression and think she was like this all the time.

I grabbed Owen's arm to get his attention. I leaned in just enough so that he could hear me, making sure to keep enough distance so that I wasn't too close. "Do you think you could find like a granola bar or something small for Claire? Just to get something in her stomach?"

He thought for a second and then nodded. "Yeah, I can go upstairs and find something. I'm sure all the guys have snacks and shit in their rooms."

"Okay, thank you!"

I left Gi and Claire for a second to go find Axe. Him and Ash had been conversing with some of the other guys while Gianna and I dealt with Claire. We had only been apart for twenty minutes, but I missed him. My sober mind raced through fear of abandonment and doubts about Axe, but my drunk mind always buzzed with all the reasons why I loved him. And right now, I was drunk.

I saw him standing near the corner, bent over while he laughed. It was the same corner where he used to stand while he watched me, before we even knew each other. The sight made me smile. His eyes caught mine and before I knew it, his strong arms were around me, hugging the life out of me. He was drunk too, but he had made sure not to get too plastered, so that he was still coherent enough to take care of me if I needed him to.

God, I loved him.

"So, how's it going between Claire and Owen?" Dylan yelled to me over the music, beer in hand.

"It's going pretty good, I think! I just sent him to go get her a snack to help sober her up!" I chuckled. Dylan laughed and nodded, taking a swig of his beer.

Axe lightly held my hand and gave a slight bow. "May I have a dance?"

"Absolutely," I smirked.

He pulled me in and kissed my forehead, swaying us side to side before spinning me around.

My smile faded as Gianna frantically approached us. I assumed she would walk straight into Ash's arms like she normally would, but this time, she didn't. She just stood in front of all of us, running her fingers through her hair.

"Have you guys seen Claire?" she shouted, looking around.

My body stiffened against Axe's. "I left her with you."

"I know, but I looked away for literally one second and when I turned back around, her and Owen were both gone."

I relaxed into Axe's arm that rested around my waist. "Oh, she probably just went with Owen upstairs to get her a snack. I asked him to get her something quick to eat to help her sober up a bit."

Gianna eased up, relieved that there was a perfectly good explanation for why Claire was gone.

"She's fine with Owen, right?" I asked Axe.

"Yeah," he nodded. "I don't think he'd try to pull anything. And if he did, then he's gonna have a problem with me."

I felt much better knowing that Axe wasn't worried about Claire being with Owen. It wouldn't take long for them to get back, and we had full faith in Owen that he wasn't the type of guy to take advantage of a drunk girl.

The boys watched and laughed as Gianna and I danced around in the corner, bouncing up and down to the music. I let go of all the stress I had been feeling, focusing solely on the present moment. It felt relieving.

But the stress returned when Owen came up to us, without Claire by his side.

"Where's Claire? I have granola bars for her," he said, holding two up. Gi and I quickly glanced at each other, both wondering the same thing as panic started to take form.

"We thought she was with you," I said, concern running through my voice.

"No, I left her by Gianna to go run upstairs."

Owen and I both looked at Gi, who shook her head, unsure of what to say. "No, when I turned around, she was gone. I just assumed she was with you."

Owen looked around, just as worried as us. Axe gripped my hand, trying to motion to me to stay calm. I gazed at him, and he softly touched my chin with his thumb and forefinger. "We'll find her. Don't worry," Axe said. He turned to Dylan and said something to him. Whatever it was, it caused Dylan to nod and start looking around the basement. "We'll all split up and look for her," Axe said to the remaining four of us. "Ash and Gianna, you guys look around the basement. Owen, you go upstairs and check all the rooms. Tate and I will go look outside."

Everyone nodded in agreement and set off for their assigned destination. It was the end of February, so it was still cold out, but my drunken and worried body didn't care. All I cared about was finding

189

Claire. There were too many bad things that could've happened to her and even though I hated thinking about the possibilities, they all ran through my head anyways.

She could've been taken upstairs by some guy and taken advantage of. She could've wandered around Fratville and gotten lost or taken or hit by a goddamn car. She could've passed out somewhere, drunk and alone.

Axel and I started in the backyard of the frat house, checking everywhere and then moving to the front of the house. It was dark and Claire was wearing a dark outfit, which didn't help. I checked my phone every few minutes, hoping to see a text from Gianna saying that they found Claire, but that text didn't come.

I covered my face with my hands. "Axe! Why can't we find her?" I cried out, desperately.

"Baby, we'll find her, okay? She couldn't have gotten far."

"What if someone took her?" I held a hand to my chest, trying to catch my breath.

He placed his arms around me, and I melted against them. "We'll keep looking until we find her, okay? We won't stop looking until we do."

"Maybe we should check around Fratville."

"Okay," he said. I could feel his warmth pressing against me, and up until that moment, I hadn't realized how cold I actually was. "I'm gonna go run inside really quick and get a jacket for you. You're freezing. Do you wanna come with me?"

"No," I shook my head, "I'm gonna keep looking out here while you're inside."

Axe nodded. "Don't leave the property, okay? You never know what creeps are wandering around. I'll be back in two minutes tops." He kissed my forehead and jogged back inside.

I took a deep breath and began to look around again, checking behind and even under cars. I walked all the way to the front of the driveway of the house, checking every inch of the property. A small figure sat on the curb, swaying side to side. I squinted my eyes, trying to identify whoever it was.

"Claire? What the hell! What are you doing all the way down here?" I ran over to her, crouching down where she sat.

Her drunken eyes scanned my face. She looked like she had been crying. "I—uh, I—I, um," she stuttered.

"C'mon, let's go back inside," I said, gripping her arm to help her stand up.

"No!" she yelled, pulling her arm back. "I'm—I'm waiting."

"Waiting? For what?"

A car pulled up to the curb and the door flew open.

"Claire, get in the car," Jason ordered.

My breath caught. I could've sworn he just said Nicole. The image of that night ran through my mind, making me uneasy.

Claire struggled to stand up, but once she did, she slowly took a step, intending for it to be towards the car, but instead, it was to the side.

I couldn't help her, though. My mind was too occupied by the nightmare running through it. Connor's face displayed in my head the moment he pulled up to the curb and told Nicole to get into the car. The moment he proceeded to pretend as if I didn't exist, as if I was nothing to him, never was, and never would be. The adrenaline rushing through my body thinking about the memory mirrored the exact adrenaline I had felt that night. My breath faltered, starting to become heavy. I zoned out of the present as everything replayed inside my head, over and over and over again.

I didn't know what happened between the time Claire took that first step until I felt Axel grab my arm. He gently pushed me back behind him, turning his attention towards Jason, who had gotten out of the car to get Claire in. But before Jason could get to her, Axe was in front of her, his jaw working under his skin.

"Don't. Take. Another fucking step," Axe breathed.

Jason's rage rested in his eyes, unaffected by Axel's warning. He stepped forward, causing Axel to take one as well, until the two were face to face, chest to chest. Axe towered over Jason, but for some reason, Jason didn't seem afraid. Or at least if he was, he wasn't showing it.

"Don't make me swing," Axe threatened, clenching his teeth.

"Do it. I'll gladly call the cops if you do and you'll get fucking arrested again."

"Axe," I said in a small voice, Jason's threat making me nervous. The last thing I needed was for Axe to get arrested. Axe didn't move, unimpressed by the threat, his vigorous gaze resting on Jason.

I slowly made my way over to Claire, who was still having trouble standing. I wrapped her arm around the back of my neck and started to move her back towards the house.

"Tate! Fucking bring her back here, now!" Jason screamed.

I glanced back at them with Claire's arm still draped around me. Axe was about to explode. I could tell he was trying his absolute hardest not to deck Jason in the face right then and there. But at this point, I almost wanted him to. If I didn't think that Jason was so serious about calling the cops on Axe, I would've encouraged Axe to fuck his face up.

"*Leave,*" Axe viciously warned.

"No. I'm not leaving without Claire."

"Yes, you fucking are."

"No, I'm fucking not!"

Axel gripped a fistful of Jason's shirt in both hands, shoving him up against the car. It wasn't until then that Jason's rage resorted to fear.

"I suggest you leave now while you're in one piece. And I'm not gonna ask you again," Axe boiled.

I needed to get Claire back inside, but I wasn't able to look away from the altercation. Jason winced and trembled, clearly afraid of what was to come next. Axe dropped him, causing Jason to scramble back into his car and drive off. Axel waited until the car was out of sight, then ran over to Claire and I.

"Let me help, baby," he said, noticing that I was struggling to hold Claire up. He took her out of my hands and picked her up effortlessly.

"I'm proud of you," I blurted out as we walked back towards the house, "for not swinging."

He took a deep breath. "I only didn't because I knew you were watching. And I didn't want you to see me like that."

"What do you mean?"

"I'm not... myself when I get into fights. I get very... aggressive and destructive and the last thing I want is for you to see me that way and then be scared of me."

"I'm never gonna be scared of you."

His soft eyes searched for mine in the dark. "God, I hope not."

I texted Gianna to come outside, informing her that we found Claire. She rushed out of the house, Ash following.

"Claire, are you okay? Jesus! Where did you guys find her?" Gianna shrieked.

"She was sitting on the curb, waiting for Jason to pick her up."

Gianna narrowed her eyes. "Jason?"

"Yep."

"I hate that fucker," she muttered with her tiny hands clenched into fists.

"Don't we all," I said.

At this point, Claire hadn't said anything since before Jason pulled up. It was evident that she needed to go to bed. Gianna rubbed her forehead, annoyed by the new information that we had just given her.

"So, you got her back before he showed up? Do you think he's still coming?" Ash asked.

"He did show up. Axe scared him off," I said.

Gi let out a heavy sigh. "I'm just gonna get her home."

"Good idea," Ash nodded. "I'll take you guys back."

The three of them left, leaving Axe and I standing alone. We weren't sure if anyone had told Owen and Dylan that Claire was found, so Axe texted them, letting them know that they could stop looking.

"You want me to take you home now?" Axe asked. I looked at the muscles bulging out of his shirt, getting the sudden urge to rip the shirt off.

"No, I wanna go home with you."

Axe smirked, knowing what I intended. He cocked his head to the side. "Let's go."

When we got back to the apartment, Ash still wasn't back yet. The second the bedroom door opened, Axel's lips planted wet kisses all over me. He slammed the door shut, then proceeded to glide his hands up and down my body, tugging at my clothes.

Soon we were both completely naked, and I climbed onto the mattress as Axel followed. He put a condom on quickly. Thank God, because we did not need another pregnancy scare, even if this one was me and not some other chick.

Within a few moments, I felt him between my thighs. I closed my eyes as he slowly slid inside of me. When my eyes peeked back open, he was already looking at me. He kissed me tenderly, grabbing at me as if he couldn't get enough of me. His hips moved rhythmically against mine and with each thrust, a bolt of electricity was sent through my body.

I could hear the apartment door open, followed by footsteps down the hall, but neither of us cared.

My hands traced along his back, fingers digging into his skin. I looked deeply into his eyes. "I love you," I said, out of breath.

My words caused him to push into me harder, groaning as he did. "God, I fucking love you," he replied, kissing my neck as another grunt escaped from his throat.

I bit my lip to try to keep myself quiet, but after another minute, I couldn't contain it. I moaned loudly, my insides tensing as I clenched my eyes shut. I pulled him closer against me, our sweat allowing us to glide effortlessly against each other.

I knew he had always wanted to be gentle with me, and now, it was clear that he had been holding back before. My uncontrollable whimpers escalated to a satisfied cry as he pressed deeper and deeper, the intensity building inside of us both.

After a while, his body became rigid, twitching as he pushed into me one last time before letting out a loud groan. He collapsed next to me, kissing me over and over again as our breathing settled down. My brown eyes studied his emerald ones, admiring them.

"You're amazing," he said.

I smiled. "After that, I think I know why so many girls went crazy over you."

"Well sucks for them because I'm crazy about you," he said, gently moving my hair out of my face.

My smile grew wider. "Sing me to sleep?"

His eyes softened and he pulled me closer, singing a sweet melody until I was sound asleep.

Chapter Nineteen
The Storm

I awoke with instant disappointment when I reached over and Axe wasn't next to me. I lifted myself up on my elbow, taking a look at the digital clock on the nightstand. It was a little past eleven. At least it was a Sunday, so I didn't have to worry about going to class. I was still naked from last night, sighing as I forced myself to get out of bed. I threw on some comfy clothes of Axel's and walked out of the room, but even more disappointment washed over me when I only found Ash, no sign of Axe.

"Where's Axe?" I yawned.

"He said he wanted to make you pancakes or some shit like that? But we ran out of the stuff he needed, so he went to the store."

"Gotcha," I said, eyeing the bagel that Ash was slabbing cream cheese onto.

"You want one?"

"Nah," I said, scrunching my nose. "I'll just wait for Axe to get back.

He nodded once, his focus shifting back to his bagel. The silence didn't last long, overtaken by an amused smirk that slowly spread across Ash's face.

"What?" I asked.

"I heard you last night."

My mind ran through the night prior. Spending the night with Axel was truly amazing, hands down the best sex I've ever had, but had we really been that loud? My cheeks flushed with embarrassment.

"You didn't hear anything," I denied his remark, refusing to meet his gaze to avoid more awkwardness.

"Oh, yes, I did," he laughed. "You guys were so loud."

"You didn't hear anything," I repeated, scratching my head.

Ash chuckled again, closing the container of cream cheese. "You know Tate, when I first made that bet with Axe—"

"What bet?"

He opened his mouth as if to say something, but then snapped it shut. His face went blank, regretting that he had said anything.

"Ash," I asked again, this time firmer, "what bet?"

He moved his hands around as he spoke nervously. "Okay, listen, don't be mad. But do you remember the night you met Axe?"

I nodded, signaling for him to continue.

"Well that night, after you rejected him when he asked you to come back to the apartment, he came back here and was pissed off and disappointed. So, I... ended up betting him that he couldn't get you to sleep with him. That's all."

My eyebrows shot up, stunned by the confession. Not only did the idea that I was originally a bet piss me off, but the fact that Axe had never mentioned this to me before just pissed me off even more.

The apartment door opened, and Axe strolled through, whistling, hands filled with bags from the grocery store. Once our eyes locked, he knew that something was wrong. His whistling ceased as he slowly set the bags down onto the ground, waiting for me to speak.

"I was a bet?"

Axe's eyes darted over to Ash, immediately heated. "You fucking told her?"

Ash winced. "It was an accident."

"How the fuck is that an accident?"

Ash pressed his lips together, stuck in regret. "Axe, listen..."

"No, you fuck!" Axe yelled, taking a few steps towards his brother, but once I started speaking, he instantly stopped in his tracks.

"So, let me get this straight. You bet Ash that you could get me to sleep with you?"

Axe cringed at my irritation. "Yeah," he admitted, unwillingly.

196

I was speechless. I felt like the entire foundation of our relationship was a lie. "And how long were you gonna wait to tell me? How long did you think you could keep this a secret? Forever?"

He rubbed the back of his neck nervously. "Kinda, yeah."

I could feel the heat bubbling up inside of me. This was not a good way to start my day. I bit my lip in anger, nodding at the realization.

"So how much?"

"What?" Axe asked, confused.

"How much did you bet on me? A hundred bucks? Fifty?"

Axe winced again, not wanting to say. I drilled my eyes into him, not backing down. "Twenty."

My eyes widened at his confession. "Twenty dollars? You bet twenty dollars that you could get me to sleep with you?"

What the hell was I? Just some prey that Axel had been waiting to capture? He probably would've done it for one dollar if it meant that he had motivation to pursue me.

"And bragging rights," he added hesitantly, raising his shoulders, hoping that adding something else would help.

I broke eye contact with him, unable to look at him with how disgusted I felt with him at the moment. "Wow. So, when you asked me on our first date to 'make it up to me for being a dick,'" I quoted, "you were really just trying to get laid, weren't you?"

Axe tilted his head, hating every second of the conversation. "Tate, that was a long time ago and I had no idea that I would fall this hard for you."

I didn't respond, still staring elsewhere. Ash was still standing awkwardly in the kitchen, wishing he never said anything in the first place.

Axe's voice softened even more. "Tate, please say something. Anything. Please don't be mad."

I whipped my head back towards him. "Oh, I'm not mad. I'm furious."

"This is exactly why I was afraid of telling you."

I angrily stomped into Axel's room and grabbed all my stuff, returning back into the living room to see Axe and Ash eyeing each other carefully, wondering what my next move was going to be. I threw my jacket over my shoulders, slipping it on. Once Axe realized that I was about to leave, he stepped towards me, reaching for me.

I put my hands up in front of me. "Don't right now," I warned him.

His nervous eyes fell to the floor. "Are you breaking up with me right now?" he sadly asked.

"No, just give me a day or two to process this."

"Okay," he said quietly, his vulnerable side showing.

"And that means don't bombard my phone with texts or calls. And don't bother showing up to my room, because that'll only piss me off more."

He gave a small nod. I was waiting for him to beg me to stay, but I think he knew better than to test me right now. I was even angrier than when I had walked in on him with Brooke, and that's saying a lot. I gripped all my things in one hand, my other hand on the doorknob, ready to walk out the door and go back to my room so that I could rip my hair out.

"Tate?" his voice made me stop, still facing the door. "Just remember that I love you, okay? And I know that that bet was shitty and I'm sorry, but I don't regret it because it led me to you."

I felt a twinge in my chest, wondering if I should just stay and sizzle down here instead of on my own. But I felt like remaining in his presence right now, unable to sort through my own thoughts, would only cause my anger to continue to build.

I took a deep breath and without saying anything else, walked out.

Claire was still having a terrible hangover when I got back to the dorms, and Gianna was taking care of her, so I didn't bother going into their room. Penelope knew something was wrong when I walked through the door, but I wasn't prepared to talk about the situation yet. I wanted to think on my own first.

I took a warm shower, trying to allow my anger to wash down the drain. I couldn't believe that Axel would place a bet on me, especially a bet that classified me as a one-night stand. But at the same time, I could believe it, because it was before we were even together, and Axe was a different person now than he was back then. Unless he was still that person that he was then, and I was just too oblivious to see it.

I knew Axe loved me now, but at what point did he stop pretending? At what point did it become real to him? At what point was I no longer just a bet? Was it before or after he took me to Amberly's for Thanksgiving? Was it before or after we had sex for the first time? Was everything leading up to New Year's Eve just a part of his plan to fulfill the bet and get me to sleep with him?

I felt used, as if all of this was just something that Axel was doing for fun, something that he was doing to prove his point that he could get any girl he wanted. Feeling this way was exactly what I had always been trying to avoid. I trusted that this whole time, Axe's intentions were real and pure, but now, that delusion of him was shattered. I didn't know which parts of our relationship were real and which parts were simply for the sake of winning his bet.

What the hell was I going to do?

I fell asleep that night with no texts or calls from Axel, no random drop-ins either. I had expected him to say something after I left the apartment, but his silence told me that he had at least carefully listened to my words earlier.

I went straight back to my room after class, avoiding any places that I knew Axe might be at. I still hadn't had the chance to talk to Claire and Gianna, and I needed to do so before I talked to Axe again.

I laid in bed as I waited for them to return from class, which felt like forever. It was already almost eight at night, and Penelope still wasn't back, so she would probably be mad that she wasn't going to be involved in our chat, but I couldn't wait any longer. I needed to talk to someone about what I had learned the day before.

I had shut my phone off and left it on my desk once Axel started calling. I needed my best friend's opinions before I talked to him again, and I was afraid that if I kept hearing his ringtone and seeing his face pop up on the screen, that I would give in and answer.

"Okay, what's up?" Gi asked as her and Claire walked in. I climbed out of bed as Claire sat on the futon, Gianna in Penelope's desk chair.

"I was a bet," I said with a straight face. The small circles under my eyes told everyone just how much sleep I had gotten the night before.

"Huh?" Claire said.

"Apparently, when Axe and I had met, and I turned him down, remember?" They each nodded, listening carefully. "Well after that, he was pissed and his little ego was hurt that for once, someone had refused to sleep with him, so Axe made a bet with Ash that he could get me to sleep with him."

Gianna's eyebrows shot up. "What the fuck?"

"I'm not surprised," Claire said from the futon, seeming confused as to why Gianna and I were. "It's Axel Burne. That's the type of shit he's infamous for. The type of shit he would've continued to do if he hadn't met you, Tate."

I furrowed my eyebrows at her, wondering what she was trying to say. She dropped her chin towards me, her brows shooting up.

"Well... what do you mean by that?" I asked, waiting for her to explain.

"Tate," she started, "he's fucking crazy about you. Didn't you hear him the other night at dinner? He wants to marry you," she whispered the last part, as if it was meant to be kept secret.

"Well to me, it feels like our relationship is based off of a lie. Like, how am I supposed to know what was real and what wasn't?"

Gianna played with her hair, trying to come up with something to say. I waited for her to speak, watching as she scratched her head.

"Tate, you *know* what was real and what wasn't. In your heart, you *know*. And honestly, to me, I think *everything* was real." I opened my mouth to respond, but she continued before I could. "Because he wouldn't have even made that bet if there wasn't something about you that intrigued him. If he hadn't felt a spark from the very first time you two met, then he wouldn't have even bothered chasing after you. He would've just moved right on to someone else."

"Facts," Claire added, pointing over to Gianna.

I thought about it for a minute. What Gianna was saying did make sense, but for some reason, I still felt unsettled about it all. I couldn't tell if it was just because I hated thinking about the fact that I was originally a bet and nothing more, or if it was the fact that the whole nature of the bet sounded like something that Connor would've done.

I held my tired face in my hands, wondering what I was supposed to do next. "So, you guys think I'm overreacting?"

Claire shrugged. "I mean, kinda, yeah. It was a long time ago. And if that bet hadn't happened, then you and Axe wouldn't have even gotten together."

"So, what am I supposed to do now, then?"

"Well, have you talked to him since you found out?" Gi asked.

I shook my head, almost mad at myself as I came to the realization that maybe I had blown all of this out of proportion. "Not since I left the apartment yesterday morning, no."

"Just sleep on it tonight and then go talk to him tomorrow after class," Gi suggested. "I can tell you're stressing out over it. And obviously, you should talk to him in person about something like this and not over text or a call."

"Yeah, you're right," I agreed.

"You've been through too much together to throw it away now," Claire said.

I nodded. "Yeah, we really have. Thanks for helping, guys."

"Text us tomorrow," Gi said as they each gave me a shy smile and walked out.

I finished the small amount of homework I had, happy that I had something to take my mind off of overthinking for a while. I didn't even bother turning my phone back on as I crawled into bed, falling asleep almost immediately from my utter exhaustion.

When I turned my phone back on, I had twenty texts and fifteen missed calls from Axel. I didn't bother texting him or calling back, knowing that I was going to go over to the apartment directly after class.

My class felt like ten hours as opposed to two, and I immediately hopped in my car afterwards, sending Axe a quick text to let him know that I was coming.

I used my key to get in, shutting the door behind me. "Axe?" I called out, unsure as to why he wasn't sitting in the living room watching tv like he normally would be. Maybe he was asleep?

I trudged towards his bedroom door, stopping as I heard the bed shaking, followed by small moans. You've got to be fucking kidding me. I wanted to walk in there and rip out the hair of whatever whore he had brought here, but I knew that if I did, I would never be able to un-see what was going on in there.

My hands shook with complete fury as I turned around and sat down on the couch in the living room, impatiently waiting for them to finish. Whoever "them" was.

Shortly after, the noises stopped, leaving me with pure adrenaline knowing that whoever was in there was about to walk out soon.

Olivia emerged, fully clothed. Her fiery red hair was in disarray, mascara smeared under her eyes. She stopped in her tracks the split second she noticed me on the couch. I stared at her, waiting for her bitchass to say something. The urge to get up and punch her in the face was growing stronger.

"Oh, shit," she muttered.

Axe walked out of the room, looking down as he buttoned his flannel. He bumped into Olivia, causing his eyes to glance up. He stopped dead in his tracks, a deer in headlights. If I didn't know any better, I'd say he just pissed himself right then and there. I raised an eyebrow at him, sending him the clear message that I knew exactly what just happened.

Olivia's eyes darted between the both of us, shifting her weight back and forth nervously. "I'm gonna go," she said.

"Yeah, you probably should," I shot back.

I watched as she anxiously speed-walked over to the door, letting herself out. I waited until I knew she was gone before turning back to Axel. He was about to feel my fucking wrath.

"Tate... I can explain."

"Explain? You don't fucking have to! Everything that I just heard, explained itself!" I yelled.

"You weren't answering... I thought you blocked my number and wanted nothing to do with me."

"You mean when I turned my phone off to stop it from ringing? I didn't block you! And even so, why wouldn't you try calling Gianna? Or coming to my room? Instead of inviting some bitch over for you to sleep with!"

Even though I was screaming, Axel's tone stayed steady. He wouldn't dare raise his voice at me. "You told me not to come to your room."

"And I also told you not to call or text a million times, but you did that anyways!"

We had never gotten into an argument that was this heated before. I could tell he was panicking, unsure of what to do or say. The anger that I had been feeling when I found out about the bet was nothing compared to the rage that currently flowed through my bloodstream.

"I'm sorry," he blurted out, his chest heavily rising and falling.

"You're sorry? That's it? That's all you have to say?"

He looked at me with glossy eyes, his mouth opening and closing with words that weren't coming out. A hand covered his forehead, trying to hide his fearful eyes.

"Well this really is just fucking déjà vu, isn't it?" I said, contemplating if I should stay around to yell at him some more, or if I should just leave now.

"I know I'm disgusting, okay? I never should've done that. And I know I don't deserve you, but I love you and I'm so sorry. I'm beyond sorry. I can't even tell you how sorry I am."

I shook my head, steps away from the door. "All those other girls were right. You haven't changed."

"Tate, I—"

"Have you been sleeping with other people since we've been together?"

He was taken aback from my accusation, a look of hurt and offense began to spread across his face as if I had just asked if he murdered someone. "Of course not. How could you think that?"

I searched his eyes for any sign that he was lying, but I couldn't find one. But maybe he was just a really good fucking liar. "How could I think that? Oh, I don't know, maybe because I just walked in on you having sex with some other girl!"

His face saddened more and more with each response I gave. He stepped towards me, reaching for me, but I backed away.

"Don't touch me. Not after your hands were all over someone else."

I was disgusted. I couldn't help but imagine him kissing her, studying her body, touching her in ways that he only touched me. I walked towards the door, about to leave and not look back.

"I fucking love you. I can't lose you."

"Well maybe you should've thought of that before you slept with someone else."

"I know... but last night, thinking that you were done with me was the worst feeling I've ever had. Thinking that I lost you made me feel the same way I felt when I lost my mom, and I never want to feel that way again. I know that's not an excuse for what I did, but can we please just talk this through?"

I felt a small twinge of pain when he mentioned his mother, but I couldn't allow that to be the reason why I stayed. "No, there's nothing to talk about," I said, opening the door and slamming it shut behind me. I made my way down the stairs and out to the parking lot, not stopping when I heard Axel running towards me from behind.

"Tate, please!" he yelled out. "Can you please come back inside so we can talk?"

When Axel realized that my feet weren't going to stop, the desperation in his voice heightened.

"You can't leave Tate, please! I'm sorry!"

I whipped around to face him right as I was approaching my car. We stood only a few feet apart.

"You're exactly like him."

His brows pulled together, his heart breaking from my words. That was probably the worst thing I could've said to him. "I'm nothing like him," he barely managed to get out. I shook my head, refusing to believe anything else that came out of his mouth. "You're breaking my heart into a million pieces right now... but do whatever you want with it, because it's yours. It's been yours since the second we met."

I shook my head slowly. "It's over."

"What?" he quietly asked, hoping that he had heard me wrong.

"It's OVER! We're done!" I screamed.

The glossiness that rested in his emerald eyes finally spilled over, tears rolling down his cheeks. It was weird that just a few nights ago, I had seen him absolutely outraged, pinning Jason against a car, and now, he was the complete opposite. Sad and hurt. I'd never seen him cry before and I fucking hated the sight. My eyes immediately swelled up. I could feel my tears about to trickle down, but I held them back as long as possible.

His eyes peered into mine. "But I love you."

My voice turned from screaming to almost a whisper as my tears finally gave way. "If you really loved me, then you wouldn't have done what you just did," I said, pointing up towards the apartment.

Axe clawed at his own hair and face, expressing absolute panic, because he knew I meant what I was saying. I loved him, but I was done. He bit his lip so hard that it looked like it hurt.

"I wasn't thinking straight."

"Well, clearly!" I replied.

"I promise this will never happen again. Just please stay," he pleaded.

"I've heard that one before."

He looked around, tears still falling. "I love you more than anything, okay? I don't want to be with anyone else ever. Please don't end this. What we have is too good."

"I've heard that one too."

"Tate, I'm fucking begging you! I'll do whatever you want me to do. I'll make it up to you in any and every way possible. I swear I'll fucking—"

"I've heard this shit before! I've fucking heard it all, Axel! I'm done! I'm done," I repeated, the second time mostly just me trying to convince myself.

"Please... you can't be done."

My tears were still falling, but my anger was back. "Well I am! Because I don't fucking trust you anymore! I trusted you... and it backfired." I wiped away my tears with the sleeve of my jacket.

Axe grabbed both of my hands, holding them in his warm ones. His voice drowned in desperation and heartache. "Tate, stop. Please listen to me. I mean it. I'm so fucking in love with you. I know I fuck up sometimes and I know I can be a complete asshole, but I also know that you are the one I've been waiting for. I've never had a real relationship before you, so when you left, I—I didn't know how to handle it."

"Just fell back into old habits, right?" I said, quoting him from the last time we had been in this situation. I pulled my hands out of his.

He dropped to his knees in front of me. "Tate... Tatum Dianne Everley, I want to be with you for the rest of my life. You *are* my life. So, if you leave right now, then my life is over. Please don't get into that car," he begged, in one last desperate attempt to convince me to stay.

I told myself that if Axe did anything that remotely resembled Connor, I would leave. I could feel my heart physically breaking inside of my chest. I wanted to stay. God, I wanted to stay so bad, but for what? So that Axel could sleep with someone else after every fight we had?

"Watch me," I said, opening my car door and climbing inside. I started the car and drove off right away, leaving Axel by himself in the parking lot.

But unlike the last time, I didn't look back in the rearview mirror.

Chapter Twenty
The Missing Half

The second I walked into my room, I immediately dropped to my knees and let out a wail. Penelope ran over and got on the ground next to me, wrapping her arms around me. She squeezed me tight as I cried uncontrollably into her arms, pain coursing through my entire body.

"What happened?"

I tried to answer her question, but I couldn't get it out. The tears were unstoppable, and it felt like there were rocks in my lungs. I could hardly breathe. My cries echoed throughout the room.

Gianna barged through the door, a look of absolute worry spread across her face. She kneeled down to where Penelope and I were on the floor. Gi rapidly wiped my tears away. "I'm so sorry," she said, trying to comfort me.

"H—how did, did you know?" I managed to get out in between sobs.

Gi adjusted her position on the floor. "Ash called me." She rubbed my back. "I'm so sorry," she repeated. I didn't respond to her explanation, only continued to weep in Penelope's arms. "Fuck Olivia, okay? She's a bitch and Axel's a bitch and you deserve better," Gi said.

"Oh," Penelope quietly said, finally understanding what happened.

I looked up at them with splotchy eyes. "What did I do?"

Gi pulled her brows in. "What do you mean?"

"What did I do to deserve this?"

"Tate... you didn't do anything. You did not do a single thing wrong. Don't even for a second think that you did."

The door slowly crept open, revealing a sympathetic Claire. She frowned as she stepped over to us, sitting.

"Hey," she softly spoke.

I turned to her, a few more tears gliding down. "Guess we're both single now," I managed to get out.

She gave a shy laugh, reaching for my hand. "Guess so."

I pushed my mouth into a line, focusing on maintaining my breathing as Gi's phone buzzed with a text.

"Tate," Gi softly said, touching my arm, "there's something you should see."

I looked up at her, my vision still blurry. She pulled up a video on her phone that Ash had sent to her.

Axe was having a breakdown, destroying the entire apartment. Debris was scattered everywhere already as Axe took his guitar and smashed it down on the coffee table, completely unaware that Ash was recording.

The video only lasted ten seconds, but by the amount of debris throughout the room, it was clear that Axe's episode had been lasting ever since I left.

I turned my head away from the video, unable to look for a second longer.

It felt like my entire universe had just been flipped upside down. I knew the second I fell for Axel that he would tear me apart in the end. But I guess I had hoped that I would be wrong.

"Tate, talk to us. Let it all out," Claire said.

I clenched my eyes shut, my heart aching as another tear fell. "I thought he was the one."

"I know," Gi sympathized.

I looked up at her. "My heart hurts," I whimpered. She pulled me in for another hug. "I just want to lay down," I said.

"Okay. You wanna be alone for a little while?" Gi asked.

I nodded, staring at the ground. The girls all glanced at each other, then stood, helping me up.

"I'll give you a bit to yourself in here," Penelope said, following Gi and Claire out of the room.

208

I collapsed into bed, my mind fuzzy. My body felt exhausted, as if I had been hit by a truck. But I would've much rather preferred to have been hit by a truck than to face the reality that I was in.

I was crumbling. And I hated to admit it, but it was the truth. After Connor left, I had become more independent. I had counted on myself for a year and a half, trying to take care of myself and figure myself out. And after spending so much time with Axel, after defying the odds of Brooke's pregnancy, after everything we had already been through, he became part of me. It hadn't been just me on my own anymore, it was us. Together. Us against the world. But now it was just me again and I felt less whole than ever before.

Connor may have chosen Nicole and left me on my own, but right now, in this moment, I had never felt more alone.

I was missing my other half.

As the next few days passed, I didn't feel like myself. I missed all my classes, having no motivation to get out of bed. The girls had to force feed me because I had a loss of appetite. All I did was stare at the ceiling or the wall, wondering that if I truly made the right choice by leaving Axe after what he did, then why did I feel so terrible right now?

I missed my loser best friend. I missed looking into his gorgeous green eyes, seeing his cute dimples when he smiled. I missed making chocolate chip pancakes with him. I missed making fun of each other and sitting around doing nothing, but still having more fun than ever. There wasn't a second that passed that Axel wasn't on my mind.

Every time I closed my eyes, I saw his face, his green eyes, his smile. Every time the room was silent, I heard him singing, playing guitar. Every time I laid in bed, it felt empty.

I had never been happier than in the moments I'd spent with Axe, but I *promised* myself that if he did *anything* that reminded me of Connor, that I would leave, and I meant it. Yes, I missed him, but I refused to re-enter another relationship that was full of unhealthy habits and cycles.

It had been three days since we ended things, and all the girls were at class while I stayed in my room again.

I felt like hell and I looked like it too.

There was a knock on my door. I hadn't been expecting anyone, but I climbed out of bed, already embarrassed for how terrible I looked. Deep inside, I wanted it to be Axe, but I didn't know who was on the other side of that door.

"Hey," Lucas said, his eyes slightly brightening when I opened the door.

"Hi," I said through my exhaustion. "Penelope's not here right now."

"Oh," he responded, nodding once. "I expected her to be." He gave a shy smile.

"Yeah, sorry. She should be done with class pretty soon."

My eyes were dry and puffy still. They had been for days and Lucas was noticing.

"Are you okay?" he asked. I shrugged, not wanting to explain. "Is it Axel?" I nodded as I looked away. His face softened. "I'm really sorry, Tate. You deserve better."

"Thanks."

He wrapped his arms around me, giving me a hug. We all knew I didn't like Lucas much, but I did need a hug from someone, and it was nice that he was being supportive.

Lucas pulled away. "I'll just leave you be, then."

"I mean, Penelope should be back shortly, so you're welcome to just hang out for a bit while you wait," I shrugged, knowing that Penelope's class was ending within ten minutes. I wouldn't have offered if I knew that it would've been any longer than that.

He smiled and nodded, appreciative of my offer. I got back in bed, wrapping myself up in my blankets as Lucas talked to me from Penelope's desk. He didn't ask anything else about what happened with Axel, which I was grateful for. I needed to get my mind off of it for a while. I could tell he was trying to make me laugh, which I appreciated, but I still wasn't in a laughing mood.

I furrowed my brows when there was another knock on the door. I figured it was Penelope returning from class, but she had a key, so why would she be knocking? She had forgotten her key in the room numerous times before though, so I wouldn't have been surprised if it happened again.

Lucas stood, about to head over to the door.

"I'll get it," I said, getting out of bed. He sat back down, allowing me to open it.

Axe stood before me, his eyes just as swollen as mine. He was wearing a black long sleeve and joggers. The same joggers that I usually never saw him wear outside of the apartment. He looked like absolute hell.

My heart stopped at the sight of him. I hadn't seen him since I left the apartment days prior. He had been blowing up my phone nonstop, and I had turned it off again to avoid the temptation of answering.

"Tate," he croaked with his raspy voice, a clear sign that he hadn't been getting much sleep either.

My eyes met the floor, feeling more tears forming. "What do you want, Axel?"

"I want you... No," he corrected himself, "I *need* you."

I bit the inside of my lip as I glanced up to meet his tearful gaze. "Some things just can't be fixed, Axe."

He shook his head as a tear escaped from his eye, but he quickly wiped it away. His gaze strolled past me to where Lucas was sitting, and Axe's facial expression turned from complete sadness to confusion and irritation.

"What the hell is he doing here?"

"He's waiting here for Penelope to get back from class."

"Are you sure that's all?"

I stood stunned for a second, shocked as to why he would ever accuse me of doing anything with anyone else, especially Lucas.

I narrowed my eyes at him. "I'm not like you, Axe. I don't call other people to come over and hookup any time something goes wrong."

I could tell my words hurt him, because his face returned back to the same sadness he had when I first opened the door. I knew he hadn't meant to hurt me, but he still did. Deep down, I wanted to jump into his arms. I had looked past everything that happened with Brooke, even with how panicked that situation made me feel. Because at the end of the day, he slept with Brooke before we were officially together. But now, he slept with Olivia when we were technically still together. And I didn't think that was something I could get past.

"You're right," he sighed. "I'm sorry."

"Axe, just—"

"You're my best friend," he pleaded. "You're my everything. I need you."

It felt like I was frozen, but the world was still turning. My heart was already shattering. But after hearing his words, the knife that was plunged into my heart was twisting.

"I just can't believe you did what you did, when I loved you so much..."

Axe winced. "Past tense?"

I placed my right hand on his cheek, looking directly into his emerald eyes, knowing that it was the last time I would do so. He brought a hand up and covered mine, still resting upon his tear-soaked cheek.

"I love you," I said, "but I can't be with you."

Axe clenched his eyes shut as another tear fell down his cheek, my tears following his lead. He put one hand on my lower back, pulling me into him for one last hug.

"I'm always gonna love you," he said. His soft lips gently kissed my forehead, a small gesture that he used to do all the time.

I covered my mouth with both of my shaking hands as Axel walked off, trying my best to mute my own sobs.

After a few more days, I forced myself to go to class. I didn't want to go, but I also didn't want my grades to suffer. Each class felt too long, and I often found myself not being able to focus, sidetracked by both good and bad memories of Axel. I walked right back to my room after class instead of going to the dining center for lunch. This was usually around the time of day that Axe and I would go together. Not only did I not want to run into him, but I didn't want the feeling of being alone while I sat at our old table, staring at his empty seat. Plus, I still didn't have a big appetite anyways.

I rounded the corner, my eyes instantly darting to a white pick-up truck parked in the lot. Normally, the sight would cause me to panic, to feel the need to run. But instead of thinking about Connor at the sight, I thought about Axel instead. I didn't know why, but I did.

When I got back to my dorm, I made sure to leave my phone on the other side of the room. Any time that it was in front of me, I found myself knee deep in old pictures and videos, only to end up making my already crying eyes cry even harder.

Claire and Gianna slowly walked in. "Hey," Gianna gently said. "How are you feeling today?"

"Like shit."

Both of their faces fell, saddened that I was still having a rough time. "Come out with us tonight," Claire proposed.

I pulled my mouth over to the side, dissatisfied by the idea. "I don't really want to."

"C'mon, it'll be fun! You didn't go out with us at all last week."

I twisted my hair around, studying it between my fingers while shaking my head. "The last place on Earth that I currently wanna go to is ATA."

I hated that I felt that way. ATA had always been fun. We had a lot of friends in the frat. But it was where I met Axe. Where we had partied together almost every weekend. It was the place I knew he would be.

"We don't even have to go to ATA. We could go to the other frats instead," Gianna offered. But I didn't want to be the reason why they didn't go to ATA to spend time with Ash and Owen. I didn't want to hold them back.

I had felt almost guilty recently. Axel and I breaking up had placed Gianna in an awkward spot. She couldn't go to the apartment without Axel asking a million questions and Ash couldn't come here without Axel wanting to come with. "And even if we did for some reason end up at ATA," she added, "Axel wasn't even there last week, so he probably won't be there again."

"Not tonight, guys. I'm sorry," I said. "But if you end up needing a ride or something, just call and let me know."

They each sighed and left me alone with Penelope. She hurriedly threw her hair up into a ponytail and sat down in front of her mirror, pulling out her makeup bag.

"Are you going somewhere?" I asked in my small voice.

"Out with Lucas," she smiled.

"Oh, okay," I said, slight disappointment taking over. I didn't want to go out, but I also didn't want to sit alone all night. "Where are you guys going?" I asked out of curiosity.

"Definitely not ATA," she joked. "Probably just Pi Rho." I nodded, taking a deep breath as I sat down on the futon. "Did you want to come with?"

I considered it for a second, but third wheeling with Penelope and Lucas did not sound like a good time. And there was no way in Hell that seeing Jason would make my mood any better, either. "No, that's okay. Thanks for asking, though."

There was one single knock on the door before it opened. Lucas walked in with a smirk and headed directed over to Penelope. She went on her tip toes to kiss him on the cheek, her smile never fading. She liked him a lot. I didn't know why, but she did.

"I'm almost done getting ready," she said. "I'm just gonna go to the bathroom really quick and then go see if I can find someone who will let me use their straightener, since mine broke," she frowned.

I stayed on the futon, sitting criss-crossed applesauce as Penelope left, leaving me alone with Lucas. He stood with his hands in his back pockets.

"So, how are you?" he asked.

I hadn't bothered putting on makeup for nearly two weeks now. The bags under my eyes were only growing, my hair tied in a messy low pony. It was obvious how I was doing.

I shrugged. "How 'bout you?"

"I'm good."

"That's good," I nodded, my lips pushed into a straight line from the awkwardness I felt. It went silent for a minute until I stood up, making my way over to my desk to grab my water bottle.

A hand caressed my lower back and I jumped, cringing. That wasn't Axel's hand. And I sure as hell didn't want anyone touching me there unless it was.

"What the hell are you doing?" I yelped.

Lucas took a deep breath as I stepped back. "I, uh, sorry," he said, rubbing his forehead. "I've been meaning to ask you, um... my frat is having this date party in a few weeks and I was wondering if you wanted to go with me?"

"You're kidding, right?"

214

His eyes shifted around, blinking numerous times. "No."

I pulled my eyebrows as close together as they could physically go, my jaw dropped. I laughed once. "You're dating my roommate!"

He bit his lip nervously. "Well, I mean, we're not like *officially* dating or anything."

I glanced around the room, wondering if he was being serious. When my eyes fell back onto him, he was still looking at me, waiting for a response. "No!" I screeched.

Disappointment stretched across his face at my denial, as if he didn't see it coming. Penelope walked back in, smiling as usual, a straightener in hand. I gave Lucas one more glare, then retreated back to the futon, turning my movie back on. I knew I needed to tell Penelope what just happened, but I didn't want to do it while Lucas was around, so I let her leave with him after she finished her hair.

About an hour and a half later, my phone rang from across the room. I paused my movie and rushed over to it, wondering if it was Claire and Gianna needing a ride.

Axe's name lit up the screen. My heart began to pound harder. Before thinking, I picked it up and held the phone up to my ear.

"Hello?"

"Hi," he said. I didn't say anything, curious as to why he was calling when he hadn't done so in over a week. "Sorry for, uh... calling you. I just wanted to hear your voice."

"Axe..."

"I fucking miss you."

I took a deep breath, those same words lingering on my lips. But instead of saying it back, I changed the subject. "Are you drunk?"

"Yeah."

I didn't hear any noise in the background, so I assumed he wasn't at ATO. I didn't know where he was or who he was with, but I hoped that he was safe and okay. "Just go to bed, okay?"

I could hear him start to weep on the other side of the phone. "I can't... my bed is too empty without you."

I hated to hear him cry. I wished I could embrace him through the phone. My eyes closed, fighting back tears. "I have to go. Please be safe," I said, hanging up the phone. Part of me expected another phone call from him, but I didn't get one. I dropped to the ground, hugging my knees into my chest as I sobbed. It seemed like the tears were never going to stop.

I studied myself in the mirror, taking in just how terrible I looked, which reflected how terrible I felt. I closed my eyes, focusing on my breathing. I needed to be strong. I needed to remind myself that the past year and a half that I was on my own wasn't useless. It taught me how to be independent and how to get past pain. I stood back up and wiped my tears away. I was a warrior. I couldn't let this destroy me.

For the next hour, I kept myself occupied doing homework and cleaning my room until it was spotless. I think it was the longest I'd gone without crying. When Gianna and Claire walked in, I forced a tiny smile.

"How was your night?" I asked, putting the broom and dustpan away.

"It was good," Gi said, nodding, noticing that I was up and about. "Well you seem to be feeling better."

I shrugged. "A little."

"We just wanted to check in on you before we went to bed," Claire expressed.

"Thanks, guys." I knew that my next question probably shouldn't be asked, but I wanted to know anyways. "Did you guys go to ATA?"

They both awkwardly nodded. "Yeah," Gi answered.

"Was Axel there?"

Gi tilted her head. "Well he was, but then when we showed up and he realized that you weren't with us and that you weren't coming at all, he left right away."

"Oh," I said, almost surprised. "Did he leave alone?" Both of them nodded.

That was probably when he had called me, after he left ATA. I contemplated telling them that he called, but I didn't want to drag on the topic for any longer. I was content knowing that he hadn't gone home with anyone, but I was sort of angry at myself for caring enough to even ask. We all knew that I wasn't over him. We all knew that I still cared, but I didn't want to. I couldn't be with Axel, so the best thing I could do for myself was to stop asking questions.

Directly after the girls left, Penelope strolled in, looking as happy as ever. I didn't know if it was the right time to be telling her what happened earlier with Lucas, but I went for it anyways.

"Hey, um, can I talk to you about something?" I asked.

"Of course. What's up?"

I took a deep breath, my hands in the pockets of my sweatpants. "Okay, um..." I started, wondering exactly what to say, "well, earlier, when you weren't in the room, Lucas weirdly touched my lower back and I backed away from him. And then he asked me to go to his frats date party with him in a few weeks."

Her face fell, stuck in thought. "No," she denied, "he wouldn't do that."

"But he did. I'm really sorry."

A flare of anger ignited in her eyes. "I don't believe you."

I raised my eyebrows. "Well, you should."

"Well, I don't."

"Look, I was just trying to be a good friend and tell you what happened."

She shook her head, crossing her arms. She laughed once. "Listen. I know you're still really upset about your breakup, which I understand, but that doesn't mean you have to sabotage my relationship," she said, before stomping out of the room.

My jaw dropped. Wow. Did she really think I was miserable enough to the point where my conscience was off? Did she honestly believe that I was jealous of her relationship to the point where I would sabotage her?

I shook off the annoyance that I felt and got ready for bed. I stared at the ceiling again, lost in thought, but I physically didn't have any more tears left to cry. My eyes were too dry, and my brain was too tired. I tried to think about happier things, more positive thoughts. I reminded myself that I've been through this before, so I could do it again. The world was still turning, and I was still alive, whether I felt like it or not.

Tomorrow would be a new day, and I would do my best to make it the first day in nearly two weeks that I hadn't cried.

Chapter Twenty-One
The "Water" Bottle

The next few days were still rough, but I tried my absolute best to keep myself together. I didn't allow myself to cry, didn't allow myself to sit and look at old pictures or videos. I didn't listen to songs that Axe and I used to listen to or watch movies that we used to watch. I avoided anything and everything that reminded me of him.

I put most of my energy into my homework and dancing, which shifted my focus in a positive way. After I finished my short essay at the library, I headed towards the dining center, where I was supposed to meet Claire for dinner. Axel and I never went to the dining center at this time of the day on Wednesday's when we were together, so I figured it was a safe time to go. I texted Claire when I got there, looking around for her.

Almost there! Find us a good table

I sighed. I hated being the first one there. I spotted an empty table on the opposite side that Axel and I used to sit at. I took a seat, setting my stuff down. But when I looked up, my heart dropped.

Axel was sitting a few tables down, a group of girls standing around him. He didn't look entertained by their presence, though. It seemed as if he was trying to shoo them all away. I didn't recognize any of the girls, but I wondered if he had been sleeping with any of them. Or

218

worse, if he had been sleeping with all of them. He shifted around in his seat, agitated as they touched his hair and tried conversing with him.

Part of me wanted to get up and punch all the girls in the face for touching him, but he wasn't mine anymore to protect.

When his eyes wandered around, they stopped on me. His face softened at the sight of me, suddenly not paying attention to the four girls who were all over him.

I swallowed the lump in my throat, wondering which one of us was going to be the first to leave. I needed to look away from him, but I couldn't. I couldn't take my eyes off of him.

As if he read my thoughts like he normally could, he stood up and strolled over to my table, placing one hand onto it and leaning in.

"I don't want any of them. I only want you. So, no, I'm not sleeping with any of them," he said, before turning around and walking out of the dining center. The group of girls stood disappointed as they twisted their hair and left.

I was stunned. I kept replaying his words over and over in my head. It was odd how he knew what I had been thinking. I didn't know if that was a good thing or a bad thing.

Less than five minutes later, Claire sat down next to me, the bright smile on her face fell as I stared down at the table.

"What's wrong?" she asked.

I snapped out of my trance and faked a smile, not wanting to explain.

"Nothing," I said, forcibly grinning.

Before I knew it, it was already Friday night. I had been hanging on by a thread. I still felt a little unsettled from seeing Axel a few days prior, especially after what he had said, but I wanted to push through it. I hadn't gone out in two weeks, so I figured I should just full send it and go. After all, Axel and I still went to the same school, so it was inevitable that I was going to see him places. I didn't want to avoid ATA forever or any of the other places we used to go to. The earlier I faced my fears, the better the outcome would be, right?

Penelope was already gone. She hadn't talked to me much since I "tried to sabotage her." I flipped through all the clothes in my closet, inspecting every piece of fabric on each hanger. I felt a heaviness in my chest when I got to one of Axel's sweatshirts. It was his black Nike one, one of his favorite sweatshirts. I knew I should give it back to him, but I hadn't gotten around to it yet, and surprisingly, he hadn't even asked. Usually, most guys would throw a tantrum if they didn't get their things back after a breakup, but for some reason, it was the last thing Axel cared about.

I held the fabric between my fingers. I wanted to put it on. I wanted to have a piece of him wrapped around my body. I placed my nose on the upper part of the sweatshirt, smelling the remainder of his cologne that rested upon it. The smell caused me to walk over to my desk. I lifted my necklace up, examining it. I hadn't worn it since we broke up. Just feeling those two things alone was enough to cause my heart to twinge in misery. Having physical reminders of Axel only made it more evident that what we had was real.

I kept my tears back, even though all they wanted to do was fall. I didn't want to ruin my makeup. I had been trying for weeks to stay strong, to be the person I needed myself to be. I tried so hard to forget about the pain, but at some point each day, it found its way back to me.

The last day that I saw Connor was absolute hell. The last phone call I received from him before he got on that plane to leave for the Marines was absolute hell. The day I found out he proposed to Nicole was absolute hell. The day they got married and I had to sit back and endure the reality was absolute hell. But for some reason, somehow, the pain I felt now was even worse. When everything happened with Connor, my heart was broken. But right now, my heart was absolutely, utterly, without a doubt destroyed. Demolished. Nonexistent.

I stared at my closet, knowing that I had an entire handle of vodka hidden in there. I wondered if I should just give in and do what my body was specifically made to do. The temptation was strong. I wanted to forget. For just a night. I rummaged through my belongings until I found the fifth. I slipped on a red velvet crop top and black jeans, then poured myself a shot. Then another. And another. And another.

I looked at myself in the mirror, realizing what I had done, but not caring. Four shots would not make me as drunk as I needed to be and the buzz that it would give me certainly would not last all night. I

220

grabbed a plastic water bottle and emptied it into the community kitchen, then refilled it with vodka.

Red lipstick was the last thing I added.

"I'm ready," I said, walking into Gianna and Claire's room.

Claire's face lit up. "I'm so happy you're coming out with us tonight!"

"Me too," I said with a deep breath as I tucked a strand of hair behind my ear.

"Same," Gi said. "We're gonna have fun tonight, okay?"

I gave her a small nod. She reached for my hand and gently squeezed it for a moment.

"Everyone's ready?" Gi asked. Claire and I both nodded. "Okay, perfect. Let's go," Gi smiled.

It wasn't until we were walking up ATA's driveway that I started to feel a buzz. Unsure if Axel was going to be there or not, adrenaline flickered around inside my body, a deadly mix with the alcohol that I had already drank.

When we got inside, my eyes were peeled. I scanned the room as we moved through the sea of people. The party room was very much alive, an entire room filled with people who had no idea what had been happening behind closed doors.

Gianna and Claire stopped in the back of the room, making a small circle for the three of us to dance in. It was nice that they didn't go straight to Ash and Owen, allowing me to give time to adjust to the party scene without Axe by my side. Because I was so used to having him there.

We danced around like idiots, trying not to bump into the people around us. It was refreshing to be out, not cooped up in my room like I had been every night for two weeks. But the second I glanced towards the corner of the room, I stopped. The euphoria that I had been feeling drained away. Axe leaned against the wall wearing his black Harley Davidson t-shirt with the sleeves slightly rolled up. There was a blonde girl next to him, trying to talk to him, but his eyes were on me, standing in the exact spot that he used to watch me in. The exact spot he stood on the night we met. It felt like déjà vu. I could feel the warmth of my slightly drunken body, but it wasn't enough for me. I needed more. I wanted to feel numb. I spun off the cap of my water bottle that I had filled with vodka, taking a few chugs. I needed it to start to take its effect quickly. I couldn't stand here with Axe that close to me for much longer without it.

"You brought water?" Gianna asked over the music.

I didn't want them to know what it really was. I didn't want them to worry about me, let alone try to stop me. It was dangerous for me to be drinking this much. There was always that possibility that I would end up like the rest of my family had around my age. My parents. My grandparents. Some of my aunts and uncles. Some of my cousins. And even my sister, goddamnit, but I needed it. And if Gianna and Claire knew that it was actually vodka, they'd take it away from me in a heartbeat.

I gave a quick nod, lying straight to her face.

"Can I have some?"

I shook my head vigorously, knowing that if she took one single sip, she would know damn well that it wasn't water. Gi sighed, but then brushed it off, leaving me relieved that she did.

I couldn't help but glimpse over at Axel every few minutes, curious as to if he was still looking at me or not. But each time, he was, which only made me more impatient as to when the extra chugs of vodka would kick in. I could feel it slowly taking effect, but it hadn't fully hit me yet.

"Hey!" Ash yelled as he approached the three of us. He placed a kiss on Gi's cheek, causing some jealousy to rise within me. Jealousy that was only there because Gianna had what I didn't anymore.

He nodded once to Claire and then to me. I hadn't seen Ash in weeks, since the morning he told me about the bet. It felt a little awkward since so much had changed since then, but I smiled anyways.

"Hey, Ash," I said.

He looked at me with genuine care in his eyes, almost brotherly. "How are you, Tate?"

I shrugged. "As good as I can be."

It seemed like there was something he wanted to say, but Gi shot him a look, as if she knew what it was and warned him to keep his mouth shut. His eyes drifted to his brother in the corner, and then his face fell as he turned back to me.

"Tate, please. He's miserable."

"Ash," Gianna warned. "Don't start."

Ash ignored Gi's warning. "I've never seen him like this. He hasn't been himself since you've left. Even *I'm* begging you. Please, just give him one more chance."

"That's enough, Ash!" Gianna yelled.

I could feel the alcohol taking over my body as I began to sway a little bit. But Ash's words weren't helping. I needed more. I took another gulp of my vodka, wiping my mouth with the back of my hand.

Gianna and Ash started arguing, but I didn't care enough to listen. Claire was trying to reason with them, to settle them down, but all I saw it as was my opportunity to wander off. I stumbled away from the three of them, pushing through people with no real destination. The bright strobe lights caused a peculiar pair of eyes to shine. Blue eyes.

Nick.

As far as I knew, he wasn't in this frat, so I wasn't sure how he got into the party, but he looked good. I hadn't seen him since before Axe and I had officially started dating. Our eyes locked and he smirked as he made his way over to me.

"I'd recognize those red lips anywhere," he said, smiling.

I blinked an abnormal amount of times, my coordination lacking. "Hey," I said, my eyes traveling up and down his body.

"Where's the boyfriend?"

I clenched my eyes shut for a second, then opened them. "We broke up."

"Oh," he nodded a few times. "I'm sorry to hear that."

I shrugged. "Yeah."

"Well would you like to dance?"

"Sure."

He grabbed my hips and pulled me into him, my backside connecting to his front. I drunkenly swayed side to side, letting his hands glide up and down my body wherever he pleased. I was noticeably drunk, losing my balance every so often. It felt almost wrong to be dancing with Nick, but I needed the distraction.

His hands explored each inch of me. I could feel the bulge in his pants rising as he held me to him, a feeling that I hadn't gotten in weeks. We were close, but I wanted him closer. After a few songs, his mouth grazed my ear.

"Do you wanna go back to my place with me?"

Axel's face flashed into my head for a second, but I pushed it away. I needed Nick's attention and affection. I craved the feeling of being touched and loved.

"Sure."

A mischievous grin appeared on his face as he licked his top lip. He wrapped his arm around me, leading me out of the party. I didn't bother telling Claire and Gianna I was leaving, mostly because I forgot to. The only thing on my mind was the desire to feel someone else's body on mine.

We stumbled around in the night as Nick attempted to pull me along with him. Fratville seemed almost empty, with no one walking along it. Everyone was at a house, partying.

Nick didn't try to make conversation, only focused on getting me back to his place. Wherever that was. His frustration was arising as it became more difficult for my body to cooperate.

"Tatum, just walk," he said.

I giggled as I staggered around, amused by my own clumsiness. "Walking," I said, my drunken high tone echoing in the night. I froze in my tracks and gasped. "Oh, no! My water bottle."

"Let's keep walking," Nick said.

"But my bottle," I complained, allowing Nick to drag me along.

"Hey!" a voice shouted from behind us. I'd recognize that voice anywhere. Nick and I both turned, his arm still holding me up. "Where the hell do you think you're taking her?" Axel said, demanding a sudden answer.

Nick was taken aback. "Why the hell does it matter to you? And who the fuck are you?"

I had only talked to Nick a few times before, and I had never heard him be anything other than sweet. But right now, the blue in his eyes looked like there was a storm brewing among the seas.

Axel disregarded both of Nick's questions. "Give her to me."

"Hell no. I'm trying to get laid tonight."

Axel got closer and leaned in, his rage stirring. "Over my dead body."

Nick clearly did not know who Axel was, because he wasn't backing down. "Why don't you just mind your own damn business?"

"She is my business!" Axel yelled.

Nick's eyes narrowed at Axe, whose patience was running out.

"Both of you, stop," I slurred.

Axe reached for me, about to pry me out of Nick's fingers, but Nick moved me out of the way, refusing to give me up.

Axel's jaw twitched under his skin, fists shaking at his sides. "Give her to me," Axel repeated.

"No!"

"You have. Three seconds. To give her to me. Before I rearrange your fucking face." The look on his face was vicious, fury radiating off of his body.

Nick glanced at both Axel and I. "You know what? Fuck this!" He released his grip on me, causing me to lose my only source of balance. I stumbled, almost falling, but Axe placed one hand on my arm, the other on my waist, catching me.

"You okay?" he asked. The rage that was building in his eyes just moments before had diminished.

"What the hell, Axel! I wanted to sleep with him!" I screamed into the night, releasing myself from his grip. I turned on my heels, trying to walk straight as I followed the direction that Nick went in.

"Oh, hell no."

"What!" I yelled loudly, not turning around, my feet still trying to move.

"I'm not letting you lose your self-respect because of me," he said, picking me up and throwing me over his shoulder.

"Put me down!"

"Absolutely not."

"Axel Edward Burne! Put me down!"

He sighed, ignoring my small fists hitting his muscular back. After a couple minutes, I grumbled as I gave up. He was too strong. There was no way I was going to win.

He continued to walk with both of us in silence. I tried to look around to see where we were, but I was upside down and drunk, so I couldn't quite tell.

"Can you please put me down?" I slurred.

"It's not like you can walk on your own anyways."

I made an angry pouty face, even though he couldn't see it. I hated that he was right. If I had tried walking entirely on my own, then I would've woken up tomorrow morning on the side of the road.

The next thing I knew, we were in the apartment. Axel gently dropped me onto his bed, then left the room. He returned with a bottle of water. I groaned as I laid there, watching Axe set the bottle on the nightstand.

"Is this my vodka?" I asked.

"Is that why you're so drunk?"

"Maybe."

"Tate, you shouldn't be drinking that much."

"Whatever."

"It's dangerous."

"Like you care about me anyways," I muttered, looking away.

"You know I care about you."

I laid there pouting in silence as Axe stood next to the bed, his hands on his hips. He studied me, thinking. I furrowed my brows at him, wondering what his next move was going to be. He eyed my jeans for a quick second before walking over to his closet and grabbing a long t-shirt.

I sat up in the bed, feeling a little dizzy. I made a pouty face as I crossed my arms, still angry that he hadn't allowed me to get my way. My eyes skimmed the bedsheets, noticing that they weren't the same ones that he used to have. He must've gotten new ones after he destroyed the apartment.

I started to giggle as Axel unbuttoned my jeans and wiggled them off of my small legs. The feeling made me want to pull him on top of me.

"Put your arms up," he softly insisted. I did as he asked, allowing him to slip off my red, velvet crop top. He was so close to me as he prepared to put the t-shirt over my head. I wanted him closer. I wrapped an arm around the back of his neck and pulled him into me, still topless and pantsless.

My drunk lips smashed onto his, my breath probably smelling like straight alcohol. He stiffened for a second, but then relaxed against my touch, kissing me back. We opened and closed our mouths rhythmically.

At that very moment, I wanted him. So bad. I still had the urge to feel someone's skin on mine, and the urge was even stronger now that it was Axe.

226

I brought my free hand down to his black belt to undo it as my other arm was still draped around his neck. I began tugging at the belt, trying to get it off with one hand, but it didn't seem to be working. His lips left mine, pulling away. He was breathing heavily.

"Tate, no."

I was baffled at his rejection, disappointed. "Why?"

"You're too drunk."

"But I want you."

His green irises glittered, longing for me. But he still shook his head. "You're too drunk," he repeated. He quickly put the t-shirt on me, his shoulders rising and falling as he took a deep breath.

"Axe?" I said as he tucked me in.

"Mhmm?"

"I still love you."

His body froze, taken off guard at my confession. He peeked over at me, locking eyes with mine. He clearly hadn't expected me to still love him after what he had done, let alone to admit it right now.

"I love you too." His chin dipped down as his beautiful emeralds eyed my lips. He slowly bent down and placed a tender kiss on my mouth, but backed away instantly after, not allowing me to continue it. "I'm gonna sleep in the living room, so just come out there if you need anything, okay?"

My head hit the pillow, still frustrated that he refused to give me what I wanted. But even so, I still craved his presence. Having my lips on his was the most myself I've felt in weeks, the most relaxed and normal I've felt. My heart started to ache as he walked towards the door. I didn't want him to leave.

"Axe?"

"Yeah?" he turned.

"Will you lay with me?"

One side of his mouth slightly pulled up into a half-smile. He kicked off his shoes and climbed into the bed. The second he was next to me, I cuddled up into him, draping one arm around his stomach and placing my head on his chest. He held me tight, maybe the tightest he's ever held me. I smelled his cologne radiating off of him. My favorite smell.

I didn't want to go to bed. I wanted to savor every moment of this.

I hadn't been to Wilmot in six months. Hadn't been home in six months. But I didn't need to be. Because Axe was my home away from home. Laying in his arms felt right.

He rubbed my back gently. I thought about what it felt like when Lucas had touched my back. Not only did it make me uncomfortable because it was Lucas, but it just felt wrong in general. It's as if my body knew the difference between the two simply by the touch.

I knew I had missed Axel more than anything, more than I had ever missed anyone before, including Connor. Laying with Axe felt so right, which was why it was making me so sad. Once morning would come, this moment would be over, and Axe and I would return to being strangers. My eyes swelled up with tears as my head still rested on his chest and as if on cue, the waterworks all rushed out at once, soaking Axe's shirt.

I may have been drunk, but even if I were sober, I knew I would've had the same reaction. I shook as I cried, then cried even harder when Axe spoke.

"Tate," he whispered as he sat up, pulling me up with him so that he could look into my eyes. "Baby, why are you crying?"

He attempted to wipe my tears away, but they were coming out so quickly that he couldn't keep up. God, I probably looked so ugly right now, mascara most likely covering my entire face. But I didn't care. My appearance was the last thing I cared about at the moment.

"I miss you so much," I said in between sobs.

He wrapped his arms around me, putting my head against his chest. I could hear the vibrations coming from his chest as he spoke. "I can't even put into words how much I've missed you. When I'm not with you, I can't even think straight. I can't think of anything other than how much I fucking miss you." I cried into his arms for another minute before he spoke again. "Take me back," he pleaded. I slowly disconnected my cheek from his chest, my eyes traveling up to meet his. I'd been crying so hard that I hadn't even noticed that he was crying too. "Please take me back." My thumb rubbed over his bottom lip, my heart yearning for his.

"Axe..."

"I promise you that I'll work hard every single day to be the man you need, the man you deserve. I don't ever want to touch a woman again unless it's you. I won't even breathe in another woman's direction, ever. I will love you and protect you at all costs until the day I die. Just, please Tate," he begged, clenching his eyes shut as another tear fell down. His eyes fluttered back open. "I'm so fucking miserable without you."

My drunken mind couldn't sort through my thoughts. If I were sober right now, I would be able to decide what to do or say. But as I sat there in Axe's arms, under the influence, I didn't have enough control over myself to stop and think. But you know what they say. Drunk words are sober thoughts.

I opened my mouth to speak, to give in, but then there was a buzzing sound coming from the nightstand. Axe reached over and picked up his phone, still holding me with one arm. Gianna's name lit up the screen.

"Yeah?" Axe said, annoyed by the interruption. He listened carefully. "She's with me. She's fine." His eyes rolled at whatever her response was. "If you think I would let anything happen to her, then you're crazy." He hung up the phone, tossing it to the end of the bed.

I yawned, my tired, drunken, swollen eyes slowly closing. Axe laid me back down, covering me with the comforter.

"Go to bed, baby," he whispered, sniffling. I wanted to stay awake. To talk to him, snuggle up next to him, feel his lips on mine, but my dizzies had returned, and before I knew it, I was already sound asleep without having told Axel that I would take him back.

But would I feel the same way in the morning?

Chapter Twenty-Two
The True Definition

I awoke to yelling coming from the living room. I quickly sat up to go see what the commotion was about, but my eyes widened when I felt my head throbbing. I winced, rubbing my forehead. I reached over for the water bottle that Axe had left on the nightstand last night, taking numerous gulps.

When I finally managed to get up, I slowly made my way out of the bedroom. Axe, Ash, and Gianna were all in the living room, voices raising.

"Why the hell would I ever do that to her? I love her!" Axe exclaimed.

"Because it sounds like something you would do!" Gianna retaliated.

"I didn't do anything to her, Gianna! You're being a bitch for no reason!" Axe yelled. I wasn't sure what the argument was about. All I knew was that I had never heard them yell at each other this fiercely. And their yelling wasn't helping my headache.

"Axel!" Ash shouted back in reaction, warning Axel to tone it down.

Axe's mouth pressed into a straight line as he shook his head. "Whatever," he said, pushing past Ash.

Ash placed a hand on his brother's shoulder, stopping him in his tracks. "Calm down. You're acting like Paul right now," Ash said through gritted teeth.

Axe whipped himself around to face his brother. "I'm *nothing* like that scumbag," he seethed.

It seemed as if he didn't even notice I was standing there, blinded by his anger as he strolled past me and slammed his bedroom door shut.

Ash and Gianna both watched me for a second, before Gianna started another argument, this time, with Ash. Usually she was so mellow, so I was confused as to why she was currently so heated. I didn't want to be caught in their wildfire, and more importantly, I wanted to make sure Axe was okay. I slowly backed out of the living room, retreating back to the bedroom, but the door wouldn't budge as I went to open it. It was locked.

I lightly knocked on the door. "Axe? It's me. Open up."

Within seconds, it was opened. Axe moved out of the way to let me in, closing and relocking the door after I entered. I touched my forehead again, overtaken by my current nausea.

"How are you feeling?" Axe asked, pretending as if the altercation in the living room didn't happen.

I disregarded the question, more concerned with getting answers to mine first. "What was all that about?"

Axe sighed. "Gianna thinks I snatched you from ATA solely because I wanted to, not because you were about to get basically raped by that dumb fuck. You were so drunk that it definitely would've been considered rape. And then she thinks I took you back here and had sex with you myself."

I didn't remember too many details from the night before, but I did remember enough to know what happened and what didn't happen. I brought my eyebrows together. "But neither of those things are true."

"I know, but she doesn't believe me."

"I'll talk to her later and set things straight," I said, holding my unsettled stomach.

Axe took notice. "Damnit and I was in the middle of making your pancakes too."

"Chocolate chip?"

The sides of his mouth slowly turned up in response to my question. "Of course."

Both of our smiles fell as the yelling from the living room got louder, and even though we couldn't hear word for word what they were saying, it didn't sound good. Axe and I quietly looked at each other as the apartment door slammed shut, followed by stomps down the hall. I jumped when there was a fist banging on the door.

"Axel! Get your ass out here now!" Ash demanded. Axe didn't flinch from his brother's aggressive tone. He placed an arm in front of me and pushed me behind him, his protective instincts kicking in, even if it was just his brother.

The door swung open and Ash stood, huffing and puffing in anger.

"What do you want, dick?" Axe calmly asked.

Ash's eyebrows flew up. "Your dumbass just got me broken up with!"

"For what! I didn't do shit!"

"Honestly, I don't even know!" Ash yelled, bringing his arms up and then smacking them down by his sides. "But now I'm fuckin' pissed!"

Axel's tone stayed calm. "Well, you're one of the reasons why Tate and I broke up. So, I guess karma's a bitch."

Ash clearly did not like his answer, his heavy breathing becoming heavier as his jaw trembled beneath his skin. "You're a dick."

"I didn't even do anything."

"You called my girlfriend a bitch!"

"Ex-girlfriend," Axe corrected him.

Ash exploded, throwing a punch at Axe, but he quickly ducked. In the blink of an eye, Axe grabbed both of Ash's arms and twisted them behind his back, ramming him up against the wall.

Ash's cheek kissed the cold wall, his facial expression still pissed as he tried to break out of Axe's hold, but his grip was too strong.

"STOP!" Axe screamed at his brother. Ash still struggled under his grasp, trying his hardest to wiggle free. I had seen Axe absolutely outraged, but I had never seen him lay a hand on Ash before now. I had no idea that Axe was strong enough to take on his own brother, his older brother. Axel's breaths were deep, his words dull. "Don't make me beat your ass right now. I don't want to, especially while Tate's in the room."

Ash's eyes drifted over to me, barely reaching sight of me under his restrictions. "Okay, okay! Just let me go!"

Axe did what was requested, backing up and away from Ash as he did so. I didn't know if now was a good time to be getting involved, but I did anyway.

"Ash, I'll talk to Gianna later for you."

He nodded once at me, smoothing out his shirt. "Thanks, Tate." His breathing was still in the process of going back to normal, a clear sign that he was still distraught, but it seemed like he was trying not to take it out on me. Ash took one last look at both Axe and I and then walked out of the room, trampling down the hall.

Axe made his way over to me, gently pushing my hair back. The apartment door slammed shut again, causing Axe to roll his eyes.

"Did he just leave?" I asked.

"Yep."

"I feel bad."

"Don't." His fingers traced down my arm, stopping when he reached my hand. He lightly squeezed, not taking his eyes off of mine. By the small bags that had made homes under his eyes, it didn't seem like he gotten much sleep last night either. I wondered if he had stayed up thinking, the same thing I would've done if I hadn't been so goddamn drunk.

"Now let's go make you those pancakes," he smirked on one side, a single dimple popping up. I couldn't help but grin too as my favorite sight stood before me.

I sat down with my plate after the pancakes were done. I hadn't been much help in the process, my hangover growing as time passed. But hopefully, eating would help.

It was odd how even after everything, being around Axe felt right. Being at the apartment felt normal. It didn't feel like anything was being forced or that there was any awkwardness in the room. Obviously, there was a peculiar tension in the air, but it was only due to the underlying circumstances.

I could feel Axe's eyes peer up at me every so often as we ate across from each other. He definitely had something on his mind, maybe even about last night, but he hadn't said anything about it. I tried to think about the previous night as I ate, small parts coming back to me as I concentrated. I knew that Axe had asked me to take him back, but I didn't remember my response to him.

Finally, he broke the silence. "Do you remember anything from last night?"

I did a one-shoulder shrug. "Bits and pieces, yeah."

He shifted around in his seat. "Do you... remember anything specifically?"

Oh, no. Had I told him I would get back together with him? Even if I did, he should've known not to get his hopes up or take my word for it considering how drunk I was.

I knew how I felt about Axel. My feelings were no secret, but I didn't know what was best for me. Did I really want to risk putting myself back in a relationship where my significant other still hadn't broken his worst habits? Was I actually ready enough to risk another possible heartbreak?

"No, I don't think so," I said, even though I vaguely did remember.

Axe sighed. "I assumed you wouldn't remember." His eyes dropped down to his plate and then back up at me. "Tate, please take me back. All I need is one more chance," Axe said, grabbing my hand from across the table. There was a longing in his eyes, a specific type of pain that no one could fake. I didn't say anything, my tired eyes stuck on him. "Because all I know is that I'm absolutely fucking dreading the moment that you leave and go back to your dorm, the moment we go back to being strangers, as if we don't know each other and never have. At the end of the day, I'll do whatever you need me to do, even if that means being miserable. I'll leave you alone forever, as long as that's what makes you happy. Because the one thing I care about the most is your happiness. But is being apart really what makes you happy?" His eyes studied mine nervously, waiting for my reply.

I thought about everything that Axe and I had been through. He had always done everything for me, treating me like royalty. He put me first, made me feel wanted, and loved me more than anything.

What I hated the most about my relationship with Connor was that because it was my first relationship, my "first love," I was put under the impression that that's what love was. That it was being treated as an option rather than a person. That it was putting someone first even after they repeatedly put you last. But after meeting Axe, after falling in love with him, it was clear what love was. Love was putting someone else's needs before your own. Love was not caring about the amount of time or money you spent on them. Love was not blaming someone for your issues or guilting and manipulating them into doing what you wanted them to do. Love was wanting the best for someone, no matter what the outcome was going to be for you. Love was forgiving someone for their mistakes.

My eyes slightly glossed over as I shook my head. "No," I quietly said. "Being apart sucks." My head throbbed as a few tears fell. As I closed my eyes, I felt Axe's arms around me.

"I hate myself for hurting you. And I never wanna be the reason for your tears ever again," he said. I stood as I buried my head into his chest and cried into him for a moment. "I'm so sorry," he added.

His hand rubbed my back, comforting me. I finally managed to stop my tears, my hungover eyes looking up at him. All I did was nod.

His eyes slightly brightened with hope. "You'll take me back?"

"Yes."

His mouth turned upwards, revealing those dimples that I loved so much. He picked my feet up off the ground, hugging me to him. When he set me back down, he kissed my face repeatedly, covering every square inch of it.

"I love you. I love you. I love you," he said in between kisses. And somehow, all my worry and sadness faded away.

We drove to the dorms, preparing to deal with Gianna. I took a deep breath as we stood outside of Gianna and Claire's room, nervous as to how Gianna would react to our drop-in.

"I'm scared," I whispered to Axe. "What if she unleashes her wrath on us?"

Axe covered his mouth as he laughed, trying to keep quiet. I playfully hit him, smiling as I brought my hand up to the door and knocked a few times.

"Hey," Gianna said when she saw me. Her eyes drifted to Axe. "Oh, you're here too."

Axe rolled his eyes as we walked in. Gi didn't seem like she had been crying. Her anger was still the main emotion that she was feeling.

"Gi, what happened?"

She opened her mouth to speak, then snapped it shut when Axe rested an arm around my waist. "Well it seems like you two made up."

"Yeah... we did," I said, swallowing my nerves to hear her reaction.

The room was silent. She didn't seem too pleased, but then the sides of her mouth slowly turned upwards. "I'm glad," she nodded at me, her eyes shifting to Axe. "But I'm still mad at you."

He dropped his chin. "Gi," I intervened, "I know you think Axe took me from ATA for his own sake and that he slept with me after, but neither of those things happened." She eyed me, trying to determine if I was telling the truth, or if I was just trying to cover for Axe. "I'm serious. You know I wouldn't lie to you, especially about something like this." She crossed her arms as she thought.

"I love her," Axe said. "I would never, ever, ever do anything like that to her. And it sort of hurts that you'd think I would," he scratched his head.

Gi let out a long exhale, her arms still crossed as she tilted her head at Axe. "Okay, I believe you."

"Good. Now tell us what happened with Ash," I insisted.

"We argued last night when he kept asking you about Axel and then we argued again when we couldn't find you. Then we argued *again* at the apartment. He kept defending Axel for everything and it was pissing me off."

"Well, all of that has been cleared up now, so you guys can go back to normal, right?"

"No, because one thing led to another and we each said things that we can't take back," she said, looking down.

I wanted to ask for specifics, for more details about what was said, but I didn't want to push her too hard. If she really wanted to tell me, she'd do it on her own without me having to ask.

"You guys can fix it, you know," I said.

"I don't know," she shook her head.

"If Axe and I can fix what happened between us, then you and Ash can too."

"But—"

"Do you want to be with him?" I interrupted.

Her eyes trailed upwards, reaching me. Her bottom lip quivered, finally releasing the tears that she was trying to hold in. I didn't know if she had been keeping them in to try to be strong, or if it was because she simply didn't want to cry in front of Axe.

"Of course, I do," she cried.

My sympathy for Gianna was growing. I knew what she was feeling. She felt torn. She felt like she had just lost her other half. The pain that I felt when Axe and I ended was excruciating and by the look in her eyes, she was feeling it too.

I looked up at Axe, compassion for Gianna resting on my face. He read my mind and sighed, letting go of the tension that he had been holding against Gianna.

"Help," I whispered.

His green eyes glowed into me as he nodded once. "Have you talked to him since you left the apartment?" he asked Gi.

She shook her head. "No. I tried calling him, but he didn't answer."

Axe scratched his head, taking out his phone. He dialed Ash's number and held the phone up to his ear, but after it rang multiple times, it went to voicemail. "No answer. So, you don't know where he is?"

"No."

"I think I know where he might be," Axe said, putting his hands in his pockets.

Axe held my hand as he drove. Gianna sat in the back, staring out the window, lost in thought. She was definitely in her head, replaying the fight between her and Ash, probably regretting some of the things that had been said.

I immediately recognized the house as we pulled up to it. The big, beautiful home that belonged to Amberly and Drew.

"Where are we?" Gianna asked from the backseat.

"My sister's," Axe replied, unbuckling his seatbelt.

Gianna had been wanting to meet Amberly for the longest time and now, she finally would. These definitely weren't the best circumstances for her to meet Amberly, but we currently didn't have a choice. We needed to find Ash. There was the possibility that he wouldn't be here, but Axe seemed pretty confident that he knew his brother well enough to know where his escape place was.

I clung onto Axe's arm as he rang the doorbell with his free hand. Gianna stood behind us, shifting back and forth nervously. She was iffy about being here, but it was clear that her desire to fix things with Ash was giving her motivation.

A smiling Amberly opened the door.

"Oh my God, Tate! Hi!" she yelped, enveloping me for a hug.

"Wow. You hug Tate before your own brother," Axe said.

She looked up at him and laughed. "Well, she's my favorite."

I giggled, happy to know that I was still on Amberly's good side. She gave Axe a quick hug, going up on her tippy toes to reach him. When they pulled away, her eyes rested on Gi. "I'm gonna assume you're Gianna."

"Yeah," Gi shyly said, stepping forward. She didn't know if she was supposed to hug Amberly or not. Her nerves were evident, but Amberly looked past them. She wrapped her arms around Gi and squeezed her. Amberly was such a motherly figure, always smiling, and always making sure everyone was okay and comfortable. Gianna's eyes widened as we walked in, just as amazed as I was when I first strode in on Thanksgiving.

Axe turned to Amberly. "Where is he?" he asked, without giving any context whatsoever.

Amberly knew exactly who and what he was referring to. "He's in the living room," she whispered.

Axe turned back to us. "I'm gonna go in there first before Gi does so that he's not too overwhelmed."

We both nodded, my heart slightly yearning as Axe walked away. I had just gotten him back and I wanted to be with him every second to make up for the time we had lost.

Gi nervously played with her hair as she looked around, taking in every detail of the house.

"Stop being so nervous," I whispered.

"What if he won't take me back?"

"I'm pretty sure he will."

"Well what if I don't want him back?"

I made a face, confused as to what she was saying and concerned as to why we were here if she didn't want him back.

"The fuck do you mean?" I yelled in a whisper.

She brought her arms up and dropped them down to her sides. "Ugh, I don't know. I don't even know what I'm saying. I don't know what I'm doing with my life."

"Just breathe," I said, placing a hand on her shoulder. She shut her eyes and took a deep breath. "You love him, right?" Her eyes stayed closed as she nodded. "Then stop doubting yourself and just be with him. The longer you try to stay away, the worse you're gonna feel. Trust me."

Gi's blue eyes flickered open. "Okay, yeah. You're right."

Axe reappeared. He cocked his head towards the living room. "Gianna, you can go in there."

She gave a subtle smile. "Okay, thanks." I watched as her feet slowly and nervously walked towards the living room. Whatever conversation was about to occur between her and Ash, I hoped it would end well.

"You wanna go talk upstairs?" Axe asked.

I felt a turning in my stomach, anxiety rushing through me as I wondered why he wanted to talk. Usually, when someone asked if you could talk, it was never good. Especially when that person was your significant other.

"Okay."

He led me by the hand upstairs, into the same room that we stayed in over Thanksgiving. The same room that we had shared a bed in for the first time.

Axe shut the door behind us. I anxiously shuffled over to the bed and sat, preparing to hear whatever Axe was about to throw at me. The second we made eye-contact, his lips were on mine. He kissed me passionately, revealing just how much he had missed me as he grabbed me and brought me closer.

"God, I missed you," he said, pulling away.

"Is that what you wanted to talk about?"

"Pretty much," he said, reaching for my hand. I let out a relieved sigh, my nerves washing away.

"When you asked if I wanted to talk, I thought you were gonna break up with me or something."

He drew his eyebrows together. "Absolutely not. I just got you back. I'm never letting you go again."

I grinned, resting my head on his shoulder. I clenched my eyes shut when my headache returned. I was still hungover.

Axe brought his lips down to my forehead, planting a gentle kiss, sending butterflies throughout me. I missed his simple acts of affection. It was one of my favorite things that he did.

"I'm glad that nightmare is over. I didn't know how much longer I could go without you," he said. His thumb softly stroked my cheek, emerald eyes studying me. "Again, Tate, I'm so sorry. I put you through so much unnecessary bullshit."

"It's okay."

"No, it's not. I let you down. You deserve the entire world and that's what I plan on giving to you."

His words made my heart happy, a feeling that it hadn't fully felt in weeks. I grinned, then gave him a quick kiss. He wrapped his arms around me, then fell back onto the bed, pulling me with him so that we were laying instead of sitting.

Axe gripped my hand, examining it. "God, I missed these tiny hands. And arms," he said, brushing my arm with his fingers. "And your cute, little nose," he added, placing a kiss on the bridge of my nose. "And your perfect lips and your pretty eyes."

"I missed you too, Axe," I giggled.

His emerald eyes studied mine. "Too bad we can't go to the arcade today. It'd cure your hangover instantly."

I grinned. "You wouldn't wanna go, anyways. I'd beat your ass in skee-ball again."

"I let you win last time."

"No, you didn't," I laughed. "You genuinely sucked."

He chuckled and kissed my cheek.

There was a knock on the door. Axe and I both sat up. "Come in!" Axe shouted.

The door creaked open, revealing a smiling Ash. Gianna stood next to him, seeming content. "You guys wanna come hang out downstairs with us?" Ash asked.

"Sure," I responded, standing up. Axe placed his hands on my hips, still seated on the bed.

"We'll be down in a few," Axe said.

Ash nodded, then shut the door. It seemed like everything had gone well between Gianna and Ash, which made me satisfied. I had gone through hell for weeks, and the last thing I wanted was for Gianna to go through that too. Her and Ash had never really had issues before now. But then again, they were not as dysfunctional as Axe and I, who each had complicated pasts and bad habits.

Axe pulled me onto his lap. His arms hugged my middle as he buried his face into the crook of my neck. I snickered at the feeling, reminded of how much I had fucking missed him. I never wanted to be without him again.

"How are you feeling?" he asked, his hot breath hitting my neck.

"Still a little icky, but it's manageable."

He had asked me numerous times throughout the day, and although it was repetitive, it was nice knowing that he cared so much.

"You should drink some more water. C'mon, let's go get you some."

I was still sitting in his lap when he put one hand under my legs and one behind my back as he stood, carrying me bridal style.

"Axe, I have my own legs. You don't have to carry me," I laughed.

"I'm just practicing for a few years from now," he winked with a smirk.

"Well, you're gonna be waiting a while."

"I'll wait however long you need me to," he said.

I smiled as I rested my head near his collarbone, content as he carried me in his strong arms, the arms that I missed so much. When we got into the living room, Gianna gave a small smile as she watched Axe lower me down to my feet.

"I'm gonna get you some water. I'll be right back." He kissed my cheek and headed towards the kitchen.

"Well, you two seem to be in a much better mood than earlier," I said.

Gi couldn't contain her smile as she sat by Ash on the brown couch, her feet resting upon his lap.

"Yeah," she said, glancing over at Ash. "Everything's good."

"Good!"

Axe returned with a tall glass of water, handing it to me.

"Thank you," I said.

He nodded once. "Make sure you drink it all. It'll help."

I smiled, taking a gulp. I liked how caring Axe was. Not only was it refreshing, but it was a feeling that I knew I wanted to have for a very long time.

Amberly trudged in, her smile never dulling. "Okay, okay, okay! I have the best idea."

Axe rubbed his eyes and then dropped his head back. "What is it?"

"Why don't you guys stay here tonight, and we can have a wine night!"

Axe and Ash traded glances with each other. "Sis, you know we're not really into wine."

Amberly rolled her eyes. "Not you two! Me and the girls."

"You want just them to stay here tonight? Not us too?" Axe raised his eyebrows.

"Yes. It's girl time."

I didn't think Amberly had a lot of girlfriends, especially ones her age. Most of her time in her late teens and early twenties was dedicated to raising the boys. And she had Drew, who was not only her fiancé now, but her best friend too.

Axe looked at me for a second before returning his attention towards his sister. A pained expression stretched across his face. "But I just got her back. I wanna be with her."

"Boo-hoo. You can see her tomorrow," Amberly said, waving it off. Axe rolled his eyes at her remark. Amberly's everlasting grin turned to a straight line, a serious look taking over her face. "Don't you roll your eyes at me, young man!"

"Sorry," Axe said, looking down.

Amberly was still a motherly figure to the boys and she had been for six years, ever since their mom passed. Since she took part in raising them, she knew them better than anyone did. And it was clear that the boys respected her for it.

"I wasn't born with any sisters, just you two idiots!" Amberly expressed, dropping her hands to her sides. "So, don't ruin my fun!"

"I'd love to stay," Gianna chimed in.

"Baby..." Ash started.

"I want to," Gi said.

I wanted to stay and hang out with Amberly, but I still felt like shit from the night prior and on top of that, I wanted to stay with Axe. But if Gianna and Amberly were going to be hanging out all night, I didn't want to be left out.

The girls both looked over at me, waiting to hear my answer on if I would join in or not.

"I want to, but I'm still really hungover, so I don't think drinking more will help," I said.

"Oh, no worries! You don't have to have any if you don't want to. And you guys can borrow clothes or face wash or anything else you guys need."

Amberly seemed so excited to hang out with us, and even though I didn't feel so great, I didn't want to let her down. After all, I didn't know if she knew what had happened between Axe and I, but I was on her good side at the moment, and I didn't want to ruin that.

"Okay," I nodded. "Yeah, I'd love to."

Amberly jumped up and down in excitement. "Oh my gosh, I'm so excited!"

She stopped jumping, glancing over at Axe with a straight face, and then Ash.

"What?" Ash asked.

"It's officially girl time. So, unless you two magically have vag's now, get out."

Axe took a deep breath, shaking his head. He wrapped his arms around me, squeezing the life out of me.

"I'm gonna miss you," he said, planting a kiss on my lips.

"I miss you already," I said as he pulled away. We walked them over to the door, my heart aching as he looked back at me once, giving a wink before walking out.

"Do you guys wanna cook or order food?" Amberly asked right away.

"I'm fine with either," I said, shrugging.

"Me too," Gi agreed.

"You know what? Fuck it. Let's go get a nice dinner. We'll make Drew pay," she laughed.

Gi and I chuckled as Amberly went upstairs to grab one of Drew's credit cards. She returned with a smiling face, and we followed her out the door.

The restaurant we went to was very nice. It reminded me of the one Axel and I went to on our first date, except Brooke didn't work at this one, so it was much better. At first, I thought I was underdressed, but most people that were dining here were wearing a nice shirt and jeans, so I figured I was okay.

"So, give us all the wedding details. Have you guys planned anything yet?" I asked, smiling.

Amberly looked down at her ring, filled with excitement. "It's going to be on June fourteenth. Most people are engaged for a full year, but we didn't want to wait."

From what I remembered, Drew and Amberly seemed very happy together. They had the type of relationship that everyone wanted. Granted, I didn't know either of them very well yet, especially Drew, but it wasn't hard to tell how strong their love was. They had been together for about four years, so it was a good time to become engaged.

"Have you picked a venue yet?" Gianna asked.

"Yeah, we chose a really beautiful outdoor venue about an hour from here. And you guys are both invited, obviously," she smiled.

I was excited to go to the wedding. It would be the first one that Axel and I attended together, but hopefully not the last.

After ordering, Amberly placed her elbow on the table, resting her chin in her hand. "So, tell me everything."

"Like, with the guys?" Gi asked, unsure if Amberly was referring to them or if she was curious about our lives in general.

Amberly nodded. "I mean, they each tell me a good amount, so I'm pretty sure I know mostly everything, but I wanna hear your guy's sides too."

I crinkled my nose as I smiled. "They tell you everything?"

"Oh, yeah." Her dusty blonde hair framed her face perfectly as she spoke. "I'm very close with both of them, which is why I wasn't surprised when Ash came by today."

Gianna's light brown hair fell in front of her face as she looked down at her lap, embarrassed that she was the reason why.

Amberly took a sip of her drink before she continued. "And Axe did the same thing," she shrugged.

I tipped my chin down towards my chest. "Axe came over too after we broke up?"

She nodded. "Yeah, it was right after he wrecked their apartment."

I thought back to that day, uneasy at the memory. I knew that Axe had destroyed the entire apartment after I left, but I didn't know that he had gone to Amberly's after. I wondered what else she knew. Maybe she already knew everything.

"What did he tell you that day?"

244

"Um," she gazed off, thinking, "he told me about the bet. He was super pissed that Ash told you. Then he told me how he fucked up and slept with some redhead and that you left."

"Yep, that's accurate," I assured her.

"I've never seen him that way, honestly."

I glanced around. "What was he like?"

"Broken," she responded shortly.

"I was too," I quietly said.

"Well, it's over now. Everything's fine now. And that goes for both of you guys. Don't dwell on any of that past stuff. No relationship is perfect. Shit happens." She scratched her head. "When it comes to those two, they're both idiots. I mean, most guys are, but Ash and Axe in particular. I'm just surprised you two deal with them."

"I'm honestly surprised that Ash deals with me," Gi said, chuckling. "I can be a handful, not gonna lie. I mean, what happened today was partly my fault too." She turned to me. "And thank you for helping me and taking me to Amberly's to fix things. I didn't get to thank you earlier."

"You were there for me when I needed you, so it's only fair to be there for you," I smiled. She squeezed my hand quickly and then released it.

"I'm glad you guys came. And I'm glad we're getting to do this. Not only is it refreshing for me to be around other females," she laughed, "but it's nice to get to know who my brother's are dating."

"Yeah, me too," Gianna and I both said in unison. We looked at each other and widened our eyes as we giggled, weirded out by our identical thoughts.

Amberly smirked. "And I just want to thank you guys for being so good to my brother's and for dealing with them, even when they're complete, confusing assholes," she said, rolling her eyes. "Ash is pretty straightforward for the most part. But Axe, on the other hand, is a little more complicated." Her attention turned directly to me. "So, bless your kind heart for putting up with him and his bullshit."

I had a feeling I knew what she was referring to when she called Axe complicated, but I wanted to hear her explain her reasoning. "You think he's complicated?"

"Definitely. When he was younger, he used to try to hide all his emotions, bottle them up, especially when it came to vulnerability, like with stuff about our parents. He still tends to do that. But for some reason, he lets it all out when it comes to you."

"Yeah, I feel like I know what you mean."

She placed her hand on mine from across the table, a very serious look on her face. "Tate, I'm telling you now. He's going to fuck up a lot. But I'm promising you, you'll never find anyone who will love you more."

Her words were reassuring, affirming that Axe did love me, and just how much he loved me. He had never had a real relationship before me, and although I only had one other than him, that one was nothing compared to Axe. My relationship with Connor was toxic, and even though Axe sometimes made mistakes, the way he loved me never changed.

It only made me more certain that I had made the right decision about giving Axe another chance. And for some reason, I wasn't scared this time.

I nodded. "I really love your brother."

"I know," she smiled. "He loves you more than anything too."

I replayed everything she had said over in my head as her and Gianna talked about Ash. My mind stopped on one detail that I had remembered regarding the day Axe wrecked the apartment. The video. The one that Ash had sent to Gi.

I waited until their conversation died down to speak again. "Is there a mall around here?"

"I think so. Why?"

"Do you think we could stop there? I really need to get something," I smirked.

Chapter Twenty-Three
The Jealousy

I sat in the living room, waiting for Axel to get back from class. I hadn't told him that I was over, because I wanted my gift for him to be a surprise. I had attempted to wrap it, which took me a long while, but even with my wrapping job, it was pretty obvious what it was.

"Hi, baby," he smiled as he walked in.

"Hi!" I said as I got up, wrapping my arms around the back of his neck. His hands rested on my lower back as he connected his lips to mine, holding them there for a few seconds.

"I missed you last night. How was it at my sister's?"

"It was good. We went out to dinner and stopped at the mall and then watched movies all night."

"So, she wasn't annoying?"

I pulled my eyebrows together as I laughed. "No, of course not."

He let out a breath. "Good."

I bit my lip as I swung my arms back and forth. "I got you something."

He tilted his head at me. "Baby, I'm the one that should be buying you gifts. Not the other way around."

I walked over to where I had placed his present behind the couch, grabbing it and handing it to him.

His eyebrows raised as he held it with one hand. "Hmm, I wonder what it is," he teased. "Tate, you really didn't have to—"

"You don't even know what it is yet! Open it."

He lifted an eyebrow as he studied the wrapping job. "I think I have a pretty good idea what it is."

I rolled my eyes. "Just open it."

The small corners of his mouth turned up as he sat next to me on the couch, his thigh rubbing against mine. He slowly tore away the wrapping paper, revealing the brand-new acoustic guitar that I had bought him. It was a newer version of the one he had destroyed.

"A new guitar. I never would've guessed," he joked.

I playfully hit his arm. "I did a great wrapping job."

He laughed, still examining the gift. "Thank you, baby. You didn't have to get me a new one."

"Yes, I did. How else are you going to play songs for me?"

He shook his head, dimples sinking deeply into his cheeks. "I learned a new one actually."

My excitement levels rose. I hadn't heard Axel sing or play guitar in weeks. His voice was my favorite sound and I couldn't wait another second to hear it.

He took a deep breath as we sat on the couch. His hands felt the strings, studying the new guitar and adjusting it before he started playing. Green eyes peeked up at me once more, dimples reappearing as his grin turned up.

The melody of "Wonderwall" by Oasis began to play, slow and steady. Axe focused on the strings, lightly strumming them with his fingers. His voice echoed throughout the room, a perfect mix of raspy and graceful.

These were the moments that I had missed the most. The ones where we were just sitting around, enjoying each other's company, no matter what we were doing. I didn't want the song to end. Listening to Axe reminded me of just how much I loved him, and each time he opened his mouth to sing the next part, it felt like the very first time he had ever sang to me. Butterflies fluttering. Smiles inevitable.

I threw my lips onto Axe's the moment the song was over. He slowly placed the guitar on the ground as I swung my leg, straddling his lap. I rested my hands around the back of his neck as our lips moved together rhythmically. His lips parted, allowing my tongue to slip inside his mouth. Axe grabbed at me more intensely from my gesture, hands sliding up and down my back.

His mouth left mine, pulling away. "Stay here tonight."

I ran my fingers through his brown hair, admiring his luscious curls. "I have class kind of early in the morning, though."

Axe's perfectly pink bottom lip stuck out, revealing his pouty face. "Please? I missed you too much and I didn't get to spend a lot of time with you yesterday," he said, burying his face into my neck.

His curls tickled my neck for a second. His warm hands gently moved my hair out of the way, face still nuzzled in the crook between my neck and my shoulder. I felt his hot breath against my skin, followed by slow, wet kisses. I sighed from the feeling, his soft lips exploring my skin, making my whole body feel warm. The tingling between my thighs was developing as the desire to move into his bedroom began to grow.

"I love you," he hummed between kisses.

"I love you too."

"Please stay. We can hang out all night and watch movies and cook dinner," he said, finally pulling away from my neck to look at me again. I groaned when the good feeling went away, my neck already missing his lips.

"What else do you have in mind?" I asked, pulling my mouth over to the side.

His hands supported my back as he lowered me onto the couch, positioning himself on top of me. One hand ran along the side of my body, starting from the side of my breast and traveling all the way down to my hip. "Loving you over and over and over again," he whispered, his lips retreating back to my neck. I moaned feeling him above me, suddenly bothered by the few layers of fabric between us.

I placed my index finger under his chin and gently pushed it so that I could place my mouth against his. He kept one hand beside my head to stable himself, the other hand digging under me to find my ass, squeezing lightly when he finally found what he was looking for.

"Stay," he said again.

"Alright," I finally agreed. "I just need to run over to my dorm to grab some of my stuff."

"Okay. Do you want me to drive you?"

"No, it's fine. I have my car with me."

"Okay, babe," he said, getting off me. He reached a hand out, offering to help me stand up. I gladly accepted it. "I'm gonna shower while you're gone."

I made a small pouty face. "No, wait for me to get back."

His sexy smirk spread across his face at my words. "I was hoping you'd say that."

I finished packing my bag after leaving the apartment, making sure I had everything I needed to spend the night and get ready for class tomorrow morning. I sighed when I looked at Penelope's side of the room, absent of her presence. She was still trying to avoid me, still mad about the conversation we had regarding Lucas. She didn't want to accept that her boyfriend tried hitting on me, so instead, she denied it. I didn't blame her, but it was frustrating.

I jumped when there was a sudden knock on the door, my shoulders rising and falling as I sighed, walking towards it.

"Hey," Lucas grinned.

I forced a friendly smile. "Hey, um, Penelope's not here. I thought she was with you actually."

"No, she's with Serena right now."

I brought my brows together, my mouth forming a straight line. "Who?"

"Her new friend from one of her classes," he said, waving it off.

"Oh, okay. Well if you knew she wasn't here..." my eyes darted around, confused, "why are you here then?"

He shifted his weight back and forth. By the look on his face, I had a feeling of what he was going to say, but I really hoped that I was wrong. I didn't have any more rejection in me to hand out to him.

"Well, I was just on my way to get dinner at the dining center. Do you want to join?"

I rested my weight against the cracked open door, making sure it was closed enough to let him know that he wasn't welcomed inside. "I can't."

"May I ask why?"

"I just can't. I'm busy right now."

"Are you sure you can't?"

"I'm sure," I gritted through my teeth.

"Is being busy really the only reason?"

Once again, he was pushing my buttons. And this time, I was out of patience. "There are numerous reasons," I said firmly. "One, you're still with my roommate. Two, I don't think my boyfriend would appreciate that. And three, I don't have feelings for you, so dates or hang outs or whatever the hell you want to call them are not going to happen."

His eyes narrowed. "Boyfriend?"

Out of everything I said, that's the only part he paid attention to?

"Yeah," I said with a straight face.

Lucas's jaw twitched, outrage growing in his eyes. He went from zero to one hundred really quickly. "Are you back together with Axel?"

"Not that it's any of your business, but yeah. I am."

He rubbed his chin, shaking his head. "Unbelievable." I rolled my eyes, taking a deep breath as I watched Lucas sizzle. "You're seriously going to be with him after what he did to you?"

"Yeah," I nodded.

"Why?"

"Because I love him," I announced.

Lucas shifted around, unhappy with my response. "You shouldn't be with him."

The conversation didn't need to be continued. Lucas didn't approve of me being with Axel. He never did and he probably never would. But I didn't care. It wasn't his relationship, and I certainly wasn't interested in his opinion.

I moved back, pushing the door closed, but a hand smacked onto the center of it, holding it open just enough for me to see the anger in Lucas's eyes. It was strange how his personality had slowly gotten darker throughout the school year. When first semester began, he was understanding about my rejection, accepting it in the moment at least, before trying again another day. But now, it seemed as if his patience was running out while mine was. I didn't know why he had such an infatuation with me, or why he seemed so unable of letting me go, especially when nothing had ever even happened between us.

"Leave," I demanded through my teeth.

"You're gonna regret this," he breathed.

"No, I'm not."

A devious grin came across his face as he lowered his hand from the door. He stood for a second as he looked at me, as if he was silently mocking me for reasons that I didn't know. I carefully watched as Lucas slowly walked down the hall, away from my room, leaving me with nothing but an unsettled feeling.

My tired eyes fluttered open the next morning. I rolled over in the sheets, immediately satisfied by the sight of Axel next to me. I knew I needed to get up and get ready for class, but I couldn't help but get sidetracked by him, studying every inch of him. His head was turned towards me, revealing his sharp jawline and messy hair. A couple of his tattoos poked out from underneath the blankets. He was still tangled up in the mess of the sheets, a clear sign of what happened in the bed the night prior. Twice. And once in the shower.

I slowly got out of bed, trying my hardest not to wake him up. I poured myself a bowl of cereal and ate quickly, then threw on my dance attire for class, tossing my hair up into a ballet bun. I tiptoed back into Axel's room, quietly making my way around to his side of the bed. I bent down, placing a gentle kiss on his forehead. I took one last look at him, his chest rising and falling peacefully. He was such a beautiful sight. And suddenly, I was overcome with a massive feeling of hope that I would be able to wake up next to him every day.

After class, I headed back towards my dorm, stopping in a café that was connected to the bookstore. The café was pretty large, tables lined up and down for students to sit and relax or do homework at. I wasn't a huge coffee person, hence why I had only been there a few times throughout the year, but I was certainly in a coffee mood now. I needed some, considering how late I was awake and how early I had woken up. Plus, dance class killed my already nonexistent energy levels.

I stood in line, patiently waiting for my turn to order. I wasn't a big fan of hot drinks, and even though the early March air was still kind of cold, I wanted an iced coffee anyways.

I felt a tap on my shoulder, causing me to swing around, praying to God that it wasn't Lucas again. But instead, an even worse sight stood before me.

Olivia's red locks flowed past her shoulders, a bitchy smile plastered across her face.

Great. Just what I needed.

"Hey, Tatum," she said, her high-pitched tone deafening me. "I heard you're back together with Axel."

I moved forward in the line as I shot her a look, curious as to why she was curious. "Yeah?"

She lifted her brows, scanning me up and down, a disapproving look coming across her face.

I narrowed my eyes at her for a second as I crossed my arms, turning back around in line. Hopefully, ignoring her would cause her to go away. I didn't want to let her presence or her words get to me. I was sick and tired of people and things getting in the way of Axe and I's happiness. Whether if it was one thing or another, one person or another, there was always something that was trying to get between us.

I ordered my coffee and within two minutes, it was ready for me. I gave a friendly smile to the barista as I paid and left a tip in the tip jar, then pushed past Olivia, pretending she wasn't there. I obviously hadn't forgotten about the morning I walked in on Axe and Olivia. It was impossible to forget something like that, but at this point, I felt like I had successfully pushed it to the back of my mind. I was determined to get things right with Axe this time and not let anything get between us. Including my negative thoughts. Ever since dinner with Amberly the other night, her words had been stuck in my head. Axe would fuck up a lot. But no one in the world would be able to love me more than him. He may have had flaws, but I did too. And it was up to us to work together to help each other break our bad habits and to accept each other's flaws.

Olivia's little annoying footsteps followed me out of the café. I sped up to get away from her, not turning around to meet her gaze, but it was her voice that caught my attention.

"Your boyfriend is really good in bed by the way! And just for the record, he said the same thing about me."

I stopped dead in my tracks, slowly turning to face her. "What did you just say?" I seethed. If people wanted to say bullshit things about me, then whatever. So be it. But once they brought Axel into the equation, that's where I drew the line.

She was still a good five feet away, but she leaned in towards me. "That your boyfriend thinks I'm good. And that I'm better than you," she said slowly.

I gave a vicious grin, the bitchiest one I could manage. I stepped closer to her, until I was directly in her face. "Yeah? And that's why he's dating me and not you, right?" Her victorious smile started to fade, which only fueled my fire even more. "You know, I'm really not the type to slut shame or make girls feel bad for sleeping around, because at the end of the day, girls should back each other up and if someone wants to have sex without being in a relationship, then that's their decision and I don't judge them for it. But when you're deliberately sleeping with a guy who you *know* has a girlfriend, then you kind of deserve it." I gave another wicked smile, still face to face with her. I could tell she was starting to back down, not having expected me to call her out this time.

"Are you calling me a slut?"

"Do you feel like one?" I asked, emotionless. She looked away, unwilling to meet my gaze or answer my question. I waited to continue until she looked back at me again. "Stay away from me. And stay the fuck away from Axel," I said, turning around and walking away, nonchalantly sipping on my iced coffee.

It was blatantly obvious that Olivia was jealous. When she first met Axel, she wanted to tame him. She wanted him all to herself.

After waking up next to Axe and studying every detail of him while he slept this morning, it was impossible to deny that he was irresistible. Easily one of the most attractive, if not, *the* most attractive man on campus. I couldn't blame other girls for wanting him, but I could blame other girls for trying to take him. And the last thing I was going to do would be to let that happen.

I sipped on my coffee all the way back to my dorm, thinking about how great it was going to be to sprawl out in bed and take a nap before my next class. This was usually the time of day where neither Penelope nor I had any classes for a few hours. Sometimes we would go get lunch or each lay in silence and nap, but knowing her and how mad she still was at me, she wasn't going to be in the room.

I took a deep breath as I made my way down the hall, slightly picking up my pace to reach my room faster. I twisted the knob, my enthusiasm dying at the sight. Everyone stopped and looked at me as I walked in.

Penelope was at her desk, while Lucas and Jason made themselves comfortable on the futon. Fire immediately coursed through my veins. Not only was I pissed that Lucas and Jason were here, but how the hell was I supposed to nap in peace now?

A tall girl sat in my desk chair, her straight blonde hair barely making it past her shoulders. Her big brown eyes lit up when I walked in, matching how perfectly straight her teeth were as she smiled. "Hi! You must be Tatum. I'm Serena," she beamed.

"Hi Serena. It's nice to meet you," I said, trying my hardest not to explode all my anger out on this sweet girl who I didn't even know. My eyes darted back to everyone else in the room, trying to divert my anger away from Serena. The only time Penelope was actually here while I was, she had Lucas *and* Jason over? I had been tolerating both of them all year, and now, I was out of patience. Having Lucas here was bad enough, especially since he was the whole reason why Penelope and I even had tension in the first place. But to bring Jason here too? After he put his hands on me and after everything he put Claire through? No, thanks. I wasn't in the mood for the bullshit.

I gestured to the guys. "You guys need to leave."

"Why?" Penelope questioned.

"Serena, I don't really know you, but you seem sweet, so I don't mind if you stay," I said. "But I live here too and I'm not comfortable having them here."

"Why do you even care? You're never here half the time," Penelope argued.

"How the hell would you know? You're never here when I am."

She opened her mouth to fight back, but Jason beat her to it. "What are you gonna do? Have your boyfriend come over and tell us to leave?" he mocked me, nudging Lucas as they both began to chuckle.

I honestly didn't understand why they thought it was funny, when they both knew that neither of them would stand a chance against Axel. "Yeah, I am actually. And I'm sure he would enjoy kicking both of your asses at the same time, so..." I paused, holding my phone up to show that I was serious.

They looked at each other, trying to determine if they should leave or stay to see what would happen next. Lucas whispered something to his best friend, prompting Jason to turn back at me with venom in his eyes. I'd be lying if I said I wasn't a little intimidated by the way they were looking at me with such hatred, but I wouldn't let it show. And I certainly wasn't going to back down. They stood, sauntering in my direction. I moved to the side, allowing them to pass. Jason walked out first, but Lucas stopped, his eyes targeting me.

"Your boyfriend can't protect you forever," he said, jaw twitching before he followed his friend's lead.

But what the hell was that supposed to mean?

Chapter Twenty-Four
The Blood

It had been a few days since I had kicked Lucas and Jason out of my dorm room, and Penelope was as pissed as ever. She purposely wouldn't sleep in the room when she knew I was there, and I was tired of her bitching every time I was, so I decided to stay the night at Axel's.

I used my key to walk in, laughter taking over me by the sight of Axe and Ash doing repeated push-ups in the living room. Axe was shirtless, his back exposed, revealing his defined muscles as the hem of his boxers stood out of his black jeans.

Goddamn.

"What the hell are you two doing?" I giggled, setting my bag down.

"Push-up contest," Ash spoke, out of breath.

I tucked my curled hair behind my ear and tilted my head, watching the show. Axe's muscles tensed each time he went down, his arms lowering him passed a ninety-degree angle. I bit my lip at the sight, enjoying the view. After another minute or so, Ash's arms began to get tired, each push-up becoming slower, harder, a bigger struggle. But Axe didn't seem to be having any issues. He moved at the same pace.

Ash dropped onto his stomach, groaning. "Damnit!" he yelled, out of breath.

Axe grinned as he stood up, laughing at Ash on the ground. He pointed at his brother. "Sucks to suck, bro."

Ash slapped Axe's ankles, and Axe jumped to escape his brother's hands as he made his way over to me.

"Is that really what you guys do in your free time?"

"Hell, yeah."

"I'm gonna fucking win next time," Ash said from the floor.

"You say that every time," Axe rolled his eyes. "How was your day?" he asked as he turned back to me.

"Boring," I shrugged, lightly running my hands over his dragonfly tattoo. "How 'bout you?"

"Boring," Axe agreed. He checked the time on his watch, his face dropping at the sight. He studied my face and then grabbed it on both sides, leaving a tender kiss on my lips. "You're perfect."

"There's no such thing as perfect."

"Yes, there is. I'm lookin' right at it," he brought his eyebrows in, an irresistible smirk stretched across his face as he walked backwards towards his room, keeping his eyes locked on me. He slipped inside for a moment, reemerging with a white t-shirt in hand.

Axe tossed the shirt over his head, hiding the perfect lines on his abdomen, along with his dragonfly tattoo. "Ash, what time are you leaving?"

"I'm gonna take a quick shower and then leave shortly after."

"Where are you going?" I asked.

He sat up, resting his arms on his knees. "I've got this internship thing at some company for one of my business classes. It's only a few days long, so I'll be back on Saturday."

"Sounds fun."

"Not at all," he shook his head, standing up.

Axe mocked his brother for a moment, until Ash disappeared into the bathroom. The pipes croaked as the shower turned on.

"I'll be back soon," Axe said, throwing his backpack over his shoulder.

"What? Where are you going?" I cried.

"I've got a chem lab. It shouldn't take too long."

"How long?"

He shrugged. "About two hours. Two and a half tops."

I made a pouty face, making it evident that I didn't want him to go, but never would I ever ask him not to. I cared about Axe and I wanted what was best for him. And being the reason why his grades would suffer would make me a selfish girlfriend. The next two and a half hours may be boring, but I wanted him to succeed, which meant he had to go to his lab.

"I'll be back as soon as possible," he said. His hands dug into his pocket, retrieving his wallet. He pulled out a hundred- dollar bill, handing it to me. "Here, baby. You can go to the store and get a bunch of snacks and stuff for us to make dinner together when I'm back."

I gave a small smile, lightly accepting the money. I hated when Axe spent so much money on me, but knowing that the money was for things for us to share, and not just him spoiling me, made me feel better.

He placed a hand on my hip, pulling me in to give me one more kiss on the lips. "Love you," I said as he pulled away.

"I love you the most," he replied, dimples accompanying his grin. He turned back to me with his hand on the doorknob. "Just call me if you need anything, okay?"

I nodded, sadness overcoming me as Axe walked out. He had been gone for three seconds and I already missed him.

I moved all my stuff into Axe's room, making sure it wasn't making a mess in the living room. I set out for my car, trying to walk as slow as possible, so that more time would pass. A few hours didn't seem like a long time, but when it was a few hours of me waiting for Axel to get back, I knew it would feel like forever.

I made a short grocery list in the car before I started driving, trying to make sure that I wouldn't forget any ingredients we would need for dinner. My car drove slowly, still waking up from its sleep in the chilly March air.

I casually scanned the aisles of the grocery store, checking everything off of my list as I hoped and prayed that I wouldn't see anyone that I knew. I hated when that happened. It always caused some sort of awkwardness to rest in the air, especially when you ran into people that you knew, but didn't know well enough to know if you were supposed to say hello to them or not. But on top of that, I hoped I wouldn't run into Olivia, Brooke, Lucas, or Jason. Throughout the year, I had made a lot of friends, but I also met people who I did not get along well with. Which was fine, I guess. That was part of life.

I placed all the bags into the backseat of the car, too lazy to pop the trunk. It had only been about an hour when I arrived back into the parking lot of the apartment, which meant that Axel still wouldn't be back for another hour and a half or so. Ash's car wasn't in its usual spot, so he had already left. I sighed knowing that I would be all alone until Axe got back.

I grabbed the few grocery bags that I had, happy that I wouldn't have to make two trips out to my car. I trudged up the stairs, getting my key ready to use. Each time I looked at my key, it gave me a warm, fulfilled feeling. Knowing that Axe wanted me to have my own key, knowing that I was welcome to come to the apartment any time, made me happy.

I jiggled the key into the lock and opened the door, flipping on the light-switch as I stepped inside.

"Lucas," I jumped, dropping the bags on the floor. I was taken off guard, immediately uncomfortable by the sight of Lucas standing at the beginning of the hall.

"Hey Tate," he said, his smug smile only causing me to become more unsettled. I normally wasn't afraid of Lucas, but right now, I was fucking terrified.

"What are you doing here?" I quietly asked, unsure if I wanted to hear his real answer or not. I remained close to the door, prepared to make a run for it if I had to.

He tilted his head to the side. "I came here for you, Tate," he eerily said.

"How did you get in?"

Lucas reached into his back pocket, holding up a keychain and dangling it in front of his face. My keychain. My lost set of keys. I had thought this whole time that I lost them, but they weren't actually lost. Lucas had taken them from my room. And then it dawned on me. The entire time that he had been with Penelope was really just his own way of getting closer to me. I wondered if he had taken any of my other things without me noticing.

A little bit of anger started to bubble up inside of me. I knew that Lucas had been interested in me all year, but I never knew how crazily infatuated with me he actually was. I never thought he would've taken it this far. I thought about all the times that I had felt followed throughout the year, all the times I felt like someone was watching me. At the mall. At the library. On the balcony at the apartment. Walking around campus at night. The way he would randomly show up places that I was at, passing it off as a coincidence. It all made sense.

"Have you been following me around all year?" I asked.

"Occasionally."

"Why?"

260

"Why not?" he shrugged.

I was scared. I didn't know what Lucas was planning on doing. And I didn't know what he was capable of. The only thing I could think of to make him leave was to threaten him.

"Well Axel will be here any minute, so your ass better be gone when—"

"Don't lie, Tate. I know Axel won't actually be back for a while."

Fuck.

My mind started racing, wondering how the hell I was going to get out of this one. Usually, each time I turned down Lucas, people were always around. And if they weren't in the exact same room as us, there were people nearby. But right now, we were absolutely alone. No one could hear me if I screamed or needed help.

If I ran now, he would easily catch me. And then I would be fucked. I thought about Axel. The last thing he had said to me was to call him if I needed anything. Lucas would obviously see my phone out, but part of me hoped that Axel would answer quickly and hear enough through the phone to know what was happening, whether I was speaking directly to him or whether I was struggling.

I swallowed the lump of fear in my throat. "What do you want?" I asked, my voice shaking. I slowly maneuvered my phone out of my back pocket, trying not to draw too much attention to my hands.

"Well Tate," he began, looking around, his voice began to get angrier and angrier as he spoke, escalating more with each word, "I've been nothing but nice to you all year, trying to do things for you and ask you out, but you always. Blew. Me. Off. Then choose Axel over *me*? Yeah, I don't like that." The insanity in his eyes was showing, true intentions becoming clearer. "And now that Axel won't be back for a few hours, now that he's out of the way for a while, you're *mine* for now."

My heart started to race harder, adrenaline kicking in from the realization of what he was planning on doing. I dialed Axel's number as quickly as possible, but right as he answered the call, the phone was ripped out of my hand. Lucas's irritation grew as he ended the call. He slammed the phone down on the counter, diverting his attention back to me as he breathed heavily.

My phone began to buzz against the countertop. Lucas's jaw twitched, clearly aggravated from the interruption. He looked down at the screen, his face distorting into disgust. Even though I couldn't see it, I had a pretty good idea that it was Axe. My heart jumped, hoping that he would know something was wrong.

"Always in the way," Lucas said, shaking his head. He picked up my phone and launched it across the room. I cringed as it hit the wall, shattered, and fell to the floor, knowing that my only source of reaching anyone for help was officially gone. He smiled menacingly for a second. "I told you he couldn't protect you forever."

I wanted to bolt out the door, but I needed to be smart. Every move mattered. I knew I shouldn't run until there was something that would prevent him from catching up to me. My adrenaline kicked up a notch as he slowly walked towards me, stopping when we were face to face. His hands pushed my hair behind my shoulders, and I clenched my eyes shut knowing what he was about to do. I let him come closer, not because I wanted to, but because I had to. His lips touched my neck, sending shivers down my spine, absolutely disgusted by the feeling. He came even closer, until we were basically body to body and that's when I knew that now was my only chance.

I hiked my knee up to his groin as hard as I possibly could and he yelped, huddling over and falling to the floor. And then I ran. I turned and made my way out the door and down the stairs as quickly as possible, not even stopping or looking back to see if he was behind me or not. By now, it was dark out, but I ran towards my car, not knowing where the hell I was going to drive to for safety, only knowing that I was going to get the fuck out of there.

I was a few feet away from my car when I felt a hand grab me from behind and before I knew it, I was on the ground. Lucas sat on top of me, holding both of my arms down. The ground was so cold as I struggled against it. I cried out from how tight his grip was. He moved my arms above my head, transferring both of my small wrists into one of his hands. I tried to kick and free myself, but it was useless. I was too small compared to him.

I screamed as his free hand traveled up my shirt, his touch making my skin squirm.

"Stop!" I demanded, turning my head away from him. "Get off of me!"

"Shut up!" he yelled, trying to silence my screams.

The parking lot was filled with cars, but no one was outside. I wondered if anyone could hear my screams, hoping that someone would. I didn't know what he was planning on doing from here. The worst things came to mind. He could either drag me back up to the apartment, throw me into his car and take me God knows where, or he could hurt me right here, right now.

"Lucas, please," I cried. "Please let me go!"

My words went through one of his ears and out the other, ignoring my pleads entirely. His jaw twitched under his skin as he tried to tame me.

"I won't even tell anyone you were here. I swear! I won't even tell Axel," I begged, hoping that he would cave.

But there was no reasoning with him. He wasn't going to let me go until he got what he wanted. A tear escaped the corner of my eye as I struggled, fidgeting to try to get free, but distressed knowing that I wouldn't. I was about to give up. My body was getting tired from trying to fight back. It seemed as if giving up and letting Lucas do whatever he wanted to me was the easier option.

Axel's face ran through my mind again. His glistening green eyes and charming smile, my absolute favorite view in the entire world. I loved him. More than anything. Thinking about Axe made me want to fight.

I could feel my wrists becoming bruised from his grip, still holding them above my head as his hand made its way down towards my crotch. I started wiggling around more, trying my hardest to keep his hands away.

Lucas looked over to his right, his eyes widening as a tall, dark figure launched at him, tackling him off of me and to the ground. I scrambled away, standing up at the realization that it was Axel.

Lucas tried breaking free as he lay under Axe, but it was no use. Even though it was dark, there were enough lights surrounding the building to pick out the rage in Axe's eyes. A specific rage that I had never seen in him before. Axe pulled his elbow back and sent his fist flying into Lucas's face with more force than I'd ever seen. He repeatedly drilled his fist into Lucas over and over again, nonstop. He began alternating fists, still not slowing or stopping. Lucas struggled underneath him, attempting to use his arms to cover his face, but it wasn't working. After a solid minute of repeated punches, he grabbed Lucas's shirt in both hands, lifting his chest off the ground and smashing his head down against the concrete. Over and over again. Lucas's body was becoming limp.

"Axe," I called out, realizing how hurt Lucas actually was. "Axe, stop! You're gonna kill him!"

But he wasn't stopping. It was as if he couldn't hear me. I was scared what would happen if I got too close, afraid that Axe might accidentally hit me, but I had full faith in him that he wouldn't.

I rushed over to him and put my hand on his shoulder. "AXEL! STOP!" I screamed.

Axe immediately dropped him at my touch, slowly raising his shaking hands up and away from Lucas's unresponsive body. Axe was breathing heavier than I'd ever seen him, his eyes widening as he gradually stood, realizing what he had done.

I took a look at Lucas as he lay on the ground, his face unrecognizable. He had cuts and bruises scattered across his entire face, a gnarly gash above his left eyebrow. Blood was pouring out of his mouth and nose, covering his whole face. A small puddle of blood was forming underneath him, most likely coming from the back of his head. Both of his eyes were already becoming swollen. He was unconscious, but I was grateful that his chest was at least rising and falling. Not for his sake, but for Axe's. If Axe got charged with murder, it would be the end.

I had never actually seen Axel in a full-on fight until now. There had been plenty of times where I watched him intimidate people, but I had never witnessed him throw an actual punch. Axe had told me that he never wanted me to see him in a real fight because he wasn't himself when he fought. And now I finally saw it for myself.

It was no wonder why everyone was so afraid of him. Axe was ruthless. He was a monster when he fought. But I didn't care if he was a monster or not. He was still Axel. And I still loved him no matter what.

Axe stood over Lucas, staring at him, still in shock over what he had done. I didn't know how long it had been since the last time he got into a fight, but he hadn't been in one since we've been together, so it must've been a long while ago.

"Axe," I said, touching his hand. "We need to leave." He wasn't budging though, as if he was still in his own world. Axe's white shirt was splattered with blood. Blood that wasn't his. Anxiety started to race through me as I realized that sooner or later, the police would be here. And they would know that it was Axel who caused Lucas's injuries. "Axe, baby," I said, panic running through my voice. I gently grabbed his chin and turned it towards me. His eyes met mine, finally snapping out of the trance that he had been in. "We need to leave. We need to go now. The police will be here eventually."

He slowly shook his head, his chest still breathing heavily. "There's no point in running."

"What?" I brought my brows together as he grabbed me by the hand and led me back inside, leaving Lucas's destroyed body lying alone on the concrete.

He shut the apartment door, resting his hands against the wood for a second before turning to me. "Are you okay?" he asked, tears stinging his eyes as he brought his hand up to my shirt.

I hadn't even noticed that Lucas ripped it. I wasn't even sure when he had. But I didn't care. My ripped shirt was the least of my worries.

I looked up at Axe. His emeralds worriedly scanned my face. My heart swelled knowing that even after what just happened, Axe was still more worried about me than he was about himself. I couldn't hold any tears back as they streamed down my cheeks. "You came back for me."

His thumbs wiped my tears away. "Baby, of course I came back for you," he said, bringing his comforting arms around me. "When I called you back and you didn't answer, I got concerned." My head rested on his chest, arms wrapped around his middle as I squeezed. He pulled away, inspecting me for injuries. "Are you okay, though? Did he do anything bad to you?"

"He took my set of keys. The ones I thought I lost. That's how he got in and then he chased me outside. He broke my phone too," I cried. "But I'm okay."

"Don't worry, baby. I'll get you a new one." He shook his head. "I should've fucking killed him." His hands cupped the sides of my face. "I'm so sorry that I wasn't here."

"Don't be. You came back for me and that's more than enough."

Axe was still pissed. And I had a strong feeling that if I had not stopped him, he would've ended up killing Lucas. He felt guilty that he hadn't been here to protect me the moment Lucas got here. But absolutely no part of me was mad at Axe. In my mind, all that mattered was that he came back. And that was more than I ever could've asked of him.

"I'm sorry you had to see me like that," he said, almost embarrassed.

I brought my hand up to his cheek. "You have nothing to be sorry for," I replied, looking down at his bloody fist. Lucas obviously hadn't been able to land a single punch on Axel, but seeing any sort of injury on him made me want to cringe, even if that injury was from beating the shit out of someone. I grabbed an ice pack out of the freezer and carefully placed it on his knuckles. He winced at the feeling.

"I don't want you to be scared of me," Axe quietly said, worry resting in his eyes.

"I could never be scared of you," I assured him.

His thumb rubbed the top of my hand, soft eyes comforting me. We looked at each other as the sirens started blaring. Immediately, my pulse quickened, but I could tell that Axe was trying to stay calm. He placed the ice pack on the counter, and we waited in silence for a few minutes, hugging the life out of each other.

There was a knock on the door and instantly, I knew who it was. Axe took a deep breath, his eyes clenching shut as he kissed my temple. He knew who it was too.

I watched as he slowly trekked over to the door, pausing for a second before opening it.

A sheriff stood with his head tilted. He looked fairly young to be a sheriff, but he sure as hell didn't look happy. His short dark hair and brown eyes reminded me of Ash.

"Axel," the sheriff said shortly.

"I know," Axe said, looking down.

"After seeing what that kid looks like, I think this is the worst you've ever done."

"But he was attacking my girlfriend. What else was I supposed to do?"

The sheriff looked at me past Axe. He eyed my ripped shirt, studying the look of fear on my face.

The sheriff sighed. "I'll see what I can do. But for now, you know what I have to do."

"But Uncle Jesse, please—"

"I don't have a choice. I have to take you in."

Uncle? No wonder why Axe's charges had always gotten dropped. Or why he swore that the cops wouldn't do anything during my birthday party when our music was blasting. Or why the sheriff looked so similar to Ash. Or why Axe said that there was no point in running.

Axe slowly turned around, trying not to make eye contact with me as he put his hands behind his back. I stood, so shocked at the reality of what was happening.

I rushed over, panic enveloping me. "You can't take him," I begged.

"I'm sorry, but I have to. I'll be in touch with you though, miss. I'm gonna need to get a statement from you."

"Please don't take him," I pleaded.

"Tate, it's okay," Axe said.

His uncle held one of Axe's handcuffed wrists, ready to lead him out of the apartment. Axe let it happen, not fighting it. He looked back to me right before walking out the door, emerald eyes longing for me.

"I love you," he said, his eyes filled with sorrow as his uncle pulled him out of the apartment.

My eyes glossed over as I stayed in place, drowning in disbelief and denial.

What the fuck just happened?

Chapter Twenty-Five
The Orange Jumpsuit

I sat on the couch, drenched in tears for the next few hours as Ash talked on the phone, pacing the room. He was the first person I called after Axe was arrested. It took me a while to get a hold of a phone, but once I did, I called him immediately. He rushed back here in a panic, not caring that he was leaving his internship behind.

My heart hurt. It hurt just as bad as it did on the day that I walked in on Axel and Olivia. It may have hurt even more than then. Because this time, it wasn't just losing Axe that hurt; it was knowing that it was my fault. If it wasn't for me, Axe would still be here. He wouldn't be sitting in a jail cell right now.

We had no idea what condition Lucas was in, and honestly, we didn't care enough to. It sounded shitty, but he wasn't my priority. Axel was my priority. And I was going to do everything in my power to get him out of there. I knew that Ash would too.

Ash hung up the phone. "My uncle is going to build a case as quickly as possible, but he doesn't know how long it will take."

A few more tears streamed down my cheeks. "Can I go see him?"

"Probably not tonight."

"Why not?" I cried, my heart aching.

"He just got there," he softly said. "They have to get him into the system and all that bullshit."

Another tear fell down my cheek. "I need to see him."

"Tate, it's almost midnight. You've had a rough day. Just get some rest and you can go within the next few days, when my uncle calls. I doubt they would even let you in if you tried visiting this late."

I wiped my tears away and nodded, knowing that Ash was right. There was no way I could visit tonight. The reality of knowing that I would be sleeping in Axe's bed alone was a slap in the face.

"Did you call Amberly?" I asked.

"Yeah. There's really nothing she can do either," Ash placed a hand on my shoulder. His eyes were tired, stress overwhelming him, similarly to me. I didn't know how many times this had happened before, but I had hope that Ash knew how to handle it. He pulled me in for a brotherly hug, trying to comfort me.

"Get some sleep," he insisted, retreating back to his phone to make some more phone calls.

I collapsed onto Axe's bed, another ocean of tears forming in my eyes. My hand rubbed the sheets on his side of the bed, feeling its emptiness.

I studied the ceiling. Axe had protected me at all costs, no matter when or where. He was always there for me, comforting me when I needed him to. He saved me over and over again, and this time, it was my turn to save him. I would do absolutely anything to get him out right now, even if it meant switching places.

I rolled over to his side, laying where he usually would. Anything to get me closer to him right now. But I couldn't fall asleep in his warm bed, knowing that he was lying in a cold jail cell.

I woke up almost an hour before my alarm went off, unable to fall back asleep. I had barely slept at all, lying awake for hours, overwhelmed with thoughts and feelings of sorrow, denial, and guilt.

When the alarm read seven, I sprang up and got ready as quickly as possible. Visitation hours started at eight, and I planned on getting there when they opened. It had only been twelve hours since Axe got arrested, twelve hours since I'd seen or spoken to him, but I missed him as if it had been years.

I didn't really know how any of the jail shit worked. I had never been arrested before, and I didn't know if they would even let me see Axe or not, but it was worth a try.

I hopped in my car and drove straight there, not caring that I would be missing all my classes for the day. My hands were clammy on the wheel, nerves racing through my entire body, not knowing what to expect. After a short car ride that felt like a long one, I jogged inside and up to the front desk, proud of myself for making it there right on time.

"Hello," the woman at the front desk said as I approached. Her short black hair framed her face as she looked up from her computer. "How can I help you?"

"Hi, um, I'm here to visit someone."

"Okay," she said, typing into her computer. "What's their name?"

"Axel Burne."

Her eyes instantly darted up at me, studying me. A slow smile started to creep onto her face. "I'm going to take a lucky guess that you're the girl he's been talking about since he's been in?"

I smirked and gave a small nod, assuring her. My heart swelled for a second. "Can I see him?"

She gave a small sigh. "He's really not supposed to have visitors yet since he's still getting put into the system and everything," she stated. My eyes fell, disappointed. "Oh...alright. I guess I can make an exception. What's your name, sweetheart?" she asked, writing on a piece of paper.

I beamed. "Tatum Everley."

The woman wrote my name down on a visitation sticker and handed it to me. I stuck it onto the left side of my shirt, beginning to become impatient to see Axe. She passed me a clipboard with a stack of papers on it.

Paperwork. Great.

"You can sit right over there to fill out these papers."

I smiled at her as I took them, even though no part of me was smiling on the inside. I sighed as I sat down, running my fingers through the thick stack of papers. My eyes skimmed through the words on each page, fully aware that I should've been reading each word carefully, but not caring. I scribbled my initials on the lines and ten minutes later, I brought the papers back to her.

270

"Thanks, honey. An officer will be out here in just a minute to take you back there."

"Thanks," I nodded to her, sitting back down in the chairs that were near the entrance. I bobbed my knees up and down, impatience and anxiety taking over.

"Hello, ma'am," an officer with short, brown hair said as he approached. "You can follow me."

I took a deep breath as I stood. The officer walked me into a room with concrete walls on three sides. On the last wall, there was a set of glass windows. Black sectors separated each window from the next, creating a small amount of privacy for each window. I cluelessly glanced over at the officer, unsure of which window to sit at.

"You can sit wherever," he said.

I slowly chose one towards the middle, nervously waiting as the officer stayed on the other side of the room, monitoring.

I watched through the glass as another officer, this one blonde, opened a door on the other side. Axe walked through it, dressed in an orange jumpsuit with his hands handcuffed. The officer held Axe's forearm, leading him over to my window.

It was hard to see him that way. He was normally so carefree, normally so independent. But now, everything was determined for him.

Axe's face lit up when he saw me, barely waiting for the officer to take off his cuffs in order to sit down. The bags under his eyes caught my attention. He hadn't slept. He was probably up all night, uncomfortable and upset as he tossed and turned in a cold and crummy jail cell. It broke my heart.

The blonde officer stepped back, positioning himself near the door that he had brought Axel through, giving us a little bit of space.

He picked up the black phone on the wall and I followed his lead, holding the piece of plastic up to my ear.

"I was hoping it would be you," he said, smiling through the glass. He had just spent the night in prison, yet for some odd reason, his smile was just as bright as I had ever seen it.

I laughed once at his words, a small piece of my heart becoming filled, but tears forming at the same time. I wished I could touch him. Kiss him. Feel his warm and strong arms around me.

"Axe..."

"Baby, don't," he said, cutting me off. "This isn't your fault. Stop thinking that it is."

"But, it is. I'm so sorry," I responded, looking down.

"No, it's not," he paused as a single tear fell down my cheek. My guilt was inevitable, undeniable. "Please don't cry," his gentle, raspy voice begged.

I shut my eyes for a second, reminding myself that this may be the only time I got to see Axe for a while, so I should be less sappy. At least for his sake if that's what he wanted.

I gave a tiny nod. "Okay."

"Tate, listen to me very carefully, okay?"

I looked up at him, curious as to what he was about to say. My eyes studied him as he spoke, dreading the fact that there was glass between us.

"Lucas will probably be in the hospital for only a few more days or so and Jason is God knows fuckin' where," his eyes drilled into mine as he emphasized his words. "So, can you do something for me, please?"

"Anything."

"Please don't go anywhere other than class and your dorm until I get out. I don't want anyone hurting you again. If anything, and I mean *anything* at all happens to you, I will never forgive myself."

I nodded, taking in every word, but confused as to how he was so worried about me when he was the one that was currently sitting in jail.

"If you need to go to the store or anything, have Ash go with you. He's the only one I trust to watch over you while I can't be there," Axe added.

"Okay." I bit my lip as I swallowed the lump in my throat. "How long do you think it'll be?"

Axe sighed. "Hopefully not long."

I took another look at him, guilt still engulfing me. I wanted him out of there. He didn't deserve to be sitting behind glass right now. He didn't deserve to be dragged around in handcuffs or thrown into a jail cell. He deserved the world. And if I could trade places with him, I would do it in a heartbeat.

"So, they really put you in a jumpsuit that fast, huh?" I joked, trying to lighten the mood.

"Well, since it's not my first offense, they got me in right away."

272

"Orange," I wrinkled my nose.

"Yeah, it's definitely not my color," he laughed.

"Tatum? Everley, right?" a voice called from behind me. I turned, still holding the phone up to my ear. Axel's uncle was dressed in uniform as he stood near the door, patiently waiting for me to respond.

"Yeah," I confirmed.

He cocked his head to the side. "Can you come with me, please?"

I turned back to Axe. His eyes were glaring his uncle down, disappointed that our talk was about to be cut short.

"I love you. I'm going to get you out of here, okay? I promise," I said, my voice shaking.

Axe's beautiful eyes softened. "I love you more than anything. And I hope you know I don't regret what I did to protect you. I would do it a million times if I had to."

My lip quivered, distress and remorse swallowing me. I placed my hand on the glass, wishing I could touch him. He brought his hand up to the glass, matching mine, eyes staying on me.

He hung the phone back up on the wall and again, I followed, waiting to get up until he did.

'I love you,' he mouthed as he stood. I watched as the blonde officer put the handcuffs back onto Axe and pulled him out of the room.

Another tear escaped out of the corner of my eye, but I caught it before it got too far. I turned as I stood, unprepared for whatever his uncle was about to do, but I didn't even care at this point. He could've arrested me too, right here, right now, and I would've have given a single fuck. If Axe was stuck in jail, then I deserved to be too.

I followed Uncle Jesse down a long corridor. He opened a door on the left, then signaled for me to go inside. There was only one small light on in the center of the room above a table. The rest of the room was dark. And empty.

An interrogation room. Fantastic.

"Go ahead and take a seat, Ms. Everely."

I nervously sat down, still overwhelmed by everything that I was feeling from seeing Axe. Uncle Jesse sat across from me, resting his hands on the table.

"I'm glad you came in. I was about to call to ask you to come in, actually, so this worked out nicely. So," he paused, "I think we have the same goal, which is to help Axe."

"Can't you get him out of there?" I nervously begged, wondering if there was anything he could do to free his suffering nephew.

"Well, no. Not directly. That's why I need your help."

"I'll do anything."

"So, here's the deal. Due to the severity of the assault and the fact that this isn't Axel's first offense, his bail is fairly high. And even if you got the money to pay it, it doesn't mean that the charges get dropped. It would only bail him out until his court date."

"Okay..." I said, trying to take in what he was saying. "So, then what can we do?"

"Well, for starters, I'm gonna need a statement from you about everything that happened. Are you okay with that?"

"Absolutely," I nodded.

"Perfect," he said, taking out a small tape recorder and hitting the button. "Go ahead. From the beginning."

I took a deep breath and explained everything, from the moment Axel left to go to his chemistry lab, to the moment he got arrested. I told him every detail that I remembered, trying my hardest to help out as much as possible. I didn't care what Uncle Jesse needed me to do, as long as it was contributing to getting Axe out.

"Wait," he furrowed his brows, "you said he attacked you in the parking lot, correct?"

"Yes. Does that make a difference?"

"Well, we can check and see if the apartment complex has cameras set up outside. If they do, then there very well might be footage of him attacking you and if that's the case, then that might be the key to setting Axe free."

"How exactly will that help, though? Won't you just be able to see the footage of Axe fighting Lucas too, then?"

"Well, it's already very clear that Axel attacked Lucas, because he has the injuries to prove it. So, the plan is to prove that Lucas attacked you. That way, when Lucas goes to press charges against Axe, you will be able to press charges against Lucas."

I nodded, finally understanding what his plan was. "How long do you think it'll take?" I asked, picking at my fingernails under the table. I wanted Axe out now. At this point, he had been in jail for less than a day and that was already too long.

"Not sure. I'm going to try to work as quickly as possible."

"Okay... Is there anything else that I can do to help?"

He raised an eyebrow in thought. "Uh, actually yes. I need you to bring in that shirt that Lucas ripped."

"I can do that," I agreed, knowing that I would go to the apartment directly after and bring the shirt back to Uncle Jesse immediately.

"You didn't wash it or anything, right?"

"No."

"Okay, good. Don't. If there's any little bit of Lucas's DNA on there, it will help build the case even more."

He was smart. He clearly knew what he was doing. I wondered how many other times this had happened, where he had to come up with and execute a plan in order to get Axe out. But knowing how many other times this happened wasn't going to get me any step closer to freeing Axe. I thought about going to the hospital that Lucas was at and trying to talk him into dropping the charges, but I promised Axe that I wouldn't go anywhere other than class and my dorm. And he most definitely would not want me around Lucas anyways.

"Do you have any injuries or anything from the attack?" Uncle Jesse asked.

I slowly brought my fingertips to my wrists, gently pressing down on my bruises. I winced at the feeling.

I rolled my sleeves up and brought my hands above the table, showing off two gnarly bruises where Lucas had been gripping the life out of me. I had almost forgotten that the bruises were even there, too occupied by what was happening with Axe to even remember my own problems.

He raised his eyebrows as he studied the bruises, impressed by how dark they had managed to become. "Do you mind if I photograph those?"

I shook my head. "Not at all. Do whatever you have to do."

He left the room for a moment and returned with a camera. He lightly moved my wrists in different directions, taking photos at every angle.

"I'll be in touch with you," Uncle Jesse said, dismissing me out of the room.

Afterwards, I went home and brought the ripped shirt back as quickly as possible. I still had one class left for the day, but I didn't bother going.

My thoughts and guilt were consuming me whole. I wasn't going to have any motivation to do anything until Axe was freed. The system was tricky, but I prayed that Uncle Jesse's plan would work, and that it would work quickly.

I walked down the hall towards my dorm room, unprepared to deal with Penelope. I had no idea if she knew what happened or not, no idea if she had talked to or had visited Lucas in the hospital. We hadn't spoken in days, and at this point, I didn't want to. At all. The only thing on my mind was Axel. My guilt and stress were at record highs, and I swore to God that if Penelope said any little thing that would tick me off, I was not going to hold in my rage. More importantly, if she said anything negative about Axe, the hurricane would be even worse.

When I opened the door, she wasn't there. I wasn't surprised and I most definitely wasn't disappointed either. I climbed into bed and laid there for a few minutes, feeling empty. Laying there made me think about how I didn't want to go another night without him sleeping next to me. I wondered how many nights I would have to go without him. I prayed that it wasn't long, prayed that the plan wouldn't fail, prayed that he wouldn't be convicted and be locked up for years.

I had already lost him before. I couldn't do it again.

I sat up when I heard the door open, relieved when I saw Ash and Gianna walk through instead of Penelope.

"Hey," Gi said, delicately.

"Aye, let's go," Ash said, cocking his head.

"Where are we going?"

"Well, I got very strict directions from my uncle that came directly from Axe, stating that I need to go get you a new phone," he explained, shoving his hands in his pockets.

A light smile came across my face. I brought my hand up to my lips, feeling gratified knowing that this demand came specifically from Axe. It amazed me how even though he was in jail, he was still somehow finding a way to take care of me.

I sat in the back of Ash's car, staring silently out the window. I wasn't in the mood to talk, wasn't in the mood to do anything, really.

"Tate," Gi gently said from the passenger seat, "how are you feeling?"

I hadn't even told anyone what happened. For starters, I didn't have a phone to do so. And second, I didn't want to. My number one priority was to get Axe out, not waste time telling people what happened. On top of that, I didn't want anyone to see Axe differently. Whether he had destroyed Lucas's face or not, he was still a good person. My perspective of him wasn't going to change, regardless of what anyone else thought.

I didn't answer Gianna, figuring that my silence would give her a pretty good idea of how I felt. I watched out of the corner of my eye as Gi and Ash traded glances.

I picked out a new phone, trying to choose the least expensive one that they had, aware that Axel would be paying for it. He spoiled me too much as it was, let alone from jail. I barely spoke the entire time, too worried about Axe to even think of anything else.

I twisted my necklace around in my fingers as I walked back into my room, stopping at the sight of Penelope in tears on the futon. Her eyes traveled across the ground and up to me.

I wanted to know why she was crying, but I didn't want to be the first one to speak. I slowly let the door shut behind me, awkwardly entering the room.

"Hey," she sniffled.

I lightly raised my eyebrows as I kicked off my shoes. "Hey," I said passively.

She covered her eyes for a few seconds before speaking again. "I, uh, went to the hospital to see Lucas."

I paused, unsure of what Lucas had said to her. That is, if he could even speak at the moment. I had no idea how bad his injuries currently were.

"Okay… And?"

"Well I had to wait two hours for him to wake up, but once he did, he told me," she cried.

My heart was beating fast. I wasn't sure if he told her what truly happened, or if he had told her his own version of the story.

"What'd he tell you?"

"He admitted that he's been trying to get with you and that he attacked you."

"Oh."

"So, I'm sorry I didn't believe you."

I took a deep breath, almost relieved at her words. I was expecting some elaborate lie, some bullshit reason for why Axel would beat the shit out of him.

Something clicked in my head. Something that might work faster than waiting for DNA results and camera footage.

I knew I should be comforting Penelope. It was obvious that they had broken up due to the truth, but I had someone else as my top priority.

"Do you think you could get him to admit it again?"

"What?"

"Could you get him to admit it again?"

She pulled her blanket up, dropping another tear-soaked tissue next to her. "I'm not sure. Why?"

"I need to get Axel out of jail. Would you be willing to help me?"

Penelope looked down for a second in thought, her wet eyes finally starting to dry. She glanced back up at me. "Absolutely."

I drove Penelope and I back to the police station to propose my idea to Uncle Jesse. When we walked in, the same woman was at the front desk as before. Her face lit up when she saw me.

"Back already?" she joked.

I gave a shy smile, pleased by her kindness. "Most definitely," I joked back, walking up to the desk. Penelope stood behind me, waiting patiently for whatever we needed her to do.

"What can I help you with, sweetheart?"

"We need to speak to the sheriff, please."

"Got it," she said. "I'll get him right away for you."

"Thank you."

"And hey," she whispered, "technically, no one is allowed to visit more than twice a week, but I'll make an exception for you."

"Thank you so much," I expressed. I wasn't sure if maybe she knew Axe from previous arrests, which was why she felt the need to let me break the rules to visit more often, or if it was just her noticing how broken I currently was.

Within a few minutes, Uncle Jesse appeared. He nodded to me once. "How can I help you, Tatum?"

I glanced at Penelope for a second, swallowing my nerves. I had no idea if he would approve of my theory or not, but it was worth a shot.

"I, um, think I have an idea for how to get Axe out faster."

"Okay," he nodded, "shoot."

"Well, you said we first have to prove that Lucas attacked me, right?"

"Right."

I shifted my weight. "Lucas admitted to Penelope that he attacked me," I said, motioning to Penelope when I realized that the two had probably never met. "So, if we could get him to admit it again, and to record it, then will that be enough proof?"

Uncle Jesse stroked his chin with the tips of his fingers, thinking about my proposal.

"Might work. We sent some detectives to the hospital an hour or so ago to speak with Lucas. As far as I know, he has not confessed. I figured he wouldn't, which was why I began planning a different solution. But if they come back with no confession, then we can try to send your friend in to get one for us."

"If we can get a confession, will it speed up the process of getting Axe out?"

He bobbed his head side to side as he thought. "In theory, yes."

That was a good enough answer for me. I wasn't an expert on the judicial system, but I still hoped that my plan would work. It was already early March, which meant Axe's birthday was in two weeks. And there was absolutely no fucking way that I was going to let him be in jail on his birthday.

A ringtone sounded, prompting Uncle Jesse to reach into his pocket and retrieve his cell. He brought it up to his ear.

"Sheriff," he said, answering the call. His eyes roamed around as he listened to whoever was on the other end. "He's in and out? Well I'm not surprised. Axe definitely left him with some damage." Penelope and I stayed silent, trying to piece together the whole conversation from only one side of it. "So, he didn't?" I rubbed my hands together nervously, waiting for him to hang up the phone. "Okay, thanks."

Uncle Jesse brought his attention back to us. "No confession," he said. He turned towards Penelope. "Are you comfortable with wearing a wire?"

"Uh, yeah," she shakily answered.

"Excellent. Let's get you set up then."

We followed him into the same room that he had interrogated me in earlier that day, sitting down at the single table in the room. He quickly set up Penelope's wire, then looked at the both of us, a serious expression on his face.

"Alright, so the plan is to get him to confess. Penelope, just make sure you're acting normal. Talk normally. Casually. We don't want him to feel like something is off. That'll lessen our chances of getting a confession."

She nodded. "Okay. Got it."

"Are you guys ready to go?" he asked.

"Yeah," Penelope said, standing.

"Actually, um, do you think it's possible if I see him one more time? Before we go?"

Uncle Jesse studied my desperation for a second, then sighed. "Technically, you're not supposed to, but I guess you can. It has to be quick, though."

My face brightened a little bit at his words, hope taking over my body. I nodded, letting him know that I understood. He led me back into the room that I had been in previously to see Axe, leaving me alone for a few minutes while he went to go let the guards know to bring Axe in.

I took a deep breath as I watched a new officer bring him in, immediately saddened at the sight of his orange jumpsuit and handcuffs. He was looking at the ground as he walked in, but once his green eyes found my brown ones through the glass, his face brightened.

I could see his mouth start moving, but then he stopped, realizing that I couldn't hear him yet. The guard undid his handcuffs as I shifted around in my seat, impatiently waiting to be able to speak to him.

Axe rolled his wrists and rubbed them for a second. I internally cringed watching, knowing that the cuffs were causing his pain.

I reached for the phone, holding it up to my ear.

"You're already back," he smiled, leaning into his elbow.

I smirked. "Guess I just couldn't stay away."

"Well, I'm glad, because I'm missing you like fucking crazy in here."

"I miss you so much. Beyond words."

His eyes sparkled as he adjusted his position. "Did Ash take you to get a new phone?"

"Yeah, he did," I said, my heart feeling warm and oddly calmer from simply listening to his voice.

"Good. I would've kicked his ass if he didn't."

"From jail?" I laughed.

"I'd find a way."

I rolled my eyes. Typical Axe. He always knew how to lighten the mood, how to take a terrible situation and make it seem less bad. I tilted my head, disheartened as I stared at him through the glass.

"I just wanted to see you again," I said.

"Well, you're welcome to come visit whenever. I'm pretty busy in here, but I guess I can make some time for you," he joked.

"I'm honored," I giggled as I rolled my eyes again.

"You look beautiful today by the way," he said.

My cheeks flushed a little, overtaken by Axe's charm, even as he sat in an orange jumpsuit.

"You too," I joked.

He turned away as he laughed, dimples sinking in. God, I loved him. I hated that he was sitting where he was.

His smile faded and his facial expression turned serious. "Can you do one more thing for me, please?" he asked.

"Of course. What is it?"

"While I'm in here, can you make sure you're still taking care of yourself? I don't want you to block everyone and everything else out. Make sure you still go to class and take care of yourself, okay?"

"Tatum?" a voice called. I turned, already knowing who it was. Time's up.

I gave Uncle Jesse a single nod, then turned back to Axe. "I love you."

"Wait, Tate. Promise me."

"I promise," I said.

"I love you," he said, eyes softening.

"I love you too." I choked back tears as I watched the officer put the handcuffs back onto Axe and walked him out. I covered my mouth with my hand, trying not to let out a sob.

"Tate?" Penelope called, standing near Uncle Jesse. I wiped my eyes quickly, shutting them before taking a deep breath. I walked over to them, nodding to signal that I was ready. "Let's catch this fucker," Penelope said, rubbing her hands together.

We made our way to hospital and up to the floor that Lucas was on. Uncle Jesse and I sat in a nearby room, setting up his equipment. Lucas had been going in and out all day, so I was praying that he would be awake for Penelope to do her job.

My hands shook as I sat, replaying everything over and over again in my head. I was still shocked about the entire situation. Shocked that Lucas attacked me. Shocked that Axe had gotten arrested. Shocked that I was sitting in the hospital next to the sheriff, trying to get a confession. Too much was on the line. The pressure was drastically high, and my anxiety was right up there with it.

We sat in silence, waiting to hear Penelope and Lucas speak. I bobbed my knee up and down, rubbing my legs with my palms. Uncle Jesse tilted his chin down towards me, raising a hand and gently dropping it, signaling for me to calm down.

"You're awake," Penelope said.

Lucas was silent for a minute before he spoke. "Yeah. Hey," he groggily said.

He sounded like hell, and I hadn't seen him, but he probably looked like it too.

"How are you feeling?"

"Pretty bad," he responded, his voice hoarse. It sounded almost as if he was trying to get over a cold. I tried remembering if Axel had hit him in the throat or not. The memory was somewhat cloudy, so I wasn't quite sure, but I wouldn't be surprised if he had. "What are you doing back here?"

282

"I just wanted..." Penelope paused, her voice shaking slightly, "to talk to you again about what happened."

Her tone made me nervous. I could tell she was uneasy, pressured to be in the position that she was in, but I didn't want her to accidentally blow our cover.

"Okay..." he slowly said. "What about it?"

"Can you just tell me... again what happened? I'm just a little confused."

It was silent for a few moments. I wished I could see what was happening, to know the exact expression that was on Lucas's face, but all I could do was try to piece together his reaction through his silence.

"I already told you," Lucas said, his scratchy voice becoming a little irritated.

"But—"

"But nothing," he said, cutting her off. "There's nothing left to say." Penelope didn't say anything, probably startled by how rude he was being. "Look," he continued, "I'm going to press charges against Axel. And when he gets locked up for a while, I'm going to be with Tatum. I know that's not what you want to hear, but that's what's going to happen."

"Fuck you," Penelope finally responded. Lucas chuckled once.

I gripped the sides of my chair, disgusted by not only how rude he was being to Penelope, but by how he could ever think that I would be with him. Especially after everything that he had done. And after everything that he just put Axe through.

"I hope you know Tatum's gonna press charges against you," Penelope hissed.

Lucas was silent again, probably taken aback by the new information. I didn't know why he would assume that I wouldn't press charges. For some reason, he thought he was invincible. He thought he was smarter than everyone else. I wanted to march into the room and confront him myself, but Axe's face flashed through my mind. He had asked me to stay away from Lucas. He didn't trust him. And neither did I. Obviously Lucas couldn't hurt me with all his injuries, plus the fact that Uncle Jesse was with me and we were in a hospital, but I still didn't want to go against Axe's wishes.

"And when she does, you're gonna go to prison for just as long as Axel does," she added.

I had never heard Penelope talk of or to Lucas negatively. It was almost refreshing. She had been on his ass since after New Year's, so it was nice that she was finally seeing him the same way I did.

"Me attacking Tatum was not nearly the same as Axel attacking me," he shot back.

I glanced up at Uncle Jesse. "Is that a good enough confession?" I whispered.

"Shh," he said, trying to listen.

"How was it different?" Penelope asked, viciously.

"Because all I did was break her phone and get on top of her. Axel attacked me like the wild animal that he is."

His comment about Axe made my jaw twitch. I clenched my hands into fists, trying to maintain my anger so that the temptation to walk into his room and scream at him would lessen.

Uncle Jesse stood. "Where are you going?" I whispered.

"To get a warrant."

I furrowed my brows. He sensed my confusion, taking a deep breath before explaining.

"He confessed. It was a weak confession, but at least it was one. I've got camera footage and DNA results coming within the next few days. Once he's out of here, I'm taking a warrant for his arrest straight to him and arresting his sorry ass."

The tenseness in my body relaxed a little, relieved that the confession was at least going to help the case. "Does this mean Axe will get out sooner?"

"Not necessarily. All the charges have to go through the system first. Both cases have to be thoroughly looked at before they could be dropped. Once they're able to be dropped, then that's when we've gotta convince Lucas to drop the charges on Axe. And even after he does, then we've gotta wait for that to go through the system before the charges are entirely gone. That's when Axe can get out."

"How long?" I asked, my heart racing.

"At least a few weeks," he said, his mouth resting in a straight line. "And that's assuming that we can arrest Lucas within the next day or so."

I dropped my face into my hands, cringing at the realization that Axe would most likely be stuck in jail on his birthday.

Uncle Jesse placed his hand on my shoulder. "Don't worry. We'll get him out."

I touched my necklace, praying that he was right.

Chapter Twenty-Six
The Plan

The days went on painfully slow. I kept my phone next to me at all times, waiting for a call from Uncle Jesse that Lucas had been arrested. But at this point, it had already been six days since Axe got arrested, and that call still hadn't come.

Each day felt like it was getting longer and every time I went to bed, I dreaded waking up because I knew that Axe would not be next to me. All I wanted was to be with him, or at least see him, but I hadn't had time to. Axe had requested that I made sure to go to my classes and do my school work, and even though I wanted to skip every day for the sake of going to visit him, I didn't. Because that's not what Axe wanted. And I would do whatever he wanted or needed me to do, because he sure as hell would do the same for me.

I walked over to the dining center with Gianna and Claire. They had been trying to be supportive, but nothing that anyone said or did could make the situation better. The only person that could make it better was Axe.

We chose a small table in the corner of the cafeteria. I sat with my plate, tracing my food around with my fork. I didn't have an appetite.

I had just gotten Axe back and now I lost him again. And this time felt almost worse. Because not only was he not here, but he was suffering from something that was partly my fault. If it wasn't for me, he wouldn't be sitting in a jail cell.

"Well," Gi started, "on the bright side—"

"There is no bright side," I interrupted.

She gave a quick sigh before continuing. "On the bright side, at least he'll be getting out soon."

"We don't know that."

"Tate—"

"He could be in there for fucking ever."

"You just have to be patient," Gi softly said.

"I'm out of patience."

"You wanna get drunk?" Claire asked.

"Dude," Gianna scolded Claire.

"What?" Claire asked.

"Getting drunk isn't—"

"Shh," Claire's eyes widened as the entire room went silent, conversations coming to sudden halts. I glanced up, noticing the drastic change of noise within the room. Uncle Jesse walked through the cafeteria, two other officers following behind him. They trudged across the room, unphased by the amount of eyes that were watching their every move. My eyes shot ahead of them, curious as to where they were heading.

"Is that Lucas?" I asked, keeping my eyes fixed across the room.

Claire and Gianna both squinted, trying to determine if my accusation was right or not.

"I think it is, and I think that's Jason sitting next to him," Claire responded, leaning forward to get a closer look. No one had told me when Lucas was released from the hospital or when he started to return to his classes. I swallowed the lump of nerves that was settled in my throat, wondering if this was the moment that I had been waiting for.

Uncle Jesse stopped in front of the table. I could see his lips moving, but he was too far to be able to hear what he was saying. One of his fellow officers held up a piece of paper as Uncle Jesse continued to speak.

Lucas slowly and shakily stood, a look of horror on his face. He hesitated before turning, his back facing the officers as Uncle Jesse placed handcuffs on him.

"Woah," Gianna said, her jaw dropping.

"Holy shit. They're just gonna arrest him right now? Here?" Claire added.

Adrenaline began pumping throughout me, my body becoming overtaken by a sight that was too good to be true. Positive thoughts flowed, wondering just how much longer it would be before Axe would be freed.

Everyone throughout the room was sitting in silence, dumbstruck at the situation that was unraveling right in front of them.

Uncle Jesse held onto one of Lucas's arms, leading him towards the exit. Lucas's eyes met mine as they walked past our table. I could finally see his injuries, clear as day, impossible to miss. His face was still pretty swollen, both eyes still fairly black. Small cuts and bruises were scattered around his face, accompanied by a line of stitches resting above his eyebrow and white tape covering his broken nose. As he walked by, you could see the large bald spot on the back of his head where he was given another lovely set of stitches.

But I didn't feel bad. Axe wasn't crazy. He wasn't a wild animal. He could control himself and wouldn't have done what he did unless he knew that it was necessary. And seeing me struggling beneath Lucas was enough for him to feel like it was.

Uncle Jesse didn't acknowledge me. I figured he was trying not to make it evident that I was involved. Either that, or he genuinely didn't know that I was there.

"I can't believe that just happened," Gianna said, snapping me out of my daydream. The room returned to a normal volume of laughs and voices, most likely discussing Lucas being arrested.

"I need to call Uncle Jesse," I said.

"Wait for him to call you, Tate. I'm sure he will be soon," Gi said.

Claire squeezed my hand. "He'll be out soon, okay? Don't worry."

"God, I hope so. He doesn't deserve to be in there."

Two hands smacked down on the table, causing all three of us to jump. Jason stood, breath faltering.

"What the hell was that?" he smoldered, eyes digging into me. "You get my best friend arrested just because your psychopathic boyfriend was?"

"Lucas got what he deserved. And unless you want to end up where he's going, I suggest you shut your mouth and fuck off," I spat back.

"Wow," he turned away, breaking eye contact with me for a split second. "Now I gotta go bail him out."

288

"Good luck trying," I responded, knowing that there was no way in hell that Uncle Jesse was going to let Lucas get released until Axe was.

Jason shot me one last look, as if Claire and Gianna weren't even there. He stomped to the door, shoving it open to complete his dramatic exit.

I could tell it made Claire a little uncomfortable, but she didn't say anything. She just continued on as if it hadn't happened.

Gianna and Claire finished eating. I hadn't eaten much, but I wasn't hungry. I had too much on my mind. We made our way back to Stanley Hall, all shuffling into Gianna and Claire's room.

"Tate, are you okay? You haven't really been talking much," Gianna asked, worry glimmering in her eyes as she sat in her desk chair. I rested against Claire's bed frame, biting the inside of my lip. My mind couldn't form words, unable to fathom a single sentence from the clusterfuck that was going on in my head.

"I'm just..." I shrugged, "you know."

"Talk to us," Claire insisted.

I messed with my hair, attempting to fill the gap of silence with meaningless actions. "I'm scared," I admitted. "And I feel guilty as hell."

"It's not your fault that Lucas and Jason are both scumbags. Sorry Claire, but you dated a fuck."

"Yeah, I know that by now," Claire stubbornly said.

"Sorry. Just stating facts," Gianna shrugged.

My back pocket buzzed, and I immediately grabbed my phone out of it, recognizing the number as Uncle Jesse's. My blood rippled around, sending my heart into a frenzy.

"Hello?"

"Tatum," Uncle Jesse said, "we've got him."

I smiled, nodding. "What happens next?"

"Well, it only took twenty minutes to convince Lucas to drop his charges against Axe. The only condition being that you drop your charges against him, which was originally the plan anyways."

"Done," I agreed. "So, Axe will be getting out soon?" I gripped the hem of my shirt, trying to prepare myself for whatever answer he had for me.

"Here's the thing. Just because he dropped the charges, doesn't mean that the prosecutor has yet. Or that the prosecutor will."

I stood up straight, my glimmer of hope fading. "What does that mean?"

"When you press charges against someone, you're reporting the crime, but you're not the one that decides if or when the investigation ends. The prosecutor decides that. Usually in cases like this, especially when the victim drops charges, the prosecutor will also drop the charges and not follow through with a trial or anything, but at this point, it's up to them."

My throat felt like it was closing, speechless by the reality that it was no longer in our hands. We did everything that we could, and now, the odds might not be in our favor. Gianna and Claire stared at me, curious to know what Uncle Jesse was saying. They traded glances a few times, sending mind messages to each other. Similarly to the way that Axe and I did. Except Axe wasn't here.

"So, now what? We just wait?" my voice cracked, glossy eyes running into another wall of frustration.

He sighed on the other end. "Pretty much. And there's one more thing."

"What is it?"

"Axe requested to get a restraining order for you against both Lucas and Jason, which I will happily do for you. But he wants it to be put in place before Lucas gets out. And Axe isn't going to get out until Lucas does. So, it might take a little longer now."

My jaw dropped. Axe was okay with staying in jail longer just for the sake of Lucas staying away from me? My stomach twisted, disrupted by how much Axe was doing for me and giving to me when I didn't have enough to give back to him, let alone having the power to get him out of jail.

"How long?" I asked in a whisper, a tear falling.

"Hopefully within the next two or three weeks. I've already started all the paperwork for the restraining orders, but you need to sign some things and they have to be approved by a judge as well."

I rubbed my forehead, reality smacking me in the face. Axe was not getting out anytime soon.

I cleaned every square inch of the apartment, doing everything I could to keep myself occupied. I had been staying there for the past couple of days. Everything had been going fine with Penelope and we hadn't had any arguments, but if I couldn't see Axe, then being surrounded by all of his things was the next best thing.

Axe had been in jail for two weeks now and Uncle Jesse was calling me every few days, keeping me updated on everything. But at this point, there was hardly anything to keep me updated on. Nothing had changed over the last week. The prosecutor hadn't dropped the charges yet and the restraining orders still hadn't been put into place.

With each day that passed, I fell deeper and deeper into a hole of guilt. I couldn't help but think about Axe sitting in a cold and uncomfortable jail cell, all alone. I felt helpless. Powerless. Unable to take his pain away.

It wasn't fair. He was getting punished for protecting me. And the worst part was that I knew that if he had to, he would do it all over again in a heartbeat if it meant protecting me.

Axel's birthday was in two days and instead of spending it together, we would be forced to spend it apart. And even worse, instead of him being able to have fun, he would be stuck in a cell, left with nothing to do but stare at a wall.

I planned on skipping classes that day to go see him, but even then, it wouldn't be the same as being able to sit next to him. Touch him. Hug him. Kiss him.

Ash's bedroom door opened, footsteps making their way down the hall. He peeked his head at me from around the corner, catching me in the middle of finishing up the dishes.

"Hey," he said.

"Hey, what's up?"

"Gianna and I were going to have a movie night if you wanted to join."

I gave a subtle smile, grateful that they were at least trying to keep me included. "That's okay. I'll probably just finish up some homework or something," I softly responded, hating the idea of third-wheeling for the night.

Ash sighed, making his way into the kitchen. I kept my eyes on the dishes, afraid that making eye contact with him would cause my water works to come rushing down.

"Tate, stop beating yourself up so much."

"I can't help it," I sniffled, struggling to keep the tears back.

"He'll be out before you know it," he said, but by the tone in his voice, I could tell he didn't believe it either. We both knew that Axe was going to be stuck in there for at least a few more weeks. "And hey, didn't he ask you to make sure not to block everyone out? C'mon, just hang out with us tonight."

I thought back to the last time I had gotten the opportunity to speak with Axe. He wanted me to make sure I was taking care of myself, doing my school work, and not blocking anyone out. The last thing I wanted was to hang out with Gi and Ash tonight. All I truly wanted to do was to lay in Axe's bed and cry, but that wasn't what Axe wanted. And when you truly loved someone, you would do anything they needed. Axe had shown me that, and now it was my turn to reciprocate it.

"Okay," I agreed. "But I get to pick the movie."

Ash laughed. "Fine, loser."

I awoke in Axe's bed, disappointed once again because the love of my life was not lying sound asleep next to me. I barely had any motivation to get up, but I forced myself to, reminding myself that the faster today went by, the closer I was to visiting Axe tomorrow.

I walked into the kitchen and rummaged through all the cabinets to find something to eat for breakfast. I spotted the pancake mix sitting in its usual place. It had remained untouched for weeks. There were a few mornings that Ash had offered to make chocolate chip pancakes for me, but each time, I turned him down. If they weren't made by Axe, and if he wasn't going to be the one eating across from me at the table, then I didn't want them.

I fixed myself a bowl of cereal before throwing on some makeup and tossing my hair into a ponytail. I only had two classes today, but I knew they were going to drag. I packed up my bag and headed off for class, dreading it.

I sat in business, zoning out as my professor rambled on about finance. I covered my yawn with my small hand, my eyes shutting for just a second before springing back open at the sound of my phone. I glanced down in my lap, reading the text from Ash very carefully.

Come back asap. Gotta talk about Axe.

I immediately started shaking, anxiety rippling through me. A million possibilities flew through my head, but none of them were good ones. His text sounded urgent, desperate.

I tossed my books back into my bag, trying not to be loud or draw attention to myself as I made my way out of class. I felt bad to be leaving in the middle of it, but I couldn't wait another forty-five minutes to find out what Ash already knew.

Uncle Jesse had mentioned that it was left to the prosecutor to decide if the charges would be followed through or entirely dropped. In that case, Axe would be tried for battery. And we all knew that he would be convicted. Easily convicted. And sent to prison for God knows how long.

I parked in my usual spot in the apartment parking lot, grabbing my bag and running in. I took the stairs two at a time, torn between needing to speak with Ash and being absolutely unprepared to at the same time.

I didn't want to lose Axe entirely, didn't want to be ripped apart if he got a long sentence, but no matter how long that sentence would be, I would be there. Waiting. Every day. For days. Or months. Or years. I was absolutely in love with him, and that wasn't going to go away whether he was in prison or not. I would wait for him until the day he got out.

I wiggled my key in the lock and slowly opened the door, taking a deep breath as I stepped inside. A familiar head of curly brown hair stood in the kitchen, tossing a handful of chocolate chips into a bowl of pancake mix.

My backpack slid off my shoulders, making a plopping sound as it came into contact with the ground. The curly haired head turned, pearly whites and dimples coming into view at the sight of me. My mind froze, dumbfounded as I attempted to decide if I was dreaming or not. There was only one way to find out.

I took a few strides towards him, my feet speeding up with each step. I jumped into him, wrapping my arms and legs around him. His cologne radiated off of him, a scent that I hadn't smelled in weeks, letting me know that I definitely wasn't dreaming. I nuzzled my face into the crook of his neck, tears helplessly falling down.

"You're here," I cried.

His hand gently stroked my hair, holding me close. "I'm here," he repeated.

"I'm so sorry," I wept into him, the guilt I had been carrying for weeks spilling out.

"Hey, look at me," he whispered. I brought my head up, meeting his green eyes with my tearful ones. "You have *nothing* to be sorry for."

"But you just spent the past two and a half weeks in jail because of me."

He slowly shook his head. "No, I went to jail because of that douchebag, not because of you."

I gazed at him, mesmerized. "So, Uncle Jesse put the restraining orders into action?" I asked.

"Yep. Neither of those dicks are allowed to come near you."

I placed my lips onto his, the puzzle piece that I had been missing for weeks finally falling into place. Axe was still holding me, not putting me down. I wondered if his arms were tired, but even if they were, he wasn't showing it.

"I love you," I said.

He grinned. "I love you more."

"Thank you for everything."

Axe stared deeply into my eyes, examining every speck of them as he shook his head again, his eyebrows slightly pulling in. "No. Thank *you* for *being* everything."

I smiled as I swung my legs down, finally allowing his poor arms to be relieved from holding me up. I wondered how he had managed to get released, but it didn't even matter. What mattered was that he was here.

I held onto Axe's left arm, leaning into him as he flipped our pancakes with his right.

"Awe, you got my text," Ash said, making his way into the kitchen.

"Yes, I did," I smiled.

I squeezed Axe's bicep, clinging onto him as if my life depended on it. The smile on my face hadn't faded for a single second. Axe leaned down, connecting his lips to my forehead.

Being able to touch him, feel his body warmth against me was comforting. And even more so, knowing that I would wake up tomorrow morning to the sight of him next to me gave me something to look forward to.

"I love you," I exclaimed, looking up at him.

Green eyes peered down at me, a charming smirk accompanying it. "I love you so much."

"Too much PDA," Ash said, grabbing his keys off the counter.

Axe chuckled, lifting his eyebrows. "You wanna see more?" he said sarcastically.

"Absolutely not," Ash replied, shaking his head as he walked out the door.

I laughed, the situation making me feel lighthearted rather than embarrassed like it normally would. At this point, I was too comfortable with both Axe and Ash to feel any sort of awkwardness.

The pan sizzled as Axe moved the last pancake off, tossing it onto a separate plate. He turned the stove off and immediately faced me, barely waiting a second to smash his lips onto mine. His hands placed themselves on my hips, applying just enough force to gently back me up against the counter.

They slid up to my waist. Axe lifted me, carefully placing me on the counter, his lips never leaving mine. I rested my hands on the back of his neck, my mouth smiling against his by how euphoric he made me feel.

"What do you want to do tomorrow for your birthday?" I asked, running my fingers through his curls.

He shrugged. "I don't care, as long as it's with you."

I grinned, admiring every inch of his face. He set his hands on both sides of my hips, leaning against the counter. My heart felt so full, overwhelmed by the amount of love that settled in the room.

"We can just hang out, spend the day together, and get dinner tomorrow night and then go to ATA," he offered.

"Sounds perfect," I said, giving him another kiss.

Axe smirked as I pulled away. His arms scooped me up off the counter, carrying me out of the kitchen.

"Axe," I giggled, realizing that we were heading towards his bedroom, "our pancakes are gonna get cold."

He bobbed his head to the side. "You're right," he replied, turning around and laying me down on the couch. He jogged back into the kitchen, causing me to instantly miss him.

"Come back," I pouted, sitting up to get a glimpse of what he was doing.

"I'm comin' baby, hold on."

Thirty seconds later, he jogged back to me, a plate of warm chocolate chip pancakes and syrup in hand. He set it down in front of me on the coffee table.

"Where's yours?" I asked.

He kissed my forehead. "I'm gonna go get mine now."

I nodded, turning my attention back towards my pancakes. I slapped some syrup on and brought a bite up to my mouth. They tasted like love. Tasted like hope. Tasted perfect.

Axe reemerged with his plate and sat next to me.

"These pancakes are the one thing I missed more than you," I joked.

"I can't even argue with that," he said between bites. "These pancakes are good as hell."

I giggled as I took another bite, still in disbelief that Axe was sitting next to me.

We quickly ate, both anxious to spend the rest of the day together making up for lost time. I had missed him beyond words, beating myself up over everything that happened. And even after it all, Axe still loved me. My sisters had said before that he was everything I had always been looking for and it was clear that they were right. Axe was my match. It might have taken me awhile to realize it, taken me awhile to open up to him after we had first met, but it was the truth. Axe was my person.

Chapter Twenty-Seven
The Birthday Boy

The sheets were still in disarray when I awoke, my body tangled up in Axe's. He was still asleep, but his arms were holding me so tight, as if he was afraid to let me go. I slowly and carefully lifted my head up, glancing at his peaceful face. His bare, built chest was exposed out of the sheets, revealing the swallows and the tattoo he had for his mother.

I lightly traced over the words with my finger. I wished I could have met his mom. She seemed like a wonderful and loving mother. I wondered if she would like me if she had met me.

Axe didn't talk about his parents a lot. The topic clearly made him upset usually, which was why I had never asked any questions. But in this moment, all I could do was feel thankful. I knew Axe's real dad was never around, abandoning Axe and his siblings at a young age. His mom, Anne, had died too young, leaving Axe parentless. But either way, the two had brought Axe into the world, had helped shape him into the incredible man that he was, and for that, I was beyond thankful.

His sleeping body shifted around, causing me to freeze until he situated himself to become comfortable again. I warily wiggled my way out of his grip, untangling myself from his comfortable grasp. Once I was free, I slipped my red, silk robe on over my thong and tiptoed out of the room. I headed straight to the kitchen, preparing to make Axe a huge birthday breakfast.

I took out the eggs, bacon, and hash-browns, placing them on the counter as I tied my hair up into a messy ponytail. I quickly washed my hands and got started, quietly playing music on my phone as I cooked. I danced around the kitchen by myself, fueled by the feeling of waking up happily for the first time in weeks.

For most couples, being apart pushed them farther apart. But for Axe and I, it had brought us closer together. We survived a rough breakup and then survived an entire nightmare of an assault and arrest, but even so, the important part was that we survived. We made it through. Together. And now it seemed like we were as strong as ever.

Once everything was done, I slowly reentered Axe's room, smirking at the sight of him still being asleep. He usually always slept in, and even though it was his birthday, today was no exception. I figured Axel would still be sleeping, so I made sure to place his breakfast into the microwave to try to keep it warm for him.

I climbed back into bed, snuggling up next to Axe. He groaned, wrapping his arms around me. His eyes fluttered open, scanning my face.

"Happy birthday," I softly said.

He squeezed me tighter, pulling me in as close as he could. "Thank you, baby."

"I made you breakfast."

"You didn't have to do that."

"Yeah, I did."

He kissed my cheek, causing me to give out a small giggle. He kissed it again and again and again, kisses traveling all around my face, sending love and electricity throughout my entire body.

He moved me on top of him. My body rested against his, puzzle pieces fitting together perfectly. His lips touched mine, hands grazing the back of my thighs. I moved my hair to one side, trying to keep it from falling onto his face. His fingertips moved up my silk robe, skimming my sensitive skin.

"Come eat breakfast," I said, cocking my head towards the door.

Axe played with my hair, a grin stuck on his face. He bit his bottom lip for a second, smoothly flipping me onto my back and positioning himself on top of me. He used his fingertips to gently push my head to the side and then brought his lips down, kissing my exposed neck. My hands rubbed his bare back, satisfied with the feeling. His back muscles tensed under my touch as he hummed against my neck. His lips

298

worked against my skin for a minute, a bulge beginning to push up against my lower half.

"Axe," I said laughing as his lips traveled down to my collarbone that was hanging out of my robe.

"Mhmm?" he hummed against me.

"Breakfast."

He finally pulled away, smiling as he sighed. "Fine."

I cupped his face with both of my hands, bringing him in for one last kiss. I watched as Axe got out of bed, slipping on his boxers, but no shirt. He studied me as I lay there, his eyes inspecting me from head to toe, stopping at my bare legs. His sexy smirk reappeared, and I instantly knew what he was thinking, but I disregarded it.

I got out of the bed and walked over to him, lifting myself up on my tiptoes to plant a kiss on his cheek. "Come out when you're ready, birthday boy," I said, heading out of the room and back into the kitchen.

I pulled Axe's plate out of the microwave. Two arms wrapped around my middle from behind me. I glanced up, feeling Axe's chest against my back. He looked down at me, his wide frame making mine look tiny.

"What's for breakfast?" he asked.

"Eggs and bacon and hash-browns."

"Yum," he said, swaying me back and forth in his arms.

"Here's your plate."

He took it, giving me a quick kiss on the forehead. "Thank you for making breakfast," he said, sitting down at the table.

"It's your birthday breakfast." I felt bad because I had figured Axe would still be in jail for his birthday, and even though I had been planning on visiting him regardless, I hadn't gotten him a gift. "Where do you wanna go today? Pick anywhere. I'm paying."

"You're not paying."

"Yes, I am. It's your birthday and I didn't get you a gift because I didn't know you'd be out. I'm paying," I insisted.

Axe's entire body stopped, fork dropping mid-bite. His gaze slowly proceeded upward from his plate, eyes meeting mine, all seriousness intended. "You're here. That's the only gift I need."

I tilted my head to the side. "Axe. You always do everything for me. Let me do something for you."

He took a deep breath. "Okay, let's go out. But we're not doing anything that would require you to spend money."

I rolled my eyes, wondering what on Earth we could possibly do that didn't require any money whatsoever. I turned around in my seat, glancing out the sliding back door that led to the balcony. The sun was out. No more snow on the ground.

I got up and roamed out to the balcony, feeling the almost-April air on my face. It wasn't cold, yet it wasn't super warm either. It was somewhere in between, a good day for sweater weather.

I overlooked the parking lot for a second, reminded of the time I saw Lucas walking around in the middle of the night. A small hint of panic overcame me at the thought, but I stopped it, instantly reminding myself that Axe was here, which meant I was safe.

"You wanna go on a walk in the forest preserve?" I asked, making my way back inside.

"You wanna go on a walk?" he raised a brow.

I shrugged with one shoulder. "It's nice out. And it doesn't require money."

"Just you and me?"

I nodded.

Axe leaned back. "Sounds perfect," he said, eyes brightening.

We finished eating and got ready. I threw on a hunter green sweater and ripped blue jeans, completing my outfit with my favorite necklace. The one Axe had bought me.

I was beyond excited to spend the day with him. It felt almost unreal that he was here, as if the entire day so far had been a dream.

Axel walked out of his bedroom, dressed in a long black sleeve, black jeans, and a grey beanie. His brown curls stuck out of his beanie, framing his face perfectly.

"Ready to go?" he asked, grabbing his car keys off the counter.

"Yep," I smiled, slipping my Adidas on.

A short drive later, we got out of the car. The parking lot was empty other than a few other cars, which meant barely anyone was here today. Axe intertwined our fingers together and led the way, heading towards the trails. The leaves were beginning to sprout on the trees, making for a beautiful shade of green to be surrounding us, matching the green of Axe's eyes.

It was silent around us, other than the sounds of nature: the birds chirping, frogs croaking in the nearby pond, trees calmly swaying back and forth. It was serene; tranquil. The most peaceful place with the most perfect person.

I was grateful that the trail was a paved one. I would've hated to be walking on a muddy trail.

My tiny hand squeezed Axe's big one. I leaned into him, resting my free hand on his bicep.

"I love it out here," I said, looking around.

"Me too. I wish this was an everyday thing."

Our steps remained gradual, leisurely enough to take everything in. "We can come here more often."

"Yeah," he paused, "I meant like an everyday thing for like...ever."

"Forever is a long time, Axe."

His gaze turned down to our feet for a second, studying each step we took in unison. "I know, but..." he trailed off.

"You really wanna put up with me forever?" I laughed, watching him.

He turned his attention back to me, our steps still continuing. His brows slightly came together, mouth turning upwards. "I'm up for the challenge."

I playfully pushed him. "A *challenge*? Maybe *you* are the challenge, mister!" I joked.

His dimples appeared, the sight sparking a rush throughout me. I never usually liked talking too far into the future. It scared me, gave me false hope. But for some reason, it wasn't bothering me right now. The subject felt more of a present topic than it did a future one, as if planning the future with Axe was a necessary thing and not just a hopeful dream.

"Alright, alright. Maybe I am the challenge."

"Yep, you are. Considering the fact that you want to tell our future kids the story about Brooke."

He tilted his head back, laughing. "It's a funny story."

"Mhmm," I said, raising my brows.

"Hey," he nudged me, "you said our future kids."

He caught me. I looked away, blushing for a second. "I didn't say that," I denied.

301

"Yes, you did," he smirked.

"No."

"Yes."

"Nope."

Axe stopped in his tracks, pulling me into him. He leaned in as he played with both of my hands. "Three kids."

I pulled my mouth to the side, trying to hide my smile. "Maybe four."

He lifted his eyebrows, his smile never fading. "That's fine with me." I looked away, giggling, unable to hide the happiness pouring out of me. "We can get started today," he said, still moving my hands around. My eyes widened at his words, disapproving them. "Kidding," he laughed, lifting both of our hands up.

"I hope you are kidding, cause I'm not gonna be popping kids out until I'm married."

He took one of my hands and spun me around as if we were slow dancing, stopping once my backside was to him. He wrapped his arms around my midsection, chin resting near my shoulder. "I love this conversation," he said, rocking me side to side.

I snickered. "Why?"

"Because it's relieving to know that I'm not the only one who thinks about these things."

To be honest, I guess I never really gave too much thought to a long-term future with Axe. I knew I wanted a future with him, but I never really thought about details until now. Partly because up until now, I didn't really like talking about the future or getting false hope. I barely had time lately to think far into the future since I was so busy with fixing the issues that were currently occurring. And now that those issues were over, I felt like I could relax.

I covered his hands with my little ones, melting under his touch. I observed our surroundings once more, taking in every detail of the moment, so that I could cherish it forever.

I turned, looking up at him. "I love you," I said.

"I love you too."

"I'm really happy I get to spend your birthday with you."

"Me too," he quietly said. "And I'm also glad I'm spending it out of jail," he added, chuckling.

"Believe me, so am I," I laughed.

302

We walked throughout the entire trail, hand in hand, heart to heart, talking about anything and everything that came to mind. One thing that I loved about Axe was that he was so easy to talk to. Not once did our conversations ever get dry. And on top of that, talking to him didn't make me feel like an idiot or judged or hurt. He always made me feel wanted, made me feel like my opinion mattered.

Once we got back to the car, we drove home in laughter, a perfect way to end our perfect day. Axe and I planned on watching a movie, hanging out for a while, and then cooking dinner before heading to ATA. We hadn't been there together in over a month. The last time we were each there, we were broken up and I was hammered out of my mind.

After numerous hours passed, I slipped on my long-sleeved, red laced bodysuit, completing the outfit with black ripped jeans and black bootie heels. There was a knock on the bathroom door as I finished curling my hair.

"What's up?" I asked.

Axe leaned against the doorframe, watching me intently. "I just missed you."

I gave out a single chuckle. "I've been getting ready for like thirty minutes."

"I know," Axe expressed, "but after being apart from you for so long, even thirty minutes feels like a lifetime." I grinned, grabbing my necklace off the bathroom counter. He nodded once. "Let me," he said, plucking the necklace out of my fingers.

Axe pushed my hair onto one side. He rested the necklace around my neck, securing the clasp in the back, before leaving a precious kiss on my skin.

"Are Gi and Ash back yet?" I asked.

"Yeah, they're in the kitchen."

I nodded, completing my outfit with red lips before following Axe.

"Hey, bitch!" Gi exclaimed, already buzzed. She drew me in for a tight hug.

"Hey," I laughed, letting go. "Are you already drunk too?" I turned to Ash.

He shook his head. "Nah, she's just a lightweight."

Gi dropped her jaw open. "Am not!"

"Yes, you are," Axe said, strolling past them to pour shots.

"Whatever," Gi rolled her eyes.

"So, Axe, big twenty means twenty shots tonight," Ash announced, leaning against the counter.

Axe chuckled once. "Yeah, if you want me to get alcohol poisoning and die."

"Please, don't," I said, grabbing a full shot glass. Axe's smirk continued to stay on his face as he poured the rest, handing one to each of us. "Okay," I started, raising my glass as my eyes stayed on Axe, "I just want to give a birthday shout out to my favorite person."

"I thought I was your favorite person," Gianna interrupted.

"Shut up," I said before continuing. "Thank you for everything that you do for me. And thank you for going to jail for me," I laughed. "I have no words to describe how much I love you. Happy birthday!" I finished. Axe's charming smile illuminated throughout the room, satisfied by my toast.

"Happy birthday!" Gi and Ash shouted.

All four of us tossed our shots back. The stale liquor ran down my throat, causing my face to twinge in disgust for a moment before recovering.

Gi leaned towards me. "We should invite Claire."

"Yeah, call her."

"You want me to text Owen?" Axe asked.

Gi and I traded glances. "Yeah, why not," I responded.

As far as we knew, Claire and Owen weren't dating. They occasionally hung out and definitely hooked up, but Gi and I both assumed that Claire wasn't looking for another relationship for a while. I respected her decision, knowing how it felt to need some time alone. Plus, we all knew that Owen was thinking about going into the military, so it wouldn't be a good idea for Claire to get attached to him now, just for him to leave. But we didn't want to leave Claire out, especially now that she didn't have Jason to hang out with while we were here at the apartment.

Claire and Owen showed up together after another half hour or so. We all pre-gamed for a while, throwing shots down. The boys made us martinis and we threw those down as well. I threw down two.

As we made our way up ATA's driveway, I could feel all the alcohol kicking in. I was fairly drunk, but I was nowhere near as drunk as

I had been the last time that I was at ATA. The same night that Axe saved me from Nick.

The room was already packed when we got in. Strobe lights were flashing, music blaring. Axe led me by the hand over to our usual corner. He twirled me around in his arms, never letting me go. I bit my lip as I giggled, overwhelmed with pure happiness.

We didn't do anything super extraordinary today for Axe's birthday, but from what I could tell, he still enjoyed it anyways.

My body didn't stop moving when I noticed a familiar head of long, fiery red hair across the room. Olivia stood next to the two blondes, whose names I had forgotten because they were so irrelevant. Her arms were crossed as she watched Axe and I, a dirty look on her face.

Bitch.

I smiled at Olivia as I brought my middle finger up high and proud, making sure she saw it. She shook her head and dropped her arms to the side before walking off, leaving me to feel accomplished.

My eyes trailed over to the DJ. I placed a hand on Axe's shoulder as I went up on my tiptoes, using him for stability. I brought my mouth up to his ear so that he could hear me clearly.

"I'll be right back," I said. I could tell he was nervous to let me out of his sight, afraid after what happened the last time that we had been apart. But I walked off before he could argue, heading straight towards the DJ.

"Hey, Tatum! What's up?" he asked. I didn't know him, but somehow, he knew me. Probably because of Axe.

"Can I use the microphone for a minute?" I yelled over the music.

"Sure," he said, handing it to me as he stopped the music that was currently playing.

Everyone ceased dancing and booed, pissed off that their vibe had just been killed.

"Hey!" I said into the microphone, getting everyone's attention over to me. "So, a lot of you probably don't know me, but I'm sure you all know Axel," I said, looking over in his direction. "It's his birthday today, so can we sing to him?"

"Hell, yeah!" everyone shouted. I picked out Axel in the crowd as everyone started singing, never taking my eyes away from him. I swayed back and forth as I sang along, feeling euphoric.

When the song came to a close, I made my way back over to Axe. He enveloped me in his arms, lifting my feet off the ground. "Thanks, baby," he said as he put me down.

I hugged his midsection, squeezing as tightly as I could, relieved to be back in his arms.

And this time, I wasn't going to let anything fuck this up.

Chapter Twenty-Eight
The Trip

Usually I was the first one to be up, but when my eyes drifted open, the first thing I saw were Axe's. He grinned when he noticed I was up, playing with my long hair.

"Good morning, baby," he said.

"Good morning," I repeated, stretching around in bed.

"So, I was thinking," he started, rolling closer to me.

"Yeah?"

"Let's take a trip."

I furrowed my brows, smiling. "A trip? To where?"

He pulled his mouth to the side, thinking for a moment. "Chicago."

I dropped my head back onto the pillow, readjusting myself. "Chicago? Why do you wanna go to Chi?"

He shrugged, green eyes still glistening. "I've never been."

My eyes widened as my mouth dropped open. "You've never been to Chicago?"

"Nope," he sighed.

Wilmot was only forty or so minutes away from Chicago, so I had been there numerous times a year, every year growing up. It was a beautiful city, almost magical the first time you went. Filled with millions of people and thousands of tourists each year, I was surprised Axe had never been.

"Okay," I agreed. "When do you want to go?"

He looked around for a second before covering my hand with his. "Next weekend? We can go for a few days over spring break."

"Sure."

Axel and I had never been on a trip together before. And now that I thought about it, the farthest place from campus that we had ever gone together was Amberly's house.

I smiled as he buried his face into my neck, his curls tickling my skin. I giggled, tracing the tattoos on his arm with my finger.

"Did you wanna invite Ash and Gianna or anyone?" I asked.

His head popped out of the crook of my neck. "Nah, let's just have some us time."

I turned onto my side as Axe draped an arm around me, my backside facing his front. He pulled me in as close as he could before kissing my shoulder repeatedly, as if he couldn't get enough of me.

The image of Chicago popped into my head. Dozens of thoughts played through my mind, happy knowing that in about a week, I would be walking around my favorite city with my favorite person.

My excitement levels were too high throughout the next week that it made the week go by much slower. I hadn't stepped foot in Illinois since leaving for school, so I was thrilled to show Axel a little bit of where I came from.

We loaded up the car with our bags, preparing for a nice weekend getaway. And like usual, I had packed way too many things.

I stared out the window, watching the highway go by. The weather had gotten nicer over the past week, spring finally setting in, so I was glad that we would be walking around the windy city in decent weather, rather than the cold.

"Whatcha thinkin' about?" Axe asked, one hand on the wheel, one on my left thigh.

"How excited I am," I responded, turning back towards him, away from the window.

His dimples sunk into his cheeks. "I'm excited too."

I gasped as one of my favorite songs came on the speaker, leaning forward to slightly turn up the volume. I yelled out all the words, laughing as Axe's eyebrows jumped up to his hairline by how terrible my voice sounded.

I turned down the volume, just enough so that Axe could hear me. "You like my singing voice?"

He chuckled, biting his lip. "I love it."

"Oh, good," I laughed. "I'm sure you're reconsidering what you said about being stuck with me forever last week on our walk."

"Not at all," he smiled, shaking his head.

"I'll wake you up every morning to the sound of my wonderful singing voice."

His eyes widened for a second. "That's okay. You don't have to do that."

I threw my head back, laughing. I covered his hand that was on my thigh with my own, grabbing it and bringing it up to my mouth. I planted a little kiss on the back of his hand, holding onto it as I placed it back into my lap.

The song changed to a slower one. My mouth turned upwards, watching Axe as he began to sing along. His voice was so beautiful. Deep and raspy, yet delicate and smooth. I turned the volume lower.

"Why'd you turn it down?" he asked, shifting his eyes between the road and I.

"So that I could hear you singing," I replied. He smirked, happy with my answer. "Do you want me to sing with you?"

"Oh, God," he chuckled.

The sides of my mouth turned upwards as he caught back onto the music, continuing to sing along as if he never stopped in the first place.

About two hours later, the skyline came into view. I could tell Axe was struggling to keep his eyes on the road, distracted by the beautiful sight of Chicago.

I used the GPS on my phone to navigate us towards Michigan Avenue. I had been to Chicago dozens of times before, and I knew my way around Michigan Avenue itself, but the roads to get there still confused me.

Axe was getting a little fed up with the city drivers, annoyed by their impatience and fierce driving. I drove all the time in Chicago, almost every time I went there, so I was used to it, but Axe wasn't. I felt kind of bad. I should've offered to drive so that he wouldn't have to deal with it.

We parked in the parking garage that was alongside our hotel. Axe had made reservations for us at the nicest hotel in the city. I told him it wasn't necessary to spend nearly four hundred dollars to stay in a hotel for a single night, but he wouldn't listen, claiming that he wanted us to have a luxurious time and that he needed the "full Chicago experience." Whatever that meant.

My jaw immediately dropped when we walked in. The tall ceilings and marble floors were most definitely luxurious, matched with the bright chandeliers that hung along the ceilings. Damn. This was double fancy.

I stood next to Axe as we checked in. Guilt consumed me as Axe handed over his credit card to the man working at the front desk, bothered by how much money Axe was spending without letting me help out.

I clung onto his arm with one hand as we brought our bags up to the room.

I set mine down and took a look around, still amazed by how nice everything was. It was hands down the best hotel I had ever stayed at. I collapsed onto the bed for a few minutes, positioning myself up on my elbows as I watched Axe stare out the window.

I got off the bed and walked up next to him, wrapping my arms around his middle. He looked down at me and beamed, bringing an arm around my waist.

"Pretty view, right?" I said.

"Yeah," he agreed, observing every inch. "Do you want to go walk around soon?" he asked eagerly.

"Sure," I said with a smile.

He checked his watch. "Okay, it's almost four and our reservation is at six, so—"

"Reservation?" I lifted a brow.

"Yeah, I made us dinner reservations."

I tilted my head. "It better not be at some crazily expensive restaurant."

"Nah," he said, waving it off. "Just go ahead and change or get ready or whatever you've gotta do and then we can go walk around for a bit before dinner." He kissed my forehead and toppled onto the bed.

Axe had his arms behind his head as he lay there, looking over at me. The gray t-shirt he had on under his blue unbuttoned flannel rode up a bit, slightly exposing his dragonfly tattoo. I couldn't help but want to rip the shirt off. But I knew I needed to wait until later tonight. We had places to go.

I quickly changed into a nice purple sweater and jeans that didn't have any holes in them. I stood in front of the bathroom mirror, brushing through my long hair before applying lip gloss.

The second we began walking around, Axe's eyes were everywhere. He took everything in, watching angry taxi drivers pass by and walking around the pigeons on the sidewalk. Axe glanced upwards at the buildings, amazed. It was cute that his first time in Chicago was with me. It made the experience even more special.

"The buildings are so... tall," he said, his eyes still lingering around.

"Good observation," I laughed. "You wanna go by the bean?" I asked as we made our way down Michigan Avenue.

"Is it around here?"

"Yeah. Right up the road."

"Okay," he smiled, his childish, adventurous side coming out.

We crossed the road, huddled in the middle of a crowd of people that were doing the same. Axe held onto my hand, not daring to let go. I led the way, knowing my way around Michigan Avenue.

As usual, giant groups of people and tourists from everywhere surrounded the bean, touching it and taking pictures. Axe was eager to get there, almost tugging me along as we got closer.

His eyes widened as we approached. "How do you think they built this thing?"

"I'm not really sure, honestly."

"And why a bean? Why not a carrot or something?"

"Or like an apple."

Axe's eyes zipped over to me. "They can't do an apple."

"Why not? Fruits are better than vegetables."

"Because it's the Windy City."

"Okay...and?"

"Not the Big Apple."

"Okay," I rolled my eyes, "I see what you mean. But fruits are still better than vegetables."

"I don't even think beans are vegetables."

"Whatever. No need to get all technical, dork. Go stand next to it," I insisted, positioning him. I slid my phone out of my pocket and backed up. Axe flashed his most charming smile as he stood next to the bean, allowing me to snap a perfect photo.

We continued to explore the city, walking into whatever stores we came across that looked interesting. There wasn't a single second that passed that we weren't overjoyed and smiling and laughing. It felt like after everything, the world was finally on our side, as if the universe was finally working in our favor.

Western was filled with people who knew Axe and I. It was filled with a handful of people who had been trying to rip us apart. But Chicago was filled with millions of people who didn't know who either of us were. Nobody here was out to ruin us.

Axe and I made our way to the restaurant. It was only a fifteen-minute walk from where we were, so we didn't bother getting a taxi. When we walked in, my eyebrows shot up. I hit Axe's arm as the hostess led us to our table.

"What?"

"You said it wasn't gonna be fancy!" I yelled in a whisper.

He waited until we were seated in our booth to respond. "It's not that fancy."

I shook my head as I looked around. "The marvelous chandeliers hanging from the ceiling say otherwise!" I took a deep breath as I picked up the menu, taking a look at all the options. My eyes jumped out of their sockets. "Fifty dollars for a steak?"

Axe grinned. "Who cares? Just get whatever you want."

"Axe. You spend more money on me than you do on yourself."

"And what's wrong with that?" he asked, skimming the menu. "Do you want the steak?"

"I mean, yeah, but not for fifty dollars," I replied, my eyes moving from the steak to the other options on the menu.

A few minutes later, our waiter appeared. "Welcome," he said, bowing his head. I zoned out for a second as he read off the specials, my mind too consumed as I studied every inch of Axe from across the table. "What can I get for you tonight ma'am?" he asked, snapping me out of my daze.

"Oh, um," I started, retreating back to the menu to repeat what I had chosen.

"We'll both have the filet please," Axe budded in. "And can we also get mashed potatoes and a ceasar salad, please?"

"How would you like your steaks cooked?" the waiter asked.

"Medium well, please," Axe responded.

Damnit. He even knew how I liked my steak.

"Very well, sir. I'll have that right out for you." Our waiter took our menus and walked off, leaving me to shoot a disapproving look at Axe.

He sipped on his drink. "What?" he asked, laughing as he put it down.

"Now you're spending over a hundred dollars on dinner."

He sighed, eyeing me from across the table. "Baby," he said firmly, "I don't care about money. Stop worrying about it, okay?"

I exhaled, letting it go. This was our trip, and I didn't want to ruin it by complaining about how nice Axe was being.

I rested my hands on the table. The scene reminded me of the first time we went out to dinner, the first time I ever got any real idea of who Axe was. We barely knew each other then, and at that point, I was too scared to get to know him better, too scared to fall for him or get too close to him. And now, we knew each other better than we knew ourselves. We had conquered everything that had been thrown at us, and we had done so together.

My taste buds were beyond happy as I ate my steak, satisfied with the fact that it was most definitely the best steak I had ever had. Axe and I finished eating, and after paying the check, we left, reentering the windy city air. It was dark out now and all the city lights were beaming, causing Axe to look around, once again amazed by the view.

After walking around and exploring the city for a few more hours, we headed back to the hotel, content with how our day went.

I shimmied off my jeans and plopped onto the bed, my feet tired from how much walking we had done. Axel placed a knee onto the bed, reaching over for me. He scooped me up and threw me over his shoulder, tickling me.

"Axe," I said in between laughs, "stop tickling me!"

He placed me down on the bed, collapsing next to me as he hugged my middle. I played with his hair, feeling more peaceful than I ever had in my entire life.

My hands slowly lingered over his abdomen before starting to tickle him. Revenge.

His limbs flailed around, trying to free himself of my touch and after a minute, he flipped over, smashing his lips onto mine.

I gripped the back of his neck as his tongue slipped into my mouth, analyzing every inch of it. He reached down and pulled my knee up towards my chest, running his hand along the inside of my thigh. I fell onto my back, allowing him to position himself on top of me as he slid my thong off. I kicked it off once it reached my ankles, diverting my attention back to his lips.

Axe's mouth broke away from mine and I impatiently watched as he stepped out of his black jeans, throwing them onto the ground along with his flannel and grey t-shirt. He slipped my purple sweater off of me, a satisfied grin appearing on his face as it joined the pile of clothes on the floor.

We woke up early the next morning and after quickly eating breakfast in the hotel, we got ready for the day.

"Where do you wanna go first?" I asked.

"Wherever," Axe shrugged. "I wanna see everything," he grinned.

I thought to myself for a second, thinking of the best places that Chicago had to offer. "Okay. I know where we should go first," I smirked.

An hour later, Axe gripped my hand as we took the elevator up to the Chicago Skydeck at the top of Willis Tower. The elevator doors opened, revealing the one hundred and third floor of the building.

I led Axe over to one of the glass cases, which gave an entire view of the city. I stepped onto it, taking in the beauty of Chicago and all its entirety. My eyes drifted down, looking through the glass beneath my feet before I turned back to Axe.

"Come on here with me," I smiled.

"It's so high," he said, unsure.

"I know that. Now come on here with me," I repeated.

"But, it's so high…"

"Oh, so now you're afraid of heights?" I rolled my eyes.

"Maybe."

"Since when?"

"Since they built that shit out of glass," he pointed.

"It's not gonna break."

He raised his brows. "You can't guarantee that."

I held my arms out. "I'm standing on it right now."

"Yeah, but you're small."

I rolled my eyes again and reached for him. "You're being a wuss. Get on here."

He finally complied, holding onto me for a minute until he got comfortable enough. His dimples began to sink in as he took a look around, finally giving him the understanding of why I loved Chicago so much.

"Would you two like a photo of you?" a voice called from behind us.

We both turned, seeing an older woman smiling at us.

"Sure," I smiled, handing her my phone. "Thank you." I leaned into Axe, placing my hand gently on the center of his chest as the kind woman snapped a photo. I had been taking pictures of Axe throughout the trip, documenting his cute reactions to the places we went, but Axe and I didn't have a lot of photos together, definitely not as many as I would've liked for us to have.

The woman handed the phone back to me. "Thank you so much," I said again.

"Of course," she grinned. She turned to Axe. "She's a very pretty one," she whispered loudly. "Sweet too. Make sure you keep her."

"Planning on it," Axe smirked. I glanced over at Axe, his eyes bringing a feeling of fullness to my heart.

"Next stop?" I asked.

"Yeah," he agreed with a beautiful smile as he gripped my hand.

After the Skydeck, we went to the Shedd Aquarium, spending a decent amount of the day there, checking out all the exhibits they had. I had been to all of these places numerous times throughout my life, but it was fun exploring the city with Axe. It was almost as if I had never been there before, as if it was my first time. He made everything feel fresh, brand new.

"Now where?" Axe asked as we exited the aquarium.

"Dinner?"

"Bet, I'm hungry. Where do you wanna eat?"

"Uno's," I replied.

He brought his eyebrows in. "What's that?"

"Pizza," I responded. "Chicago pizza."

Axe nodded, taking his phone out of his pocket. "I'll turn the GPS on."

"We don't need that thing," I waved it off. "I know where I'm going."

"You sure?"

"Yeah," I ensured him.

We swung our intertwined hands back and forth, walking towards Uno Pizza. It was one of the best places to get some genuine Chicago deep dished pizza, so it was necessary that Axe tried it. After all, he kept claiming he wanted the "full experience."

"I like it here," Axe said, glancing around.

"Me too. Greatest city in the world."

"Well—"

"You can't change my mind," I insisted.

"Guess we might have to just live here someday," he said, his eyes dropping from the buildings to me.

I raised my brows. "City living? Eh, I don't know if I could do it."

"What? Why not?"

"Too many people. So expensive. You gotta walk everywhere and we all know I can be lazy."

"The laziest," Axe said. I shot him a glare. "You said it!" he chuckled. His eyes wandered around again, brows coming together as he took a look around us. "Are you sure you know where we're going?" Axe asked.

"Yeah, yeah," I waved him off.

"Tate, do you really, though?" he chuckled.

"I mean, I've been here before," I shrugged.

"But have you gotten there from the Shedd Aquarium before?" he questioned.

"Well... not necessarily... but I know where we're going."

"You do realize we passed this same exact t-shirt shop fifteen minutes ago."

"It's Chicago. There's the same store a couple blocks apart throughout the entire city."

"Yeah, but does every t-shirt shop have a guy standing outside of it wearing a shirt that says, 'Fuck you, I'm from Chicago'?"

"Well...no..."

Axe stopped in his tracks, causing my feet to stop as well. "You got us lost, didn't you?" he said, the sides of his mouth slowly turning upwards.

"We're not lost," I insisted. "I just wanted to take the long way so we could go sight-seeing."

"Mhmm," he hummed, swinging our hands.

"We aren't lost."

"You can admit that you got us lost," he smirked.

"We're not lost," I said as I continued to walk on.

Axe shook his head. "So stubborn."

It took us a while, but once we finally got to the restaurant, Axe stopped before going inside. I curiously watched as he looked around, deep in thought.

"What is it?" I asked.

He pulled his mouth over to one side, still thinking. "How far did you say your hometown was from here again?"

"Like forty or so minutes. Why?"

"Let's go there."

I scrunched my nose. "Why?"

He shrugged. "I mean, you've seen where I grew up. I wanna see where you come from, too."

I scratched my head with my free hand, my other still holding onto Axe's. I thought about Wilmot for a minute, trying to imagine it. I hadn't been there in nearly eight months, since before school even started. I had been avoiding going home all year, afraid of the flashbacks that going there would cause. My initial reaction would be to say no, but after everything that Axe and I had gone through, no flashback or flood of negative feelings of Wilmot could ever be worse than what he and I had already surpassed. I couldn't avoid Wilmot forever. And if I had to go back, then I wanted him to be there with me.

317

"Okay," I agreed, reluctantly, swallowing the lump of nerves in the back of my throat. "We'll leave in the morning."

Chapter Twenty-Nine
The Peanut Butter Cookies

I knew how to get home from the city and Axe had already driven the two hours to Chicago, so I offered to drive.

As we got closer, my heart started racing, hands sweating against the steering wheel. I didn't know what to expect. I wasn't sure what old friends I would run into from high school. I wasn't sure if the town was going to look the same. I wasn't sure if I would have flashbacks or not.

Recognizing all the familiar buildings felt strange. They all looked the same, yet somehow different. I tried keeping my eyes solely on the road as we passed my old high school, but knowing it was right there even though I wasn't looking at it, made me uneasy.

Don't get me wrong, this town gave me some great memories throughout my life, but it also housed my deepest fears and worst moments.

"You okay?" Axe asked from the passenger seat, sensing my shakiness. The second he spoke, I was instantly more relaxed.

"Yeah," I assured him.

I pulled into the driveway, giving out a long exhale as I turned off the car. I had called my parents the night prior, giving them a heads up that Axe and I would be coming. They happily agreed, excited to see us, but I could tell they were mostly excited to see Axe. They loved him.

My parents were already at the door, ready to greet us as we walked up. Charlie and Buddy were next to them at the door, barking and wagging their tails in excitement. I hadn't missed Wilmot, but I definitely did miss my two fluffy golden retrievers.

They jumped all over us as we walked in, unable to calm themselves down. I smiled, bending down to pet them before I gave each of my parents a hug.

Axe gave my mom a kind hug, following it up with a firm handshake with my dad. Watching them interact was soothing. They got along so easily.

"How was the drive?" my mom asked, standing with her hands on her hips.

"Not bad," I shrugged.

She gave another smile. "Awe, I'm *so* excited you both are here! It's about time you came home."

"I know," I said, breaking eye contact.

"Go ahead and bring your stuff upstairs, honey. And the guest room is all ready for Axel to sleep in."

I furrowed my eyebrows at her. "Mom, I'm nineteen."

Axe stood next to me, trying to keep his laughter in. God, my mom was embarrassing.

She looked back and forth between Axel and I, then sighed. "Well, alright. I guess it's okay."

"You guess?" I said, grabbing my bags that were resting at my feet.

I dropped my bags onto the floor of my room and Axe did the same. My eyes silently scanned the entire room. It was exactly how I had left it. Not a single thing was out of place. The pictures of all my friends and I still hung on the grey walls, along with all my dance awards. My blue and grey comforter was perfectly laid upon my bed, my blue teddy bear resting against the organized pillows.

Axe picked up my bear, lifting a brow as he smirked. "Teddy bear?"

I stomped over and ripped the bear out of his hands. "His name is Berry."

"Berry?" he chuckled.

"Yeah, because he's blue like a blueberry, not because he's a bear. I'm not that mainstream."

He brought his hands up in front of him. "Okay, okay."

I hugged my bear to my chest as if I was five again. I used to do it all the time actually. Every time Connor had made me cry, I had squeezed my bear.

I sat down on my bed, slightly overwhelmed by everything, but maintaining control over it.

"So," Axe said, rubbing his hands together, "show me around."

"You want me to show you around Wilmot?"

"Yeah."

"You want me to show you around a tiny town that barely covers a tenth of a centimeter on a map?"

"Yes."

I sighed, standing up. "Alright," I agreed, motioning for him to follow me back downstairs. I was slightly reluctant about walking around town, a little nervous about how I would feel knowing that I had been uneasy during the car ride here, but I knew that if I was with Axe, I had nothing to worry about.

I walked into the kitchen to let my parents know that we were leaving. "I'm gonna go show Axe around," I said.

"Okay. Just don't be too long. Your sisters are coming over for dinner," my mom said from her usual spot on the couch.

"All of them?"

"All of them," she nodded.

I bit the inside of my lip, trying to hide my smile. I hadn't seen Kendall and Macey since they came to Western to visit, and I hadn't seen Brynn since school started. She was the only one who hadn't met Axe yet, so I was excited for her to do so.

My town was small, so there wasn't really much to show Axe. We walked along Main Street, stopping in some of the local shops to look around. One thing that Wilmot did have was an amazing burger joint with even more amazing milkshakes. I knew that my mom would be pissed if we ate since she was making dinner, so we stopped inside and just got shakes.

Axe and I sipped on our shakes all the way to the pier. Wilmot might have been small, but the massive lake in the center of our town made up for it. It had been a huge attraction for years, outdoing the other nearby lakes by plenty with its size and depth.

We hung our legs over the side of the dock, letting our feet rest in the water. The water was still cold, not yet warmed up after the long winter, but it wasn't too terrible. It was pretty refreshing.

"It's really nice out here," Axe said, glancing around at the sun beginning to set over the lake.

"Yeah, it is," I agreed, dropping my head onto his shoulder as my feet slowly splashed around in the water.

"You wanna jump in?" Axe asked.

"Absolutely not."

"Why not? C'mon, it's not even that deep here."

"Yeah, that's the issue."

"How?"

"You wanna jump in so that our feet can touch the nasty seaweed at the bottom and then we can smell like lake for the rest of the night when we get out? Cause, I'll pass."

"We can shower when we get back," he winked.

"Oh, yes, because I so want to be caught in the shower with you by any of my family members."

Axe laughed, shaking his head. "You know, Tate," he started, "before I met you, I never understood how anyone could be in a relationship and stick to that one person."

"Oh, I know," I mocked him, fully aware of how many girls he had been with before me.

He smiled as he shook his head. "There's that stubbornness I know and love."

"Well, I'm glad you've realized that it's never going away."

"I realized that a long time ago," he chuckled. I playfully nudged him before he continued. "But anyways, after I met you, and after I started having feelings for you, the world just... looked different to me."

I stared into his eyes, lost in them. "I know what you mean," I said, planting a kiss onto his soft lips.

We stayed on the dock until the sun went down, then headed back home. I wasn't sure if my sisters would be there or not before we got back, but I prepared myself for it anyways. Axe had only met my parents at a single time, and had only met two of my sisters at a single time, so I hoped that having both of my parents and all three of my sisters there wouldn't be too overwhelming for him.

Everyone sat around the dining room table, digging into the chicken and brussel sprouts that my mom had prepared.

"How was your trip to the city?" my mom asked.

"It was really good," I said.

"What'd you guys do?" she asked.

"We walked around a lot, went to the bean, Skydeck, all the touristy places," I smiled.

"Of course, of course," she nodded.

"It was my first time there actually, so it was really nice to be able to go with Tate," Axe said.

"First time ever?" Brynn asked.

"First time ever," he nodded.

"How'd you like it?" my mom asked.

"Loved it. I tried to convince Tate that we should live there one day, and she shot the idea down really quickly," Axe chuckled.

"Well," I shrugged, "too expensive, so many damn people, and the walking, oh God the walking," I rolled my eyes.

"God forbid you get some exercise," my mom said, throwing a bite of chicken in her mouth.

"I get plenty of exercise," I said.

Macey leaned into me. "Sex doesn't count," she whispered. I lightly smacked her with the back of my hand, praying that neither of my parents heard her comment.

"She's right about the city, though," Brynn chimed in. "It's a pain in the ass. The bars are a fun time though, I'll admit."

I turned to Axe. "Brynn lives in the city."

"It's fun... most of the time," she said, taking a sip of her drink.

"So, Axel, when are you proposing?" Macey interrupted.

I dropped my silverware onto the table and covered my face with my hands. "Macey," I warned.

"What? It's a genuine question," she said.

Axe couldn't contain his embarrassed, yet insanely cute smile. "Probably right after graduation," he responded.

My head shot up, looking around to see if I had heard him correctly. I was taken aback by the fact that he had an actual answer for her. Did he really think about marriage that often?

"Your graduation or her graduation?" Macey asked, demanding to know when she should be expecting a ring on my finger.

"Uh," he looked over at me, thinking carefully about his answer, "whichever one she wants."

"Good answer," Kendall smiled.

Brynn nodded once to me from across the table. "He's a keeper," she said with a grin.

Heat rushed to my cheeks by the fact that this conversation was happening in front of my entire family. Macey seemed satisfied by his answer, her attention dropping back down to her plate. I shot her a look, waiting for her to look up and see it. She shrugged when she did, not giving a second thought to how embarrassed I had become. I glanced over at my mom, who had a smug smile on her face. My dad pretended like he hadn't heard, continuing to eat without reaction.

The rest of dinner went smoothly, filled with laughter and conversation, which thankfully, didn't involve any more embarrassing questions.

I took a quick shower, which felt quiet, due to the fact that Axe wasn't in there with me. We showered together a lot of the time, but there was no way in hell that I was going to risk getting caught in the shower with him by one of my family members. The embarrassment of that would've been a million times worse than it was earlier.

Axe showered after me, leaving me to sit in bed for a bit, thinking about absolutely everything. My mind played through the entire story of Axe and I, taking into account all the ups and downs that we had been through. And now, when I looked in the mirror, I saw someone who was loved instead of someone who was left.

I felt sort of at ease having Axe here in Wilmot with me. It was almost as if he was repainting all my memories of Wilmot, taking them from tainted to beautiful. At first, I had been nervous about bringing him here. Wilmot was so small that I had been to basically every single place with Connor at some point, and if I hadn't, then I had seen Nicole there, or both of them. But now, Axe was fixing my view of those places. And instead of them being places I had gone to with Connor, they were places I had gone to with Axe.

I used to not be able to see the end of my symptoms, stuck in thoughts that the pain would never end. But Axe had given me the stepping stones to get out of the hole I had been in. No more crying. No more fears.

Rewriting my worst memories into beautiful ones with Axe felt good. And suddenly, I couldn't wait to wake up in the morning to show him around some more.

My mom made us breakfast in the morning when we woke up, and quite honestly, her pancakes were not as good as Axel's. I ate them anyways, slightly disappointed.

We each gave my mom a hug before we left, and then we set off around Wilmot. I took Axe to all my favorite places growing up, and we even stopped at my high school to visit some of my old teachers and my old dance coach.

The day went well, filled with positive vibes and no flashbacks. I was even surprising myself, pride radiating off of me from the fact that I was winning. I was beating the C-PTSD that had been drilled inside of me. I was controlling it instead of letting it control me. And if I could face Wilmot, the place that would give me the worst flashbacks imaginable, I could face anything.

We sat in my room after a long day, looking through my old scrapbooks. Axe was amused by all my old, middle school pictures, laughing at how awkward I looked with braces. I playfully hit him each time he did, but honestly, I couldn't blame him for laughing. Those pictures were awful.

The sun was about to set, and we had just eaten dinner, but suddenly, I got a strong craving.

"I want peanut butter cookies," I exclaimed, jutting my bottom lip out.

"Are there any downstairs?"

"Nah, probably not."

"We could make some," he shrugged.

I smiled, immediately thrilled by his idea. "Yes, please."

I grabbed his hand and led him downstairs. My parents were sitting on the couch, watching tv when we came down.

"Do we have stuff to make peanut butter cookies?" I asked, praying that they would say yes.

My mom brought her hand under her chin, thinking. "No, I don't think so," she replied. My face fell, true disappointment overpowering me. "But you guys can go run to the store and get some," she offered. I peered over at Axe, checking to see if he was up for the cookie ingredient run.

"I'll do whatever," he said, soft eyes glimmering into mine.

"Okay, I just need to change."

We ran back upstairs really quick so that I could replace my sweatpants with jeans and my old dance t-shirt with an off the shoulder, maroon top. I usually didn't put too much thought into what I wore when I ran out somewhere, but since we were in Wilmot, it would've been very embarrassing if I ran into people from high school wearing my sweats.

The second we got to the grocery store, I opened up my phone, checking the list of ingredients that we needed.

"Okay, let's divide and conquer," I said, checking the list.

"Got it. What should I grab?"

"Hmm, I know we have some of this stuff at home like flour and sugar, so you go get butter and peanut butter. I'll go get baking powder and baking soda."

He nodded and we separated to grab each item that I had assigned. I made my way down the baking aisle, keeping my eye out for the ingredients that I needed. I scanned each section, my face lighting up when I found both items that I had been looking for.

I turned on my heels, ready to go find Axe. A familiar pair of eyes caught my attention, and sure enough, they were staring right back at me.

Every muscle in my body froze. My heart was beating at an abnormally rapid pace and my throat felt like it was closing. It was as if the room was spinning as I stood there, unsure if what I was seeing was real. The past four years flooded back to me, every ounce of pain, heartbreak, and defeat rushing through me at once. My breathing was becoming irregular, lungs overwhelmed. Adrenaline took over, sensing the danger, but even so, I stayed still.

Anxiety. Fear. Panic.

I needed to run, but my body would. Not. Move.

Where the fuck was Axel?

326

Chapter Thirty
The Moment

Connor stood tall, his buzzed hair a different look than the last time I had seen him. His malicious smile rested on me, eyes doing the same.

My body started shaking, worse than it ever had before. I could feel tears swelling up in my eyes as I stood, facing my perpetrator for the first time in two years. My mind was on a loop as it crashed, like a computer whose system was overloading.

Within another minute, Axe was by my side. He had both butter and peanut butter in one hand, the other was reaching for me. I could hear the sound of Axe's voice, but I was so in shock that I couldn't make out what he was saying.

He dropped the items and crouched down in front of me, his hands gently shaking me back and forth to snap me out of it.

"Tate. Tate. Tatum. Tatum," he kept repeating, over and over, lightly shaking me.

I squeezed my eyes shut at the feeling, recognizing that this was the present and not the past. Axe brought a hand up to my face, cupping my cheek. I looked down at him, taking into account the worry in his eyes.

"Baby," he whispered, "are you okay?"

I nodded as a single tear fell, watching out of the corner of my eye as Connor strode over in our direction. Axe turned as he stood. The two made eye contact and once they did, Axe immediately knew who he was.

Axe put an arm around my frontside and pushed me behind him, prepared to protect me if it came down to it. I clung onto his arm, standing more so to the side of him rather than behind, so that I could see what was happening.

I was still shaking a fair amount as I glanced down, noticing the ingredients all over the floor. I guess I had been so in shock that I hadn't even realized I had dropped them.

Connor walked straight up to us, nodding once at Axel.

"Who's he?" he asked, looking Axe up and down.

I squeezed Axe's arm, too afraid to say anything. Axe looked over at me once, recognizing the fear on my face.

"Okay," Connor said emotionlessly, rolling his eyes at our silence. He leaned to the side a little, trying to get a glimpse of me as I hid behind Axe's arm. "You look really good by the way, Tate."

"Don't look at her," Axe spat.

"I'm guessing you're a new boyfriend."

Axe eyed him viciously. "And last she'll ever have before she has a husband."

Connor was starting to get bothered, and he most definitely didn't like Axe's previous answer. "Interesting," he said, lifting his chin. His attention turned back to me, waiting for me to finally say something. "So, what brings you in town, Tate?"

"None of your goddamn business," Axe said.

"I wasn't talking to you," Connor seethed.

"Where's your wedding ring?" Axe calmly asked, pointing to Connor's empty left hand.

Connor's eyes darted to me for a second, almost nervously, but trying not to show it. He looked back at Axe, taking a step closer to him. "None of *your* goddamn business."

I didn't know where Nicole was or why she wasn't here, but I didn't care. I probably would've ripped her raggedy hair off of her head if I saw her. I wasn't sure why Connor wasn't wearing his ring, and I wouldn't have been surprised if it was because they were getting a divorce. But I also wouldn't have been surprised if it was because he was trying to find other girls to sleep with. He had a tendency to cheat.

Axe didn't flinch with how close Connor was, completely unafraid of him. He reached into his pocket and pulled out his keys, maintaining eye contact with Connor the entire time. Axe felt for my hand, placing the keys in my palm.

"Baby, go wait in the car, please," he requested.

I clutched the keys, not moving. The tension in the aisle was rising and as anxious as I was, there was absolutely no way in hell that I was leaving Axe there.

"Tate," Connor said, "I don't like this guy. He doesn't seem good for you."

"I'm better for her than you ever were," Axe shot back, standing his ground. His breathing picked up, becoming heavier. I could see the anger flaring in his eyes and hear it stirring in his voice, similarly to all the other times he was about to fight someone.

Connor's anger was also starting to bubble, jealousy coursing through his veins. He got in Axe's face, trying to intimidate him. "I'm in the Marines. I'd watch your mouth if I were you."

"You think I give a damn?"

"You wanna take this outside?" Connor offered.

Oh, no. The ruthless against the Marine. This was not going to end well.

I gripped Axe's hand before he gave an answer that someone would regret. I tugged on it, forcing him to look at me. "If you get arrested again..." I whispered, trailing off.

I hadn't seen or spoken to Connor in two years. At this point, he had been in the Marines for that long, and I had no idea what he was capable of. He was stationed in North Carolina, so I wasn't sure why he was in Wilmot in the first place, but I currently had more things to worry about than to figure out what he was doing here.

Axe's eyes softened as they looked into mine. He caved, allowing me to drag him out of the store, leaving Connor and all our cookie ingredients behind.

The second we got onto the road, I sensed something was off. I glanced in the side mirror, my heart catching in my chest from the sight of a white pick-up truck trailing behind us.

"Shit," I muttered.

"What's wrong?" Axe asked.

"He's behind us," I swallowed.

329

Axe's eyes dashed to the rearview mirror, outrage immediately taking over by the sight. He gripped the steering wheel, stepping a little harder on the gas.

We took backroads and made sharp turns, trying to lose Connor, but it wasn't working. His truck chased behind us the entire time, riding our ass.

The image of his car trailing behind Nicole and I as Bianca drove flashed into my mind, feeling the déjà vu. We all knew how that night ended. Not good for me.

"I've gotta pull over," Axe quietly said as we entered my neighborhood.

"What?" I questioned, hesitant about his decision.

"I'm gonna pull over," he repeated, bringing the car to a stop in front of the playground in the middle of my neighborhood.

The second Axe stopped the engine, he was out of the car, ready to handle the bullshit. Panic was still rushing through me, but Connor was *my* mess, not Axe's. So, there was no way I was going to let him face Connor alone.

I took a deep breath as I opened my car door and stepped out. The two of them were already chest to chest and in each other's faces, both of them riled up.

Connor shook his head as he clenched his fists shut, the sight causing me to immediately run over to them, unsure of what Connor was about to do. I shoved myself in between the two of them.

"CONNOR, I SWEAR TO GOD IF YOU TOUCH HIM!" I screamed in his face. It was the first thing that I had said to him since we had seen him, the first thing I had said to him in two years. Connor took a step back, taken off guard at my words. His face fell from anger back to jealousy.

He brought a hand up to his chest, lifting a brow. "You're defending him over me?"

Axe took a step forward and I put my hand up, signaling for him to stop. I wanted to handle this. There were so many emotions that had been built up inside of me over the past four years, but I never had the courage to say any of them. It felt like I had been waiting all this time to speak up, as if this was meant to be my moment.

Connor had never wanted me to move on. He always used to say that if I dated anyone else, he would beat the shit out of them. Back

330

then, I thought it was cute how protective he was. But now, it was clear that he just always wanted control. Axel and Connor saw protection very differently. Axel protected me when I needed to be protected, whereas Connor was just trying to protect himself.

In Connor's mind, I was always going to be his property. In his mind, I would always choose him, always love him, and always belong to him. But that wasn't the case. I chose myself now, and in choosing myself, I chose Axe. I loved Axe. I belonged to Axe.

Axe had done everything in his power to protect me, and now, it was my turn to do the same.

"Yeah," I admitted to him, nodding.

Connor's jaw worked under his skin, his eyes moving back and forth between Axe and I. "Do you love him?"

I looked him dead in the eyes, my heart feeling just as full as it ever had. "With every ounce of my entire being."

He didn't seem to like my answer, causing him to shift his weight side to side for a moment. "Do you love him more than you loved me?"

"Absolutely," I responded, without a single drop of hesitation or doubt.

Connor slowly nodded, displeasure and outrage still resting on his face. I always used to worry about what Connor thought, used to wonder if he would approve of what I did or said, but right now felt different. I didn't feel like his opinion was relevant. I took his silence as an opportunity to speak my mind freely, not worrying about what he would think.

"You," I seethed, putting my pointer finger to the center of his chest, "are the most narcissistic, inconsiderate, and emotionally abusive *fuck* that I have ever met. And not stopping you from marrying somebody else was the best decision I've ever made. Axel is twice the man that you'll ever be. He loves me more than you ever did or could. And he's a million times better at everything than you, including sex, so I hope that ruins your fucking ego," I said, grabbing Axe's hand and leading him back towards the car. "And just for the record," I paused, turning back to him, "your wife's a bitch."

I opened the car door and climbed inside, feeling a weight suddenly become lifted off my shoulders. The second Axe got into the driver's seat, he burst out laughing, smacking the steering wheel.

331

"That was the best thing I've ever seen," he cried out.

I eyed him intensely with a straight face for a moment, before the corners of my mouth started to turn upwards. I dropped my forehead into my hands as I laughed, unable to contain the sense of pride I felt.

Axe started the car and drove off, not caring to look back. He made a right turn instead of a left.

My eyebrows pulled in, confused. "Where are you going?" I asked.

"We gotta make those cookies somehow," he said, his charming smile appearing as he headed back towards the store.

I grinned, looking out the window. I didn't bother checking to see if Connor was following us this time. Because either way, it didn't matter. The only thing that mattered was the person sitting next to me now.

Chapter Thirty-One
The Epilogue

I smoothed out my blush pink dress as I sat in the front row, next to Gianna. Red ribbon was tied around the back of every chair. White and red roses decorated the entire outdoor venue, petals scattered across the aisle.

Amberly stood across from Drew at the altar, her smile as bright as I had ever seen it. A braid was perfectly draped into her updo, a few curled hairs sticking out at the front to frame her gorgeous face. I studied her elegant white dress. It was made of lace that trailed all the way down her arms and body, the train of the dress resting neatly on the ground. She looked absolutely stunning.

Drew held her tiny hands in his, not taking his eyes off of her as they began to exchange their vows. My eyes shifted over to Axe as he stood next to Ash, with Drew on the other side.

I couldn't help but think about everything that we had been through. When we first met, I wanted nothing to do with him. I was afraid of him because I didn't trust myself. And I surely didn't trust others either. I fought my feelings, trying to hide them away, but they kept resurfacing. Axe kept reappearing and no matter how hard I tried, I wasn't able to make him stay away. I fell for him. Hard. Maybe even too hard. People tried to keep us apart, tried to tear us away from each other, but at the end of the day, they couldn't. No matter what tore us apart, we kept finding our way back to each other. Whether if it was a pregnancy, a terrible breakup, a bitchy redhead, a psychopathic stalker, jail itself, or Connor, we survived it all.

I used to think that I knew what love was. But reality is, I had absolutely no fucking clue until I met Axe. Love isn't necessarily something that you're told, it has to be shown. It has to be experienced in order to fully understand it. Love was a deep concept, a difficult one to fully grasp, and even though it was often complicated, it was usually worth it.

Love was not jealousy or manipulation. Love was consideration and kindness. Love was soft and wholesome. Love was what was standing in front of me.

I needed to go through what I had in order to become the person I was today. And above all, it was beyond clear that everything bad that happened was only put into place by the universe in order to strengthen Axe and I.

We made each other better. We challenged each other in a positive way. We were there for each other when we needed to be, and we loved each other no matter what. The universe brought us together for a reason. We were meant to be together, and we sure as hell were stronger together than we ever were apart.

I took in every detail of Axe as he stood there. His curly hair was perfectly placed on top of his head as he stood tall, shoulders broad with his hands resting in front of him. Green eyes wandered over to me, shining in the sunlight. He gave a light smile, forcing me to mirror his expression.

'We're next,' he mouthed to me, motioning to the wedding itself. I smiled wide, unable to contain the happiness that poured out of me at his words.

I loved that man more than anything. I'd give up my life for him if it ever came down to it.

Watching him stand up there now, on that altar as a groomsman, made me think about the day it would be our turn. And suddenly, I couldn't wait for that day.

Axe constantly ignited a flame inside of me that I had been missing for four years prior. And now, that flamed burned brighter and stronger than it ever had. It was a flame that I wanted to always be there, and I had full faith that it would. It was a love that I knew would burn forever.

Acknowledgements

First, I would like to thank you, the reader, for finishing my novel. It means the world that you read through the entire thing.

Now, I would like to thank everyone who took part in helping me create this book.

First, thank you to Chloe and Gia, who inspired the characters of Claire and Gianna. Not only that, but thank you for encouraging me to keep writing and assuring me that my work was not as bad as I thought it was.

Thank you to my parents and siblings who always support everything that I do.

Thank you to Liv and Ms. Shogren for helping me with the editing process and giving me the corrections and critiques needed to make my book better.

Thank you to Daria, my soul sister, for being to first person to finish reading my book and supporting me through it.

Thank you to Summer, Alyssa, Bailey, Kate, Dany, and Antonella for always sticking by my side and encouraging me to continue doing what I love.

Thank you to Maggie, my sweet angel.

Thank you to Ryan Tippery for designing a beautiful cover that I am absolutely in love with!

Thank you to Paige for being the inspiration behind Penelope.

And again, if you made it all the way through this, a huge thank you to you! I hope you enjoyed reading the book as much as I enjoyed writing it!

Made in the USA
Middletown, DE
06 May 2021